ETTIE SMITH AMISH MYSTERIES: 3 BOOKS-IN-1

SECRETS COME HOME: AMISH MURDER: MURDER IN THE AMISH BAKERY

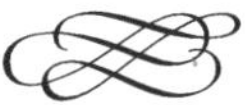

SAMANTHA PRICE

SECRETS COME HOME

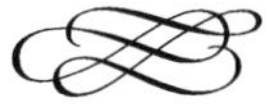

BOOK 1 ETTIE SMITH AMISH MYSTERIES

Secrets Come Home

This is a work of fiction. Any names or characters, businesses or places, events or incidents, are fictitious. Any resemblance to actual persons, living or dead, or actual events is purely coincidental.

CHAPTER 1

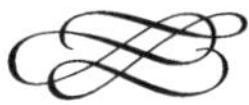

"Why would you have to go to the reading of the will, Ettie?" Elsa-May stood behind her sister and dusted her shoulders.

"I don't know, but if Bishop John says to be there, then that's exactly what I'll do." Ettie pushed Elsa-May's hand away. "Enough, there's nothing on my dress."

"There are tiny pieces of lint all over you. And please tie the strings of your prayer *kapp* together." Elsa-May breathed out heavily. "You look untidy."

"Then I'll be untidy. Ever since you've gotten those new glasses you've been on a cleaning frenzy."

Elsa-May folded her arms over her chest. "Agatha's most likely left you something in the will. That's what it sounds like to me."

Ettie adjusted her prayer *kapp*, pushing some loose strands of her white hair underneath it. "I don't know about that, but then again, Agatha had no family to speak of."

"Do you want me to come along?"

Ettie pushed her lips together. *"Nee, denke*. I've got Eli collecting me." Eli was the bishop's eldest son.

"What am I supposed to do by myself, then?"

Ettie turned and glared at her sister. They didn't have to go everywhere together, did they? It was bad enough that they shared the same house; they didn't have to be joined at the hip. "Knit like you usually do. Or you could water the vegetables for me before the sun gets too hot."

Elsa-May scoffed, sat down and picked up her knitting. "That's your job. You know how the insects like me."

A giggle escaped Ettie's lips. Elsa-May was right. For some reason the mosquitos and anything else that could sting or bite found their way to Elsa-May's ankles, while leaving Ettie well alone. "I won't be long. I'm guessing she left me that china set of hers. She noticed me admiring it recently and asked me if I'd like it when she died. I laughed and said I'd be gone long before she would. I never had any reason to wonder why she asked me if I wanted it. Do you think she knew she was going to die soon?"

Either not hearing or not listening, Elsa-May stared at her hands and then looked up at Ettie. "I won't be able to keep knitting very much longer. Do you see the size of the fingers on my right hand?" Elsa-May held out a hand to Ettie.

Ettie walked a few paces to get a close look. *"Jah,* it looks swollen or something. Did you get stung by a bee?"

Elsa-May frowned at her sister. "It's called arthritis, Ettie, and when you're as old as I am you'll know what it's like when you can't close your hand fully."

Ettie grabbed her coat off one of the pegs by the door. "Nonsense, I'm nearly as old as you, and I don't intend to get arthritis or anything of the kind. Didn't you hear that I just asked you a question and you ignored me?"

Elsa-May frowned. "What question?"

Ettie sighed. "I asked you if you thought that Agatha knew she was going to die soon."

"How could she possibly know something like that?"

Ettie pulled on her coat. "I thought it odd that she asked me if I wanted her china set, when she's much younger than I am – or was much younger, I should say. Or is she still younger than I?" Ettie sat down on the couch facing Elsa-May. "Do you count someone as a certain age when they're dead?"

Elsa-May looked up from her knitting. "Have Eli stop by the store on the way back, would you? I wouldn't mind some candy. We've run out again."

Ettie sighed once more. Elsa-May hardly listened to her. Now with Agatha gone, she had one less friend to talk to, and she did like to talk. "You know that stuff's not good for you. That's probably what the insects are attracted to, all that sugar you eat."

"Just have him stop, will you? It'll save me getting a taxi out later today."

Ettie shook her head at her sister. They didn't have their own buggy anymore and taxis were an expense they could barely afford. They grew most of their own vegetables and lived as thriftily as they could. Elsa-May ate the candy far too quickly these days; Ettie was lucky to see one tiny piece. That was just one of the things that Ettie had to contend with when living with her sister. But still, nothing in life was perfect.

She and Elsa-May were now in their early eighties. They'd both lost their husbands many years ago, and after living on their own for years had sold their farms and moved in together.

Agatha was just one more friend in their community whom they'd lost recently. She died at home, of natural causes, the doctor had said.

Ettie hurried over to the front door, opened it and peered out; there was still no sign of Eli's buggy. "He's running late," Ettie said, more to herself than her sister.

"You know the young don't care about time like we do."

"That's true, but it's not like Eli to be late, and he's not that young anymore." Ettie wondered why Elsa-May chose to respond to murmurs when she ignored direct questions.

"Get me some of those soft caramels, too. *Nee,* not the ones that are covered in chocolate, the ones that are firm. *Jah,* firm caramels."

"I'll try to remember, and I'll stop if Eli can spare the time." Ettie left the front door open and sat down to wait.

"Very well, but if he can't spare the time, and if you don't come back with them, you know I'll have to go out myself and get them, don't you?"

The sound of horse's hooves was music to Ettie's ears.

"That'll be him now," Elsa-May said.

Ettie sprang to her feet and headed for the door.

"Don't forget–"

"I won't," Ettie said before she closed the front door behind her and hurried over to Eli, who was waiting in his buggy.

"SORRY, ETTIE," said Eli. "I had a problem with the buggy wheel. I had to change buggies at the last minute."

"What happened?" Ettie asked as she climbed into the passenger seat.

"I'm not sure – I'll have a better look at it when I get back home."

"*Denke* for driving me to town, Eli."

"Anytime, Ettie. You know that."

"Do you know who else is going to be there?"

Eli looked over at her. "In the lawyer's office?"

Ettie nodded.

"*Dat* didn't say. He just asked me to bring you. He's going to be there because he is a trustee of Agatha's estate. He couldn't take you there himself because he had things to do before and after seeing the lawyer."

"I understand. I could've got a taxi. Isn't it unusual for a lawyer to work on a Saturday?"

"I can't answer that, Ettie. I don't know too many lawyers."

Ettie pressed her lips together and wondered if she should write a will. When she sold the farm, she gave her children most of the money to help them toward buying places of their own, so she didn't have much left. She only had the house she shared with Elsa-May. That, she'd surely have to leave to Elsa-May because what good would it be to her children to have half a house? They wouldn't be able to sell it and leave their aunty Elsa-May homeless.

"You're awfully quiet today, Ettie."

Ettie gave a low chortle. "I'm getting closer to going home to be with *Gott,* and all my friends are leaving before me. Agatha was only sixty."

"*Gott* knows we want you to be here for a long time, Ettie."

The buggy stopped and Ettie looked to her side. "We're here already?"

"*Jah,* we are. When you get out, I'll move the buggy and park it in the parking lot around the corner. Do you need help to get down?"

"A hand would be good." Ettie hated needing help. Eli got out of the buggy and headed around to Ettie's side. "I'd hate to fall. Delma fell last winter and ended up in the hospital for six months. I have an extreme dislike for hospitals after a particularly bad experience a couple of years ago when I had pneumonia."

"I remember you were in the hospital for a time." Eli held her arm and released her when she was solidly on two feet. "There you are. I'll be waiting for you just around the corner there." Eli pointed in a northerly direction.

"*Jah,* I do recall you said that a minute ago. I might be old but I haven't lost my mind." She looked at Eli, hoping he hadn't taken offense. When she saw that he was smiling she added, "I'll see you soon, then. And after that, on the way home, do you think we could stop by the store? Elsa-May has asked me to get a few things for her."

"Of course."

CHAPTER 2

Ettie stood in front of the red brick building and stared up at it as a wave of heat from the pavement swept over her. She fanned her face with her hand. She could see from the signage in the window that Andrews Lawyers was one flight up. One flight of stairs would be no problem as long as there was a handrail. She was most likely the last one to arrive, so she hurried on in.

When she found the office, she pushed the glass door open and was pleased to be surrounded by cool air from the air-conditioning, a luxury she rarely enjoyed. She walked further in and stood in front of a red-haired receptionist.

"Are you Mrs. Ettie Smith?"

"I am."

"Everyone's in Mr. Andrews' office now." The receptionist rose to her feet. "Follow me."

What Ettie had thought was a cream pullover that the woman was wearing, she now saw was a slim-fitting dress. Ettie followed the lady and studied her hair. *How can she make it stand so tall on her head like that? Would hairspray alone be able to hold it? And her hair has to be colored artificially; no one has hair that color.*

The woman opened a door and said, “Mrs. Ettie Smith has arrived.” She then stepped aside to allow Ettie through.

Ettie looked at the people in the room. The first person she saw was her Amish bishop who then introduced her to Mr. Andrews. Mr. Andrews was older than she'd expected, around sixty years of age, thin with large, black, heavy-framed glasses. She already knew Ava Glick, a young woman from the community.

Ettie took the spare seat next to the bishop. The lawyer's office was as she'd thought it would be, given the exterior of the building. The furniture was dark and heavy, and dark wallpaper lined the walls behind the bookcases, which were heavily laden with books.

“We should begin,” the lawyer said.

“Sorry I'm late. There was a problem with one of Eli's buggies.”

“It's quite all right,” Mr. Andrews said. “We're all here now.” He glanced at his watch. “I could read out the will, but to sum things up and for the sake of time, I'll tell you what she left to each of you.” The lawyer looked at Ava and then Ettie. “I'm sure you're anxious to find out.”

Ettie pushed her bottom lip out. There were only the two of

them? Surely there would be more people Agatha would have left things to since she had no family. She had many friends.

"Mrs. Smith, Agatha King left you her house, all of its contents, and fifteen thousand two hundred dollars."

Ettie's hand flew to her mouth in shock. "There must be some mistake. Her whole house?"

"That's right, Ettie," the bishop said. "There's no mistake been made; I was there and witnessed the will when she signed it."

"There are conditions," the lawyer continued. "She has requested that you allow Ava Glick to continue to lease the apartment adjoining your house for the same sum she's paying now." He took his glasses off and looked directly at Ettie. "Legally, it's not a 'condition'; no one can enforce that on you. What she meant was that she would like you to do that. She'd like you to allow Ava Glick to continue living there as long as she wishes."

"Yes, of course." Ettie smiled at Ava and Ava's blue eyes crinkled at the corners when she smiled back. Agatha had mentioned finding someone to lease the *grossdaddi haus,* but who had leased it had never come up in their conversations.

"And Ava, Agatha King left you the sum of five thousand two hundred dollars and fifty six cents."

The young woman gasped. "Oh, that was so kind of her. I don't know what to say. I can't even thank her."

"I can't believe it at all." Ettie sat there stunned with her hand covering her mouth. The next thing she knew was that everyone was looking at her.

"That's it then, Ettie. You have a house, another house," the bishop said.

Ettie saw the bishop stand and realized it was time to go.

"I don't know what to say." She pushed herself to her feet.

"One more thing," the lawyer said as he rose from behind his desk. He opened a drawer and picked up a set of keys. "You might as well take these now. The papers will take some weeks to process, but the place is as good as yours. I'll try and push it all through quickly for you. There are going to be some charges for the transfers. Would you like me to take that out of the money she left you?"

"Yes, please do that." Ettie put her hand out for the keys. "Thank you." She stared down at the bunch. There must have been twenty keys tied together on a rope. It was just like her thrifty friend to buy a quality china tea set and save money on something trifling like a keychain.

"We're neighbors now, Mrs. Smith. You're my new landlord."

Ettie smiled at the young woman who she guessed was in her mid twenties. "Call me Ettie, everyone does." Quite surprised by her friend leaving her so much, the next thing she was aware of was walking down the stairs. When Ettie reached the front of the building, Ava was nowhere to be seen. Ettie made her way to Eli's buggy and told him what had happened.

Before they got too far away from the lawyer's office, Eli said, "You had to stop by the store, Ettie?"

"Jah, the store. *Denke* for reminding me. I need to get some important things for Elsa-May."

An hour later, Ettie burst through the front door of the house she shared with her sister. Elsa-May was right where she'd left her. "Elsa-May, you'll never guess–"

"Wait! Did you get my candy?" Elsa-May lowered her knitting into her lap.

Ettie handed her the bag of candy and waited until Elsa-May had a piece in her mouth before she continued. "Agatha left me her *haus,* everything in it, and some money."

"Really? She left everything to you?"

Ettie nodded. "Mostly – she left some money to Ava Glick. "

Elsa-May screwed up her nose as she unwrapped another sweet. "Who?"

"You know, Ava – Joel and Karen's eldest *dochder."*

"Ach, I know."

"Agatha requested that I let her live there as long as she wants in the *grossdaddi haus."*

Elsa-May stared into the bag of candy. "Well, that sounds good."

"Did you hear me?"

"Jah, let Ava stay in the *grossdaddi haus."* Elsa-May looked up at Ettie and the bag of candy fell into her lap. "Wait! You're not going to move into Agatha's *haus,* are you?"

Ettie sat on the couch. "I don't see why not. With the money she left me, and the rent coming in from Ava, I'd be able to afford the upkeep of it."

Elsa-May's shoulders drooped. "Would you leave me here all alone?"

Ettie hadn't thought the whole thing through. Was she supposed to invite Elsa-May to live with her? The two of them under the same roof in the small house had been fine for a time, but as the years wore on they were getting on each other's nerves more and more. Ettie longed for some peace and quiet without her sister's constant jibes and niggles. "I don't know what I'll be doing yet." Ettie looked down at the keys in her hand.

"Those the keys?" Elsa-May asked.

"Jah."

"Let's go and have a look at the place."

"What, now?"

"Jah."

Ettie frowned. "We'd have to get a taxi and that would eat into our weekly budget."

"Didn't you just say you inherited money?"

A smile tugged at the corners of Ettie's lips. They'd no longer have to be careful of every dime. "I'll call the taxi."

Ettie hurried outside and called the taxi from the phone in the shanty outside the Millers' house a few doors down. The Millers let everyone in the street use it, and the money for the calls was placed in a jar and was collected by Mr. Miller every few days.

CHAPTER 3

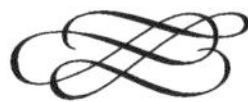

A waft of warm, stale air flowed over Elsa-May and Ettie as they pushed open the front door of Agatha's old house. The place smelled of dust and mold.

"Open some windows, Ettie."

Ettie made her way around to the windows in the living room. "It's surprising how musty it can get in such a short time. Agatha's funeral was a week ago, and the *haus* couldn't have been closed up for more than a fortnight." After she opened the windows, Ettie placed her hands on her hips. "Just as she left it."

"I wouldn't know; I haven't been here in a while," Elsa-May said as she too looked around the living room.

Ettie narrowed her eyes. "I just said it is. I wasn't asking you anything."

"No need to snap at me," Elsa-May said.

"I wasn't. I was simply saying that the place looks just the same."

"Well, why wouldn't it?"

Ettie shook her head and said nothing more. She caught sight of Agatha's rocking chair and walked over to it. "And here's her chair." She ran her fingers over the wood on the top rail of the rocking chair.

"It's her *haus* – why wouldn't her chair be in it?"

"It's my house now." Ettie gave a little giggle knowing her sister couldn't argue with that. She pictured her dear friend still alive and sitting in the chair.

"That's just what I need, a rocking chair." Elsa-May pushed past Ettie and sat in Agatha's chair. As she did, something on the floor caught her eye. She leaned forward to pick it up.

"What is it, Elsa-May?"

"I thought it was little bits of dirt, but it appears you might have woodworm or something of the sort."

Ettie leaned down to have a look. There were small holes in the floorboards. "It looks as though something's been eating it. It might be white ants."

"I'll have Jeremiah come and take a look."

"Denke, that would be good, and while he's here he can see what else needs to be done. The whole place looks rundown."

"We can go straight to his place now. These things shouldn't be left too long."

Ettie nodded and hoped she hadn't been left a liability. What if the whole house was infested with white ants and was about to fall down? It was convenient that her great nephew, Jeremiah, was a builder and lived so close.

ELSA-MAY LED her grandson into the house and showed him the holes that concerned them.

"It's not looking good." He knocked on the floor. "They've been eaten through." He knocked on the surrounding boards. "It seems to be just these few here, which is odd."

"Why is that odd?" Elsa-May asked.

"These boards appear to be made of different wood from the rest of the floor. I'd say there would have been some repair at some stage on the house and they've used a softer wood."

"Can you fix it?" Ettie asked.

Jeremiah looked up at Ettie from his crouched position. "I've got some boards in my barn that are pretty close to these others." He nodded toward the good floorboards. "If it's only those few boards that need replacing, I should be able to do it tomorrow. Oh, tomorrow's Sunday – I'm glad *Gott* tells us to have a day of rest. I'll do it first thing Monday."

"Okay, please do it," Ettie said.

"If you aren't in a hurry, I can get my tools out of the wagon and make sure it's only these few. Then I'll get under the house with a flashlight and have a look."

Ettie looked at Elsa-May.

"We're in no hurry," Elsa-May said.

Ettie nodded. "That would be excellent, Jeremiah."

Jeremiah headed out to his wagon and Elsa-May and Ettie sat down.

"This wasn't what I expected when I came over here," Ettie said.

"Best you know so you can get it fixed."

"What if they start eating the rest of the *haus?*"

"I'll ask Jeremiah; there's surely some way to treat them to ensure that they go and don't come back."

"I'll make us a cup of tea." Ettie headed to the kitchen, and when she got there she looked out the window. Jeremiah was talking to Ava. *Ah, they're about the right age for one another.* Ettie giggled as she remembered what it was like to be young and carefree. She took her mind off days gone by and put the pot on the stove. When she sat back down next to Elsa-May, she heard noises underneath their feet, indicating that Jeremiah was under the house.

Ten minutes later, Jeremiah came back inside. "I think we need to call the police."

"Why, what's the matter?" Ettie wondered if the house violated some kind of building code, but if so, why did the police need to get involved?

"There's a body under the house." Jeremiah pulled his hat off his head.

"A *dead* body?" Elsa-May asked as she made her way to stand beside Ettie.

Jeremiah nodded. "A dead *person*."

Elsa-May and Ettie stared at each other. Who would they call, now that their old friend Detective Crowley had retired?

Elsa-May looked back at Jeremiah. "Do you know who it is?"

He shook his head. "A man. Looks as though he's been dead for some time. He's wrapped up tight in plastic and covered in a blanket or rug of some sort."

Elsa-May grimaced. "Are you sure it's a man?"

Jeremiah scratched his chin. "*Nee*. I just assumed, that's all."

"Well, you go and call the police then, Jeremiah. We'll wait here," Elsa-May instructed.

Ettie and Elsa-May stared at each other again. If the man was wrapped in plastic, he'd been murdered for certain.

HALF AN HOUR LATER, an ambulance, police cars with flashing lights, and a detective were outside the house.

"Are you coming outside, Ettie?" Elsa-May asked over her shoulder as she went to have a closer look.

Ettie shook her head. "*Nee*. I'll wait here."

When Elsa-May was out of the house, Ettie peeped out the window to see Elsa-May already speaking to a detective. She sat down to the sound of banging and scraping from underneath the house as the crowd's chatter hummed in the background. Would she feel comfortable moving into this house knowing that a dead body had been under the floor? She wondered how long the body had been there. *Who could the dead person be?*

CHAPTER 4

Ettie couldn't bring herself to go out and watch what the police uncovered. A small crowd of neighbors and the press had gathered. When the ambulance took the body away, Elsa-May joined Ettie inside the house.

"Let's go home, Ettie."

Ettie looked up at Elsa-May. "What did they find?"

Elsa-May took a deep breath. "It was a man. They don't know who he is at this stage. From his clothing, it looks like he was Amish. The body's been taken to the morgue to be examined. They'll try to identify him. He had no wallet or anything on him – nothing."

"Why was he here?" Ettie turned to look at the floorboards that had led to the grisly discovery.

Elsa-May followed Ettie's gaze, and said, "Jeremiah said he was directly under those boards."

Ettie's mouth fell open. "That's right where Agatha sat; he was right underneath her feet."

"It seems so." Elsa-May slowly nodded.

"Is Jeremiah ready to go?"

"Jah, the detective's finished talking to him."

"Who's the detective?" Ettie asked.

"He's a young man, Detective Kelly. Keith Kelly, I believe he said."

"Have we met him before?" Ettie asked.

Elsa-May shook her head. "I don't think so. He's not been in the area long. He's Crowley's replacement."

"It'd be good if Crowley was still around. He was so helpful."

"Sometimes he was and sometimes he wasn't. He wasn't always eager to help when we needed it," Elsa-May reminded Ettie.

Ettie stated, "He always came through in the end if I remember correctly."

"Hmm." Elsa-May pressed her lips into a thin line, and then said, "I'm certain he wouldn't mind if we called him and told him about the dead man under the floor of your new *haus."*

Ettie shook her head. "There's no reason. I'm sure Detective

Kelly will be able to wrap things up without Crowley's help. Let him have his retirement in peace."

IT WAS Monday when Elsa-May and Ettie got a visit from Detective Kelly. Elsa-May answered the door. "Ettie, it's the detective I told you about. The one who took over from Crowley." She looked back at him. "Come in and have a seat."

The detective walked a few steps into their living room and sat on one of their rickety wooden chairs. "You two ladies knew Detective Crowley?"

"Yes, we did," Elsa-May answered before Ettie had a chance.

The detective turned his attention to Ettie. "You knew Agatha King well?"

Ettie's heart pitter-pattered at a quicker rate. The man wasn't a bit like Crowley, this man was much younger and seemed not nearly as friendly. "Yes, very well. We both knew her; she's part of our Amish community." *If only Crowley were still around.*

"She left you her house, I understand, Mrs. Smith?"

Ettie nodded.

"Did you find out who that poor man was, Detective?" Elsa-May asked.

"He was Horace Hostetler."

Ettie and Elsa-May gasped and looked at each other.

The detective leaned forward. "You knew him?"

Ettie nodded. "He disappeared many years ago. Horace and Agatha nearly married some years back."

"Many years ago." Elsa-May put her hand to her head. "I had a dreadful fear that it might be Horace."

Ettie looked at her sister and frowned. "You never mentioned that to me."

Elsa-May looked at Ettie and remained silent.

The detective made a sound in his throat, and then pulled a notepad out of his pocket. He looked up at Ettie. "When was the last time you saw him?"

Ettie ignored his question, and asked, "How do you know it was Horace? I heard that there wasn't much left of the body."

"His mother reported him as a missing person some years ago. We had his dental records on file from that time. We knew the body was dressed in Amish clothing and we don't have many reports of missing Amish men, so it didn't take as long to connect the dots."

"But he went missing when he was on *rumspringa*. So he wouldn't have been in Amish clothing," Ettie said.

"Well, Ettie, he could have just come back to the community, like we'd heard, and been killed then," Elsa-May said.

The detective raised his hand. "In or out of the community, it doesn't matter to me. Neither do the clothes he was wearing when he was murdered, except for the fact it enabled us to speed our identification of him." The detective looked between the two of them. "Now, I shall ask you again, Mrs. Smith – when was the last time you saw Horace Hostetler?"

"It was many years ago, Detective. I'd say that Agatha would've been just a girl, nearly a young woman."

"That's right, they had both left the community and Agatha returned. They were to marry before they left, and then Horace came back, but he left again suddenly. Is that how it happened, Ettie?"

"From memory, I think that's correct. I know they both left around the same time. They were going to marry, then they just up and left the community before they did, and only Agatha returned."

Elsa-May chimed in. "Obviously he'd come back or he wouldn't have been in those clothes."

The detective frowned. "They left the Amish together, then? Agatha came back, followed by Horace, and then Horace suddenly left again?"

"I had heard Horace would return and they'd continue with their plans of marriage, but he never did. Now, hearing about the clothing, it appears he did return and then he must have been murdered straight away," Ettie said.

"Could you both please keep your answers to the point?" The detective raised his eyebrows and scribbled something in his notebook. He looked up at them. “Did they get along well, Agatha and Horace?”

“As well as any couple who were going to get married,” Elsa-May answered.

“Why do you ask, Detective? You don’t suspect that Agatha had anything to do with his death, do you?” Ettie asked as she leaned forward.

He stared at Ettie and blinked a couple times. “Well, the man was murdered. He was found under her floor. When we have a murder, the first person we look at is the spouse – or, as in this case, the significant other. When you put two and two together, Mrs. Smith, you wind up with four.”

“But not always,” Ettie said before she could stop herself. When the man frowned at her she realized what she’d said. “I mean, two and two make four, of course they do. Well, except if you draw a two, and then you draw another two, and then two and two make twenty two. Very often the most likely or the obvious answer is not…”

As Ettie struggled to finish her sentence, Elsa-May chimed in. “What Ettie is trying to say is that it’s a ridiculous notion to think that Agatha was capable of hurting anyone. No one in our community would be capable of doing such a thing – that’s my opinion. I suggest, Detective, that you start looking outside the community for your murderer.”

Worried that they were getting on the wrong side of the man, Ettie changed the subject slightly. “How was Horace killed, might I ask?”

"A blow to the back of the head. Looks like it came from a broad, flat object. As there wasn't any flesh left, the coroner could only gather evidence from the skeletal remains."

Ettie grimaced at the image his words conjured up.

"Have you spoken to Horace's family?" Elsa-May asked.

"They've been informed, but they haven't been formally questioned yet."

Ettie scratched her chin. "I guess that explains why they've not heard from him in years."

"Tell me, Mrs. Smith, did Agatha ever marry?"

"No, she didn't."

The detective continued, "Did she have any gentleman friends who might have been jealous of Horace's attention toward her?"

Ettie stared into the distance and rubbed her top lip with her index finger while she thought. "If she did, I didn't know about them."

"Well," Elsa-May added. "That means 'no' because Ettie is the one person who always knows what's going on in our community. She talks to everyone – she's friends with everyone and she's always talking."

"You're making me sound like a gossiper, Elsa-May, and I'm not."

"You do talk with everyone."

Ettie frowned. "Not everyone, I don't."

The detective stood up. "Well, thank you, ladies. I might have some more questions for you at another time."

Elsa-May and Ettie stood as well. "Anytime, Detective," Elsa-May said as she showed him to the door.

Ettie walked up beside her sister and they watched him get into his car. When the sisters were alone again, they sat down.

"He thinks Agatha had something to do with Horace's death." Ettie exhaled loudly.

"It certainly sounds that way."

"I wonder how he got under the floor like that. Who do you think did it, Elsa-May?"

"I don't know anyone that would have a reason to kill him, but we don't know what happened when he was on his *rumspringa*. Many a young man has gotten himself into trouble when he ran around with the *Englischers*."

Ettie sighed. "She came back to the community without him."

"And that was after her *mudder* died and left her the *haus?*"

Ettie nodded. "Her *mudder* died when Agatha was sixteen, I remember that. It was always just the two of them with Agatha's *vadder* dying years before."

"How old was Agatha when Horace left?"

"She would've been eighteen and Horace would've been around the same age."

"And living in that place by herself?"

"*Jah*. What are you thinking?" Ettie asked her sister.

"It seems odd that a stranger would kill him and then put him under her *haus*. Wouldn't it have been easier to dump a body somewhere else rather than wrap the body and bury it under the *haus?*"

"Seems it was a good place to hide it. No one found it for forty years, and if it weren't for you spotting those holes in the floorboards, he might never have been found."

"Possibly." Elsa-May scratched her neck.

"You're not thinking Agatha did it, are you?"

"Don't you think it odd that her rocking chair was directly over the body? It's an odd place for a chair, to be placed in the middle of the room like that."

Ettie breathed out heavily and cast her mind back to her many visits with Agatha. She'd always considered it most strange for the rocking chair to be where it was, but then again Agatha did live alone. It wasn't as though she had to be mindful of others and keep the centre of the room clear. "That's what we have to do then, Elsa-May."

Elsa-May lowered her eyebrows and looked at Ettie over the top of her glasses. "What?"

"We have to find out from Jeremiah how the body would've got there."

"How would he know? He wasn't even alive back then," Elsa-

May said before she realized what Ettie meant. "Oh, I see. Did the floorboards have to be taken up for the body to be placed where it was, or was the body simply dragged under the house? That would explain why those boards were different, perhaps."

"Exactly." Ettie nodded.

"It seems obvious to me that the boards were taken up, but then the person would have had to have access to the *haus*. Well, we shall do that. First thing tomorrow we'll go and see Jeremiah."

That evening, as Ettie watered her vegetables, she cast her mind back to dredge up what she could remember about Horace and Agatha. Agatha and she weren't close back in those days. Agatha was a young single girl, and Ettie was busy with her own large family. She knew that Agatha had returned to the community, and had heard talk of Horace returning and that was all. Perhaps she should make her own enquiries with Horace's family. They'd know if Horace had spoken of having crossed or accidently wronged someone, and they might know if he'd had any enemies.

A smile crossed Ettie's face as she bent down to look at her tomato plants. The first tomato had formed. It was the size of a large cherry, and it was still green. "It's a wonder I didn't see that before," she murmured to herself. When she finished the watering, she placed the watering can by the back door. Elsa-May could be heard rattling around in the kitchen making dinner.

Ettie decided that when Elsa-May went to her Wednesday knitting circle, the day after tomorrow, she would visit Horace's family alone. If God willed it, they would find out more from Jeremiah tomorrow about how the body was placed. With that knowledge she could go to Horace's family with a little more information up her sleeve.

CHAPTER 5

Ettie and Elsa-May's taxi came upon Jeremiah's buggy just as he was leaving his house.

"Where are you two headed?" Jeremiah asked when the taxi drew even. "I could take you."

"We're coming to see you, but you could take us home and we can talk to you on the way," Elsa-May said.

"Fine." Jeremiah agreed.

After they paid the taxi driver, the two elderly ladies climbed into the buggy.

"What did you want to talk to me about?" Jeremiah clicked the horse onward.

"We were curious about the body," Ettie began.

"Jah," said Elsa-May. "How would it have been placed there?

Would it have been lowered from above? You did say you thought that some of the floorboards were different from the others."

"What are your thoughts, Jeremiah?" Ettie asked.

"It could have been dragged under the *haus,* but it's a tight fit and would've been hard to do. It would more likely have been lowered from above. And the boards there are different, but I'm not sure that's the reason. They could have still used the old boards. Lifted the boards up, lowered the body, and then nailed the boards back down."

"Would the boards normally be damaged when they lifted them up?" Ettie asked.

"Unlikely; not if someone knew what they were doing. It's not hard to lift some boards up," Jeremiah said.

"So the person who did it might have split the boards and had to replace them and that's why the boards are different?" Elsa-May asked.

Jeremiah rubbed his jaw. "It's straightforward – I don't think anyone would make a hash of lifting boards up."

"They were damaged somehow, and because the body was right underneath those replaced pieces of wood, it seems likely that's when it was done."

"Jah, it would be an extreme coincidence – the softer wood being directly over the body, and all," Jeremiah said.

"Precisely," Elsa-May commented. "So we can guess that the

person who placed the body under the floor was not good at using tools."

"A woman perhaps?" Jeremiah said, causing the sisters to glare at him. He quickly added, "I mean to say, not all women can use tools, but I'm certain there are many that can."

As soon as Elsa-May's friend, Deidre, came to fetch her for the knitting circle, Ettie hurried along the road and called a taxi. She would go to her new house and gather her thoughts before she headed to Horace's mother's place.

The ride in the taxi was a fast one and no sooner had Ettie paid the driver and got out of the taxi than she saw Ava hurrying toward her.

"Ettie, I'm glad you're here."

The taxi sped away.

"What is it, Ava? You look dreadful."

"There was a man hanging around the *haus* last night. I heard some scratching noises, so I looked outside and saw a dark figure. I opened the door and called 'who's there' and he ran off."

"Did you see who it was?"

Ava shook her head.

"I called the police first thing this morning."

"What did they say?"

"They said if I'm scared I should get a dog or a personal alarm. That's after they found out I didn't have a telephone."

"What time did you see the man?"

"Around two. I couldn't sleep and when I got up I saw it was a few minutes past two. I went to light the lamp, but before I could, I saw someone over near the front corner of your *haus*. They were crouching down."

"The police didn't come out?"

Ava shook her head. "They might have if I'd been able to call them at the time. Agatha had always talked about getting a phone in the barn, but she never did anything about it. Do you know it's in the papers?"

"What – Horace's murder?"

"Jah, the story was in the paper yesterday. When I gave the police our address, the officer said it was in the paper."

Ettie tapped her fingers on her chin, wondering if the newspaper article had caused them the unwanted attention.

"You know the police think that Agatha did it?"

Ettie looked up at her. "I thought she was a suspect, but I didn't think they thought she was a killer. Surely not."

"I'm convinced of it. They asked me to go to the police station so they could ask me some questions."

"Did you go?"

"Yes, I went yesterday."

"What did they ask you?"

"They asked me what kind of things Agatha spoke to me about, how well I knew her, if I knew any of her close friends, and if she'd ever mentioned Horace."

"Had she ever mentioned Horace to you?"

"She had. She told me there's no right man and I shouldn't wait for one. I asked her how she knew and she told me about Horace and that he disappointed her – she thought she loved him. I'm sorry now that I didn't pay more attention to what she said."

"That's sad, very sad. She was waiting for him to come back and he never did. She would've thought he didn't love her when all the while he was right under her feet."

Ava nodded. "I guess it is sad when you look at it like that. Are you going to move in or are you thinking of selling?"

"I don't think I could sell. Agatha wouldn't want me to do that, not when she said she wanted you to stay. I was seriously thinking of moving in until all this happened."

"Please move in, Ettie. I'm a little scared now. It'd be nice to have you living close by."

"You're frightened?"

"More unnerved, I'd say. There's a dark, gloomy feeling hanging over the place – Agatha's gone and now this discovery under the boards..."

"Do you want to come inside?" Ettie asked. "I can't stand for too long before I get tired."

"Okay."

Ettie and Ava walked into the house and sat down in the living room. "It's unfair that Agatha isn't here to clear her name," Ettie said.

"Nothing about the law is fair, Ettie. It's not fair that people who have no money are severely disadvantaged. Some people are in jail who wouldn't be there if they had money for bail. I heard of a man who was in jail waiting for a trial for three years and he was totally innocent – he just didn't have the money for bail."

"That is unfair."

"The world's justice system is unfairly slanted to disadvantage areas of... Oh, I'm sorry, Ettie; I'm sure you don't want to listen to my tirades."

"*Nee,* I do. I'm interested in what young people think."

Ava leaned forward. "I've done a few legal studies. I got my GED and started college, without anyone in the community knowing. It was Agatha who encouraged me."

"I won't tell anyone," Ettie said wondering what Ava's parents would have to say on the matter.

"I didn't think you would." Ava giggled.

"What happened with your studies – you said you started?"

"It's not a practical thing to do. I don't want to leave the community; I struggled with what to do for a while, before I decided to stay. I thought I might be able to do a lot of good if I became a lawyer or maybe a case worker, but then Agatha pointed out that a person can do good wherever they are and whatever they're doing."

"That's true enough. She was a smart woman."

"It's a loss, for sure and for certain. She became a good friend," Ava said before giving a sigh.

"I never saw you around when I visited her."

"I kept in my *haus* when I saw she had visitors. We respected each other's privacy like that."

Ettie chortled. "You probably didn't want to get stuck talking to old people."

"*Nee,* it's not that at all," Ava said.

Ettie slapped her hands together. "I was on my way to talk to Horace's *mudder* to see what I can find out."

"She's still alive?"

"*Jah,* she's Doris Hostetler. Horace's sister, Sadie, never married and she's still living at home."

"*Jah,* I know Doris and Sadie. I didn't realize they were related to the man who was killed. There are so many Hostetlers in the community. Can I come? I can drive you in my buggy to save you getting a taxi."

"That would be *wunderbaar; denke,* Ava. Keep your eyes and ears open. We have to find some clue that will help clear Agatha's name."

"I hope we do."

"Me too."

CHAPTER 6

When they approached the Hostetlers' place, Ettie saw Sadie sweeping the porch. "There's Sadie."

"How old would Sadie be?"

"She'd have to be sixty, and Doris, her *mudder,* is much older than I am – in her early nineties, I'd say."

"Sadie always looks so unhappy. In a scary kind of way."

"She does. She's a spinster and not to happy about it. She had two men she liked but they ended up marrying other women."

By the time they got out of the buggy, Sadie had disappeared.

Doris came to the front door and waited for them. "Ettie, Ettie." She reached out her hands toward her and Ettie took hold of them. "You heard?"

Ettie nodded. "I'm sorry, Doris."

"That's why he never came back. I always wondered if I should've done or said something different – I always blamed myself. I never could have done anything about him not coming back. I feared something bad might have happened so I reported him to the police as a missing person some years back, but I still heard nothing." Doris looked over at Ava and then back to Ettie. "Elsa-May's not with you?"

"*Nee,* she's at a knitting circle. I'm afraid I didn't tell her I was coming here, but she'll visit soon, I'm sure. You know Ava, don't you?"

"*Jah,* I do. Morning, Ava."

"Good morning."

"Ava lives in Agatha's *grossdaddi haus."*

"I'd heard that. Come in, Sadie's got the pot boiling so we can have a nice cup of hot tea."

Doris had a tight grip on Ettie's arm as she pulled her inside.

After they made polite small talk, Doris informed them the funeral was set for the day after tomorrow, on Friday. "It will be a closed casket." The lines in Doris' face depended as she frowned and looked up at the ceiling.

"*Jah,* of course," Ettie said, thinking they could do it no other way. "Did the police say anything of who might have done it?"

Doris stared at Ettie for a without answering her, making Ettie regret her sudden question. Sadie placed a tray of tea and cookies on the small table in front of them and sat down. Ettie could see that Sadie was disturbed by her brother's death. She looked paler than she usually did and her cheeks were drawn in, almost as though she hadn't eaten anything or even had anything to drink in days. The dark grape-colored dress Sadie wore under her white apron did nothing to improve her complexion.

After everyone had a cup in hand, Doris eventually answered Ettie. "They consider that Agatha was the most likely person to have done it. I told them that was nonsense."

"I see," Ettie said before bringing the tea to her lips.

"Don't you think it nonsense, Ettie?" Doris asked.

"I absolutely do, but do you have any idea who might have done it? He was on *rumspringa* at the time, I believe. Did he come back and visit you?"

Doris and Sadie exchanged glances. "He visited twice early on while he was still on *rumspringa,*" Sadie said, contributing to the conversation for the first time.

"Did he talk of anyone – anyone who had cause to harm him?"

"He did have an argument with Agatha," Sadie said opening her blue-green eyes widely.

"He did?" Ettie asked.

Sadie nodded. "He said he was coming back to the community and went to tell Agatha, thinking she'd be happy, and they had a terrible row."

Doris scrunched up her nose.

"Did he tell you that?" Ettie asked.

Sadie nodded. "He came to say goodbye straight after he'd seen her, and told me they'd had a terrible argument. Then he told me he was going away for a long time, heading up north. Before he left, he said he'd go back and try to make amends with her just one more time. That was the last time I saw him."

"Did you tell the police that?" Ettie asked.

Sadie nodded.

"You've never told me that, Sadie," her mother said looking at her in disbelief.

"I didn't want to upset you, *Mamm.*"

"The police questioned us separately. I wondered why they thought Agatha did it. Now they think she did it because of what you said, Sadie."

"I had to tell the truth, didn't I?" Sadie scrunched up her face and looked as though she would cry.

Ettie couldn't imagine how hard it would be to have a sibling disappear, not knowing if they were dead or alive.

"*Jah,* of course you had to tell the truth," Doris said, trying to calm Sadie.

"You must have missed your *bruder* over all these years, Sadie," Ava said.

"They got on so well," Doris said.

"We all missed him," Sadie said before she gave a sniffle.

"Did the police talk to the rest of your *kinner?*" Ettie asked Doris, trying to recall just how many children she had. She was certain it was six – or was it seven?

"They said they wanted to talk to them, and I gave the police all their addresses. They might have talked to them already."

"What about friends of Horace? Did you know any of Horace's *Englisch* friends?" Ava asked.

"There were two boys – well, men – he brought with him the second time he came here. He showed them the farm. I don't know their names now, but he said he worked with them."

"Doing what?" Ettie asked, hoping to have a lead.

"Building. Building new homes. It was a construction company."

"Do you remember the name of it?" Ava asked.

Doris looked at her daughter. "You'd remember it, Sadie; you've got such a good memory for names and such."

Sadie shook her head. "*Nee,* I don't remember."

Doris frowned at her. "We were talking about it just yesterday." Doris' gaze turned to the ceiling. "It was the name of a bird. Finch Homes? *Nee,* it wasn't that."

"Sparrow?" Ettie suggested.

"Wren?" Ava added.

"*Nee,* none of those. Starling, that's what it was Starling Homes. Wasn't it, Sadie?"

"That's right it was, *Mamm*. Starling Homes."

Doris took a sip of tea.

Sadie peered at Ettie. "Why are you asking all these questions, Ettie?"

"Agatha was a good friend and I want to clear her name."

Sadie asked, "How?"

"By finding out who killed your *bruder,*" Ettie added.

Doris leaned forward. "Perhaps you should leave things well alone, Ettie. He's gone and nothing will bring him back. No one in the community thinks that Agatha would do such a thing. Leave it well alone."

"What *Mamm* said is right, Ettie. He's gone; it won't bring him back."

Ettie shook her head. "*Nee,* I can't. I owe it to Agatha to clear her name. She'd want me to do that."

Ava turned to Sadie. "Was Starling Homes a local business?"

Sadie nodded. "It was, but I couldn't tell you where it was located."

Once they were in the buggy and driving away from the Hostetlers' home, Ava said, "That was interesting."

"*Jah,* it was. What part did you think was the most interesting?"

"I haven't had much to do with them, since they're so much older. I didn't know they'd be so nice and friendly."

Ettie shrugged her shoulders, wishing she'd brought Elsa-May with her instead of Ava. Still, she was pleased she had someone with her. "Now we need to find out what we can about the building company Horace worked for."

"Are you going to talk to people Horace knew back then?"

"Jah. We can look it up in a phone book at the local store on the way home. Hopefully the firm will still be in business."

"Very good." Ava nodded.

Ten minutes later, Ava returned to the buggy with a phone number and address. "Excellent," Ettie said, staring at the contact details. "We should visit and find out who they employed all those years ago."

"Would they tell us that? Wouldn't they consider that private information? And wouldn't the police be doing all this?" Ava asked.

"That's a good question. Let's go and visit Detective Kelly right now and I'll ask where he's gotten with everything."

CHAPTER 7

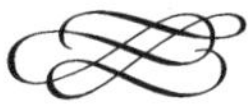

"Ah, Mrs. Smith and Ms. Glick, have a seat,"

After they sat down opposite him, Ettie looked around the office. He was in Crowley's old office sitting behind Crowley's old desk. She glanced at a framed photograph on his desk. It was an attractive dark haired woman with a dog. "Is that your wife?" Ettie asked nodding her head to the picture.

The detective frowned and tilted the picture away from sight. "Have you come with any information regarding Horace Hostetler?"

"We were hoping you might have found something out. Ava drove me here to see you because I'm a little frightened of living in the house by myself. Do you know who killed him yet?"

"It's still under investigation, but it's looking more and more like a lovers' quarrel. I'm afraid it happens more than anyone would like to think. Things got a bit heated and without thinking Agatha whacked him over the head with a frying pan; then she panicked and hid him under the floor."

"Are you certain? Agatha was such a small woman and Horace was well over six feet. If he were standing, how would she reach his head? And if sitting, wouldn't he notice her moving around him with a frying pan in hand? How would she have managed to bind his body and then place him where he was?" Ettie said.

"As I said, Mrs. Smith, it's still under investigation. I think you'll be safe enough in the house; I'd say whoever murdered that man would be long gone."

"What about the prowler I saw last night?" Ava asked.

The detective raised his eyebrows forming lines in his forehead. "You had a prowler?"

"Yes, I called here early this morning. You weren't in and they said they'd pass the message along."

The detective studied Ava for a moment before he spoke. "No, I wasn't informed."

"I asked them to tell you about the person I saw because of what had happened. I told them about the body found under the house, and they said they'd heard about it."

"What happened – did we apprehend the trespasser?" Kelly asked.

Ava shook her head. "No one came out."

"Ava said that there's never been anything like that happen at the house since she's been living there. Do you think it's got something to do with the murder, Detective?"

He shook his head. "There's a small section of the population, the criminal element, who lurk around at night looking for harmless mischief. I can't see that it's related to your friend."

Ava and Ettie looked at each other, and then Ettie said, "Someone mentioned you were going to speak to Horace's family and friends from back then?"

"We're still trying to track down a few people." The detective's eyes fell to a scrap of paper on his desk. He picked it up and asked, "You don't happen to know a Terence Wheeler, do you?" He let the paper slide from his fingers back onto the desk.

Ettie pressed her lips together and her eyes flickered upward. "No, I can't say that I do. Was he a friend of Horace's?"

"We're not sure yet. It's a name we've heard a couple times during our investigations."

"He's not from the community," Ettie added.

"We know that much. Horace's family hadn't heard of anyone going by that name."

Ettie licked her lips. "Have you looked into the building company that Horace worked for?"

"Do you have some information that we don't know about?"

"No, I don't." Ettie's eyes were glued to the detective, waiting for his next response. "Unless you didn't know about that job."

"We've got no plans to, and we did know about that." Detective Kelly leaned back. "In a case like this, this old, it's unlikely his killer will be found unless we're lucky enough to find some tangible evidence." He placed his hands out, palms up. "So far we've got nothing."

"What about looking for enemies he might have had?"

The detective laughed. "Leave the detective work to us, Mrs. Smith."

"I just thought that–"

"I know what you're saying, Mrs. Smith, but if we had any reason to believe that there was a crazed killer on the loose we'd be on to it. I think we already have a good idea who killed the man, but we'll probably never be able to prove it." The detective pushed back his chair and stood up. "Now, if you ladies will excuse me, I've got work to do."

WHEN THEY WERE outside the police station, Ava glanced at Ettie, who was staring down at her hands. "What are you thinking, Ettie? You've gone quiet."

"I just would've preferred it if the detective had treated us with respect."

"I know two reasons why he treated us that way."

"Jah, we're Amish and we're women," Ettie said with a glint in her eyes.

"Exactly." Ava laughed and then said, "Agatha couldn't have, and wouldn't have, hurt anyone in any way."

"We know that, but I don't think we've got any way of making the detective see it," Ettie said.

"Try not to get upset – we'll get to the bottom of things."

"Who do you think Terence Wheeler is?" Ettie asked.

Ava shrugged. "No idea. Are you moving into the house? I'd feel much safer if you were there."

"I shall. I'll stay there tomorrow night if that'll make you feel better. You're quite welcome to stay with me and Elsa-May tonight. We've only got a small *haus* but we have a comfortable couch."

"Nee denke, Ettie. I'll be all right. I'll sleep with a light burning."

"The offer's open if you change your mind."

"Shall I fetch you around noon tomorrow and we'll go and visit the office of the building company?" Ava asked.

"Noon will be fine."

"I've got to help my mother at the markets in the morning, but I should be done by eleven."

When Ettie walked through the front door of her old house, she smelled something delicious cooking, and then she saw Elsa-May seated and glaring at her.

"Where have you been, Ettie? I've been waiting all day."

Ettie closed the front door and sat on the couch. "You haven't. You were at the knitting circle."

"You know what I mean. When I came home I expected you to be here. And who brought you home just now?"

"It was Ava Glick. We went to the police to see what they were doing about Horace's murder. They seem to think Agatha did it."

Elsa-May raised her eyebrows. "They do?"

"*Jah.* We also visited Horace's *mudder* and *schweschder.* Sadie told the police about an argument that Horace and Agatha had. It's unlike Agatha to argue – she was so mild tempered."

"People can argue, but that doesn't cause them to kill."

Ettie nodded. "Now the police think that Horace and Agatha had some kind of lovers' tiff and she hit him over the head and killed him. Then they think she somehow managed to hide him under the floor."

"Do you think Sadie lied to the police?"

Ettie stared at Elsa-May and thought carefully about her answer. She didn't want to think of anyone as less than truthful. "*Nee,* I don't think she would lie."

"Maybe she believes what she said about the argument. That could be how she remembers things. It was a long time ago."

Ettie sighed. "I'm so tired. My mind's not working properly. Anyway, I'm going to stay at Agatha's *haus* tomorrow night."

"Do you want me to come with you?"

Ettie shook her head. *"Nee,* I'll go by myself."

"All right. It'll be strange to be here without you."

"I haven't been by myself for quite some time either." Once again, Ettie breathed in the aroma of something nice cooking. "You've got dinner on already?"

"Jah, I've got a pot roast with carrots, onions, potatoes, and turnips. Deidre gave us an apple pie."

"Goodie. I just realized how hungry I am."

"I watered the vegetables for you."

"You did?"

"I had to do something when I came home."

"Denke." Ettie leaned back in her couch and considered how much easier it was to live with another person. Elsa-May and she always shared the chores, and if she moved into Agatha's house she'd have to do everything herself.

CHAPTER 8

It was Thursday when Ava and Ettie took a taxi to the building company on the other side of town.

"How are we going to ask them about Horace, Ettie?"

"I haven't thought things through."

"I'm too nervous to say anything," Ava said.

"Best you keep quiet and let me do the talking," Ettie said. "I think an older woman will seem less threatening if anything happened back then."

Ava nodded.

The company office looked more like a lumberyard. The taxi pulled up outside eight-foot high wire fences topped with barbed wire.

"Here you are, ladies. Do you want me to wait for you?" the driver asked.

"No – we don't know how long we'll be." Ettie paid the driver, wondering if she should've asked him to wait. When she looked through the open gates she could see some kind of trailer home, which had the word 'office' printed on it in large block letters.

There was a worker on a forklift at one end and someone with a notebook in his hand walking away from them at the other. They were the only people visible as Ettie and Ava made their way to the office. Once they walked around the side of the makeshift building, they saw the office door was open. Ettie peered in. "Hello?"

"Yes," came a gruff male voice.

Ettie stepped in and saw a man who looked to be in his late thirties. "Hello, are you the boss?" The way the plump man was seated behind the desk told her that he was.

He looked Ettie up and down, then stood and extended his hand. "Yes, I'm Bill Settler."

"Ettie Smith, and this is my friend, Ava Glick."

He smiled at them as they made their way through the door.

"How can I help you?" he asked.

"We were wondering if we could take a few minutes of your time to ask you about someone who worked here many years ago."

"A few minutes? I can spare a few minutes." He smiled nicely and gestured toward some chairs. "Please, take a seat."

When they were both seated, Ettie began. "Many years ago – I'd say it would be before your time – a man by the name of Horace Hostetler worked here."

The man nodded. "I saw the piece in the paper. Someone said he once worked here. Sorry about what happened to him – was he a relative of yours?"

"A good friend."

"How can I help you?"

Ettie's mind went blank. Why was she there? She opened her mouth to speak hoping her brain would kick into gear.

"Who are you?"

The shrill voice belonged to an old woman. Ettie turned around to see an elderly lady at the door of the office.

"Oh no," Bill muttered to himself. "Excuse me for just one moment." He walked the elderly lady away, but not far enough. Ettie and Ava could hear their conversation.

"Ma, you drove here? You know the doctor told you not to drive."

"Forget that. Who's that in your office?" The woman sounded so cranky that Ettie and Ava raised their eyebrows at each other.

"It's no one, Ma. No one."

"Billy, you promised me you'd have no more to do with that woman."

"There are two women in my office and I don't know either of them. They're strangers; I've never met them before. They're after donations for charity. I'm writing out a check and then they'll leave. Now, you go home and I'll come and see you after work."

"You're sure you don't know them? Not lying to me again, are you?"

"No, ma, I'm telling you the God's honest truth."

"I've got some lunch for you and Chad in the backseat. Be a dear and fetch it?"

"We order lunch in. Just stop fussing. We're not going to take the food."

Ettie stood and looked out the small window to see Bill put his hands on his hips.

He continued, "I'm going to have Tony drive you home, and he'll bring your car back here." The old lady didn't look too happy when Bill called one of his workers over to drive her home.

"But–"

"No. No more. I'll come over when I finish work today. Will that make you happy?"

"Make sure you do," Bill's mother said.

Once Bill was back with Ettie and Ava, he said, "Sorry about the interruption."

"Was that your mother?" Ettie asked.

Bill smiled and sat down. "Since my father died she's been – I don't know what the word is – overprotective, perhaps?"

Ettie laughed. "We never see our children as grown up. They'll always be little ones in our eyes."

"I suppose you're right." The corners of Bill's eyes creased as he smiled. "I'm not much better. My boy wanted to leave school early and I insisted he work with me for a year before he goes anywhere else. He just seemed too young to be out in the big world."

"If you don't mind me saying, Mr. Settler, I overheard what your mother said. Do you know some people in our community?"

"We've had many Amish people work here, mostly when they're on their *rumspringa*. My mother's losing her mind and doesn't know what she's saying half the time." Bill laughed.

Ava put their conversation back on track. "We're here because we want to know if anyone who worked here might have known Horace Hostetler."

"I'm certain they would've, but I wouldn't know who knew him or who didn't. As you said, it was many years before my time. We've always had workers come and go." He raised his eyebrows slightly. "But you're in luck."

Ettie's face lit up and she leaned forward to hear why they were in luck regarding news of Horace's employment while he was on *rumspringa.*

Bill continued, "I've got records from back then down in one of the storage units. My father never threw anything away, and I'm afraid I've taken after him in that regard. Now we've got our records computerized, but I haven't been able to find it in me to throw the old paperwork out."

"Would you mind if we went through it?" Ava asked.

"It might take me days to find the exact year you're looking for."

Ettie told him the approximate years Horace would've worked there.

He looked at each of them in turn. "Can I ask you ladies what's so important?"

Ava and Ettie looked at each other.

"Are you trying to find out about his murder?" he asked before either lady could respond.

Ettie nodded. She didn't want to give too much away, but she had to say something to get the man to look for the information.

Bill leaned back in his chair. "You're trying to find who killed him and you think the man who killed him might have worked here? Is that it?"

Ava jumped in. "No, we just want to ask questions of people who knew him back then when he had left the community."

"Aren't the police doing that?" Bill asked.

"They have their own theories," Ettie said.

"The police haven't been by. Do you think they'll come around here asking questions?"

Ettie shrugged "I'm not sure."

"I'll help you all I can. I'll go through the records this afternoon. So you want a list of names of people who worked here at the same time as the man who was murdered?"

"Yes, Horace Hostetler."

The man grabbed a piece of paper out of the printer behind him and clicked on the end of his pen. He pushed the paper and pen toward Ettie. "You'd better write that name down for me."

Ettie wrote Horace's name and handed the paper back to Bill.

"Give me a couple days, and I'll have some names for you."

Ettie frowned. At first he said he'd look into it that afternoon and now he was saying two days? He didn't seem to be aware of the urgency. "Is there any way we can get those names sooner? We don't mind going through some old boxes or wherever you've got the papers stored."

Bill raised his brows. "That important, is it?"

Ettie and Ava nodded.

"I'll have my son, Chad, take you over to the storage shed where the records are kept. They've got the years on the end of the boxes. Now, as well as employee records there are sales receipts, taxation records – I'd ask you not to disturb anything."

"Thank you so much. You've been very helpful," Ettie said.

The man chuckled. "Well, you can put a good word in for me with the old guy upstairs."

Ava and Ettie smiled at him.

Bill walked past them and opened the door. Ettie could see a man standing not too far away and she wondered if he had been listening in.

"There you are, Chad – you were supposed to be on the forklift today."

"Just taking a break, Pa."

"These ladies here need to be escorted over to the unit where we keep the old files. They're looking for people who worked here 'round the time of that guy they found under that house – the one that was in the paper."

Chad nodded. "Okay."

Bill pushed the door open for the ladies to walk out. "This is my son, Chad."

The ladies said hello.

Bill said, "Follow him, and please don't make a mess of the records. My father was meticulous, so please, leave everything where you find it."

Ava asked, "Might we borrow pen and paper to write with?"

"Of course you can." Bill went back into his office and came out with an empty notebook and two pens.

"Thank you, Mr. Settler. You've been so helpful."

He laughed. "I've been called many things in my time, but helpful – not so often." He looked at his son. "What are you waiting for?"

"This way," Chad said to the ladies.

CHAPTER 9

Ettie's eyes fell on the right box immediately – the years were written in large black letters on the end. She pointed at the box, knowing Horace had worked there in the mid-seventies. "There."

Chad pulled the box out for them. He leafed through the files until he found the ones with the employees. He handed some folders to Ettie.

Ettie leafed through them. "Here he is, Horace Hostetler. Write down these names, Ava." Ettie handed Ava a stack of papers. Each page contained an individual employee's name and address.

"That's going to take some time," Chad said. "Why don't you photocopy them?"

"Do you have a photocopier?" Ava asked.

"In my father's office, but he probably won't let you use it. You can take them with you and bring them back when you're done."

"Your father seemed protective of these records. I daren't take anything," Ettie said.

Chad shook his head. "We're only required to keep records for so many years – I think it's seven or something like that. We don't need to keep all these ancient ones." He flung his hand toward the rows of boxes. "I'll copy them for you, and I'll bring them by when I finish work."

Ettie looked at Ava. "What shall we do?"

Ava looked down at all pages in her hand. "Well, there's an awful lot here, Ettie."

"We've had a lot of people work here. People come and go all the time, always did. I don't mind doing it. Just tell me your address."

"It's on the other side of town."

"That's okay. I just got my license and I need the practice."

"That's awfully kind of you. Ava, why don't you write down our address for Chad?"

While Ava wrote, Chad asked, "What are you trying to find out?"

"The police think that Horace was killed by our friend who died recently. We know she didn't do it," Ettie said.

"You're trying to find out who really did kill him? Aren't you scared?"

"No, not a bit," Ettie admitted.

Chad's eyes widened. "You think one of these people killed him? Someone who used to work here?"

Ettie shook her head. "No, we just want to talk to someone he knew back then. You see, he left our Amish community briefly on what we call a *rumspringa* – that's when young people can leave our community for a time and they are free from following our rules. Anyway, we want to talk to people who knew him, people other than our Amish folk."

"I know, my father told me about the Amish. I hope you find something out. Why do the police think your friend did it, then? Surely they'd have to have some kind of evidence to suspect her."

"Someone told the police about an argument our friend had with him," Ava said.

Chad nodded. "I read about how the body was found under the floor of the house. Funny that the body was there for so long without anyone knowing. You'd think that a body would smell after a while. It would rot or something, wouldn't it?"

"He was wrapped up," Ava said. "In plastic."

"That's awful. I'd hate to have that job – the job of unwrapping the body. Who had to do that?"

Ettie pushed out her lips. "I don't know. I stayed inside when they were doing that."

"You were there?" Chad asked.

"Oh yes. It's my house." Ettie realized the boy didn't know the full story. "My friend left me the house, and my sister noticed something wrong with the floorboards so she had her grandson come take a look. He's a builder – my sister's grandson, my great nephew."

"Go on," Chad urged, his eyes wider still.

Ettie continued, "He lifted up a board, then went under the house and he found the body directly under the boards – the ones that weren't right."

"And did he – your sister's grandson – unwrap the body?"

"No, that's when we called the police."

"I read in the paper he was covered in plastic, but I thought he'd still stink. And wouldn't someone have looked for what was causing the smell? If I wrapped a dead animal in plastic, I'd reckon it would stink after some time."

"I don't know anything about that. I didn't know my friend very well back then," Ettie said.

Chad pushed his dark hair away from his face. "What did they find with him?"

Ettie frowned. "Like what?"

Chad shrugged his shoulders. "I don't know. I just think it's odd that he was under the house like that. The paper said he had no identification on him, nothing."

"That's right. Well, we better go now. Thank you for being so helpful," Ava said, handing him their address.

"I'll have these to you later on."

"Thank you, Chad. Where might we go to call for a taxi?" Ava asked.

He pulled a cell out of his pocket. "I'll call one for you."

"We'll wait outside." Ava put her arm through Ettie's.

When they were out of the front gates, Ava said, "What a strange young man."

Ettie had to agree. "What do you make of him asking all those questions?"

"I don't know, but I didn't like it."

"I think he might be right about the body having an odor even though it was wrapped in plastic. I wonder why Agatha was never bothered by the smell?"

"Maybe she just didn't know what it was," Ava suggested. "Do you think that might be partly the reason the police think she did it?"

"Possibly. I know she wasn't the kind of woman not to look into something like a strange smell."

"Shall I see what I can find out? I know someone who works at a funeral home. I could ask him some questions and find out what would be expected in a situation like Horace's."

"*Jah,* do that," Ettie said.

"Okay. Do you think that young man asked too many questions?" Ava asked.

"Murder doesn't happen often around these parts. You know what people are like; he was probably just curious with it being in the newspaper and all."

CHAPTER 10

Ettie was alone in Agatha's house when Chad knocked on the door to deliver the photocopies as he'd said he would. When Ettie opened the door she was pleased to see him.

"There you go." He handed the pages to Ettie.

"Thank you. It was so kind of you to do this for us."

"No problem." He pinched the front of his loose white shirt and shook it. "It's so hot. Do you think I could have a glass of water?"

"Yes, come in."

Ettie headed to the kitchen with Chad close behind her. She placed the papers down on the kitchen table and proceeded to the sink. "I'm sorry I can't offer you chilled water." She turned away from the sink and was surprised to see him right behind her.

"This is fine," he said taking the glass from her. He drank quickly and handed her the empty glass. "Thank you. I hope you find what you're looking for. I'll leave you to it." He turned and walked toward the front door with Ettie close behind. When he was in the middle of the living room, he stopped. "Where exactly did they find him?" His gaze swept across the floor.

Ettie thought it macabre that he would want to know, but like she'd said to Ava, he was probably just curious. "Around this area," Ettie said with a sweep of her hand. She had moved the rocking chair to the side of the room.

The boy pulled a face then looked up at Ettie. "A terrible way to go."

Ettie nodded, then walked past him to the front door, hoping he would follow. She opened the door and he walked out. "Thank you once again, Chad."

"Bye, Mrs. Smith."

Once he was gone, Ettie wasted no time in flicking through the stack of papers. Something about Chad struck her as odd. What if he'd left some names out? But why would he do that? Now Ettie regretted taking up his offer of delivering the copies to her home. He'd acted strangely and she was certain that she couldn't trust him.

Before long, Ettie heard Ava calling to her from the back door.

"Door's open, Ava."

Ava joined Ettie at the kitchen table. "I see Chad's been here?"

Ettie looked up from the pages. "Yes, and he asked where the body was found."

Ava shivered. "Weird."

"Anyway, did you speak to your friend from the funeral home?"

"Jah. Myles said that the body would still smell even though it was wrapped in plastic. He told me about a murder victim last year. The people living in an apartment block complained of a dreadful smell coming from one of the apartments. That's how the authorities were notified – because of the smell. And that body had been wrapped in layers of plastic."

"So the smell would've been bad. Well, there are no close neighbors here, and back then it was just Agatha living in the house by herself with no one living in your *grossdaddi haus."*

ELSA-MAY AND ETTIE arrived at the cemetery for the funeral of Horace Hostetler. The bishop was getting ready to give the message at the graveside when Ettie saw two cars amongst the buggies. She had to find out who the *Englischers* were.

"Ettie, are you looking at the cars?"

Ettie turned around and saw Ava, who continued, "Do you think that they might be some friends he had from all those years ago when he was on *rumspringa?"*

"How would they know about his funeral?"

"It was in the local paper. I've got a copy of it in my buggy.

There's another article that came out in the paper this morning along with a picture of Horace as a young man – must've been taken when he was on *rumspringa*. It gives the whole story and gives the address of your *haus*."

Knowing the Amish didn't read the *Englisch* papers, Ettie asked. "How did you know it was in there?"

"I didn't. Myles, my friend from the funeral home, told me. He came early this morning and asked if I wanted him to come with me today. I said no, but he did give me a copy of the paper if you want to see it."

"I'll have a look at it later," Ettie said. The outsiders were never hard to spot amongst the Amish. Ettie's gaze swept over the crowd. "Ava, there are two *Englisch* men standing over there. Why don't you go talk to them?"

"Why me?"

"Because I want to have another talk with Sadie."

Ava looked around as though she were looking for Sadie. "Here?"

"*Jah,* now go. We've no time to waste."

While Ava went off in the direction of the *Englischers,* Ettie caught sight of Sadie. Ettie walked toward her then stood close to her until she caught her eye.

"Hello, Ettie."

"Hello, Sadie. I see your cousins from Ohio are here?"

"*Jah,* the whole *familye* have come."

Ettie nodded. The look of sadness in Sadie's eyes deterred Ettie from asking her anything regarding Horace or Agatha.

Ettie was all too familiar with loss. She'd lost her parents, then her husband years ago, and two weeks ago she lost her constant canine companion; her loving dog, Ginger. Ettie rubbed Sadie's arm in an affectionate manner and Sadie smiled sweetly. Her talk with Sadie could wait for another day. Today was her time to say goodbye to the man she'd grown up with as her brother. There were other people heading over to talk to Sadie, so Ettie walked on and stood to the side where she'd get a good view of the people attending the funeral.

Ava appeared deeply involved in a conversation with the two men who looked like they knew each other. Could they be two men that Horace had worked with at the building company? Even though Horace would've known many more people when he was living as an *Englischer,* the building company was the only place they knew that he had worked.

When Ava came back, Ettie asked, "What did you find out?"

"One's a reporter and the other is an off-duty policeman."

Ettie was disappointed that they weren't people who knew Horace.

The bishop stood by Horace's grave plot, and then coughed loudly to draw everyone's attention. Four Amish men carried the coffin to the graveside. Ettie admired how fine they looked in their black suits and hats. They rested the coffin by the freshly dug grave while the bishop gave a lengthy talk about the meaning of this life and the life hereafter. Ettie stood next to Elsa-May, and while Ettie was being careful to appear as though she was listening to what the bishop had to say, she studied everyone in the crowd. She knew most of the Amish folk with the exception of Horace's Ohio relations.

Ettie's attention was drawn to a car that had just parked nearby. She strained her eyes to see who was getting out of the car. It was a man dressed in a dark suit and when he leaned against his car, Ettie was certain it was Bill Settler.

Elsa-May followed her sister's gaze. "Who's that?" she whispered.

"It's Bill Settler from the building company where Horace once worked. He's Horace's old boss' son."

"Hmm. It's awfully nice of him to pay his respects."

Ettie nodded and wondered why Bill stayed a distance away, and on further thought wondered why he'd come at all.

CHAPTER 11

Once the funeral was over, Elsa-May asked, "Are you coming home tonight, Ettie, or staying at the new *haus?*"

"I'll stay at Agatha's *haus.* Ava's a little worried about being on her own. She feels safer with me there."

"Very well. Jeremiah's driving me home. Are you going home with Ava or shall I have Jeremiah take you?"

"I'll go with Ava, *denke.*" Ettie looked around to see if Mr. Settler was still there, but his car had gone. Turning back to see Elsa-May walking away, Ettie called after her, "I'll come by tomorrow."

"Are you ready to go?" Ava asked.

"Oh, there you are, Ava. Did you see Bill Settler standing by his car?"

"*Nee*. Where was he?"

"He parked his car just behind that white one. He watched from a distance for a few moments before he disappeared."

"Are you sure it was him?"

"Pretty certain. *Jah*. As certain as I am that I'm looking at you right now."

Ava walked toward her buggy and Ettie walked alongside. "I've been thinking about a few things, Ettie. How was the body wrapped exactly? Was it only in plastic? They said they couldn't get any DNA material from the skeleton or something of that nature. So does that mean he was only a skeleton?"

"I took it that they meant they wouldn't have any DNA material from the killer because he had rotted away so much."

"How could we find out?" Ava asked.

Ettie chuckled. "I'm not going back near Detective Kelly anytime soon."

"Would Jeremiah know?" Ava asked. "I'm mean, since he was there at the time?"

Ettie drew her eyebrows together while she thought. "Elsa-May was outside when the police came. She didn't talk about it, though. I wonder if she knows more about the body. I'll ask her when I go home tomorrow. I'm going to Agatha's tonight and tomorrow I'll visit Elsa-May."

"It must be confusing. I guess you'll have to pick a place soon, where you want to live."

"All in good time. I've come to learn that when you give things time, the right decisions become obvious. I used to make quick decisions when I was younger – I was always in such a rush – but now that I'm older and moving more slowly, I realize that things always have a way of sorting themselves out."

"I guess that makes sense. If you live a little bit in both places, you'll soon know where you're happiest."

"Something like that, dear, something like that."

Ava dropped Ettie by her front door and then continued on to the barn to tend to her horse.

Ettie pushed her front door open, and she didn't go more than two steps when she saw something was wrong. She gasped and walked two more steps. The whole living room had been destroyed. Every floorboard had been taken up. She walked farther and looked down at the dirt below the house. Only the cross joists remained.

She hurried out the door to fetch Ava. "Ava, come quick."

"What is it?" Ava said as she jumped down from the buggy she'd just stopped near the barn.

Between gasps, Ettie said, "All the boards in the main room have been taken up. Go call the police. Try to speak to Detective Kelly; tell him it's urgent."

"The floorboards?"

"*Jah,* Ava, hurry – go now."

While Ava raced to the end of the road to call the police, Ettie sat on the front steps of her new home. It was an uncanny feeling, knowing that someone had entered uninvited and violated what had been a peaceful home for her friend of many years. She looked down the road to the nearest neighbor, now grateful that she and Elsa-May had people living close on either side. If there had been people living closer to here, they would've been sure to hear some noise. But Agatha had liked her large parcel of land, which allowed her to keep a few animals and have a large barn.

If Elsa-May hadn't gotten those new glasses and seen the marks on the floor, they might never have known that Horace was under the house. Pulling herself to her feet, Ettie decided to walk around the house to see what she could see. The disruption that had come to the house since it had been given to her made her wonder if she should continue to live with Elsa-May. It was nice to have family around in emergencies.

"Are you all right?"

Ettie looked over to see that Ava had returned.

"*Jah,* I'm okay. Did you talk to the detective?"

Ava nodded. "They're coming soon. Wait in my place while I put the horse and buggy away."

Ettie walked into Ava's *grossdaddi haus* and put the pot on the stove. A cup of tea always made her feel better. When she sat at the table, Ava came through the door. "Ava, I know you said you talked to the detective, but did you speak to Detective Kelly directly?"

Ava shook her head and slumped into a chair. "Nee, but I told them my message the other day was not passed on. I insisted they tell him, and they said they would. They told me someone would come out straight away."

"Tea?" Ettie asked.

"Jah, that would be nice."

Ettie and Ava sat drinking tea while they waited for the police.

"They take a long time." Ettie looked up at that moment, and heard a car pulling up outside. "Ah, that must be them. Let's go."

Ettie was pleased to see Detective Kelly. At last he was taking things seriously. She showed the detective and the two officers with him the destruction to her house.

"What do you think, Detective?" Ettie asked.

The detective got as close as he could and looked at the damage. "I'd say it was some crazed souvenir hunter. We've had them before; very often they try to find something to auction online." He looked back to Ava and Ettie. "They wouldn't have found anything. I had my men comb the area the day after we found the body."

"They didn't find anything?" Ava asked.

"No."

"Shouldn't you take fingerprints or something?" Ettie asked.

The detective looked at Ettie and then walked toward the front door. He leaned down and said, "No sign of forced entry." He directed the two officers to walk around the house and find the point of entry.

"I didn't lock the door," Ettie said.

The detective's mouth fell open. "Why not?"

Ettie pulled a face. "I never do when I go out during the day. No one locks their doors around here." When Ettie saw the detective looking at her in disbelief she added, "I lock it at night when I go to sleep."

Detective Kelly shook his head. "I know you trust your neighbors and you're surrounded by your Amish people, but anyone can come into the area."

Ava said, "They could've just as easily come up through the floorboards, couldn't they? If they were looking for something under the house?"

The detective ignored Ava, kept looking at Ettie, and took a deep breath. "I suggest you find yourself somewhere else to stay tonight."

"Stay with me, Ettie." Ava placed a hand on Ettie's shoulder.

"I might as well since I'm here already. Will you have the fingerprint team go over the place for evidence?" Ettie looked up at the detective who towered above her.

He shook his head. "Trespassing and damage to property are crimes, but Mrs. Smith, you left your front door open."

"Unlocked, Detective. The door was closed."

Kelly heaved a sigh. "I'll see what the men have found and I'll make a report." He looked back over his shoulder at the loose boards that had been thrown in a corner. "Do you have someone to fix this?"

"I've got my great nephew, Jeremiah. He's a builder."

"He's the one who found Horace," Ava said.

"Ah, yes. I met him the other night. Well, very good." He looked at Ava. "And you'll look after Mrs. Smith tonight?"

Ava nodded. "I will. She'll be fine with me."

The detective walked out the door.

Ava put her arm around Ettie's shoulder. "It's nearly dinnertime. I'll heat us up some soup."

"Tomorrow morning do you think you could tell Jeremiah what happened and have him come as soon as he can? I don't like to leave it like this for too long."

"*Jah,* I will. Don't worry about another thing. You can sleep in my bed tonight and I'll take the sofa."

"*Nee,* I can't put you out like that."

"I won't hear another word, Ettie – you're taking the bed."

Ettie smiled and nodded, then tried to remember if she'd told Elsa-May she'd be back that night, or whether she told her she'd be staying at Agatha's house.

CHAPTER 12

Ettie woke to hammering coming from the main house. When she saw how light it was she knew she'd slept in. The noise had to be Jeremiah already at work fixing her floor. She got up and looked around for her dress. Ava had been good enough to loan her a nightgown. She closed the bedroom door and saw her dress hanging on a clothes peg. After she changed into her dress and *kapp*, she looked around the *grossdaddi haus* for Ava. When she realized Ava wasn't in any of the rooms, she peered out the window and saw Ava's horse was gone, too.

Ettie went straightaway to see how Jeremiah was getting along with the work. She pushed her door open and saw Jeremiah leaning over, placing the boards back. He looked up when he saw her.

"Aunt Ettie, I found something." He placed his hammer down, stood, and stepping on the joists, made his way over to the side of the room. Ettie stepped forward to see what it was. Jeremiah picked something off the windowsill and made his way over to hand it to her. "There's a key inside." Jeremiah wiped his sweaty forehead with the sleeve of his shirt.

Ettie examined the small, rectangular envelope in her hand. It seemed brittle and she was almost afraid to handle it. It was undoubtedly old from the yellowing of the paper. The number 157 was printed on the outside.

"There's a key inside," Jeremiah said.

"Yes, I heard you, but I'm still looking at the envelope. From the look of it, it's been here for some time. Where exactly did you find it?"

"It was taped flat to one of the boards inside a strip of brown paper. At first I didn't see it because it was the same color as the wood."

Ettie opened the envelope and dropped the key into the palm of her hand. It was unlike any key she'd seen before. "I think the detective needs to see this."

"Does it open something around here, do you think?" Jeremiah asked.

"Nee, Jeremiah. I would say most certainly it doesn't."

The sound of a buggy outside told Ettie that Ava was back. Ettie hurried out of the house to Ava, who had just pulled up outside the barn. When Ettie reached her she said, "Ava, *denke* for fetching Jeremiah this morning."

"That's fine, Ettie. I went early and stopped by the markets on my way home. Is something wrong?" Ava stepped down from the buggy.

"Ava, Jeremiah found something. He found a key. I'm sure that's what the people were looking for."

"The ones who ripped up the floor?"

Ettie nodded. "I'm certain that they were looking for this key." Ettie passed Ava the key and she turned it over and studied it carefully.

"Why weren't the police able to find it? They were under the house for some time looking for evidence."

"It was taped flat, Jeremiah said, hidden by brown paper that matches the boards. They might not have been looking for things like that. They were most likely looking for things in the ground, or under the dirt."

Ava nodded.

"Can you drive me to show Detective Kelly?" Ettie asked.

"*Jah,* okay. Can I have breakfast first? I've brought us some fresh baked bread from the markets."

"*Wunderbaar,* and I'll see if your chickens have laid eggs."

"They aren't my chickens, Ettie."

"They aren't? Are they mine?"

Ava laughed. "I don't know, Agatha didn't say who she wanted to have the chickens."

"I'm too old to look after chickens, and I know enough people who give Elsa-May and me eggs all the time. You can have them if you want them."

Ava smiled. "*Jah,* I'd like them."

"That's one thing settled," Ettie said. "Hopefully by the end of the day we'll have a few more things settled around here."

"IT'S JUST A KEY, Mrs. Smith. I'm sure if you dig under any house in this county you'd find a key or two," Detective Kelly said. He barely looked at Ava or Ettie. By the way his mouth was clamped tight and his cheeks sucked in, Ettie knew that he was severely annoyed they'd come to see him. He hadn't asked them into his office, but with an armful of files clutched to his chest, spoke to them at the front desk in earshot of everyone nearby.

Ettie offered the yellowed envelope to the detective so he could inspect it and the key. "This doesn't look like just any key, and it was hidden, taped onto a board – underneath the floor. This might be what they'd come back to find."

The detective slammed down the folders he was holding onto the front desk. "Look, Mrs. Smith, we do like the support of the community, but you're crossing the line and bordering on being obstructive. You seem to think that we're doing nothing. I've had our evidence technicians comb the area and we've taken samples of dirt from under your house. The matter is heavily under investigation." He leaned his body forward and stuck out his lower jaw. "You're not being helpful, you're being a hindrance." He straightened up and tipped his head to the side and stared at Ettie. "Now, if you'll excuse me, I've got work to do."

Ettie pushed out her lips.

"C'mon, Ettie," Ava said tugging at her arm.

"Do you want to take it in as evidence, at least?" Ettie asked. "It's an unusual shaped key. Won't you just take a quick look at it?"

The detective rolled his eyes before saying, "I'm done."

Ettie and Ava stood there watching as the detective walked away. The two seated policemen staring at them from behind the front desk caught Ettie's attention.

Ettie stepped back and whispered to Ava, "It's time to do our own investigations."

Ava raised her eyebrows. "How?"

"That name the detective gave us the other day – Terence something."

"Terence Wheeler?"

"*Jah,* that was it. Why don't we start by looking up that name on the library computer? You can look up the Internet, can't you?"

"*Jah,* of course I can, but what about the key?"

"The key isn't going anywhere for the moment." Ettie stuck the envelope containing the key up her sleeve.

Ava nodded. "Let's go then. The library's only down the road."

"I've used the computer at the library before, but I'm sure you'll be faster and more capable."

Ava giggled. "Ettie, you're full of surprises."

AVA PUNCHED some things into one of the library computers and read what was on the screen. "Terence Wheeler was incarcerated numerous times for robberies. He specialized in jewelry and diamond theft."

"It pays to specialize, they say." Ettie peered over Ava's shoulder.

"He's dead," Ava announced suddenly.

"Really? What else does it say about him? When did he die?" Ettie sat down in the chair next to her.

"In 1975 he was arrested for the Tonkins jewelry heist, but charges were dropped. He was identified as being at the scene of the crime, but the jewelry was never recovered."

"That was around the same time Horace disappeared. Look up the Tonkins jewelry heist, see what you can find out," Ettie ordered.

"Okay, let's see now." Ava pressed the keys on the computer

while Ettie leaned back in her chair. "The Tonkins were a wealthy couple visiting from England. They had jewelry and diamonds they'd just purchased in an auction. Until they left town they were kept in a safe at the hotel where they were staying. Just before they booked out, two of the hotel staff were taking the jewelry back to their suite when two men wearing black masks held them up at gunpoint. Some of the hotel staff recognized Wheeler as being in the hotel that morning."

"Hardly grounds for arrest, I would think," Ettie said.

"A huge coincidence, though. Why would he have been at the hotel when he had a home in the area?"

"He could've been visiting someone, or having a meal. Does it say anything else?"

Ava scrolled down the screen. "That's all it says. The jewelry was never recovered and they had to drop the charges against the man."

"I wonder if Crowley was around back then…"

"Your old detective friend?"

"That's the one. I think it's time to pay him a visit." Ettie wrote down a number for Ava. "Here, phone this number and tell Crowley that I'd like him to come to my place this afternoon. Give him my new address."

"Okay." Ava took the number from Ettie and headed to the public telephone in the foyer of the library.

Minutes later, Ava returned. "He'll be there at two."

"We best get back to the house."

AVA LEFT Ettie to talk to Crowley alone. He'd been retired a while and she looked forward to seeing him again. She sat in the living room until she heard a car, then she opened the front door for him.

"New house, Ettie?" Crowley asked as he walked toward her.

"A good friend left me this house. It's a long story."

"Elsa-May's well, I hope?"

"She is." Ettie patted Crowley on his arm. "It's nice to see you again."

"Likewise."

"Well, come in." Ettie walked inside and when Crowley followed she closed the door after him. "Come through to the living room."

When Crowley sat, he said, "It seems bigger than your old house, but it looks as though there are lots of repairs needed." He frowned as he looked around the room.

He was right; both the inside and the outside sorely needed painting, the gutters needed fixing and judging by the uneven floor, the footings – or at least some of them – needed attention.

"Your friend said you wanted to see me urgently?"

Ettie told Crowley everything about Horace and Agatha and then what had happened to her floor.

"Wheeler was a known criminal. He was often arrested but we weren't able to make any of the charges stick. I helped work on one of his arrests, but I'd only just joined the force, so I was only shuffling papers on the case. We were going after Wheeler and another criminal, Settler. They were adversaries. The two of them hated each other, that was well known."

Ettie handed him the small envelope. He tipped the key into his hand.

"This is what my great nephew found when he was nailing my floorboards back. He's a builder, you see, and he's Elsa-May's grandson."

He held the key up. "This is a safe deposit box key."

"Good. And what's that?" Ettie asked.

"If someone wants to keep something safe, they can lease a box from the bank. Many people keep important paperwork or private things in their boxes."

"Jewelry?"

"Certainly. Coins, jewelry, gold, all those kinds of things." He turned the envelope over. "With any luck, the number on this envelope will correspond with the number of the box. They don't normally have the number on the key."

"You've seen these keys before?" Ettie asked.

Crowley nodded. "They're all usually square like this, with

these flat grooved edges." He ran his finger along the key to show Ettie what he meant.

"I think the person who destroyed my house was looking for this key."

"You mentioned Terence Wheeler before – what did Detective Kelly say about him?"

"He asked if we'd heard his name. We said no, and that's all that was said."

"We?" Crowley asked.

"Ava was with me. Ava lives in the *grossdaddi haus* attached to this place. It's like a small apartment. Anyway, Ava and I went to the library to look up Terence Wheeler and we found out that he might have been involved in a big robbery."

Crowley nodded. "Yes, the one involving the English couple who were robbed at their hotel."

"Do you think this might be Terence Wheeler's key? Maybe Horace knew something and was killed because of it."

"Did Horace know Terence Wheeler?"

"I don't know; Detective Kelly didn't say. All he said was that his name had come up in his investigations around Horace."

"You said the key was taped to one of the boards?"

Ettie nodded. "So it was unlikely that it was dropped – it was hidden deliberately."

"It seems so, Ettie."

"Why would Wheeler hide the key under my house?"

"He could've been coming back to get it. He died not long after his arrest, and from what you've said that corresponds with the time that Horace went missing."

"Do you think Wheeler killed Horace?"

Crowley shook his head. "From what you've told me so far, there's not enough evidence to say anything of the sort."

"Tell me more about these boxes. If someone loses the key can't they just go to the bank and say they've lost it? And the bank opens it for them?"

"It's not as easy as that. The person would need to sign a stack of paperwork; it would take about two weeks before the bank could arrange to have the box drilled open. Not the best way for someone to hide stolen jewelry."

"He's dead now, so no one will be getting into his box, I guess. Not without the key."

"Sometimes a bank will shut down someone's box when they know someone's died. It's hard for relatives to get the contents out; there's a lot of red tape involved."

"How can one tell which bank the key belongs to?" Ettie asked.

"You can't. Detective Kelly would have to get a warrant and start with the local banks. Not all banks have safe deposit boxes. I'm certain only one in town does." Crowley looked down at the key. "I'm guessing it's too late to bother with prints?" He looked across at Ettie.

"I'm afraid so. I'm sorry, but we didn't realize the importance of it. We've both touched it, Ava and I, and so has Jeremiah."

Crowley slipped the key back inside the envelope before placing it in his inner coat pocket. "It'll be very interesting to find out who this key belongs to."

"I don't know if you'll have any luck speaking to that new detective," Ettie said.

Crowley scratched his neck. "Don't you worry about that, Ettie."

Crowley stood and disappeared out the door. Ettie was happy that someone was finally listening. Crowley had been a little like Detective Kelly when she first knew him.

Ettie had just sat down with a cup of tea when she heard a knock at the door. She knew it wasn't Ava because she always came to the back door. Maybe Crowley's forgotten something. When she flung the door open, there before her stood Sadie.

"Sadie, how nice to see you. Come in. Come through to the kitchen – I've just made a pot of tea."

"Denke, Ettie." Sadie followed Ettie into the kitchen, dragging her feet. When Sadie was seated, she began. "Oh, Ettie, I'm just so upset over everything that's happened. I'm too upset to live."

"Life has its low points, but don't go saying things like that. How's your *mudder* coping now?"

"Still upset. Your visit the other day cheered her up. I always thought he had died, and that's why he never came back." She balled her hand into a fist and held it against her stomach. "I felt he was dead." Sadie looked up at Ettie. "I didn't want it to be true."

Ettie racked her brain, trying to come up with words of comfort. "There, there, Sadie. He's at home with *Gott,* and he's happy now."

Sadie nodded. "Oh, Ettie, I hope you don't mind me coming here to talk to you. I don't have many close friends and if I talk to *mamm* I know she'll start crying all over again and not be able to stop."

"That's perfectly all right. Talk to me whenever you want. I remember how close you always were to Horace."

"You do?"

Ettie nodded.

"Jah, we were close, weren't we?'

"You were." Ettie desperately wanted to ask her questions but feared now was not the time to do so.

"There's another reason I came here today."

Ettie raised her eyebrows.

Sadie continued, "I was hoping that you might have found something here in this house that belonged to Horace, since he was so close to Agatha. I'd like a memento, something to remember him by."

"Wouldn't he have left all his belongings at your *haus?* Surely all his possessions were left there."

"*Mamm* threw everything out a long time ago when he didn't come home. She thought he was living as an *Englischer* so she wanted to rid the place of his memory."

"I can sympathize with you, and your *mudder.* I've been through the pain of losing someone many a time." Ettie thought about her dog that had just died. No one or nothing would be able to replace him. "But, as Bishop John would say, death is a part of life."

"*Jah,* but why did he have to go so soon?"

"*Nee.* He was still very young, but none of us knows when our time will come."

As Sadie sipped her tea, Ettie noticed Sadie's red-rimmed eyes and her paler-than-usual skin. She remembered the pain of losing her own brother. "There was a key found near him."

Sadie gulped on her tea, then wiped her mouth with her fingers. "A key? Where is it?"

"On its way to the police. They should have it by now," Ettie answered.

"Why the police?"

Ettie decided not to tell her about the floor being taken up. "Evidence I suppose, much like his clothing."

Sadie nodded. "Do you know what the key is for, what it unlocks?"

"*Nee,* I don't." She paused. "All that's happened shows us that we have to appreciate those we have, while we have them."

"That's true, Ettie."

A loud knock sounded on the door. Ettie opened it to see a young man dressed in black. "I don't want any trouble, lady, I just want the key."

"What key?"

The young man reached behind him and pulled a gun from his back pocket. "I want the key and I know you've got it."

"I did have a key, but I gave it to the police. A detective was here and took it to them."

Sadie stepped forward. "Put that gun down! It's true; she doesn't have it."

The man shifted his weight from one foot to the other. The gun shook when he said, "You better not be lying to me lady or I'll be back." He glanced over his shoulder with the gun still shaking in his hands. He looked back at Ettie and then ran away.

Ettie stepped outside and looked to see the young man get into the passenger-side door of a black car before it zoomed away.

Ettie put a hand to her heart to try and stop it from racing. "The way you spoke to him just now – Sadie, why weren't you scared of him?

Sadie sighed. "Sit down. It's a long story and I need to unburden my heart."

Sadie helped Ettie to a chair.

"Just before Horace disappeared, he told me a little of what was happening. Horace's boss was also running another business – against the law."

"Stealing things?"

"Jah."

"What was his boss' name?"

"Settler, Bertram Settler."

Ettie's eyes flew to the ceiling. *Bertram Settler would've been Bill Settler's father. Bill Settler, from the construction company.* "I didn't mean to interrupt you, Sadie. Continue; I'm listening."

"His rivals – well, Horace called them his boss' enemies – were Terence Wheeler's gang. I urged Horace to come back to the community; I knew no good would come of him knowing people like that."

"Go on."

"I heard from someone Horace knew that a man called Terence Wheeler said a key was hidden with Horace's body, but where no one would be able to find it. That's the first I heard that Horace was dead."

Ettie gasped and her mouth fell open. "Who told you about all of that? And do you know what the key opens?"

Sadie hung her head.

"Do you know who sent that man?" Ettie persisted but still Sadie made no reply.

Ettie frowned, pushing her lips together. "Who was that young man and why did he listen to you?"

Sadie shrugged. "He didn't listen to me."

"It certainly seemed that way. Look, Sadie, if you know anything, anything at all – and it appears that you do – it's best you talk about it. If you don't want to tell me, tell the police, but someone needs to know."

Sadie stared at Ettie with large, round eyes.

Ettie continued, her voice louder. "That man just now, or whoever sent him, must want whatever that key opens, and judging by the gun, they might be prepared to kill for it. I don't know about you, but I'd rather die of old age since the Lord's spared me for this long."

"Do you think someone else might get killed?"

Ettie nodded. "We need to tell the police about this. And you need to tell them everything you know – do it now."

Sadie stood. "You're right, Ettie, of course, you're right. I'll go and see them right away."

Ettie took a deep breath and put her hand on her heart. "*Jah*, okay. I'll sit here and try to recover. If they want to talk to me they can come here, or I'll go into the station tomorrow. I can't do any more today."

After Sadie left, Ettie had a lie down on the bed in Agatha's spare room, trying to get images of the gun out of her head.

It was just before dinnertime when Ava knocked on Ettie's back door. Ettie couldn't sleep and was glad for the interruption. She ushered her in and told her everything that had happened with Sadie and the man with the gun.

"Ettie, you poor thing! Let me cook you dinner."

"That would be *gut, denke*. I feel so much better now that Crowley's involved. He's taking the key to Kelly and hopefully he'll get a search warrant for the box at the bank."

"How would the man know you had the key?" Ava asked.

Ettie said, "There were only four of us who knew. You, me, Jeremiah, and Crowley – but then again, Detective Kelly did have us talking at the front of the police station."

"That's true, and you said you found the key stuck to the boards. Anyone could have overheard it."

"There were the two officers behind the desk, and people coming and going. I don't remember anyone in particular that seemed to be listening. Sadie knew of the existence of a key, she'd heard those rumors regarding Terence Wheeler, a key and Horace's body. I wonder why she never told the police that before now."

CHAPTER 13

Ettie again spent the night with Ava in the *grossdaddi haus.* The next morning, Ava had left early to help her mother with some work at the farmers market. When Ettie heard a knock on the door, she looked out the window to see Crowley.

"Come in," she said as she opened the door.

"Oh, good, you're here. The young lady who lives here told me where you were."

"I stayed here last night after everything that happened." Ettie stepped back to allow Crowley to step through.

As he walked in, he said, "I've got some good news. Kelly finally agreed to get a warrant. Mind you, I was with him most of the day trying to persuade him, and then he had me helping him go over all the evidence."

"Good. Have a seat." Crowley and Ettie sat at the small kitchen table. "Then you would've been there when Sadie told Kelly all about the man with the gun?"

Crowley frowned. "About what?"

"I thought you would've heard."

"No, I've heard nothing. There was a man with a gun?"

"Sadie came here yesterday, and while she was here a man came and pointed a gun at me. He demanded the key. Somehow he'd heard that I had it."

"Ettie, you should have called the police straight away."

"Sadie said she was going to go straight to the police station when she left here."

"Well, she didn't. I was with Kelly most of the day and no mention was made of it." Crowley sprang to his feet and whipped his cell out of his pocket. "I need to make a call." Crowley strode outside.

Ettie hadn't had a chance to tell him the rest of her news.

Crowley came back. "There was no report made by her at all." Crowley rubbed his furrowed brow.

"Is there some mistake? Perhaps she called instead of going there in person."

Crowley shook his head and placed his hands on his hips. "Tell me exactly what happened."

"I haven't told you everything. Sit down." When Crowley sat,

Ettie said, "The man said he knew I had the key and Sadie stepped forward and said that I didn't. He believed her and not me. I thought that odd."

Ettie saw by the detective's face he didn't think that it was particularly odd.

"And, what's more, she might have been hinting for the key, too, before the man got there. She asked if Horace had left anything at Agatha's, saying she wanted something to remember him by. Then after the man with the gun ran away, she told me that someone told her that a man called Terence Wheeler said that he'd hidden a key with Horace's body. She wouldn't tell me who told her that."

Crowley groaned. "Kelly's sending someone to talk to her now, then we'll know more. Do you believe what she told you, Ettie?"

Ettie blinked rapidly. "I have no reason to believe otherwise." Ettie pulled her mouth to one side. "I wonder why she didn't go to the police when she said she would. What about the young man who pointed a gun at me?"

Crowley nodded. "I'm sure that Kelly will want you to have a look at some mug shots."

Ettie pulled a face, but when Crowley remained quiet, Ettie nodded. "I will if I have to, but I wouldn't recognize him again. He just looked like any other young man, and all I was looking at was the gun."

"Why don't you go back home with Elsa-May until all this is

over with? It's too much for you to stay here with everything that's happened."

Ettie wondered if that might be best. She did miss Elsa-May – even though she was dominating and overbearing at times, it was nice to have her company.

"Come on. I'll take you there now."

"Thank you. I'll leave a note for Ava. She might be scared on her own too, but I'll let her know to she can stay with me if she gets frightened."

"Okay. There's no rush; I'll wait in the car. I've got some calls to make."

Crowley drove Ettie back to the home she shared with Elsa-May. She hoped Elsa-May had been watering her plants, and wouldn't be too cross with her for not being there.

When he stopped the car in front of the house, Ettie said, "Do come in; Elsa-May has most likely just baked something."

Crowley smiled. "I've missed her cooking, and yours too, Ettie. It wouldn't hurt to have a small sample."

Ettie laughed. "We'll fatten you up yet."

He followed Ettie into the house.

"Elsa-May, I've got Detective Crowley with me."

Elsa-May came out of the kitchen smiling. "It's good to see you again. Have you come to help us find out who killed Horace? I told Ettie to let you have your retirement in peace."

Ettie frowned at Elsa-May. She was the one who'd said to let him have his retirement in peace. She didn't want to argue in front of Crowley, but she'd certainly give Elsa-May a piece of her mind when he left. "He's helping us and that's that."

"I don't mind. The first few months of peace and quiet were good, but then the days wear on and they're pretty much the same."

"You're okay with helping, then?" Ettie asked.

"I'm pleased to be back in the swing of things."

"I'll put the pot on the stove, then, and see if I can find some cake." Elsa-May hurried back to the kitchen.

After Crowley sat down, Ettie said, "See, I told you there'd be cake."

Before long, they were all seated with tea and fresh orange cake while Ettie told Elsa-May all the events she'd missed.

The sound of Crowley's loud ring tone from his cell caused Ettie to jump.

He sprang to his feet. "Excuse me, I'll take this outside."

When Crowley was gone, Elsa-May said, "You're awfully jumpy, Ettie."

"A lot's happened. I had a gun pointed at me."

"*Jah,* you told me. That can't have been good."

Crowley walked back through the door. "It appears that Sadie Hostetler never came home last night. She's disappeared."

Ettie's jaw fell open and her hand flew to her mouth. "Do you think she's in danger?"

"We can't be too careful, but you did say that the man put the gun down when she told him to. I think we can safely assume that she's involved in some way with this whole debacle."

"It wasn't like that. She told that young man I didn't have the key, then after that he left." Ettie nibbled the end of her fingernail.

"Young man?" Elsa-May asked Ettie.

"The one who pointed the gun at me." Ettie shook her head at Elsa-May – hadn't she been listening?

The two ladies looked back up at Crowley and he sat down.

"Looks like there's a whole lot more to this than first appeared," he said.

"I'm sorry to drag you into all this now that you've retired," Ettie said.

Elsa-May jutted out her bottom jaw. "That's what I said in the first place. Leave him be; he's retired."

Ettie rolled her eyes.

"Anytime you need me, I'm always there," Crowley said with a smile tugging the corners of his lips. He reached for his teacup.

"Yes, you've been good to us in the past." Elsa-May glanced over at Ettie who narrowed her eyes at her.

"I wonder where Sadie could've gone to," Ettie said.

Elsa-May said, "Would her mother know?"

"I don't know. I don't think she'd want her mother involved. Doris is too old to cope with the worry, which is why I'm surprised that Sadie's disappeared." Ettie turned to Crowley. "Do you think she's in danger? Maybe that man with the gun didn't leave and he was lurking up the road."

"Let's not think about that for now. The police are doing everything they can."

"Poor Sadie. Things never seem to go her way. She was jilted by two men before she was twenty."

Elsa-May's eyebrows raised. "Ettie, stop it. You like to gossip far too much. That's how rumors start. Rumors are spread by people with too much time on their hands and not enough sense in their heads. Anyway, I heard she was only jilted by one man."

The lines in Crowley's forehead deepened. "Ettie, you said Sadie seemed to be familiar with the man who had the gun, and didn't seem afraid?"

"She wasn't scared at all. He insisted I had the key and then she came next to me and said the police had it."

"When she stood next to you, did he point the gun at her?"

Ettie shook her head.

Crowley took a notepad out of his pocket and made some notes.

Ettie licked her lips. "I don't know what to think anymore."

"Would it be possible she knew the man?" Crowley asked.

"No, I don't think she knew him when I think about it now. But that's what my first thought was. Anyone else could have overheard us at the station when I was talking to Kelly and trying to have him take a look at it."

"Hmm," Crowley said. "This does put another slant on things." He stretched out his arm and took another piece of orange cake.

"What do we do know so far?" Elsa-May leaned forward in her chair.

When Crowley swallowed his mouthful of cake, he said, "Leave it to Kelly. He's getting a search warrant for the deposit box – we're taking a guess that it's the local bank, since there's only one in town with box facilities."

"How long will it take them to get a warrant?" Elsa-May asked.

"He'll have to gather enough evidence to prove to the judge that there are grounds to sign off on a warrant."

"Someone's dead – wouldn't that be grounds enough?" Elsa-May asked.

"It's a key, but it might not be related to this whole thing. The judge will have to be convinced that this key is related to Horace's murder. It will help him get the warrant now that someone with a gun was after it." He looked at Ettie. "I think you'll have to make another visit to Kelly."

"I'll go tomorrow," Ettie said, not looking forward to doing so.

THE NEXT MORNING, Ettie was feeling guilty about leaving Ava alone in the *grossdaddi haus* after all that had happened. She made Ava the first stop of the day before she went to visit old Mrs. Hostetler.

When she got out of the taxi, she saw that Jeremiah was working inside her house. She stepped through the door. "Jeremiah? I thought you'd finished."

"Hiya, Aunt Ettie. I should have this done by lunchtime. I'm just going over the nails, making sure they're safe and filling the cracks. I had another job to get to yesterday so I couldn't finish this. I'm going to give it a light polish when I'm done. It'll look great."

"It's looking good already. *Denke,* Jeremiah." Ettie heard from the sound of the hoof beats passing the house that Ava was pulling up in the buggy. She went out to meet her. "Where have you been so early?" Ettie asked.

"I'm coming home. I stayed at *Mamm's* last night. I was a little scared to stay here alone."

"You got my note?"

"I did, and I didn't want to intrude. *Mamm* was happy for my company."

Ettie walked beside Ava's buggy up to the stable. "You'll never guess what's happened."

"What?"

Ettie told Ava everything that had happened in her absence, and then added,

"Sadie's disappeared. The last thing she told me was she was going to the police and she didn't. When they went to her home to question her, they found she'd disappeared."

"Oh, Ettie. Do you think she's frightened? Or maybe the killer's got her?"

Ettie shrugged her shoulders. "Don't know. I'm on my way now to see old Mrs. Hostetler to ask if she knows where Sadie is. Detective Crowley said I should go and make a report about the man with the gun who was after the key, but I'll do that later."

"Well, I best take you both places."

Ettie smiled. "I was hoping you would."

AVA AND ETTIE'S first stop was Doris Hostetler.

"Ettie, and Ava, I wish I could tell you both. It would be such a burden lifted from my shoulders. I made a promise to certain people that I wouldn't breathe a word of what they told me." Mrs. Hostetler said.

Ettie could feel Ava's eyes on her; they both knew it was a long shot that Sadie's mother would tell them anything. "Who did you promise?" Ettie asked.

Mrs. Hostetler shook her head. "I can say no more. I've already said too much."

"Did you tell the police anything?" Ettie asked.

Doris Hostetler shook her head.

"Do you know where Sadie might be?" Ava asked one more time.

Doris dabbed at the corners of her eyes with a handkerchief. "I knew something bad would come of keeping secrets. I warned them."

Ettie leaned forward and patted Doris on her shoulder. "Who's 'them', Doris?"

Doris shook her head once more.

"You'd feel better if you unburdened yourself and told us exactly what's happened. Is it something to do with Horace's death?" Ettie asked.

Doris howled into her handkerchief at the mention of her son. Ettie knew that they could not ask her any more questions.

"Why don't I make us all some nice hot tea?" Ava stood up.

Doris looked up at her.

"May I?" Ava asked.

Doris nodded.

It was another three hours before Ava and Ettie left Doris' house.

As the horse pulled the buggy down the tree-lined street, something occurred to Ettie. "It seems Horace told Sadie quite a bit of what was happening in his life. I wonder how she's involved in it all."

"I'm worried that she might be in danger."

Ettie scratched the side of her face. "There's always that possibility." A cold shiver ran through Ettie. "Anyway, Jeremiah should be finished with the floor by now."

"Good. Let's go and see how it looks," Ava said.

When they got back to the house, Detective Kelly was in his car waiting for them.

"Oh no. We forgot to go to the police station. He'll be here to ask me about that young man and also to take me to have a look at those mug shots. Leave the horse here and come with me?"

Ava and Ettie got out of the buggy and went straight to the detective who was still in his car.

"Afternoon, Detective," Ettie said through his car window.

"Good afternoon, ladies," the detective said. "We haven't been able to locate Sadie Hostetler. Mrs. Smith, I'd like you to come to the station to make an official report regarding the information you gave Crowley."

"I'll drive you, Ettie," Ava said.

"Thank you, dear." Ettie smiled at the younger woman.

"I also owe you an apology, Mrs. Smith."

"Oh?"

"About the key you found. It seems as though it belongs to a safe deposit box. We've taken it to the bank and they've told us that much."

"Crowley did say it was one of those keys."

"I'm afraid there's been another development, which might explain why your friend Sadie has disappeared."

Ettie leaned closer. "And what would that be?"

"While we were in the process of getting a warrant to open the safe deposit box, we discovered the box is held in the name of one Sadie Hostetler."

CHAPTER 14

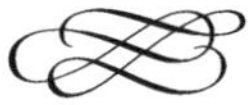

Ettie looked at Ava, who looked just as shocked as she herself felt. Ettie rubbed her chin while she tried to make sense of the fact that the safe deposit box was in the name of Sadie Hostetler, Horace's sister. She had expected it to be in Horace's name or perhaps in the name of one of the gangsters. Maybe even in the name of Terence Wheeler.

Seeing the looks on their faces the detective said, "It came as a surprise to us as well."

"It seems odd, that's all. The key was found here, and I don't know that Sadie ever visited Agatha's house. Sadie kept to herself. I wonder if she opened the box because someone asked her to – or forced her – but why would she come around here looking for the key?"

"We won't know anything further, I guess, until Sadie returns," Ava said.

Ettie shook her head. "She told me some story about someone telling her that Terence Wheeler hid the key with Horace's body. But how would Terence Wheeler have gotten the key from her? Did Sadie know Terence Wheeler to give him the key?"

"Well, we've got people on it." The detective looked at Ettie and narrowed his eyes. "Would you have any idea where Sadie Hostetler might be?"

Ettie raised her eyebrows, deepening the lines in her forehead. "I wouldn't have any idea. We've just come from her mother's place and she –"

Ava butted in. "She was very upset that Sadie's disappeared."

Ettie knew Ava's quick thinking just saved Mrs. Hostetler being interrogated by the police; the woman was in no state for that.

"When do you think you'll get the warrant?" Ettie asked.

"I'm hoping for tomorrow, once all the paperwork's done. I'm hoping the judge will sign off on it. I'm certain he will."

"Do you want to come inside, Detective Kelly?" Ettie asked, hoping he wouldn't ask any more questions.

He shook his head and his eyes glazed over. "I don't know where all this is headed, but we'll know more once we get into that box at the bank." The detective nodded his goodbye before he got into his car. Ava and Ettie stood side by side in silence and watched him drive away.

"Where could Sadie be?" Ettie asked Ava.

Ava shrugged her shoulders. "You know her better than I do."

Ettie pushed her front door open. Jeremiah was gone and the floor looked clean and polished.

"Back to normal," Ava said.

"Yes, back to normal." Ettie took a deep breath. She missed her friend, Agatha, but was glad that she wasn't here to live through the dramas that were unfolding. "It occurs to me that since Sadie and Horace were so close, he had Sadie go to the bank and open a box. Horace is the connection between Sadie and the box."

"You think that's what happened? What if she wanted to open a box for herself?"

Ettie scrunched up her nose. "For what?"

"*Jah,* I see what you mean. She wouldn't have had any valuables or anything to hide, not while she was one of us plain folk."

"He must have persuaded her to do it. Or someone else got her to do it. I guess we won't know until she tells us."

"Why wouldn't Horace have leased a box for himself? Would Horace have been involved in shady business?"

Ettie scratched her neck. Ava was right; if Horace had Sadie open the box, it meant that he was involved in some crooked business. That was not the Horace she remembered. "I don't know anymore. Nothing makes sense."

"Like the detective said, it'll make sense when we see what's in the box."

"Or when Sadie tells us. The best thing I can think of is that if

Horace got involved with those crooked men somehow, or knew what they were up to, he might have put the stolen goods in there intending to notify the police."

"Ettie, do you think so? Really? He would've just taken it to the police station, wouldn't he?"

"*Nee,* they might have killed him for that."

Ava shook her head. "There are probably a thousand scenarios we could come up with. Do you think they'll find valuables in the box?"

Ettie nodded. "I do. Now, I'd hate to think that Horace was involved in anything dishonest, but we know from what Crowley and Sadie said that he knew criminals. He could very well have been involved in some way."

"*Jah,* in some way that ended up getting him killed. Do you think maybe his boss had him hide the stolen goods on his behalf?"

"We probably won't know until they open the box. They might be able to trace the stolen goods to the owner and then the police will be able to piece together what happened."

"Don't forget you have to go to the station to look at mug shots and make that report."

"That's right, and we might find out more if I can identify the man who pointed that gun at me. I'll do it tomorrow."

When Ettie and Ava were approaching the police station the next day, they saw Sadie being walked into the station between two large police officers. Sadie had her head down and didn't see them.

"I hope she's all right. Do you think we should call her *mudder?*"

Ettie shook her head. *"Nee,* I don't think Doris can take any more upsets." Ettie sat down in a chair in the waiting area while Ava approached the officer at the desk to tell him why they were there. She was told that Detective Kelly was busy and they'd have to wait.

When Ettie saw that the officer didn't even make a move to tell him they were there, she walked up to him. "Please do tell the detective that we're here. I'm sure he'd like to know."

The officer stared at Ettie for a moment and then said, "Very well. I'll let him know."

"Thank you kindly," Ettie said before she took a seat.

It was another fifteen minutes before the detective came out to speak to Ettie. "I'm sorry to have kept you so long, Mrs. Smith, but I've been run off my feet."

Ettie stood. "I saw Sadie being brought in. Is she all right?"

"We're just asking her a few questions. We found her at a bus station; she was leaving town."

"Could I speak to her?"

"I did ask if she wanted anyone present and she said no."

"I'm sure she'd want me there. Would you ask her if I could sit by her?"

Detective Kelly put his hands on his hips, and his mouth downturned. "I guess I could ask her. She's quite entitled to have someone with her at this stage, since she's only here for questioning."

"Thank you."

The detective disappeared down the long corridor and a minute later, he beckoned Ettie from the corridor.

"I won't be long," Ettie said to Ava as she stood.

Ava replied, "Take your time; don't mind me."

Before Ettie entered the room where they were holding Sadie, the detective whispered to Ettie, "She says she has things to say that only a woman should hear."

Ettie pursed her lips and nodded before she entered the room and sat next to Sadie.

"Ms. Hostetler, I'm going to have a female officer sit in. I'll leave the room, but I'll be outside listening and as I've already said we'll be recording everything you say."

Sadie's mouth quivered as she nodded to the detective.

"Ms. Hostetler, the tape can't pick up body language or gestures. I'll say again, we'll be recording everything you say. You've heard that, and you understand?"

"Yes, Detective Kelly, I understand," Sadie said.

The detective continued, "I'll fetch the officer now."

When the detective walked out, Ettie grabbed Sadie's hand. "Everything will be all right," Ettie said.

Sadie put her other hand over Ettie's and sniffed.

Detective Kelly returned with a young woman in a police uniform. "This is Officer Willis. Just tell her all that happened."

The young policewoman sat opposite Ettie and Sadie.

Sadie looked up at the detective. "So Ettie can stay? I'd feel better if she did."

"Yes, that's why she's here. And please, none of that Pennsylvania Dutch prattle, just speak in plain English."

Sadie nodded, then said, "Yes, Detective Kelly."

When the detective walked out, Ettie said, "Well?"

"I can barely speak. I haven't spoken of this in years."

Ettie waited in silence while Sadie composed herself.

"Would you like some water?" Officer Willis pushed a glass of water closer to her.

Sadie shook her head then stared at Ettie. "I'll start at the beginning."

"It's always best to start there," Ettie said.

"It was many years ago when I found out that Horace and I were expecting a child."

Ettie gasped, felt her throat constrict; then she felt she would be sick.

"Ettie, you knew we weren't real brother and sister, didn't you?"

Ettie's eyebrows flew up. She rubbed the side of her face. It had happened so long ago that she'd forgotten. The Hostetlers suddenly had a baby girl when Horace would've been just a baby himself. Horace and Sadie were the youngest of the children. The talk was that Sadie had been an unwanted baby from an unwed mother. She was raised along with their other children. "I knew, yes, I did, but it was so long ago. I had forgotten." Ettie put her hand to her fluttering stomach. Horace had been engaged to Agatha.

Sadie kept her eyes focused on the desk as though she couldn't look into the face of anyone who might judge her.

After clearing her throat and then taking a mouthful of water, Sadie continued, "He was to have gotten married to Agatha when we found out, and then he didn't know what to do. He knew he should marry me for the sake of the child. He said he had to get away from the community to clear his head. Agatha followed him, not knowing why he'd left so suddenly. He must have told her the truth of it all because she came back to the community not long after." She lifted her gaze to Ettie.

Ettie swallowed hard and tried to remain stony-faced. "Go on; what happened next?"

"While Horace was away, he went to work for a builder and he was a bad, bad man. I warned Horace – I just didn't trust the man."

"How did you know about him – the builder?"

"Just from things that Horace told me."

"So, you met with Horace regularly after he left the community?"

"About once a week," Sadie confessed. "After months went by, Horace still wouldn't marry me. I knew he loved Agatha, but I was the one having his *boppli.*" Tears trickled down Sadie's face.

"What happened then?" Ettie asked.

"I'll go back before then. I guess that wasn't the beginning. I'll go back to the very beginning." She cleared her throat again. "I was so young and was running around with Joshua Yoder, he said he wanted to marry me and we became secretly engaged. Then he told me days later he liked someone else." She looked up at Ettie with tear-filled eyes. "Joshua Yoder ended the relationship with me and then only one week later, he announced his engagement to Peggy Schroder. Why was our engagement a secret, but with Peggy he announced it straight away? I told Horace about it; he was my closest friend. Horace was comforting me, one thing led to another..."

"Well, we don't have to go into all that now," Ettie said, not wanting to know all the intimate details of the indiscretion.

"Okay, but I thought he loved me too, and then I found out that he didn't love me either. I thought he had changed his mind about Agatha just as Joshua had changed his mind about me." Sadie wiped her eyes.

Ettie wanted to say that Horace had crossed the line, especially when he was due to marry another. She shrugged off her judgmental thoughts. One indiscretion was as bad as another in God's eyes – she knew that to be true. She resisted the urge to shake sense into Sadie, but it was too late for that. The situation explained why Agatha never married Horace – she must have found out.

Sadie continued, "I went away for the birth; I hid my pregnancy right up to that time. Horace was there; he stayed with me for a week after William was born. Then I told him he had a decision to make. And I thought… I honestly thought he would choose me, and our baby. I wanted us to be married, be a real family, and then go back home after a few months with William."

Ettie wondered what had become of their baby.

Sadie looked down at her hands, which she was wringing in her lap. "Horace said he couldn't marry me. He came up with the idea that he'd have someone look after the baby for six months and then I would take him back home with me saying it was a relative's baby. I didn't want it to be that way, but Horace didn't care about that. He didn't care about me, not as much as he cared about her."

Ettie felt her pain, but even she didn't believe her next words. "I'm sure he did."

Sadie shook her head. "If he had, he would've married me. *Nee,* he wanted to be with Agatha – that was plain to see."

"What became of William?" Ettie finally asked.

Sadie looked into Ettie's face. "William is Bill Settler."

Ettie gasped. She added up the ages, the years, and it all fit. It was all possible, but could it be true? "Mr. Settler senior and his wife adopted him, then?"

Sadie shook her head. "They stole him from me. They agreed to look after him for six months. That's what the arrangement was, but then when Horace went to collect him after the six months was up they wouldn't hand him over."

Ettie took a deep breath. All this happened right under her nose all those years ago and she hadn't known a thing about it. She'd always thought she knew all that happened in the community.

"At first, I didn't believe Horace. I thought he was lying because it would've been easier for him not to be bothered with the baby and to pretend he wasn't the boy's father. I went there myself, to the Settlers' house, and they wouldn't talk to me. They said that he was theirs now. I told them I was going to go to the police."

"And did you?" Ettie asked, trying to imagine large Bill Settler as a baby.

"No, because they told me the baby would end up in a home for unwanted children if I did that. Then they asked if I had money to fight a court case. They said it would cost me thousands and take years, and all that time William would be in the care of strangers who might treat him poorly."

"So they kept William and brought him up as their own?"

"They did. Horace was so angry. He said if he couldn't get the baby back for me legally, he'd play 'their game'. He knew the Settlers were into illegal goings on. He'd heard about their robberies and at one time they'd tried to get him involved. Mr. Settler told Horace that all his workers did 'jobs' for him. Horace refused to do anything of the kind. But then he stole from Mr. Settler and told him he could have the goods back when they gave William back, but they never did."

"And that's when Horace asked you to open a safe deposit box at the bank? To keep the goods he stole?"

Sadie nodded. "That's right. He came by one night, knocked on my window and handed me a black velvet bag. I opened it, the bag, to see what was inside. There were big diamonds and other stones. I thought they were too big to be real, but he assured me they were. There was a big diamond necklace, and packets of smaller diamonds and so many large ones. Then there were pretty red and green gems. They were so pretty; I couldn't take my eyes off them. I spread them all over my bed, I held them up to the light – they were beautiful things I'd never seen the like of."

"What did he have you do with them?" the officer asked.

"He said to go to the bank. He gave me a bundle of cash and said it would be enough to keep the box for a long time if need be. Then he told me exactly what to do and say when I got to the bank."

"And you followed his directions?" Ettie asked.

"I told him he should never have gotten involved with people like that. All of it was my fault."

"No, it wasn't. It wasn't your fault at all. Sometimes things happen and then bad things just follow and we're powerless to stop them." Ettie wasn't sure what she was saying, only that she was trying to comfort Sadie and help dull the pain that she'd obviously lived with for years. "Who was the man who pointed the gun at me? You seemed to know him."

"I haven't told you, have I?"

Ettie shrugged. "There's more?"

Sadie's mouth turned down and she took a deep breath. "Bill found out he wasn't a real 'Settler' and he set out to find Horace and me. Bill sought me out about three years ago. We meet every so often. He knows about the box at the bank – about it being in my name. He was trying to protect me by stopping the police from finding out. He wanted to get the key before the police found out the stolen goods were under my name at the bank."

"How was he trying to do that? By sending someone to get the key from me, from the house?"

Sadie nodded. "I guess so. I knew Bill would do something silly to protect me – we've developed a bond. Well, I've always had the bond, the connection with my child, but now it's different when he feels the same pull toward me."

"How did Bill know I had the key?"

"Eyes and ears, Bill calls them. He says he has them everywhere thanks to his *vadder* – I mean, father." Sadie corrected herself so the police could understand her.

Ettie knew that someone at the police station must have overheard mention of the key connected to Horace's murder.

Sadie continued, "I told Bill everything, about those people he calls his parents and how they tricked Horace and me."

Ettie wondered if Bill wanted that key for himself since the box held possibly half a million dollars' worth of gems, according to the Internet search.

"But they're the people who raised him, so I didn't want to say too many bad things about them," Sadie said.

"It must be hard for you, Sadie."

"It was heart-breaking. I used to sit outside his school whenever I had the chance. I watched him grow up from a distance."

The female officer asked, "You think that Bill, your biological son, was trying to protect you from the police? He had someone come to this lady's house with a gun? Is that correct?"

Sadie nodded. "I had stolen goods in that box."

"Why keep the stolen property all these years when the people refused to give the baby up?" the officer asked.

"I didn't," Sadie blurted out. "I didn't have the key. Horace told me that without the key you can't get into the box, and that's what they told me at the bank. They said if I lose the key they have to go through all kinds of legalities to get the box opened.

I gave the key to Horace straight after I placed the goods in the box and I never saw him or the key again."

"Bill knew that there was a key somewhere, and knew what the box contained?" Ettie asked to confirm the events.

Sadie nodded.

The officer reminded her that she must speak her answers for the recording.

"Yes," said Sadie.

Ettie pulled her mouth to one side while she tried to figure it all out. "Horace took the diamonds as ransom so they'd give your baby back. If that had worked, you were going to take the baby back to the community, raise him yourself and tell everyone he was a close relative?"

Sadie nodded, caught herself, and then said, "Yes." She turned her attention to the female officer. "Will I go to jail?"

"I can't answer that." The officer stood. "I'll get Detective Kelly – I'm sure he'll have some more questions for you. I'm now leaving the room, and the recorder will be turned off."

When the officer walked out the door, Sadie leaned over and clasped Ettie's hand. "It's such a mess, Ettie, such a mess."

Ettie patted her hand. "Don't worry. It'll all get sorted out." Ettie heard the door open behind her. She turned to see the policewoman come back into the room.

"Detective Kelly is down at the bank."

"The warrant came through, then?" Ettie asked.

She nodded.

"Do we just wait here?" Sadie asked.

"You can wait here or wait in a cell."

Sadie grimaced. "Here would be better."

Ettie frowned at the officer. "Is Sadie going to be charged with something? She's free to go, isn't she?"

"Not until Detective Kelly comes back." The woman turned and left the room.

Ettie looked back at Sadie and patted her hand again, wondering why the female officer had been so rude. She had seemed sympathetic earlier when she heard Sadie's sad story. "It'll all work out." Ettie held her mouth tight, hoping it would. "Do you have any idea who might have killed Horace?" Ettie asked Sadie.

"Agatha would've been angry to find out about the baby. Then there were Terence Wheeler and his people. Horace said that his boss had stolen the diamonds from Wheeler and his lot. They were the rightful owners of the diamonds. Well, not the rightful owners, because the goods were stolen."

"How did Horace get a hold of them, then? Wouldn't they have been in a safe or something?" Ettie asked.

"I don't know, I can't answer that. That's as much as I know."

"You best tell Detective Kelly all that when he gets back."

Sadie nodded. "Oh, do you think I've got William into trouble now?"

"I guess they'll bring him in for questioning. I'm sure there's a law against sending someone somewhere with a gun." Ettie grimaced; Sadie sure did have a way of finding trouble.

Half an hour later, the detective walked through the door looking as though he'd been sucking on a lemon.

Both ladies waited for him to speak.

He planted both hands on the table and leaned over to Sadie. "We went to the bank, opened the box that was in your name and what do you think we found, Ms. Hostetler?"

"The diamonds?"

He shook his head. "Nothing. The box was empty."

CHAPTER 15

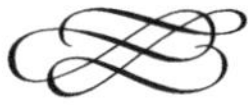

Sadie's face contorted. "That's not possible. I placed the diamonds in there myself and they said that no one but me could access it."

"Could Horace have taken the diamonds out? He had the key, after all," Ettie said.

The detective straightened up. "There's a lot you're not telling us, Ms. Hostetler." He pulled a piece of paper from his inner coat pocket. "I have here evidence that you accessed the box one month after you opened it."

"But that's not true. I didn't. I opened the box, paid the money and never went back. I gave the key to Horace straight after."

"I put it to you that Horace stole the gems from his employer, had you open the box, then you killed him and kept the stolen goods for yourself."

Ettie jumped to her feet. "Detective, that's not possible. It's simply untrue."

Sadie put her head in her hands and sobbed.

"Keep quiet, please, Mrs. Smith. You're only here out of respect to Detective Crowley."

"Yes, well, Detective Crowley would know to trust what I say."

"Sit down, Mrs. Smith," he said through gritted teeth. "Or you can wait outside."

Ettie sat, finding it hard to keep quiet.

Sadie sniffed back her tears and said, "It's not true. What you're saying is not true. I told Ettie the truth of what happened. He took the gems from Mr. Settler so they would give us our baby back, but they still wouldn't give him up. I went to the bank like Horace said to, then I gave him the key."

The detective sat down. He looked at both women, and said, "You had a baby with your brother that was brought up as a Settler?"

Ettie realized he must have missed some of Sadie's confession while he was at the bank with the warrant. "They weren't brother and sister, not by blood. Bill Settler, from Starling Homes, is Sadie and Horace's child. That's why Horace took the gems from Settler, so he would give him back the baby in exchange for the gems. The Settlers had agreed to look after their baby for six months, only then they wouldn't give him back."

The detective pulled his head back as though trying to absorb all the information. Then he looked at Sadie. “What Horace did was illegal, and you’re an accessory to his crime.”

Sadie pushed her lips together and then looked at Ettie with pleading eyes.

Ettie remembered from the Internet that the police couldn’t make charges stick to Wheeler all those years ago due to lack of evidence. “An accessory to what, Detective? You said yourself the box was empty.”

The detective glared at Ettie for a moment before his eyes traveled to Sadie. “This is by no means over, Ms. Hostetler, but I think we’ve kept you long enough today. We’ll need to speak to you again.”

The detective stepped back. Ettie put her arm around Sadie while she stood up. “Let’s go, Sadie.”

While Ettie and Ava ushered Sadie out of the police station and into a taxi, Ettie recalled that the detective had forgotten about her looking at the mug shots and she still hadn’t made a statement. Then she wondered what the detective would do now. Old Mr. Settler, the man who’d raised Bill, was dead, and so was Terence Wheeler.

On the way back to Sadie’s house, Ettie’s thoughts drifted to Bill Settler and the visit to his office. *When Ava and I went there to find out about Horace he must have known all the while we were inquiring about his birth father. That also explains why his mother was irate to see him talking to us*

Amish folk since Sadie and Horace had been trying to get baby Bill back from her and her husband. She must have known that Bill had learned who his parents were.

When the taxi stopped at Sadie's house, Ettie asked Sadie, "Does your mudder know the truth of everything?"

"I told her some things years ago, but not everything. I couldn't hold the truth in any longer. It was my hope that by telling the truth Horace might come home."

"Truth of what?" Ava asked.

Sadie looked at Ava, then back to Ettie. "You can tell her, if you want. I suppose everyone will find out soon."

Ettie nodded. "Didn't you say that someone told you about Terence Wheeler? And something about hiding Horace's body and the key along with it?"

Sadie hid her face in her hands. "I made that up. I didn't want anyone to find out about the jewels in the bank. I don't want to talk about it anymore today."

Ettie was a little upset with Sadie. Here she was trying to help her and she wasn't helping herself. "Do you want me to come inside with you?" Ettie asked.

"*Nee. Denke* for everything you've done today, Ettie. Goodbye, Ava, and Ettie."

Ettie and Ava watched until Sadie disappeared into her house.

"Where to now?" the taxi driver asked.

Ava looked at Ettie who let out a long slow breath. "Ava, what's the address of Starling Homes?"

"Really?" Ava raised her eyebrows.

Ettie nodded and then Ava gave the address of Starling Homes to the driver.

Ettie gave a laugh.

"What's so funny?"

"You've got a good memory."

Ava smiled. "I do for some things. What do you hope to find out by going to Starling Homes?"

"I'm hoping to talk to Bill."

"I guessed that much, but about what? And what did Sadie say you were allowed to tell me?"

Ettie took a deep breath and wondered where to start.

BILL SETTLER WAS LOCKING his office when Ava and Ettie pulled up in the taxi. When he saw it was them, he gave a wave.

They hurried toward him as he gave a final turn of his key. When he spun to face them, he placed his keys in his pocket and said, "How can I help you ladies today?"

Ettie walked close to him. "Did you send someone over to my

house to get a key? A man with a gun?" Ettie looked into Bill's face. She couldn't see any resemblance to Sadie, but he did have Horace's eyes, and his heavy frame. When he hesitated in answering, Ettie added, "Your birth mother seems to think that you did."

Bill's mouth fell open. He closed his mouth. "You'd better come inside and have a seat." He turned around, unlocked the door and pushed it open. "After you."

Ettie and Ava sat down.

When Bill was seated he asked, "You've spoken to my mother?"

"Which one?" Ava asked.

Ettie said, "We spoke to Sadie and she told us some interesting information."

"What do you want to know from me if Sadie's told you everything?"

Ettie bit on the inside of her mouth while she wondered how to get some information out of him. "Did you send someone with a gun to get the key to the deposit box?"

He looked down at one of his large hands and dusted something off it with his other hand. "Guilty." Then he looked at Ettie. "She told me the box was in her name. I knew what was in the box because she'd told me about it."

"Do you mean what was supposed to be in the box?"

Bill drew his eyebrows together. "What do you mean?"

"The police got a warrant and when they opened the box today there was nothing inside. It was empty. They had a record of Sadie accessing the box a month after it was opened." Ettie could see he was genuinely surprised by the news. She hoped that meant his intentions had been good.

They all heard the sound of a car driving right next to Bill's office. He jumped to his feet when he saw it was the police. Ettie drew her mouth in a straight line and bit her lip. She knew they wanted to ask him about sending someone to her house with a gun. Sadie had said she was certain he'd sent that young man, and Bill had confirmed it.

"I'm sure they just want to ask you a few questions," Ettie said as she stood and pulled Ava to her feet. She knew Detective Kelly wouldn't be pleased about them being there. To Ettie's relief, it wasn't Detective Kelly that stepped out of the vehicle, but two uniformed officers.

"William Settler?" one of the uniformed officers asked as Bill stepped out of his office.

"That's me. What's all this about?"

"We've got some questions, and we'd like you to accompany us to the station."

"Very well. Give me a moment?" The policeman nodded. "I'll have to lock the office. Do you ladies want me to call you a taxi?"

"Yes, please," Ava said.

After Bill called for a taxi, he locked his office before heading to the police car with the policemen on either side of him.

As Ava and Ettie strolled to the front entrance, Ettie whispered, "Looking at Bill walk away, I see he looks just like Horace. He's got the same large frame, and the same square shoulders."

"They're being polite to him. He doesn't look like he's in too much trouble."

"Not yet," Ettie said.

While they waited out the front for the taxi, Chad walked up to them. "Hello, again, Mrs. Smith." He nodded at Ava.

Ettie smiled. "Hello, Chad."

"Did my father just get taken away by the cops?"

"The police have some questions for him."

Ava added, "Yes, it's nothing to be concerned about."

Chad frowned. "Questions about what?"

Ettie breathed out heavily. "I'll let your father tell you."

Chad pulled a cell phone out of his pocket. "I'll call him and see what's going on."

Ettie looked up the road willing the taxi to hurry. "Let's go to my old house before we go to our place. I haven't seen Elsa-May in a while."

Chad had his head down still talking on his phone when the

taxi arrived. Ettie looked back at him when she got inside the taxi but still, he didn't look up.

While Ava gave the driver directions, Ettie hit her fist on her forehead.

"Ettie! What are you doing?"

"What aren't we seeing, Ava?"

CHAPTER 16

"What aren't we seeing?" Ava repeated. "For one, it would be nice to know why Sadie doesn't remember going to that safe deposit box. Do you think she's got something wrong with her? I've read about people doing things and then they have no memory of it." Ava looked out the window of the taxi.

Ettie shook her head. "It's more simple than that, I'd say. What if it wasn't Sadie at all? What if it was someone who forged her signature? Crowley said they check the signatures against the ones held at the bank. All someone would have to do is dress in Amish clothes and write a signature that looks similar to Sadie's."

"They'd most likely need identification. Someone could have stolen her ID card and forged her signature, but who?"

"Not just who – how did they get the key back to Horace, since it seemed he was the last one to have it?" Ettie said.

"I can't believe she made up the story about Terence Wheeler hiding a body and a key," Ava said.

"Well, she admitted that was a lie."

"What else is she making up, then?"

Noticing that the taxi driver was leaning back toward them, Ettie said, "Let's finish this conversation when we're with Elsa-May."

After Ettie and Ava told Elsa-May everything that had happened, Ettie leaned forward. "I can't believe it. I mean I do, but it's so hard to believe. Poor Sadie's been through a bit. Nothing seems to work out for that girl."

"Well, what are your thoughts on everything, Elsa-May?" Ava asked.

"I'm shocked about Horace and Sadie, truly shocked." Elsa-May took a deep breath. "I knew she wasn't a Hostetler, but then there was the matter of Horace about to marry Agatha."

"I never would've thought it either, but what are your thoughts on the things besides that?" Ettie asked.

Elsa-May began by saying, "The money's gone–"

Ettie interrupted, delighted to be able to correct her sister. "It wasn't money, it was diamonds and gems."

Elsa-May narrowed her eyes at Ettie. "You know what I mean."

A giggle erupted from Ettie's lips.

"Ettie, this is serious." Elsa-May shook her head.

"I'm sorry, continue."

"Might I?" Elsa-May asked full of sarcasm.

Ettie nodded.

"As I was saying, the goods were gone from the box. Bill was maybe trying to help his birth mother, or maybe he was trying to get whatever was in that box for himself." Elsa-May turned to Ettie. "Who are the suspects?"

"Who killed Bill?"

Elsa-May gasped. "Is Bill dead too?"

"*Nee,* I meant to say Horace. You mean, who killed Horace?"

"Did the same person who took the gems kill Horace?" Ava asked.

Elsa-May and Ettie looked at each other.

Ettie was the first to speak. "I don't know, but it occurs to me that if Sadie didn't collect the goods from that box, it had to be a woman who did it, posing as Sadie."

Elsa-May placed her knitting back in the bag by her feet. "And who would have been the same age and who would have known about it?"

"Old Mrs. Settler, the one who raised Bill – although she wouldn't have been old back then. I think she would've been older than Sadie was, though, by maybe ten years. Mrs. Settler didn't want to give the baby up and she knew what Horace had stolen because he was using it as blackmail."

Ava added, "Jah, and she was very upset to see us there talking to Bill the first day we went there, wasn't she, Ettie?"

"She was, and she seemed to be talking as though Bill knew us. She could've thought I was his mother; that I was Sadie. All she would've seen is our Amish clothes from where she stood."

"You need to talk to Sadie again," Elsa-May said.

Ettie breathed out heavily. "Some things she just clams up about. Do you think we should go and talk to old Mrs. Settler, Bill's mother?"

Elsa-May said, "Most definitely."

"Ava, do you think you could find her address?"

"I do have a friend who works at the DMV. I'm certain I could get the address."

"Then we'll visit her tomorrow, if you can find where she lives by then."

ETTIE KNOCKED on Mrs. Settler's door with Ava standing next to her.

The door opened a crack with the security chain still attached. "What do you people want?"

"We'd just like to ask you some questions, Mrs. Settler. Bill's birth mother is a good friend of ours and she's just told us about him."

"And?"

"Could we talk to you? We won't take up much of your time."

The woman closed the door; they heard the clicking and sliding of the chain and then the door opened wide. "Come in, only if you're going to be brief." They followed Mrs. Settler through to a garden room at the side of the house. When they were seated, Mrs. Settler asked, "What do you want to know?"

Ettie licked her lips and looked over at Ava. She hadn't expected Mrs. Settler to speak to them, so she hadn't come prepared with questions.

Ava said, "Bill was given to you by an Amish couple?"

"They gave him to us and then they wanted him back." She folded her arms across her chest.

"They claim the arrangement was only for six months."

"No, it wasn't. They're lying. Anyway, Billy already told me he found his birth parents. Now he tells me that man – Horace – turned up dead."

"That's right," Ettie said. "He is deceased."

"Anyway, they lied to us. Bertram, that's my late husband, said they didn't want him. He said they couldn't have him because they were Amish and unmarried. That's what I was told and that's what I believe. There was nothing said about six months. I was upset that the woman came here wanting him back. Billy was happy and settled."

"Did you know about Bill's father taking money from your husband? I mean, not money – it was diamonds," Ettie asked.

"They said we could have him and then they changed their minds. How would you feel? We looked after him for months thinking we'd have him forever and then that man comes calling, trying to take him from us. After that, she turns up."

"Did your husband tell you Horace stole some things and tried to blackmail you?"

She looked at the two of them. "See, that Horace wasn't an honest man. An honest man wouldn't have done that."

Ettie had to stop herself reminding Mrs. Settler about her husband's dubious reputation. It didn't escape Ettie's attention that the woman was the same height and weight as Sadie. She would've done anything to keep the baby, and that would include stealing back the diamonds that were used as blackmail against her. Did Mrs. Settler pose as Sadie at the bank?

Ettie didn't know whether it was old age causing her impatience or if she was simply frustrated by not knowing the truth. "Mrs.

Settler, did you go to the bank posing as Sadie Hostetler and remove the gems from the safe deposit box?"

Mrs. Settler stared at Ettie with an open mouth before she said, "I certainly did not. How dare you accuse me of such a thing? You've got a thundering cheek."

"We're sorry, Mrs. Settler, but I'm sure the police are going to come and ask you the very same thing."

"They are? Do they think I killed him? I wouldn't do it. I wouldn't have killed my son's birth father even if he were a horrid man. Neither would I have stolen anything out of a deposit box – I wouldn't even know how to go about doing such a thing."

Just then, the three women heard cars screech to a halt outside the house. Mrs. Settler stood up and peered through the trellis of the garden room. From there she had a clear view to the front of her house. "It's the police." Tears fell down her face. "I'm not strong enough for all this. I've been through too much already."

"Did you kill Horace, Mrs. Settler?" Ettie asked.

She hung her head. "No, but I know who did."

CHAPTER 17

Before Mrs. Settler could tell Ettie and Ava who killed Horace, the police were at the door.

When she opened the door, Detective Kelly looked straight at Ettie, who was standing behind her. He frowned and then looked back at Mrs. Settler. "We'd like to ask you a few questions, Mrs. Settler."

She folded her arms and leaned against the doorframe. "About?"

"I'm sure you'd prefer to discuss the matter in private."

"Is Bill in some kind of trouble?"

"Mrs. Settler, can we come inside?" the detective persisted.

"No, I have nothing to say."

She closed the door on both the detective and the officer who was standing beside him. Ettie had never seen anyone so bold as Mrs. Settler. But then, since her husband had been a villain, she wouldn't have much respect for the law.

Mrs. Settler turned back to Ettie. "Where were we?" Before Ettie could speak, Mrs. Settler looked through the peephole at the police. "Good – they're going." Mrs. Settler walked back to the garden room and sat down.

Ettie followed after her, and when she was seated, she asked, "You said you know who killed Horace? "

Mrs. Settler looked down at the terracotta tiles on the floor.

Ettie ran through all the suspects in her mind to see if she could guess the name in the seconds before the woman spoke. There were Sadie, Agatha, Mr. Settler senior and Terence Wheeler, or one of his men.

"I'm certain it was that woman."

"Which woman?" the two women said at the same time.

"The woman who gave us the baby and then wanted him back."

Ettie pulled a face and then stared at Ava.

"Now you both must go. It's just too much for me."

Ettie knew she'd get no more out of the woman. "Thank you for telling us all that you have, Mrs. Settler."

She led them back to the front door.

Once they were outside, they walked up the road hoping to find a taxi.

"Kelly wasn't happy to see me. I think we should go straight to the station, make that report and look at those mug shots."

"Ettie, don't you ever get tired? Or hungry?"

"Jah, I could eat."

Ava smiled. "I was hoping you'd say that." Ava pulled her in the direction of a small coffee shop that she'd sighted down at the end of the street.

When they were seated with coffee and bagels, Ettie said, "I'm sorry to drag you into all this, Ava."

Ava smiled. "I have to help to clear Agatha's name. Do you still think the detective thinks she had something to do with it?"

Ettie finished the mouthful she was chewing. "Not now. Not since all this has come to light about the key, and then Horace and Sadie having a child together."

Ava took a sip of coffee. "They could think that Agatha was upset with him for what had happened between him and Sadie and then she hit him over the head."

"People have killed for less, I suppose. At least now the police have a few more things to sort out. At the beginning it was only Agatha, and now they've many more people to consider."

Ava stared into the distance.

"What are you thinking?"

"Oh, Ettie, how can you ever trust a man? I'm shocked about Horace and Sadie – it just seems so awful. There's Agatha, thinking she would marry Horace and have a family with him, and then she finds out he's having – or has had – a *boppli* with someone Agatha would have considered as Horace's *schweschder.* It's all so awful, too awful."

"It is, but so are many things in life. It's how we deal with these challenges that's important. We can't judge – it's not up to us to do that."

Ava nodded, then stared into her coffee.

"Why have you never married, Ava? You must be about twenty five now."

"Twenty three. It just seems marriage is for other people. I haven't met a man who makes me feel that I can totally be myself when I'm with him."

"What about Jeremiah?" Ettie said with a twinkle in her eye. "He'd be over twenty now, I'd say. I've got so many great nieces and nephews it's hard to keep up."

"He does seem nice, but he's never been anything more. I mean, he's never asked me to spend time with him, so I don't know how I could get to know him better. I feel too old to go to the singings – they're more for the younger people."

"Why don't Elsa-May and I have you two to dinner?"

Ava giggled. "Ettie, don't you dare do that. It'll be so obvious that I'd be embarrassed."

Ettie pouted. "If you want something to happen, Ava, you have to do something about it. You can't just sit down and hope that a man will come to you if that hasn't happened already."

"Forget I said anything. I'm okay as I am. I'm happy living alone."

Ettie raised her eyebrows at her and Ava looked away.

"The greatest joy in my life was having a family. Seeing the miracle of birth as the little ones come into the world – there's nothing like it."

"I've got my horse, and thanks to you, now I've got chickens."

Ettie giggled, and covered her mouth with her hand as she burst into all-out laughter.

Ava giggled too. "Besides, Agatha seemed happy and she never married."

"That's true; we can find happiness wherever we are." Ettie patted her mouth with the paper napkin. "Ah, that was nice. *Denke* for suggesting it. Now, are you ready to face Detective Kelly?"

"It's you who'll have to do that," Ava said with a smirk.

ETTIE APPROACHED the sergeant at the front desk. "I'm Ettie Smith. Detective Kelly has been waiting on me to look at some photographs and to make some kind of a report."

With just a glance up at her, the sergeant picked up the phone and talked to the detective. "I've got a Mrs. Smith here to make a report and look at some photos." When he hung up the receiver he said, "Follow me."

Ava sat in the waiting area while Ettie followed the gruff sergeant into an empty room. An officer came in and took down her statement over what happened when Sadie visited her. When she was done with that, she had to look through a series of photographs. She was unable to identify the young man with the gun.

"Is that all for today?" Ettie asked, hoping she could leave.

"Detective Kelly would like a word with you."

That was what Ettie had feared. She waited while the officer went to fetch the detective.

When he came in, he sat before her and said, "What were you doing at Mrs. Settler's house?"

She opened her mouth to speak when he raised his hand to stop her. "I know exactly what you were doing. You were asking her questions. And if it weren't for you, she would've spoken to us when we got there."

"No, I'm sure –"

"Mrs. Smith, I could have you arrested for obstructing justice."

"But I –"

"There have been some developments."

Ettie raised her eyebrows. Had they found out some things from Bill Settler?

"Since you insist on sticking your nose in where it doesn't belong, have you found out anything?"

Ettie scratched her neck, not sure what she should reveal. "I know a great many things about a lot of people, but I'm not sure which of it would be of interest to you."

"I'll tell you something and then you might see how vital it is that you stay out of my way. After we got a warrant for Mrs. Settler's bank accounts, we found that exactly a week after the box in Sadie's name was accessed, over three hundred thousand dollars was deposited into her account."

Ettie raised her eyebrows. "Really?"

"Yes, really. We'll also be charging Bill Settler. He admitted to sending someone to your house with a gun to get a key from you."

"How would he have known?" Ettie asked.

The detective ignored Ettie's question. "A warrant for Mrs. Settler's arrest has just come through – that is, if she hasn't already been spooked by your visit and disappeared. Our plan was to visit her and talk to her about what her son had said, hoping the warrant would come through while we were with her. But you ruined that for us. We'll have to hope that she's still at the house."

"You could've had her watched."

"Manpower, Mrs. Smith, manpower – it's not an unlimited resource."

"I'm sorry, Detective. I didn't mean to get in the way. I'm just trying to clear my friend's name. She'd do the same for me."

The detective stared at her blankly as though he wanted to admonish her some more.

"I should go, I suppose. I've looked at the photos and I've made that report."

"Very well. Please stay out of this whole thing, Mrs. Smith. I know you're trying to help your friend and I can understand that, but you are getting in our way."

Ettie rose to her feet and gave him a nod. She left the detective sitting and hurried out to meet Ava in the waiting area.

CHAPTER 18

"It doesn't add up, Ettie. There are too many things that just don't make sense," Ava whispered to Ettie behind a cupped hand so the taxi driver wouldn't overhear.

"I've been thinking that myself. Sadie's been lying, so what else has she lied about?"

"Do you think she was the one who went to the box?"

"*Nee.* Why would she come looking for the key, then? And then there's all that money that appeared in Mrs. Settler's account." Ettie scratched the side of the cheek. "Let's talk to Sadie some more, shall we? I'm going to pretend we have some information about her. Just follow my lead."

Ava leaned over and gave the driver Sadie's address.

The taxi stopped in front of the house and as Ava paid the driver, Sadie came outside and walked toward them.

"Can we talk, Sadie?" Ettie asked.

"Mamm's asleep. She's been very upset about everything. Mind if we sit on the porch so we don't wake her?"

Ettie and Ava followed Sadie to the porch. When they were seated, Ettie began by saying, "Sadie, it's been found out that it was you who went back to the safe deposit box."

Sadie looked down at her hands in her lap and remained silent. Just as Ettie was about to continue speaking, Sadie said, "I did it for my baby. It was my last chance. I thought if the Settlers could see all those diamonds and everything they could have, then they would give me back my baby."

"You got everything out and took it to them?" Ava asked.

Sadie nodded. "Mr. Settler wasn't home. Mrs. Settler said she wouldn't give the baby back for all the money in the world. I tried to make her see that he was my baby and I loved him more than she would ever be able to imagine. I said I'd go to the police, and then she said I'd go to jail for stealing." She looked at Ettie with tears brimming in her eyes. "What use would I be to my son if I was in jail? It was Horace's fault; he'd made another mistake involving me in robbery."

"What happened to the gems you took out?"

Sadie shrugged. "I knew I couldn't get my baby back. Horace was useless and I couldn't go to the police, and I had no money for a lawyer."

"Why didn't you go to the bishop?" Ava asked.

"What? Then I'd be shunned and where would I go? I don't think the community would've been able to help me." Sadie looked into her palms. "I left the gems with the woman whom my son would grow up to call his mother. They were no good to me if they weren't going to get my son back. I wondered if I should sell them to pay for a lawyer to get him back, but they were stolen goods and I might have gone to jail if I was caught."

"You gave Mrs. Settler the gems?"

"I made her promise that she would always take care of William. She promised me that, and they kept his name – his first name. She said she would open an account with the money the gems brought in and the money would be for William. She said she wouldn't tell a soul of it. Not her husband, not William –no one. She asked me to stay away from them and I agreed."

"Then you left and forgot about him – or tried to forget?" Ava asked.

"I could never forget my *boppli,* never. He was everything to me."

"Don't say another word, Sadie."

All heads turned to see Mrs. Doris Hostetler at the front door. Sadie flew to her feet. *"Mamm,* go back to bed."

"Nee, don't say another word."

"It's too late for that. It'll all come out now."

Ettie leaned closer.

"Ettie and Ava, please leave my property."

Ettie looked at Sadie. "Why did you pretend to be shocked when the police found nothing at the bank?"

"Don't say anything, Sadie," Doris ordered.

Sadie turned away from them.

"I've asked you both to go."

Ava and Ettie stood up, walked down the steps and headed to the main road. Ettie looked back to see Sadie's head hanging low as her mother spoke crossly to her.

"What do you make of that?" Ava asked Ettie.

"It explains a few things."

"But not who killed Horace."

Once they got off the Hostetler property and onto the main road, they saw a buggy heading toward them.

"I wonder who this'll be," Ettie said.

"I think it's Jeremiah."

Ettie's face lit up.

"Don't you dare say anything, Ettie. Don't invite him anywhere or anything like that. Ettie?"

Ettie nodded.

"What are you doing out this way?" Jeremiah said as he stopped the buggy.

"We were visiting Sadie," Ava said.

"And you're going to walk five miles home?"

Ava and Ettie looked at each other. They couldn't tell him they were just ordered off the property and didn't have a chance to ask to call a taxi from the phone in the barn.

"Are you going our way?" Ettie asked.

"Looks like I am now."

They got into Jeremiah's buggy.

"Aunt Ettie, do you like the floorboards as they are? I could put a varnish on them and have them shiny."

"They're good as they are. You must let me know what I owe you for doing all that work."

"*Nee,* I'll not charge one of my own."

"It took you too long to do and I want to pay you for your time, the same as you'd charge anyone else. That's fair."

"*Nee,* aunty. I'll not do it."

"You must come to dinner then, at my old house with Elsa-May. We'll cook up a *wunderbaar* meal."

"That I'll say yes to." Jeremiah turned to Ettie and Ava in the back seat and smiled.

"You come too, Ava."

Ava dug Ettie in the ribs. "I've been fairly busy these days, helping *Mamm* get things ready for the markets."

"Come on, Ava. You can spare just one night, can't you? I'll fetch you and bring you home," said Jeremiah.

Ettie looked at Ava with a huge grin and nodded.

While frowning at Ettie, Ava said, "Well, I'll see if I can."

CHAPTER 19

It was the next day that Crowley knocked on the front door of Agatha's old house.

"Come in," Ettie said. "Tea?"

"Always." He followed Ettie to the kitchen. "The floor looks much better."

"It does, thanks to my great nephew." As she put the pot on the stove and lighted the gas, she asked, "Have you been following what's happened?"

He nodded as Ettie sat at the kitchen table opposite him. "Kelly's interview with Mrs. Settler revealed some interesting things, which led to Sadie being brought in for questioning earlier today. She admitted to giving Mrs. Settler the goods from the deposit box, which means she's also admitting to being the one to take the goods out of the box."

"Yes, and she denied that up until now." To avoid another lecture, Ettie did not tell Crowley that she'd been to see Sadie the day before.

Crowley said, "She lied about going to the box the second time and she lied about someone telling her that Terence Wheeler hid Horace's body along with a key."

"What did Mrs. Settler have to say, exactly?"

"She said Sadie gave her the money for her son and said that Horace was gone, which leads me to believe that Sadie knew who killed him, or at least knew he'd been killed."

"She did say at one point that Horace told her he was heading north. She might just have meant 'gone' as in 'never coming back'."

"That's true."

"Anyway, can you believe what Mrs. Settler says? The woman stole Sadie's baby."

The retired detective heaved a sigh. "According to Sadie, she didn't give the baby back after six months, but according to Mrs. Settler, that was never the arrangement. How do we know that Horace didn't tell the Settlers one thing, and tell Sadie another?"

"That's what I've been thinking, but if that had been the case then why would he have been blackmailing the Settlers to get him back?"

"He could've changed his mind once he saw how upset Sadie

was. He might have realized he'd made a huge mistake and tried to right his wrong," Crowley said.

Ettie tapped her fingers on the table. "That could very well be the case." The sound of the water boiling drew Ettie's attention. She rose to her feet to make the tea. "I can offer you fruit cake?"

"Just the tea will be fine, Ettie, thanks."

"Elsa-May made the fruit cake."

"Did she? I'll just have a small piece, then."

Ettie chuckled. The detective did like his food, and anything Elsa-May made was always a winner. Ettie cut two small slices of cake while the tea steeped. "There you go." She sat again once she'd placed the tea and cake on the table. "It's hard to know who's lying and who's telling the truth."

"Each woman was convinced that the baby should've been with her. I don't think we'll ever know what Horace arranged."

Ettie blew on her tea. "Poor Sadie. Horace left and she didn't have him or her baby."

Crowley took a small bite of cake.

"Something's just occurred to me." She stared into the distance.

He swallowed his cake and said, "What is it?"

"If Sadie admits to taking the goods out of the box, doesn't that put her in the possession of the key? And the key was found with the body."

"But not on the body. If it had been on the body, then that would have been incriminating, but it wasn't."

Ettie breathed out heavily and placed her teacup back into the saucer. *Did Agatha leave me her house hoping I'd find Horace's murderer? But that would've meant she knew he was under the house. How odd that, for all those years, she sat on the rocking chair in the middle of the floor, directly over him.*

"What are you thinking, Ettie?"

He jolted her out of her daydreams. "Just thinking, and wondering, what became of the key after Sadie went to the bank. If she had it then, what became of it? She lied about Terence Wheeler hiding a key with Horace's body. Did she give the key to Horace at some point after she took the gems out? She did say that Mrs. Settler agreed to keep the matter of the money to herself."

"Ettie!"

"What?"

"You spoke to Sadie? You knew about this?"

Whoops! "Well, yes, I did speak to Sadie before she spoke to the police about it. I went to see her yesterday and she admitted some things, but then her mother came to the door and asked Ava and me to leave. I didn't tell you when you first arrived because I knew you'd tell me to keep out of things."

"Ettie."

"I know, I know. I've already gotten into trouble from Detective Kelly about talking to people. Please don't tell him."

He shook his head. "I'll have to think about that." He took the last bite of cake.

Ettie put her teacup to her lips and took a small sip then lowered it to the table. "She can't have been telling the truth about anything. She admits taking the money, so she would've had the key. If she did have it, then she knew about Horace being under the floor because the key was hidden close by him. Although she'd taken the gems out, so I suppose she didn't want the key found because it was in her name and would possibly link her with stolen goods. Perhaps she thought it would make her look less guilty if someone else had gone and taken the gems out. She could've wanted the police to think someone posed as her."

"What was Agatha's involvement, then? This is her house."

"*That* we'd only find out from Sadie's lips."

"You need to tell the police what you know, Ettie."

"I don't know anything that the police don't know now." Ettie pulled a face. She hadn't exactly made best friends with the new detective.

"You know a lot, and if you tell Kelly everything there might be some tiny piece of evidence that you don't know you have."

Ettie gulped. "Will you come with me?"

"I'll drive you."

Ettie looked at the empty cups and the crumbs on the plates. "Will I have time to do the dishes and freshen up?"

Crowley stood. "I'll take care of the dishes while you freshen up. Then I'll call ahead and let him know we're coming."

CROWLEY AND ETTIE waited in an interview room for Detective Kelly.

"I need to warn you, he's not happy with me," Ettie said. "Don't leave me alone with him."

Crowley smiled. "He'll be all right."

Kelly came through the doorway with a large folder and kicked the door closed behind him with a backward flick of his foot. He nodded hello to both of them before he sat on the other side of the large table.

Kelly began by saying, "What we know so far, Mrs. Smith, is that Sadie has admitted to taking the stolen goods back out of the safe deposit box. She claims she lied about it in the beginning because she knew the goods were stolen and she thought she'd be charged." He murmured, "Which is still to be decided." He went on, "We have a confession from Mrs. Settler that she accepted the stolen goods from Sadie Hostetler, sold them, and then placed the money in an account for her son."

Ettie closed her eyes. Did Sadie say that she sold the gems and gave the money to Mrs. Settler? She couldn't be certain of that so she remained silent on the matter.

Crowley added, "That places the key in the possession of Sadie Hostetler."

"Which was found near the body," Kelly said. Crowley nodded as Kelly stood and said, "I'll get a warrant prepared for her arrest."

"What?" Ettie pushed herself to her feet. "Don't you want to hear everything I know so you might be able to find a clue somewhere?"

Kelly exchanged glances with Crowley before he sat down. He scratched his head in an agitated manner, then said, "Look, Mrs. Smith, I'm grateful that you're trying to be helpful, but I don't have time to listen. Haven't you told me everything you know already?"

Crowley said, "Since Ettie – Mrs. Smith – knows everyone involved, she could very well know something that could be vital to the case."

Detective Kelly closed his eyes. "If you'll wait here, I'll be back in a moment. I'll have someone else pick up Sadie Hostetler."

When he was out of the room, Ettie asked Crowley, "Do they have enough information – I mean evidence – to arrest her?"

He nodded. "She was in possession of stolen goods and that can be proven when we find out where the goods were liquidated."

"Don't they have to find that out first?"

"Just trust the process, Ettie."

Ettie couldn't help scowling at Crowley. He's the one who got her there to talk to Kelly and Kelly obviously had no interest in what she had to say. What could she tell them that they hadn't already found out? Ettie stood up. "I'm old and I'm tired. I don't think that man wants to listen to anything I have to say, and quite frankly, I'm annoyed by the whole thing."

Crowley jumped to his feet. "Don't be like that, Ettie."

"Would you mind driving me home?"

He breathed out heavily. "You wait here, I'll find Kelly and tell him we're leaving."

"He won't be upset about that," Ettie murmured under her breath. Once Crowley was out of the room, she sat back down and studied her surroundings. The large mirror on the wall reflected the sterile gray interior. Was that a two-way mirror? She wondered if someone on the other side was watching her. But who would want to listen to what she had to say, or look at an old lady? She wasn't guilty of any crime and hadn't done anything wrong, so surely there'd be no one behind that mirror. Not knowing if there was anyone behind it unnerved her.

Ettie walked into the corridor and opened the door to the room next-door. She peeped in to see that it was empty and it was not the door that led to the other side of the mirror.

Just as she was closing the door she heard Kelly's voice behind her. "I hear you want to leave now?"

Ettie jumped and saw Kelly right there with Crowley a little way behind him. "Yes, I'm a little tired. Maybe I could come back and talk to you another day?"

"I'll look forward to it," he said in a sarcastic tone.

"Let's go, Ettie."

Ettie followed Crowley out of the building.

When they were outside, he turned to her. "What were you doing in that other room?"

"Do you think Kelly noticed?"

"I think he's got so much on his mind that he didn't recall which interview room we were in."

Ettie relaxed. "That's good."

"Well?"

"I was just wondering if there was anyone behind the two-way mirror."

Crowley's stern face softened into a smile. "It's accessed from a room on the other side of the building. And I don't think there would've been anyone interested enough in what we had to say to watch us."

"That'd be true enough. Detective Kelly seemed most put out at the thought of having to listen to me tell him everything I knew."

"Yes, I'm sorry about that, Ettie. That's not the way I would've done things. Everyone has their own way of doing things, I guess."

Ettie nodded.

"Well, come on. The car's this way."

CHAPTER 20

Ettie had Crowley drive her back to Agatha's old house. She stood at the door and watched Crowley drive away. A quick look in the paddock told Ettie that Ava had taken her buggy somewhere. At last she could have a time to sit in peace and empty her mind of all the dreadful things she'd heard.

She had kept the door locked since she'd had the incident with the intruder who'd ripped up her floor. She reached into her sleeve and pulled out her front door key, pushing it into the lock and turning it. Once she pushed the door open she stepped inside, hoping that everything was okay.

She took a few steps further, slowly, until she saw that nothing was out of place. After she checked every room she finally felt she was able to relax. She kicked off her boots, placed her slippers on her feet and headed to the kitchen. Ettie smiled when she saw how tidy Crowley had left things in the kitchen – even the dishtowel was carefully folded and left adjacent to the sink. After she made a cup of tea, Ettie headed to the living room.

Ettie looked around – it didn't feel like her house. It would always be Agatha's home. She sat in Agatha's rocking chair holding her teacup, careful not to spill a drop. After looking around the room, she put the cup to her lips. She slurped her tea, glad that Elsa-May wasn't there to tell her to stop. Hot tea tasted much better when it was slurped. "Did you play a part in this nasty business, Agatha?" she asked her late friend, wishing Agatha could tell her exactly what she knew. Agatha had to have known something about Horace being under the floor, Ettie was now convinced of that.

A knock on Ettie's front door startled her. She hadn't heard anyone approach the house. She set her tea down on a small side table and peeped out one of the front windows. It was Sadie. *The police are going to think I'm meddling again.*

With Sadie sobbing as she waited for the door to open, Ettie had no choice but to let her in. Once the door was open, Sadie put her arms around Ettie's shoulders and sobbed. Ettie instinctively patted her on the back.

"Oh, Ettie. I'm so upset."

"Come inside. I've just boiled the water." As Ettie closed the front door she looked up the road. No sign of the police.

She sat Sadie at the kitchen table while she made her a cup of tea. "Do you want to tell me what's going on, Sadie? I was at the police station earlier today and I believe I heard them saying they're getting a warrant for your arrest."

Sadie sniffled and shook her head. "I don't care anymore. I don't care what happens to me now. My life is finished."

Ettie placed a cup of tea in front of her. "Did you come to talk to me?"

"I don't know what to do."

"You could start by telling the truth before the police think you had something to do with Horace's murder."

Sadie's eyelids flickered as she avoided Ettie's gaze. Ettie wondered if she did have something to do with his death. "Correct me if I'm wrong, Sadie. Horace gave you the stolen goods and had you open the deposit box at the bank. You never gave him back the key, did you?"

Sadie sniffled, closed her eyes and said, *"Nee."*

"You heard Horace was returning to the community to marry Agatha. You were furious; he was the cause of you losing your baby so you wanted to confront him. You drove past and saw he was here at Agatha's house. You came to the door to talk to him, possibly to tell Agatha about the baby you'd had with Horace. You hit him hard in anger and killed him."

With both hands clutching her stomach she asked, "Did Agatha tell you?"

Ettie slowly shook her head. "Agatha kept your secret. Although she loved him, he'd betrayed her as well as you. She couldn't have been happy with what he'd done. Neither could she marry him."

Sadie sighed. “It’s just as you said. Only Agatha was right here when I hit him, and she saw the whole thing. I didn’t mean to kill him. I was so upset with him and how he’d trusted those people with William. He’d lost me my baby because he wouldn’t do the right thing and marry me.”

Ettie patted her on the arm.

Sadie continued, “Agatha knew it was an accident and that’s why she helped me hide his body. We figured nobody would find him there. We had a pact, Agatha and I. We didn’t like each other, but we had both loved Horace. We made certain to stay a distance from one another after that, in the hope that no one would suspect that we had worked together to create his disappearance.”

“Did Horace know you cleared out the safe deposit box?”

Sadie shook her head. “It was after Horace had gone and I realized I was never going to get my baby back. It was me who took the gems out of the bank. I sold all that I could – there were some that were too big to sell quickly. I took the big diamonds and the cash to Mrs. Settler hoping that when she saw all that money and those big diamonds she’d give me my baby. When I realized she wouldn’t give my baby up for anything, I left everything with her. What else could I do? That was all I could do for him; the last thing I could do for him.”

“It must have been hard for you to keep that secret all these years.”

“It was. I told mamm some of it.”

"What happened to the key after that?"

"I gave the key to Agatha and asked her to hide it where no one would ever find it."

"Ah, and she hid it close to Horace."

"She never told me where she hid it. When I heard that Horace was found I asked Bill to help me find the key. I knew that the police would've combed the place and if they found the key it'd be only a matter of time before they pieced everything together. I had to tell Bill about the box and that I might go to jail if they found out that key was in my name. He came here the other night to look for it, but he told me someone spotted him. Then he heard that you had the key and he sent someone to get it."

"He was doing what he could to take care of you, Sadie."

"Now I've probably gotten my own son into trouble."

Ettie heard cars pull up in front of her house. She walked to the front window and pulled the curtain aside. She called out to Sadie who was still in the kitchen. "It's the police – looking for you, no doubt."

Sadie rose to her feet and joined Ettie by the front door. "I'm ready for them."

Ettie opened the door just as Detective Kelly was walking up the porch steps followed by two policemen.

The detective looked past Ettie to Sadie. "Sadie Hostetler, I have a warrant for your arrest."

She stepped forward and Ettie noticed one of the policemen had handcuffs in his hands. He stepped forward. "Put both of your hands out."

"Is that necessary, Detective?" Ettie asked. "She's not going to run off anywhere."

"Very well." The detective gave the officer a look, which caused the officer to clip the cuffs back onto his belt. "Let's go, Ms. Hostetler."

"Will you be all right, Sadie?" Ettie called after her.

"I'll be fine, Ettie. I'll tell them all that I told you."

The detective looked up, stopped in his tracks, turned around and glared at Ettie.

Ettie took a step back, wondering what she should say. Before anything came to mind, the detective turned again and continued to the waiting car.

WITH ALL THAT had happened that day, Ettie decided that Agatha's house held too many sad memories, and so she went back to stay with Elsa-May that night.

After dinner, while she was doing her needlework and Elsa-May was knitting quietly, Ettie remembered her words to Jeremiah. "I told Jeremiah we'd have him over for dinner. And I invited Ava over too."

Elsa-May looked over the top of her glasses. "No good comes from meddling in other people's lives, Ettie."

"It's just dinner. Whatever the two of them do after that is none of my business."

Elsa-May scoffed. "You make it sound like they're going to run off and do something bad."

"You know that's not what I mean. Once they get to know one another a little better they might find that they like each other."

"And if they do it's well and good." Elsa-May nodded firmly.

Ettie smiled and looked back at her needlework as she planned what they'd cook for the dinner. "Perhaps we should have that dinner next week?"

Elsa-May kept her head down. "Whenever you'd like; a week or more would give us enough time to plan for a nice dinner."

CHAPTER 21

The next day, after completing their chores, Elsa-May and Ettie had settled down for a quiet day when someone knocked on their door.

"I'll get it." Ettie rose to her feet and hurried to the door, hoping it would be someone from the community with news of Sadie. She'd not been brave enough to go near Detective Kelly since he'd arrested Sadie the day before.

"Ah, I'm glad it's you. Come in." Ettie ushered Crowley through the door and sat him in the living room.

"Thank you, Ettie. That's one of the best receptions I've ever gotten."

"Ettie's been anxiously waiting to find out what happened to Sadie. Is she still arrested?"

Ettie didn't mind Elsa-May speaking on her behalf today. She looked at the retired detective, waiting, hoping he knew something.

"I've just come from the station. Sadie was arrested for the murder of Horace Hostetler after her confession. Her son, Bill Settler, posted bail."

"She's out?"

Crowley nodded.

"Will she go to prison?" Elsa-May asked.

Crowley sucked in his lips before he said, "She didn't have the intention to kill him and there were extreme circumstances, but I guess it depends on the judge and the jury on the day. With the waiting periods it might be two or three years before she stands trial."

"What about Mrs. Settler? She took what Sadie gave her; will she be charged?"

"I'm not certain, but most likely she'll be charged. They're still sorting through the evidence."

"Well, you were right about one thing, Ettie," Elsa-May said.

"I was right about a lot of things." Ettie glared at her sister. She reckoned she'd done pretty well piecing everything together.

"I meant you were right about Agatha not killing Horace."

"There was never any doubt in my mind about that." Ettie smiled, feeling good that her sister had finally given her a compliment. "I knew Agatha had no violence in her, but keeping a secret, that would be something she'd do. She was a good and loyal friend these past ten years, since we grew close."

"The Settler family's not short on money, I can assure you of that. With Bill looking after her, Sadie will get the best legal team money can buy."

"The son now looks after the mother that never got a chance to look after him," Elsa-May said, her voice filled with sadness.

"It's awful for Sadie that she lost a son. It would've been sad for Agatha too, but she didn't lose a child, just a man. There were many others she could've chosen over the years." Ettie wiped away a tear.

"That's what secrets will do. What would've happened if Sadie had been able to tell the truth about having a baby? Surely what she would've gone through would be less painful than what finally happened?" Crowley asked.

Ettie and Elsa-May looked at each other. "Most likely they would have had to have confessed their sin in front of the community on a Sunday, in front of everyone."

"Would they have been shunned?" Crowley asked.

"Depends if they'd been baptized or not. The young usually wait until just before marriage to get baptized," Elsa-May said. "They would've had to live with the shame. And they'd have had to marry."

"It probably all came down to Horace not wanting to marry Sadie," Crowley said.

"Well, he should've," Elsa-May said flatly. "After what he did, he should've."

Crowley nodded. "It would've been easier to marry Sadie than to end up under a house."

"Well, once again we owe you many thanks, for helping Ettie with all these goings on," Elsa-May said.

"Yes, thank you. I don't know what I would've done without you stepping in once that key was found. I haven't made a very good impression on Detective Kelly." Ettie ran her finger around the top of her teacup.

Crowley chuckled.

Ettie stared into her nettle tea. What would she do with Agatha's house? All those years of being a good friend to Agatha and she never breathed a word of what had happened to Horace. Then the scripture came to Ettie's mind: Luke 8:17. *For nothing is secret, that shall not be made manifest; neither any thing hid, that shall not be known and come abroad.*

"All secrets come home," Ettie muttered to herself while Crowley and Elsa-May reached as one for the last piece of cake.

AMISH MURDER

ETTIE SMITH AMISH MYSTERIES BOOK 2

This is a work of fiction. Any names or characters, businesses or places, events or incidents, are fictitious. Any resemblance to actual persons, living or dead, or actual events is purely coincidental.

CHAPTER 1

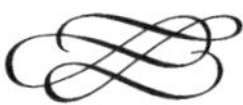

"She must've made someone angry. Not many people get killed by staying in their own homes and minding their own business," Ettie said to her sister, Elsa-May.

Elsa-May looked at her over the top of her glasses. "Who? Camille Esh?"

Ettie frowned. "How many other women do we know who've been murdered recently?"

"I was only half-listening. *Jah,* you're right about that. People do get murdered in their own homes, but usually by more violent means."

Ettie dropped her sampler into her lap. "She must've known the person who killed her. They must have slipped the poison into her food; maybe even when she was in her apartment, which means she might even have entertained her killer."

Elsa-May shivered and then shook her head.

"What is it?" Ettie asked.

"The whole thing's awful, and anyway, who would've wanted her dead?"

"You didn't know her as well as I did. There was more to that girl than first met the eye. She could've stepped on some toes when she left our community."

Elsa-May continued knitting at a slower pace than usual. They'd just finished cleaning up after breakfast and had settled in for a quiet day. "I'd say you're right. I know Camille's stepmother, Mildred, always had a rough time with her. The two never got along. How is Camille's *bruder* Jacob now? I haven't seen Mildred or Jacob since Camille's funeral."

"Jacob's coping, but Mildred's missing her husband. Nehemiah wasn't even that old."

"Much younger than both of us," Ettie added. "And it was a shock that Nehemiah died, and just weeks later, Camille was murdered."

Elsa-May glanced down at her knitting and then looked back up at Ettie, not missing a stitch of the intricate pattern she'd learned by heart. "I've been meaning to ask you, have you thought about what you're going to do with the *haus?*"

Ettie had recently been left a house by her dear friend, Agatha.

"I would sell, except Agatha wanted her young friend, Ava, to stay in the *grossdaddi haus* forever – for as long as she wanted."

Ettie placed her needlework in her lap again and looked across the small living room at her older sister. "That's my only sticking point. I'll have to keep the *haus* longer for that very reason. In the meantime, I'll have Jeremiah, your favorite grandson, do some work on the house for me."

Elsa-May chuckled. "You can't say he's my favorite, Ettie. I don't have any favorites."

"The first *grosskinner* always holds a special place, and don't even try to tell me otherwise."

Elsa-May shook her head at her sister and remained silent.

Ettie kept talking. "He's such a *gut* builder. Not only that, he's so handy with other odd jobs. I don't think I could live in the *haus,* though. I'd forever be thinking about Horace being killed and hidden under the floorboards for so many years."

Ettie had been turned off the idea of living in the house. She'd been happy when she found out Agatha had willed her the house, but when Jeremiah found Agatha's old beau, Horace, buried under the floor, the discovery brought with it a disturbing chain of events.

Elsa-May nodded. "That's good. I don't think you'd get the best money for the *haus* the way that it is."

"Remind me to go there tomorrow and have a look so I can make a list of everything that needs doing. I'll see your Jeremiah on Sunday, and ask him to come out and give me a quote." Ettie looked at her sister's smiling face. "Are you happy I'm staying on here in the *haus* with you?"

The corners of Elsa-May's mouth suddenly turned downward. "Please yourself."

Ettie frowned at her. She knew Elsa-May would have missed her if she had moved to Agatha's old house. Why was it so hard for Elsa-May to admit it?

With the exception of the loud tick of the old wooden clock that hung on the wall, the next moments were silent.

Ettie finally spoke. "We should have Jeremiah and Ava over for dinner again. If the two of them got married that would solve my problem of her living in the *grossdaddi haus.*"

Elsa-May chortled and pushed her glasses further up her nose. "Unless Jeremiah moves into it too."

"*Jah,* I hadn't thought of that. It might be best if I lease the main house out, then I'd have no worries."

"That sounds a reasonable solution." Elsa-May continued knitting, moving her elevated sore leg slightly.

Elsa-May and Ettie spent a great deal of their time in their living room with Elsa-May knitting and Ettie concentrating on her needlework.

The sisters stared at each other when a loud knock broke through the silence.

"Who could that be?" Elsa-May asked.

"I didn't hear a buggy. I'll go see." Ettie placed her needlework on the chair next to her and hurried to open the door. They rarely got visitors who walked to their house, and the neighbors, although they were close, mostly kept to themselves. When Ettie swung the door open, she was faced with a stern-faced Detective Kelly. She frowned at him, wondering if she'd done something wrong. Detective Kelly had never been as nice to them as Detective Crowley. There was something about Detective Kelly that Ettie wasn't comfortable with.

"Good morning, Mrs. Smith. May I come in for a moment or two?"

"Good morning, Detective. Certainly." She stepped aside to give him room to move through. "Come in."

"Thank you." Two strides further and he was in the living room of the small home. "Good morning," he said to Elsa-May with a nod.

"Morning. Have a seat, Detective," Elsa-May said, still sitting.

Once the detective sat down, he rocked a little on his chair. "It's not going to break, is it?"

Elsa-May smiled. "I don't think so. I'll have my grandson, Jeremiah, take a look at it."

"Yes, good idea. I know Jeremiah. I met him before at Mrs. Smith's other house."

"We were just talking about the whole business with Horace." Before Ettie took a seat, she asked, "Would you like some hot tea, and cake?" He shook his head, and sat down on a creaky wooden chair.

Ettie sat down on their only couch while she waited to hear why he was there.

He looked from one to the other. "I'm hoping you ladies might be able to help me."

The sisters glanced at each other with raised eyebrows. Just a few months back he'd warned Ettie to keep out of his way. He sure hadn't wanted their help back then.

Elsa-May leaned forward. "Regarding what?"

Ettie had an idea why he was there. The only reason could be that he wanted their help over the recent murder of Camille Esh.

Detective Kelly rubbed his lined forehead and said, "Do you know Jacob Esh and his family?"

"You're here about Camille?" Elsa-May asked.

He nodded. "We have reason to believe that her brother might have killed her."

Elsa-May shook her head. "That's nonsense!"

"We've got reason to believe that..."

"What would possibly give you reason to believe anything of the kind?" Ettie interrupted the detective. She was outraged he could think such a thing.

He held his hands up. "I'm not here to argue back and forth. I'm here because I need your help. Before I go any further, I need to tell you that I do believe the man's innocent. No one in your community will talk to me, so there's my problem right there. I need some of you Amish people to answer my questions. I've been ignored completely – others have shut themselves in their houses and refused to come to the door."

"What would you like us to do?" Ettie asked. "We can't make them speak to you."

"I'd like you to find out a few things for me. That's all! It'll have to be 'off the record', of course. But once I know what's happened, then I'll be in a position where I can help Jacob."

"We'll do whatever we can to help him," Ettie said.

Elsa-May nodded enthusiastically.

The detective leaned so far over that he placed his elbows on his knees. "If we don't find out what happened soon, Jacob could go to jail for a long time, or worse." He straightened up. "Tell me, what do you know about Jacob and the relationship he had with his sister?"

The elderly sisters started talking at the same time, then stopped and looked at each other.

"You go first, Ettie."

Ettie smiled, and then turned to the detective. "Jacob and Camille left the community as soon as they could. Jacob…"

"Jacob left when he was eighteen, I believe, and then two years later, Camille followed when she was around the same age."

Ettie turned and stared at her sister. "You told me to go first."

"So they were both out of the community for a good twenty years?" the detective asked.

"My goodness, is Jacob around forty now?" Elsa-May asked.

The detective nodded. "He is, and his sister was two years younger than he is."

Ettie was quick to answer before Elsa-May butted in again. "To answer your question correctly, Detective, she came back to the community around two years ago. I'm a good friend of Camille's stepmother, Mildred. Poor Mildred – Camille never liked her right from the start. Anyone would think a young girl would be pleased to have a stepmother after her mother died. Surely it would be better than no mother at all. Nehemiah married Mildred two years after Mary's death. Camille was five at the time."

"Mildred was Camille's stepmother, then?" the detective asked.

"Yes." Ettie answered.

"The detective doesn't need to know all that, Ettie."

Kelly looked at Elsa-May. "Actually, it might be helpful." He looked back at Ettie. "Camille didn't get along with Mildred when she was five years old? I would've thought that a child that young would've adjusted better than that."

"To everyone on the outside it appeared that way, but Mildred told me what had gone on behind closed doors. It would surprise even you, Detective. She was a very different girl when no one was watching."

The lines in Kelly's forehead deepened. "Go on."

Ettie rubbed her neck. "I feel terrible. Mildred told me these things in confidence."

Elsa-May frowned. "What things?"

"Anything you tell me could help Jacob," the detective said. He nodded, urging her to continue.

"To put it bluntly, then, the girl used to do dreadful things at home and make it look like Mildred did them. She did everything she could to turn her father against Mildred. She broke Mary's china clock, which Nehemiah had given her on their wedding day. Mary was Camille's mother. It was a beautiful thing with tiny pink rosebuds the entire way around the face of the clock."

"Get to the point, Ettie," her sister said.

Ettie glanced at Elsa-May then looked back at the detective. "When Nehemiah got home that night, Camille told him that Mildred broke it in a fit of temper. He didn't think for one moment that Camille might have broken her mother's clock."

"You never told me about all of that," Elsa-May said.

Ettie nodded. "Camille did things like that all the time. At first, Nehemiah believed Camille, and I believe it caused a rift in Nehemiah and Mildred's marriage in the early days. Then one day, when he overheard Camille talking to Mildred, he knew Camille had been lying about everything."

"Children do go through stages and she was dreadfully upset about her mother's death," Elsa-May said.

"I know that," Ettie said. "And Mildred and Nehemiah tried to be understanding, but she never got along with Mildred. Ever."

"Did Jacob get along with Mildred?" the detective asked.

"Oh, yes, but Jacob and Camille never got along. Not as far back as I can remember. The pair were always at odds with one another, but that doesn't mean he'd kill her."

"Of course, a great many siblings don't care for each other," Detective Kelly said.

Elsa-May said, "I remember they were always competitive, each telling the other they could do better at any given task. I remember, years back, one day at one of the softball games…"

"The detective doesn't need to know that, Elsa-May." Ettie was pleased to mirror Elsa-May's former comment right back at her.

Elsa-May narrowed her eyes at Ettie.

"I do, if it's relevant," the detective said.

"It's not," Ettie said abruptly, making sure to avoid Elsa-May's stern gaze.

The detective looked at Elsa-May, raised his eyebrows, and then turned back to Ettie. "What about Camille's more recent history?"

"As I said, she'd left the community many years ago, and then once Nehemiah had started getting frail, Camille came back to run the farm. She told him she had business experience, so Nehemiah handed things over to her. He really had no choice with Jacob gone. Normally sons take over from the father, but with Jacob not in the community Nehemiah handed the running of the farm over to Camille."

"So when did Jacob come back to the farm?" the detective asked, tipping his head slightly to one side.

Elsa-May said, "Camille came back two years ago, like Ettie already told you. Jacob returned around six months ago. So I imagine in those last few months the siblings both tried to run the farm together. As you probably know already, Camille and Jacob's father died only weeks before Camille was killed."

Ettie continued, "The two were still at odds with one another, just like when they were younger, according to Mildred. When I say 'the two', I mean Camille and Jacob. I think Mildred was used to the fact that Camille was never going to like or accept her into the family. It was hard for Mildred, especially since she never had children of her own."

"Camille was murdered in the apartment she'd moved into, so we know that she'd left the community again by then," the detective said.

"Camille left after Nehemiah died," Ettie said.

The detective repositioned himself in his chair. "What do you mean?"

Ettie took a deep breath, waiting for Elsa-May to jump in and speak for her as she normally did whenever she hesitated. Ettie frowned at Elsa-May when she made no attempt to speak, and continued, "Each thought they knew how to run the farm better. Nehemiah wasn't happy with how Camille had done certain things and he complained to Jacob. Nehemiah let Camille know that she was no longer running the farm and gave the job to Jacob."

The detective sighed. "No, I wasn't asking about that. I want to know why Camille left after Nehemiah died."

"Well, that's what I'm trying to tell you – this is how it happened. Jacob stayed and Camille left. In the will, the farm was left solely to Jacob."

Now Elsa-May interrupted, "So, she had no reason to stick around. Nehemiah was pleased to have his son back before he died. Wasn't he, Ettie?"

Ettie nodded. "Yes, he was pleased that Jacob came back to run the farm. After that, Camille had even more reason to resent poor old Jacob." Seeing the detective open his mouth to speak, Ettie added, "Jacob would never hurt a fly."

After Detective Kelly took a deep breath, he said, "That's my next question. Did Jacob ever show signs of violence or anger toward anyone?"

Both Elsa-May and Ettie shook their heads.

Ettie said, "Not while he was a part of our community. I believe he hasn't got a mean bone in his body."

"But you both wouldn't know him very well if he left when he was eighteen and he only came back to the community recently," Detective Kelly said, looking pleased with himself.

"I believe a person's personality is formed very early in life. Jacob was always a kind boy in his youth." Before the detective could speak again, Elsa-May quickly added, "You said you thought there was some kind of proof that Jacob killed Camille, so what do you have that you're calling 'proof'?"

"No, Elsa-May, I believe the detective's words were that he 'had reason to believe' that Jacob might have killed Camille. He never said anything about having proof." Ettie turned to Kelly. "Isn't that right, Detective?"

"That's correct, Mrs. Smith; that's exactly what I said. We don't have proof, as such, but what we do have is someone who's willing to testify that Camille told her that she suspected Jacob was trying to kill her."

"Utter rubbish," Elsa-May blurted out.

The detective whipped his head around toward Elsa-May. "Are you certain?"

"Yes, why would he kill his own sister? Besides, Jacob's the one who inherited the farm. There was no reason for him to kill her – no monetary reason."

The detective looked between the two of them. "According to the both of you, they didn't get along. A lifetime of not getting along with someone could be the only reason he needed. It's not uncommon for a perfectly sane person to kill another in a fit of rage. It happens every day. Most often people are murdered by someone close to them, such as a spouse, or a family member."

"You did say you thought he was innocent, Detective?" Ettie asked.

"Yes, and I'd like you ladies to help me prove that. I've got pressure on me to solve this case. I'm up for a promotion, and it wouldn't hurt if I could wrap this one up quickly."

Elsa-May huffed. "You didn't want Ettie's help when she tried to help with Horace's murder."

The detective turned to Ettie. "This time, Mrs. Smith, I'd be grateful for your help." He looked at Elsa-May. "And yours too, of course."

"I'm afraid it'll just be Ettie. With my sore leg, I can't do anything. I can't walk very far." Elsa-May rubbed the top of her leg.

"Nothing serious, I hope."

"No, just a niggle."

The detective tilted his head to one side. "A niggle?"

Elsa-May chuckled. "Something that's annoying."

"I'll be glad to help you prove that Jacob is innocent, Detective," Ettie said.

"People will talk to Ettie," Elsa-May said.

"That's what I'm banking on." The detective looked back at

Ettie. "When none of your people would talk to me, naturally I thought of you ladies."

Elsa-May asked, "Do you have any leads at all on the murderer?"

Kelly rubbed his nose. "No. We're still waiting for forensic results to come back. I do have a statement from that woman Camille spoke with."

Elsa-May laughed. "You had me worried for a minute. I thought you were about to lock Jacob away."

Ettie noticed the detective swallowed rather hard at Elsa-May's comment, which made her wonder if he was keeping something from them. Did he have some evidence he didn't want to share with them? He did look kind of guilty at that moment.

The detective rose to his feet. "Can I leave it to you ladies to see what you can find out?" He looked at Ettie. "I guess it'll be just you asking around?"

Ettie pushed herself up from the couch. "I'll do that for you, but you're leaving me in the dark. What exactly do you want me to find out?"

"I need to know what the exact situation was between brother and sister. Did Jacob have any motive in the slightest to want Camille dead? For that matter, did anyone else have reason to want her gone?"

"I'll see what I can find out," Ettie said, walking the detective to the door.

"Goodbye," Elsa-May called out.

Before Kelly had a chance to say goodbye to Elsa-May, Ettie explained, "It hurts Elsa-May to stand with her bad leg."

"Yes, she mentioned that." The detective nodded goodbye to Elsa-May. He then turned to Ettie. "I do appreciate your help, Mrs. Smith. I know we haven't seen eye-to-eye before, but let's let bygones be bygones, shall we?"

"Of course, we can do that."

The detective stepped out the door and walked down the steps toward his car. Ettie watched him all the while.

CHAPTER 2

When Detective Kelly left, Ettie wasted no time in visiting Mildred. The last time she'd seen her was the day after Camille's funeral.

Just as Ettie knocked on the door, Mildred swung it open.

"Ettie, I'm so pleased you've come."

Ettie gave Mildred a quick hug before Mildred ushered her into the living room. "Can I get you something?"

"*Nee denke.* I've just had a visit from a detective." Ettie figured the straightforward approach would be best.

Mildred scowled. "About Camille?"

Ettie nodded. "Jah."

"Why did he go to you?"

"He knows me because I met him when poor Horace was found

under Agatha's floor. Anyway, the detective thinks... Well, he's got some crazy notion that Jacob is involved somehow."

Mildred looked away from her. "Impossible." She looked back at Ettie. "Why should we talk to him? Is that why you're here, to get us to speak to him?"

"Nee. I'm not here to ask you to do that. The truth of the matter is that he wants me to find out what I can about the whole thing." Ettie tapped her chin. "Would you talk to him?"

Mildred shook her head.

"Do you have any idea who might have done it?"

"Not at all. I mean, she didn't have many friends."

"You mean she had no friends?"

Mildred groaned. "Nee, she did have a couple of friends, but they were *Englischers.* She still kept in contact with two people. I never met them, but she'd receive letters from them, and I think she used to meet them in town. People would tell me they saw her speaking with *Englischers.*"

"I might have a cup of hot tea," Ettie said.

"Come with me and we can talk while I make it."

Ettie followed Mildred into the kitchen. "I'm just glad that Nehemiah's not here. He'd never be able to get over Camille being murdered. Especially the way it happened."

Once Mildred put the pot on to boil, they both sat at the kitchen table.

Ettie asked, "From what you told me before, Camille and Jacob had an argument over Nehemiah's will?" That's something Ettie could have told the detective but didn't.

"Nehemiah didn't like the way Camille ran the farm. Among other things, we started losing money and we'd never lost money before. She never was good with finances and that's one of the reasons Nehemiah left the farm to Jacob. She had told her *vadder* she had management experience but it soon became clear she had none. Nehemiah had given her a good chance and she'd been running the farm for nearly two years before Jacob came back to us."

"Jah, you told me that before, about Camille not running the farm to Nehemiah's liking." Ettie raised her eyebrows. "Pardon me for asking, but the whole farm was left just to Jacob?"

Mildred nodded. "Nehemiah discussed it with me before he made the will. I said I didn't want a share. All I wanted was to live in the house here for the rest of my days. It makes sense since I was never blessed with *kinner,* and would never even have *kinskind* of my own." The corners of Mildred's mouth drooped.

Ettie couldn't imagine not having children or grandchildren. Although Ettie didn't see her own that often, they filled her life with a sense of purpose and wellbeing.

Mildred continued, "Better to leave everything to Camille and Jacob. Nehemiah knew that if he left the farm to Camille she'd see to it that I was put out on the street without anything to live on, and Nehemiah didn't want me to end up homeless when he was gone."

Ettie nodded, knowing that Jacob and Mildred had a bond like mother and son, and Jacob would look after her.

Mildred sighed. "After Nehemiah died, Camille found out she wasn't getting the farm and she and Jacob had some terrible rows. She carried on so badly that Jacob ended up offering her half the farm."

"That was generous of him."

"Camille didn't think so; she said she wanted the whole farm. She accused him of only coming back to take the farm from her."

"What did she mean by that?"

"I suppose she meant that he knew his father was close to the end and he chose to return at that time only so he'd inherit the farm. You see, it wasn't until Nehemiah died that she found out she didn't get the farm; he didn't let her know beforehand that she wasn't going to get it. I suppose Nehemiah didn't want to be the victim of one of her outbursts. That girl had such a temper. When she found out that she didn't get the farm, she left the community and leased an apartment in town. She told Jacob she would see him in court."

"She did? You never told me she sued him."

"I don't think it came to anything. We never heard from a lawyer or anything. If she stayed here she might have been safe. She moved to that apartment and that's where they found her."

Ettie rubbed her chin. She hadn't liked to ask Mildred too many questions when she'd learned about Camille's death. Camille threatening to start legal proceedings might have given Jacob motive, but then again, he'd already offered her half the land. Surely a court wouldn't be more generous than Jacob had already been. Did she really expect the courts would award her the entire farm and leave her brother with nothing?

"I know what you're thinking, Ettie. It's like the story of the prodigal son returning."

"I wasn't thinking anything of the kind. Anyway, Camille and Jacob's situation was a little different since Jacob inherited everything and Camille was left with nothing."

"Nee, I never said she got nothing."

Ettie tilted her head to one side. "What do you mean? Did she get left something?"

"Nee, but she did have a trust fund that Nehemiah set up for her when she was twenty five. He was concerned she wasn't married so he set up the fund. He had a lot of money in the bank and the man at the bank said he should do something with it. That's when he thought that Camille should have something, some kind of security."

"Did she have access to it?"

"I'm not certain about any of it. I do know that Nehemiah put Jacob in charge of the money."

"Jacob was the trustee?"

"Is that what you call it when someone can't get at the money unless the other person allows them?"

Ettie nodded, and then pulled a wry face. Jacob probably wasn't the best choice of a trustee since he and his sister had never gotten along. "And has Jacob inherited the money now that Camille's gone?"

"I'm not certain. Whenever Jacob tells me about business matters or money I just block my ears." Mildred covered her ears with the palms of her hands.

Another motive, if Jacob inherited the money from Camille's trust fund.

"Oh, the water's boiling." Mildred got up to pour the tea, and as she did so, something out the window caught her eye. She pulled the heavy curtain aside.

"What is it, Mildred?" Ettie asked, getting up to see what she was staring at.

"Just that pesky fellow from next door. He's been bothering Jacob to sell the farm, and before that, he was pestering Camille when he thought she might have had some say. He can't leave things well enough alone."

"He shouldn't be upsetting people like that." Ettie peeped out the window to see a stout man who appeared to be in his fifties, standing just beyond the property line. "He's an *Englischer?*"

"Jah, his name's Ronald Bradshaw."

"Why does he want the farm so badly?"

"I don't know."

"Has he told Jacob why he wants it?" Ettie asked.

"You'd have to ask Jacob about that. I'd dare say he wants to increase his own farm size, since land around these parts is getting scarce."

Ettie looked out again at the man who now had his hands on his hips gazing at the house. "What's he doing just standing there like that?"

"Beats me. He's probably putting a hex on the place or something, since we won't sell."

Ettie giggled. "Have you ever spoken to the man yourself?"

"*Nee*. He's never come to the door. He's spoken to Jacob when he was out in the fields." Mildred moved away from the window and continued making the tea.

After taking one last look at the man, Ettie sat back down at the table. Mildred placed a cup of tea in front of Ettie and then sat down next to her.

Ronald Bradshaw had to live on the farm with the white house and the red roof, Ettie figured. They were the only *Englischers* that had a property neighboring the Eshes' farm.

Once Ettie took a sip of tea, she placed the cup back on the saucer and looked directly at Mildred. "Do you have any idea who might have killed Camille?"

With a slight raise of her brows, Mildred said, "I don't, but I think she was the type of person to make enemies. Normally I never talk ill of people, but she did have some people who weren't too happy with her. Not that I know anything for certain, I just happened to overhear some conversations she had with people when she was talking on her cell phone."

"She had a cell phone here?"

Mildred nodded. "She never gave up all her *Englisch* ways when she came back to the community. I was sure I heard her talking in her room and I was certain she must've had a phone. I found the phone when I was cleaning her room. I was frightened to talk to her and have her yell at me again, but I knew I had to say something so I did. She spoke real nasty and told me never to tell anyone about it, and I didn't. I never even told Nehemiah about the cell phone. He wouldn't have liked her having something like that in the *haus,* and Camille knew that."

"Nee, nee, of course not." Ettie frowned and thought back to a couple of years ago when she and Elsa-May had kept a cell phone for emergencies. Until one day they had a visit from the bishop and he let them know he was aware of their phone. Elsa-May decided they should get rid of the phone after that. "And you heard her talking on her phone, arguing with someone?"

"Jah."

"Did you hear enough to know who it was, or what the argument was about?"

Mildred moved uncomfortably in her chair. "Some woman, I think it was. She was upset with Camille about something from the sounds of it. That's all I know."

"Interesting," Ettie said. "How did you know it was a woman she was speaking with?"

"The voice was loud enough for me to hear that it was a woman's voice."

Ettie sipped on her tea, knowing her next stop had to be Ronald Bradshaw, the neighbor who was so interested in the farm.

The rattle of a wagon, and loud sounds of horses' hooves, told the ladies that someone had pulled up outside the house.

"That will be Jacob come home for the midday meal."

"Is that the time already? I must be on my way."

"Stay! Ettie, you'll stay won't you?"

The back door swung open and Ettie leaned forward to see Jacob taking off his boots. He looked across into the kitchen. "Ettie."

"Hello, Jacob."

When he took his hat off and ran his large hand through his thick black hair, Ettie couldn't help comparing him to Nehemiah; the two were so similar in appearance.

"You're staying to have a meal with us, Ettie?" Jacob asked when he stepped into the kitchen.

Ettie looked back at Mildred who nodded, urging her to stay. "*Jah, denke*. I'll stay."

"After we eat, Jacob can run you home instead of you taking a taxi," Mildred said.

"I'm happy to do that, Ettie. I've got my wagon and horses just outside and you don't live that far away, do you?"

"Not far at all." Ettie smiled and thanked Jacob, but wasn't too happy that her visit to Ronald Bradshaw would have to be delayed until the next day. She could hardly ask Jacob to take her to the neighbor's farm and wait there while she talked to him. Besides, she couldn't let Mildred and Jacob know she intended to talk to their unfriendly neighbor.

While Ettie enjoyed Mildred's cooking, she felt a little bad for leaving Elsa-May on her own with her bad leg. She should've been there to help her get something to eat at least. Elsa-May would be able to make it to the kitchen, but it would be difficult.

CHAPTER 3

While Jacob drove her home in his wagon, Ettie knew she'd have to ask him some difficult questions if she was going to be any help to him. She bit the inside of her lip and tried to muster up some courage. "You know, Jacob, it doesn't look good for you that your *schweschder's* been murdered and the pair of you were known to fight all the time."

Jacob frowned at Ettie. "Arguing is one thing, Ettie, and murder is another. I couldn't kill anyone. I wouldn't have returned to the community if I didn't want to follow *Gott's* ways. I held no bad feelings against my *schweschder;* it was she who had bad feelings toward me. I let her know I didn't like the way she spoke to our *mudder.*"

Jacob always referred to his stepmother as his mother, never making the distinction that she wasn't his birth mother.

"*Jah,* I know that. I'm just saying how it looks for you. Sometimes when the police have no suspects their attention turns to the most likely person. Then, rather than innocent until proven guilty, it becomes a matter of having to prove that you are innocent."

Jacob looked over at Ettie and smiled. "Ettie, you're worrying too much about things. *Denke* for your concern; it's nice to know you care so much."

"I think you should be concerned."

"Why? The police questioned me and I told them everything I know. They seemed to be satisfied and I haven't done anything wrong."

Ettie sucked her lips in.

Jacob glanced at Ettie's concerned face, and then tipped his straw hat slightly back on his head. "You must tell me if you know something I don't. I know you've got contacts with the police since you've been involved with things like this before. I heard what happened to Horace, and *mamm's* told me about a few other things you've been involved in as well."

"I can tell you this: no matter what they've said to you, or wanted you to believe, it's clear that you're one of their suspects. I know that much. Well, most likely their only one so far, and that's why the detective has been out here trying to question people. No one will talk to him, apart from you it seems, and that's why he, the detective, asked me to help. Detective Kelly doesn't believe you did it, but I don't think he knows enough about Camille's life to know who could have done it or where to look for the person who killed her."

"The person who took her life might not have known her. It could've been a stranger, someone passing through."

"Possibly, but I believe she was the type of person to clash with people."

"Probably, because she was never happy at home. She never called Mildred *'mamm' or 'mudder;'* she always called her 'Mrs. Esh', if she had to call her something at all. Behind her back she would call her 'it' or 'the thing', but never if Mildred or *Dat* could hear her."

"I didn't realize things were that bad."

"They were. When *Mamm,* our real *mamm,* got sick, she beat Camille a couple of times. That's when *Dat* took our *mudder* to the doctor and found out about her mental illness."

Ettie gasped. "She was beaten? The poor little mite."

Jacob nodded. "Beaten and treated badly. I was older and out of the *haus* a lot with *Dat,* so that's why I escaped a lot of *Mamm's* nastiness."

"I had no idea things were like that."

"*Mamm* couldn't help it. It was the illness that made her act like that."

"All the same, it's awful for Camille to have gone through something like that."

"I think that's why she never took to Mildred. I don't think she could ever trust anyone."

"It's dreadful to think that one of the people who were supposed to love and protect her would do something like that."

"My *mudder* couldn't help it, Ettie. She was sick in the head," Jacob repeated. "I feel guilty that I didn't protect Camille."

"You shouldn't feel guilty. You were still so young yourself."

"Maybe that's why she hated me, because I wasn't there to look after her like a big *bruder* should've. Camille only got along with *Dat.*"

"That's dreadful."

Jacob nodded. "Anyway, I try not to think about the past. I try and remember my *mudder* how she used to be before she got sick."

Ettie nodded. "That's best."

"Now, no need to worry yourself about me, Ettie. Seems like I'm in the clear if the detective knows I didn't do it."

"He needs to investigate the thing properly. Do you know anyone who had the slightest possible reason to kill her? Did she have any arguments or disagreements with anyone that you know about?"

Jacob laughed. "She argued with *Mamm* every day of her life."

"I know they never got along."

"It was never *Mamm's* fault. She's always done everything she could to be a proper *mudder* to us."

"Did she have any disagreements with anyone apart from Mildred?"

"My *schweschder* and I were never close, as you know. I didn't know her well enough to know the enemies she made. I'm guessing there were a few."

"Do you know that for certain?"

"*Nee,* I'm just guessing, going by what type of person she was." Jacob glanced over at Ettie. "She wasn't a happy person, and the only time I saw her smile was whenever she was making someone miserable. The last days before she left the community, she had my *mudder* in tears every single day."

"That was after your *vadder* died?"

Jacob nodded. "*Jah,* she was much worse when she found out that the farm was left entirely to me."

"Mildred tells me you offered Camille half the farm?"

"She told you?"

Ettie nodded.

"*Jah,* I offered her half. It wasn't as though I talked *Dat* into leaving it all to me, but that's the idea Camille had gotten into her head. I didn't know who he was leaving it to; he never even talked of having a will. *Dat* left me a letter with his will telling me he was leaving it to me because he didn't want Camille interfering with the running of it, and he wanted Mildred to be able to stay on. I didn't exactly offer Camille half; I offered her forty nine percent so I could keep a controlling interest, and also that way *Mamm* wouldn't be turned out of the *haus.*"

"I heard your *vadder* had money put away for Camille?"

Jacob glanced over at Ettie. "How did you know? *Ach,* I suppose *Mamm* told you that too. *Dat* had over two hundred and twenty-five thousand dollars for her."

Ettie gasped in shock and her hand flew to her mouth. "I never dreamed it would be so much."

"Dat's life savings. *Mamm* only wanted to live in the *haus;* she wasn't interested in money. She knew I'd take care of her."

"Who does the money go to now that...?"

"Camille left everything to me. I was a little pleased that she must've liked me deep down."

Ettie frowned. "That is a surprise, but I suppose her *vadder* dying gave her cause to think of writing her own will. She must have had a change of heart, then, where you were concerned. Perhaps it was your generous offer regarding the farm?"

"Nee." Jacob laughed and then moved the wagon over closer to the side of the road so a car could pass. When the car had zoomed past, Jacob said, "She didn't see my offer as generous at all. She wanted the whole lot and thought I was the one who was being unreasonable."

"Did she know why your *vadder* left the farm to you?"

"She never saw the letter *Dat* wrote to me if that's what you're asking. Camille knew *Dat* wasn't happy with the job she'd done of running the farm when she was in control of it."

"Surely she should've been happy with the money?"

Jacob shook his head. *"Nee,* she wasn't happy with anything, but that's the type of person she was."

"I suppose it does make sense that Camille left everything to you, after all, you were her only relative. And according to you and Mildred, she didn't make friends easily."

Jacob shrugged. "I guess she must've cared about me after all, in some way at least."

They were getting closer to Ettie's house and she had only a small amount of time left to talk to him. She needed to get as much information as she could. "So, can you think of anyone at all who might have wanted her gone?" She'd asked the question before but in a slightly different way. Ettie wasn't expecting a different answer to the one he'd already given her, but she was hoping.

He shook his head. "I've no idea."

Ettie pointed up the road. "It's the one up there on the left with the white fence."

When Jacob stopped his wagon right in front of Ettie's house, he jumped down to help her out.

"Denke. That's quite a distance for an old lady."

Jacob chuckled.

"Will you come in?" Ettie asked.

"Nee, I must get back home. I've got some men working for me today. I've got to get back to tell them what to do next. Say hello to Elsa-May for me."

"I will." Ettie stood at the gate and watched Jacob lead his two horses to turn the wagon around and head back down the road.

CHAPTER 4

Ettie started out bright and early the next morning to get to Ronald Bradshaw's house. She had the taxi drop her up the road so she would avoid being seen by Mildred and Jacob Esh.

When Ettie knocked on the door of the Bradshaw house, she waited and there was no answer. She knocked and waited again, but when there was still no answer she walked around to the back of the house.

"What are you doing?" a man's loud voice boomed, causing Ettie to jump.

Ettie's heart pounded, and she turned around to see the man she'd seen the day before when he was staring at Mildred's house. "Oh, forgive me. I was looking for a man named Bradshaw."

The man had a smudge of dirt across the left side of his face.

Ettie tried not to look at the odd combination of frayed cut-off shorts and huge work boots he was wearing.

He took a couple of steps toward her. "That's me – Ron Bradshaw."

"Nice to meet you; I'm Ettie Smith. I've come to talk to you about Camille from next door."

"She died, didn't she?"

"I'm afraid so. I hope you don't mind if I ask you a few questions?"

The man frowned at her. "Depends what kinda questions you might be askin'."

"Did you ask Camille if she'd sell you the farm?"

"Ask?" he shook his head. "She came to me and said she'd sell it and asked me how much I'd pay. I've had my eye on that piece of land for years."

"Did Camille know that?"

"I wouldn't know, but I asked her father a couple times if he'd sell. He might have told her I wanted it, for all I know."

"I see. That's interesting."

"That woman and I agreed on a price and once the old man got sicker, she wanted more money."

"Really? But it wasn't hers to sell."

"She said the old man was dying and she'd get it when he kicked the bucket."

Ettie nodded and wondered whether Camille had used those exact words.

"Yeah. She was a nasty piece of work, that old woman." The man looked Ettie up and down. "You a friend of the family or somethin'?"

"I am." Ettie licked her lips. "Did you mean you were talking to Camille or her mother? Camille wasn't that old."

The man scratched his balding head. "Dunno. The one I was talking to was around forty or fifty. She said she was the daughter." He shook his head. "I'm no good with women's ages. Why do ya want to know?"

"Surely you know who's who if you've lived here for a long time. Camille grew up next door."

The man shook his head. "They keep to themselves. I've only noticed one woman there lately."

"Did you only talk to one woman from next door?"

The man nodded. "Are they thinking of sellin' now?"

"I don't think they are. They seem happy to keep it; it's been in the family for generations. The son inherited it from the father." Ettie breathed out heavily. She had to find out which woman he'd been talking with. Surely he wouldn't call Camille 'old'. What if he'd been speaking to Mildred thinking she was

Camille? "Camille would have been around forty and her stepmother, Mrs. Esh, is in her late fifties."

"Can't help you." The man scratched his cheek. "I hear they think the woman – Camille – was murdered?"

Ettie nodded. "That's right."

He scratched his head. "That explains why she didn't get back to me." He stared at Ettie with his blue eyes piercing through her. "How did they do it?"

"Poison, I believe."

"Can't say I blame who did it. Shame she didn't sell me the farm first." He rubbed his gray stubbly chin.

"You didn't, or rather, you don't know the people next door very well at all, by the sounds."

His mouth turned down and he shook his head. "I talked to the old man maybe twice, I've spoken to the son about the same, and that woman a few times when she was offering to sell me the farm. That's it."

"You don't know Camille other than her talking to you about selling the farm? You've had no other dealings with her?"

"No, why should I?"

"Well, you lived in this house, on this farm, when Camille and her brother were growing up. You've been here for a long time, haven't you?"

"I've been here all me life. The missus and me raised the kids here. You should know that you folk keep to yourselves. I knew there were a couple of kids living there some years ago. When the woman came knocking on the door, I didn't even know who she was until she told me. After that, I saw her in town having an argument with some woman, and that was the only times I seen 'er."

"So only when she was talking about selling the farm to you, and the one time you saw her in town?"

"Yeah! That's right."

"She was arguing with someone, you say?"

"Yeah, a woman."

"Can you remember what the woman looked like?"

He shrugged his shoulders. "Never took much notice." He stared at Ettie and she noticed his eyes opened wider. "Do you think that woman might have been the one who done away with 'er?"

Ettie shrugged. "Do you remember how long ago it was?"

"Not long ago, not long ago at all. Couldn't say exactly when. I go into town on a Tuesday mostly, so yeah, it must've been a Tuesday."

"Thank you. You've been helpful."

"Why are ya askin'?" He repeated his earlier question: "Do ya think the one she was arguing with did away with her?"

"I couldn't say." Ettie swallowed hard. The man had been polite enough, but Ettie had a feeling the man might have another side to him. He scared her a little. "I'm just a friend of the family, and I was a friend of Camille."

"Humph. I didn't think the woman would've had any friends. She was a liar and a cheat."

"Because she didn't get the farm in the will? I'm sure she would've kept her word to you if she had."

The old man chuckled. Was he happy that Camille didn't inherit the farm even though it meant he missed out on buying it?

"Is there anythin' else I can do ya for?" he asked, narrowing his eyes at Ettie.

"No. Thank you," Ettie said as she walked a few steps away, and then said, "Do you mind if I borrow your phone to call a taxi?"

"I'll call one for you," he said.

"Thank you. I'll wait down by the road."

The man nodded and Ettie headed to the road. Her first stop would be Detective Kelly to tell him what she'd learned so far.

CHAPTER 5

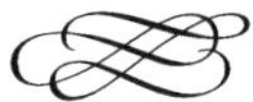

When the taxi pulled up at the police station, Ettie hoped the detective would be about. She climbed up the steps and walked inside. Before she could ask the officer behind the front desk if Detective Kelly was in, he walked up behind her.

"Mrs. Smith."

Ettie turned around to see Kelly with a takeout coffee in one hand and a white paper bag in the other.

"Detective, I've come to see you."

"Good. Come through to my office."

Ettie knew the way. His office used to be Detective Crowley's office before he had retired. When she sat in the chair opposite Kelly, she said, "I hope I'm not interrupting your lunch."

"Not at all. Not if you don't mind if I eat." He glanced at his watch. "I've got appointments the rest of the afternoon."

"Please, eat away. Don't mind me."

Detective Kelly smiled as he ripped open the white paper bag to reveal two donuts. One had pink icing with sprinkles and the other was covered with a thick layer of chocolate.

"Detective, I hope this isn't your lunch?"

Kelly frowned and looked a little guilty as he stared at the donuts. "I have few pleasures in life, Mrs. Smith. Don't make me feel bad about one of the few things that makes me happy."

"I'm not saying don't eat things like that, but for lunch? That's not going to sustain a busy man like you with all the stress you must have."

Kelly pressed his lips together and flipped off the lid of his coffee. "And I suppose coffee's bad too?"

Ettie pulled a face. "Depends how many cups you have a day."

"Why have you come, Mrs. Smith? Have you found something out for me already?" he asked before he broke off a portion of his pink donut.

"I didn't pick you to be a cake-eater. When I asked you if you wanted tea or cake yesterday at my home, you turned it down." Crowley had never once turned down her or Elsa-May's cakes. "That's why I'm so surprised to see you eating something like this instead of a proper lunch."

Kelly finished his mouthful and said, "I don't know – I could've just eaten before I arrived, I can't recall. Does that bother you, that I didn't eat your cake?"

Ettie gave a little laugh at how ridiculous that sounded. "It's just that I formed an opinion of you and now I realize I was wrong."

The detective nodded. "I've learned never to form an opinion of anyone too early. Also, even if you know someone well, they can always do something that surprises even themselves."

"I suppose that's a good lesson to learn."

Kelly's glance at his watch prompted Ettie to get to the point of why she was there. "I went out to visit Camille's mother yesterday, and then today I talked to the neighbor, Ronald Bradshaw. It seems that the neighbor wanted the land. Camille had agreed to sell it to him when she thought she'd be getting the land when her father died."

"How did the old man die?"

Ettie frowned. "He's not dead. I just talked to him this morning."

"No, not that one – Nehemiah Esh."

"Oh." Ettie's gaze flickered to the ceiling. "Old age, I'd say. Wait a minute, he might have had a problem with his heart or something along those lines."

"Hmm." Kelly popped the last of the pink donut in his mouth. Ettie couldn't help frowning at him in disgust. "Was there an autopsy?" he asked.

"No, nothing like that. I don't think so. Come to think of it, I don't know the answer to that. Why? Do you think he might have been killed as well?"

"No." The detective shook his head then looked across at Ettie. "Why? Do you?"

"I've never given any thought to it."

"It's interesting when you talk about the will, and people waiting to pounce on the farm right after the old man dies."

Ettie said, "I don't think it was like that. There was no one waiting to pounce. According to the neighbor he'd asked them before if they wanted to sell. I don't think anyone was waiting for Nehemiah to die. The neighbor said he talked to Camille, Nehemiah, and Jacob separately about wanting to buy the farm."

"Was it a sudden death?" Kelly picked up the chocolate donut and took a huge bite.

"Nehemiah's?"

The detective nodded and Ettie pretended not to look at the chocolate sprinkles that clung to the sides of the detective's mouth. "I believe he was sick for quite some time. He went downhill rapidly and was in quite a bit of pain. Come to think of it, I think Mildred mentioned it was his heart."

After Kelly swallowed, he said, "I didn't think that was painful."

Ettie shrugged. "I'm certain it is."

Kelly licked his lips, and then wiped his mouth with a paper napkin. “What else did you find out?”

“I talked to Jacob and found out that after Camille discovered he’d been left the farm, she was terribly upset. Jacob even ended up offering her forty nine percent of the farm.”

The detective nodded before he took a mouthful of coffee. “Yes, that’s what he tried to tell us.”

Ettie raised her eyebrows. “Tried to tell you? You mean you don’t believe him?”

“There’s no proof, is there? It seems a generous offer for someone to make.”

“Anyway, she turned it down,” Ettie said. “She wanted the entire farm – one hundred percent.”

“We’ve only his word on that,” Detective Kelly said. “Do you know about the money she inherited?”

Ettie said, “To be accurate, I don’t think that she inherited it. It was banked for her well before Nehemiah died.”

“Are you talking about the trust fund?”

“Yes,” Ettie said.

“Jacob told us about the trust fund and you’re right, it wasn’t an inheritance. It was a trust fund that her father set up for her. The thing was that Jacob had control of it. Nehemiah Esh wasn’t a smart man.”

“Detective!”

Kelly took a mouthful of coffee and then brought the cup down to the desk. "You've got two siblings that don't get along; you don't put one in charge of the other's money. Not a smart move."

"He most likely had his reasons."

"Only if he wanted them to hate each other more."

Ettie wasn't pleased that the detective knew that Jacob and Camille didn't get along. That wouldn't be good for Jacob.

"I'll make a note to look into that fund and see how much of it's left." The detective had another mouthful of coffee. "I'm sorry, do you want tea or coffee? I'll have someone make you one if you do. It mightn't be very good – that's why I get mine from the coffee shop down the road."

"No. I'm fine, thank you." Did Kelly think Jacob might have spent some of Camille's money?

The detective rubbed his hands together, picked up a pen and wrote something down on his notepad. When he finished, he looked up. "Did you find anything else out?"

"Yes, it seems that Camille had quite a few people she didn't get along with. She was seen in town arguing with a woman, and Mildred heard her speaking on a cell phone arguing with a woman as well."

The detective screwed up the white paper takeout bag and tossed it in the trash basket. Once he had his pen in hand again, he asked, "Do you have any names?"

"No, I don't, but that's good, isn't it? She had other people she didn't get along with."

"Good for Jacob?"

"Yes."

The detective stared at Ettie before he took another mouthful of coffee. "We'll see." He rose to his feet with his coffee in hand. "Thank you, Mrs. Smith. You've been a great help. I'd still like you to keep your eyes and ears open. I might still need your help depending on how things go."

"I'd be glad to help anytime." Ettie stood up, said goodbye, and walked out the door. She suddenly turned and walked back into Kelly's office.

Kelly was now sitting down at his desk. He looked up at her. "Yes, Mrs. Smith?"

She studied his face. Could he be keeping something from her? "Nothing, Detective." Ettie walked away feeling she was getting far too suspicious of people.

CHAPTER 6

Ettie was pleased to get home and she told Elsa-May every detail of the conversations she'd had and all she'd found out that day. "Well, what do you make of it all?"

Elsa-May was knitting as usual and had her sore leg elevated on a chair. "The man next door doesn't seem sure who he was speaking with. Was he speaking with Camille or was he speaking to Mildred?"

"That's what I wondered at first, but Mildred said she had no interest in the farm and only wanted to stay on there. She didn't feel the need to own the farm or have any part of the ownership. I don't think she'd be running over to the man next door to do a deal behind everyone's backs. She didn't want to be left anything. She didn't even want any money. *Nee!* The neighbor must have been speaking to Camille because she had expected that she'd inherit the farm."

"Strange."

"Do you think that's strange?"

Elsa-May nodded. "A little strange that she didn't want to own the house or anything when she's got a stepdaughter like Camille who'd be pleased to see her off the property. She was taking a risk relying solely on Jacob."

"I disagree. Jacob will always look after his *mudder.* Jacob and Mildred are like real *mudder* and son."

"Even so, she seems a little naive."

"How so?"

Elsa-May rubbed her leg. "From what you told me, the detective might think that someone killed Nehemiah since he was questioning you about his death."

Ettie regretted telling Elsa-May so many details. "*Jah,* I think he might."

"And it sounds like Camille had many enemies."

"I'm hoping that Jacob's in the clear. Kelly said he believes he's innocent."

Elsa-May added, "I hope that's right."

"Well, I'd better go and fix the dinner. Speaking about food, you should have seen what Kelly ate for lunch. I was so surprised and you would've had something to say about it if you'd been there too." Ettie told Elsa-May about the detective's eating habits and Elsa-May had a good chuckle. "It's dreadful, Elsa-May. It's not a laughing matter. He can't go on eating like that every day."

"Hmm. Why don't you cook up some extra dinner tonight, and then take him some food tomorrow? I'm sure he'd appreciate a decent meal rather than having sweets."

"That's a good idea. I'll do that."

THE NEXT DAY, Ettie had fixed some sausage and egg casserole to take to detective Kelly, and since he had a sweet tooth, she'd gone to the trouble of making him some blueberry muffins. She placed the bowls in a cloth bag and walked down the road to call for a taxi. As soon as the taxi stopped, a small man in long cream-colored pants and a matching short-sleeved shirt sprang out and opened the front passenger-side door for her.

"Such service! Thank you."

"No problem at all, lady."

He seemed such a happy man that Ettie was certain she was in for a pleasant drive, but as soon as she sat in the seat, heavy cigarette smoke invaded her nostrils. She wound down the window and inhaled some fresh air before the driver got in the car. Normally Ettie didn't mind a little smoke, but the odor in the taxi was overpowering. She glanced down at an overflowing ashtray between the two seats and crinkled her nose. She was glad the muffins in her lap were covered in heavy cloths and the casserole was in a tightly-lidded glass bowl so they wouldn't pick up the smoky smell.

"Where to?" the driver asked while he fastened his seat belt.

Ettie was tempted to make a comment about him fastening his seat belt but not being concerned how many cigarettes he was smoking. She held her tongue.

"Where to?" he asked again glancing over at her.

"The police station."

He flicked the meter on while he pulled away from the shoulder. When he turned onto the main road, he lit up a cigarette. He drew in a long breath, and then blew it out the partially opened window. Ettie glanced in his direction to see smoke wafting out of his nose in waves. Then she looked directly ahead hoping the fabric in her clothes and her prayer *kapp* wouldn't pick up the smell.

Suddenly the taxi driver asked, "Are you a relative of the Amish man who was arrested last night?"

"What man?"

"I heard it on the radio. Some Amish man was just arrested for murdering his sister."

Ettie's mouth fell open. It could only be Jacob who had been arrested. There had been no other murder in the Amish community. "Put your foot on it, driver!" Ettie yelled.

The man did as instructed.

"I'm not a relative. I'm a good friend and I believe I've been double-crossed."

The taxi driver gave her a sideways look and remained silent the rest of the trip. When the taxi pulled up, Ettie threw down some money hoping it was enough to cover the fare. The driver got out of the car to help Ettie out, but by the time he reached the passenger side of the car she was halfway up the steps of the station.

Once she was through the door, she hurried to the man sitting behind the front desk. "Where's Detective Kelly?"

The man looked up at her with a bored face, and drawled, "He's busy at the moment, ma'am."

"I need to see him immediately. Let him know Ettie Smith is here, would you? Now?"

"What's it regarding?"

"He'll know."

"Take a seat and I'll call him." The officer picked up his phone and talked to Kelly, and when he placed the receiver down, he called out to Ettie, "He'll be out as soon as he can."

"How long will that be?"

He shook his head. "I'm not sure."

Ettie stood up with the bundle of food still in her arms, and walked over to the officer. "Then I'd like to speak to Jacob Esh."

"Who?"

"I believe you have him here somewhere. He's just been arrested."

"No, you can't talk to anyone in custody. Please take a seat and Detective Kelly will be out to see you as soon as he can."

Ettie narrowed her eyes at the officer, and then turned and took a seat. It was an hour later when Detective Kelly finally came out to see her.

"Come through," he said, motioning to her with his hand.

Ettie followed him through to his office with the bag of food clutched in her hands. Once he was seated, she placed the food on his desk without any explanation of what it was, sat down, and then asked, "What's going on, Detective? You've arrested Jacob?"

He interlocked his fingers, placing them under his chin. "We have him in for questioning. He's not under arrest, not at all."

"The taxi driver said he heard on the radio that an Amish man was under arrest for killing his sister."

"I said he's not under arrest. I'd hardly think a taxi driver is a reliable source of information." The detective sniffed the air. "Do you smoke?"

"No, I do not." Just as she'd feared, her clothes had picked up the odor in the taxi.

"I can smell cigarette smoke. I'm sensitive to the smell. I've given them up."

"Congratulations," Ettie said sarcastically before she regretted her tone. She licked her lips, about to make an apology and explain about the smoke-filled taxi she'd ridden in to get there, when the detective spoke.

"I'm afraid there was more to things than I let on to you."

Ettie tipped her head to one side. "What haven't you told me?"

"The kind of things that made it look like Jacob Esh murdered his sister."

Ettie pulled her mouth to one side. "I didn't know there were things that made him look guilty. You said…"

"There are."

"Can you be more specific?"

The detective leaned back in his chair and scratched his forehead. "We had dealings with Camille before she died. She'd had shots fired into her apartment. Someone drove past and shot into her home three times. More accurately, it was a drive-by shooting and three shots were fired."

Ettie gasped.

The detective nodded. "Someone tried to kill her."

"You think it was Jacob?"

"Evidence strongly points to him. He'd hardly be sticking to your Amish rules if he was about to kill someone. He could've paid someone to shoot her, or he could've borrowed a car and done the job himself. I know you were just about to point out to me that he doesn't own a car."

"Were the gunshots to scare her or kill her?"

"I don't know what you're getting at, Mrs. Smith, but when someone has a gun fired into their home, we take it that the person or persons involved who were doing the shooting were aiming to kill."

"Was it while she was living in her apartment? Because Mildred never mentioned anything about a gun being fired into her home."

"It was after she left the house and started living in the apartment."

"So after her father's death, then? Because that's when she left the house, when she found out she hadn't been left the farm."

"Yes, that's right."

"There's no motive for him to kill her. He already had the farm."

"There's the money. People have killed for a lot less."

"So, you've got Jacob here still?"

"He's still being questioned. I've already grilled him but he's sticking to the same story so I'm letting someone else have a crack at him."

"Have you considered that he might be telling the truth?"

"Someone's dead, Mrs. Smith. If the brother didn't do it, then who did?"

"In just one day I found out that Camille had enemies; two people told me that. Why don't you look into those people?"

Kelly sighed. "I thank you for your help, but I think you've done all you can do. I hoped you'd uncover something we didn't know, but it seems there is nothing we didn't already know."

"You think he's guilty, and you thought he was guilty all along, which means you tricked me into believing you were trying to help him."

"I had to make you think I was on his side. I knew you wouldn't help if you thought otherwise."

Ettie rose to her feet. She bit her tongue while thinking of all the things she wanted to say to the despicable person before her. "I can't speak the words on my mind right now." She pushed the food she'd brought toward him. "Elsa-May thought you should have some proper food at lunchtime." Ettie turned and walked out the door without saying goodbye.

She heard him call after her: "Wait, Mrs. Smith."

Ettie turned around.

"I couldn't tell you. It would have influenced your thinking when you were finding things out for me."

Ettie folded her arms firmly in front of her chest. "That's something Crowley never would've done. He was always honest with us and we respected him for it."

"Mrs. Smith, I do appreciate your help, but I'll handle things from here."

"You told me you thought he was innocent. That's the only reason I helped you."

"Like I said, I had to tell you something to get you on my side."

Ettie opened her mouth in shock. "That's unethical and downright disgusting."

Kelly smirked. "I didn't want to deceive you; it's just part of the job sometimes. Often it's the only way we can get things done."

"So you do think Jacob's guilty for certain?"

"Have you come up with any other suspects?"

"I told you; there's the neighbor, and the woman Camille was seen arguing with in town. Maybe there were two people she was arguing with, because Mildred heard her arguing with someone on her phone and the neighbor saw her arguing with a woman in town."

"Hearsay and conjecture. It's too fuzzy a lead to follow up. I need something concrete."

"Everything is fuzzy until you follow the leads and see where they take you."

"Are you telling me how to do my job?"

"Yes, I suppose I am. Because if you think that Jacob is guilty, you're not doing a good job right now."

"You think he's innocent because he's a part of your community?"

Ettie shook her head. "It's not that."

"I think we're through speaking for today."

"What? Until the next time you need my help?"

The detective frowned and threw his hands in the air. "It doesn't please me that I had to lie to you, but that's just what had to happen."

Ettie pressed her lips together. "You don't mind if I follow some leads that you're ignoring, do you?"

"As long as you don't get in my way you are at liberty to do as you wish."

The detective reached out and grabbed a piece of paper from his desk. He motioned for her to come forward and she did so. "I'll tell you what. Since you're so upset with me, I'll give you a peace offering." He tossed the sheet of paper to Ettie. "This is a list of names and addresses of the people Camille talked to most often from her cell phone."

Ettie took hold of the paper and stared at it. There weren't many names on it. She looked up at the detective. "Isn't this against some kind of law, letting me have this list?"

The detective smiled. He swiveled in his chair and turned his head away. "I can't help it if the list disappeared from my office. If I need the list, I'll just print out another one. Maybe I never printed one out at all."

Ettie looked down at the paper, holding it tightly, and then disappeared out of his office without saying goodbye. He didn't deserve a goodbye. Ettie was mad with herself for not figuring out what Kelly had been up to from the start. She wasn't normally fooled so easily, and now she was so upset she was nauseous.

CHAPTER 7

After Ettie left the station, she hailed a taxi, knowing she had to go and see her dear friend, Mildred.

When the taxi pulled up at Mildred's house, she could see the bishop's buggy leaving. Well, at least she had someone to speak with this morning. When Ettie's taxi drove off, a teary-eyed Mildred met her at the front door. "I'm so glad you've come. You've heard what's happened?"

"I have." Ettie put her arm around Mildred as she broke down and sobbed. "Come on, let's sit inside."

Once they were sitting down in the living room, Mildred sniffed back her tears. "They came here with so many police cars; lights were whirling and flashing, and then they stormed in here and said they had a search warrant. Then they went right through the house, and the barn, and took things away with them."

"What kind of things?" Ettie was amazed that Kelly had never mentioned the search warrant or the fact that the police had taken things.

"I didn't see exactly what they took from the barn, but they took all Jacob's hunting guns that he had kept in the house for safety. They think that Jacob killed Camille, but she wasn't shot. Why would they take the guns?"

"She had gunshots fired into her apartment. She didn't tell you?"

Mildred opened her mouth wide. When Ettie saw the hurt in Mildred's eyes she regretted asking the question. Ettie knew how painful it was for Mildred that Camille resented her. Of course Camille wouldn't have told her about the attempt on her life.

"I don't know how to help him, Ettie. I found a card from a lawyer amongst Nehemiah's things." Mildred stood up and walked over to a small bureau, found a business card, and brought it back to Ettie.

Ettie took the card and read the name. "Claymore Cartwright." Ettie looked at the back of the well-worn card and read the address. "He's just in town, if he's still in business. I'll go with you if you want to see him."

"Would you, Ettie?"

"*Jah.* Do you want me to call now and make an appointment?"

Mildred nodded.

Ettie rose to her feet with the card in hand. "I'll do it right away. You stay here and take some deep breaths. Do you want a cup of tea?"

"*Nee,* I had tea just now with the bishop."

"*Jah,* I just passed him when I came through your gate."

Ettie made her way to the barn. She pushed the door open and saw things scattered everywhere. The police must've done this. No one would keep their barn in a state like this. She stepped over things and made her way to the telephone on the other side of the barn. She picked up the receiver and dialed the number on the card. Ettie was pleased when she heard it ring – that meant the man was still in business.

After a couple of weird dial-tone and clicking sounds on the other end of the phone, a male voice answered. It was the lawyer himself. Once Ettie explained the situation to the lawyer, he had them come in immediately. Ettie called for a taxi, placed the receiver back on the hook, and hurried to tell Mildred.

ETTIE CONVINCED Mildred to take the taxi in to visit with the lawyer rather than taking the buggy, figuring they should get there as fast as possible.

When they arrived in town, the taxi dropped them right outside the address that was on the old business card.

They took the elevator up to the fourth floor. When the elevator doors opened, they stepped out and followed the corridor around the corner. They were looking for the office of Claymore

Cartwright, but it was nowhere to be seen. All the offices appeared to be empty. When they walked up to the end of the corridor, Ettie was pleased to see an open door. Ettie walked two more steps and when she peeped in she saw a young man behind a desk in a sparsely furnished office. The man was dressed in casual clothes and wore a bright green baseball cap.

He smiled and rose to his feet. “Mrs. Esh?”

Ettie was surprised that the man was so young. He had to be the lawyer, as he’d known Mildred’s name. Given his name and the aged business card she had expected a much older man. Ettie nodded and pulled Mildred forward. “This is Mrs. Esh. I’m her friend, the one who called you. Ettie Smith.”

“Please, come in.”

Ettie had never seen a lawyer in casual clothes. She’d only seen them wear dark suits and ties.

“I heard that your son was arrested. Are you here because you want me to represent him?”

Ettie spoke first. “He’s not been arrested, although the news stations seem to think so.”

“Yes, they do like news - bad news, anyway - about the Amish.”

“Seems so.” Ettie continued, “He was taken in for questioning, and the police had a search warrant and took a great number of things out of Mildred’s home and out of her barn.”

Ettie glanced at Mildred, hoping she didn’t mind her speaking on her behalf. Mildred wasn’t used to doing things for herself because Nehemiah, or Jacob, had always been around to do things for her. Ettie looked back at the lawyer and continued, "Mildred found your card amongst her late husband's things, and we really need some legal advice. We're not too sure how these things work."

Claymore looked at Mildred. "I set a few things up for your husband."

"The bank trust fund?" Ettie asked.

"Yes," the lawyer said with a sharp nod. "I also helped him write his will."

Mildred finally spoke. "They took Jacob in the early hours this morning and searched all through our house and also our barn. The police took things away with them."

The lawyer leaned forward in his chair. "What did they take?"

"They took so many things. They asked about firearms, so I told them where Jacob kept his hunting rifles and they took all of them. Some were his father's, and some didn't even work. They also took things from the barn; I'm not sure what."

Ettie spoke again, "Before all this happened, the detective, Keith Kelly, asked for my help because no one in our Amish community would talk to him. He told me he thought that Jacob was innocent. I was only to find out later that he thought nothing of the kind."

The lawyer looked at Mildred. "Where's your son now?"

"He's at the police station."

"He shouldn't be questioned without a lawyer. I'll go and see what I can do."

"Could you do that?" Mildred asked.

"Yes, I'll see what I can find out."

"Have you done this kind of thing before?" Mildred asked.

Ettie knew Mildred was asking because he didn't look like a lawyer and his office didn't look like any lawyer's office she'd ever been to.

Claymore smiled as though he'd often answered that question. "Yes, I have. I do a bit of everything."

While the lawyer asked Mildred some background questions, Ettie took in her surroundings. There were only two small offices and no receptionist. He appeared to work by himself. There was no one in the other office, and from what she could see when she'd walked past it, it was bare. Ettie turned her head to view the small reception area through the open door of the office. There were a few filing cabinets and some ten large white folders on a bookshelf. Nothing about the office was plush or expensive.

As the lawyer stood up, he said, "Don't you ladies worry about anything. I'll go and see him right now and I'll give you a phone call this afternoon to let you know what's happening."

"Thank you, Mr. Cartwright," Mildred said. "Oh, and there's the matter of your fee."

The young lawyer waved his hand in the air. "Let's talk about that later. Don't concern yourself with that now. I can sort something out with your son."

The lawyer smiled at them as Ettie stood up and helped Mildred to her feet. Mildred looked as though she would cry again. Ettie wanted to get out of the office so Mr. Cartwright could lock up and go to see how he could help Jacob.

All Ettie could do was take Mildred home and wait for a call from the lawyer. They'd opened the barn door so they could more easily hear the telephone while they sat in the room closest, which was the kitchen.

"*Ach,* Ettie. I've already lost Nehemiah and Camille was always lost; I can't lose Jacob as well. What if they've arrested him?"

"The detective didn't say he'd arrested him. In fact, he said he hadn't arrested him. I'm sure Jacob will be home as soon as they finish questioning him. At least he's got a lawyer with him now."

Mildred nodded. "I suppose I should've called a lawyer first thing when they took him." Tears trickled down Mildred's cheeks. "I don't know what I ever did to make Camille hate me so much."

Ettie leaned over and rubbed Mildred's arm. "I don't think she hated you. She was probably so upset over her *mudder's* death that she never got over it."

Mildred shook her head. "I don't know. She used to look at me with such hatred in her eyes." Mildred looked across at Ettie. "I've never seen anything like it. She used to scare me. I thought one time she was going to hit me."

"I didn't know things were that bad."

"I couldn't tell anyone how mean she was to me. Whenever she'd walk past me she'd push me or bump me. I didn't know whether it was my fault, if I'd done something to upset her, but Jacob was never like that toward me and I always treated him in the same way that I treated her. I gave them both the same discipline when they needed it and I tried to give them all the love that Mary would've."

The sound of a car humming up toward the house met Ettie's ears. Mildred sprang to her feet and peered out the window.

"It's him. I think it's the lawyer. I can see two people in the car."

Ettie joined her at the window, and then Mildred sprinted to the front door. Ettie managed to catch up to her as Jacob got out of the lawyer's car. He straightened himself up. He looked dreadful. His face was white and he had deep circles under his eyes.

Mildred ran to him. "Are you all right?

"I am now that I'm home."

Mildred hugged Jacob and he put his arm around her shoulder. "It's okay, *Mamm*. Everything's gonna be okay. But right now I just wanna get some sleep."

"What happened? Didn't they feed you? Oh, you were there for so long. You looked dreadful."

Jacob shook his head. "I can't talk about anything right now. I just need to sleep." He nodded hello to Ettie, and then said, "Excuse me, will you?"

"Certainly," Ettie said.

Jacob turned around and shook the lawyer's hand.

"I'll be in touch." The lawyer slapped Jacob lightly on his back before Jacob walked into the house.

"Thank you for getting him out," Mildred said to the lawyer.

"We're not out of the woods yet. They didn't have anything to hold him on, but they seem pretty confident that they're getting some evidence soon. They're running ballistics tests on the bullets they found. And they mentioned they found fingerprints in Camille's apartment that didn't belong to her. They've taken his prints."

"So they didn't arrest him?" Mildred asked.

"They questioned him, or rather, grilled him. You should've called me sooner. He could've refused to answer."

"He's got nothing to hide." Mildred started blubbering again, so Ettie did her best to comfort her.

"He's home now," Ettie said. "Safe and sound."

"I've made a time with Jacob to come here tomorrow and go

over a few things. All the guns they took from here have Jacob's prints on them."

A lawyer who makes house calls? Ettie then noticed that he was wearing different clothes than when he saw them in his office earlier that day. "You changed your clothes from this morning?"

"It was my day off. Your call was diverted to my mobile. I thought it sounded serious enough to forgo my free time."

Ettie smiled. "Thank you."

"Oh, we didn't know. That was so good of you."

He chuckled. "I changed my clothes before I went to the station. I always keep a suit in my office."

The lawyer said goodbye and the two ladies watched as his car hummed down the driveway.

"Such a nice young man, and handsome too," Ettie said.

"Jah, if only I was young again," Mildred added.

Ettie and Mildred looked at each other and giggled. "Well, at least we can find something to laugh about," Ettie said.

"You do cheer me up, Ettie. Will you stay for dinner?"

"Nee denke. Normally I would, but I'll have to get home to see Elsa-May and fix her dinner. She's got a bad leg and can't walk very well."

"What's wrong with her leg?"

"I'm not certain. It started giving her some trouble a few days ago. If she keeps it elevated she says it doesn't hurt as much."

"Has she been to the doctor about it?"

"Nee." Ettie pulled a face. "Why? Do you think she should?"

"I have heard that blood clots can give people sore legs. They can be very dangerous, and sometimes people even have to have their legs amputated."

Ettie gasped. It hadn't occurred to her that her sister could be in danger of something like that. "Well, it's too late to take her to the doctor now. I'll take her first thing in the morning."

On Ettie's way home, she stopped by Ava's place to see if her young friend could help with the list of names and addresses that Kelly had given her.

"I'M HERE to ask you to help me with something. You helped me before with Horace, so I was hoping you'd be able to help me again." Ettie filled Ava in with what she knew so far about Camille's murder and her life.

"I'll help in any way I can. What do you want me to do?"

Ettie pulled out the list of names that Kelly had allowed her to take. "I'm going to work through these one by one and see what I can find out. These are the people who Camille was speaking to from her cell phone. These are the names of the people she called, and those who called her."

"What do you want me to do? Come with you when you speak to them?"

Ettie passed the list to Ava and then said, "Firstly, I'd like you to see what you can find out about each one. I've been told she was having arguments with people, so…"

"How could I do that? You mean on the Internet?" Ava looked at the list.

"Jah, that, and have you still got that helpful friend who works at the DMV?"

Ava glanced up at Ettie. *"Jah,* I do."

"I'm hoping your friend can get us photos that match these phone numbers. And also verify that the addresses are current."

"I'll see what I can find out. I'm certain he'll help."

Ettie nodded. "Very good. Before I go home, I'll have a quick look through the *haus* to see what repairs need doing."

"Do you want me to come with you?"

"Nee, you look like you're busy cooking."

"I'll talk to my friend tonight, if I can, or first thing in the morning. I'm guessing you want the information quickly?"

Ettie smiled. "You know me well." After Ettie left Ava, she walked around to the front door of the main house. She bent down to fetch the key from under the potted fern at the front door. Once she pushed the rusty key into the lock, she turned it to the right and heard a loud click.

Ettie pushed the door open and a waft of stale, warm air swept over her. "I must air the place out," she mumbled to herself. When Ettie walked further in, she realized how much she missed her dear friend, Agatha. They used to sit for hours and talk. Ettie wiped a tear from her eye and was a little sad that she'd never be able to live in this house. Not after they found poor old Horace dead under the floor.

The rocking chair was back in the middle of the floor where Ettie had left it last time she was in the house. The chair had always been placed right over poor old Horace. "I'll see you again when *Gott* takes me home, Agatha," Ettie muttered. Ettie blinked hard and reminded herself why she was there. There was no time to reflect on sentimental nonsense, not when Elsa-May was waiting for her to cook the dinner.

Ettie walked through the house, making a mental note of all the repairs she'd have to get Jeremiah to do. There were kitchen doors coming off their hinges, the ceiling had peeling paint, and some of the windows didn't open. There was mold in one corner of the living room, and she had noticed when she'd been unlocking the door that the boards on the porch needed replacing.

Ettie sighed. "So many things to do." Thankfully Agatha had also left her money. She could use that to fix the house, and then she'd lease it to a nice Amish family.

CHAPTER 8

Over dinner with Elsa-May, Ettie brought up the subject of visiting a doctor.

"*Nee,* definitely not! I've had problems like this before and it just goes away."

"But what if it's something more serious this time?"

"Like what?" Elsa-May's eyebrows drew together.

"Mildred said it could be a blood clot."

Elsa-May's eyes opened wide. "Really? She's had experience with that kind of thing?"

"She's heard of it."

"Perhaps I should go."

"I think that's for the best. You haven't been yourself lately."

"I have been tired."

"And vague," Ettie added.

"Have I been vague?"

Ettie nodded. "And that's not like you."

"I have been concerned about Mildred being all on her own if something happens to Jacob."

"She'll be okay," Ettie said.

"She's quite frail, you know. I don't mean physically. She's relied on her husband all the time for everything, and now that he's gone I guess she's relying on Jacob. What will happen if…?"

"We can't think about that," Ettie said. "We'll have to keep our thoughts off the bad things."

"*Jah,* Ettie, you're right. And anyway, there are so many people in the community to help her and there's all the ladies in the knitting circle."

"I forgot she was in your knitting circle. And there's something else I forgot to tell you about."

"What is it, Ettie?"

"The detective gave me a list of names of the people who Camille called from her cell phone. And the people who called her."

"He just gave it to you?"

Ettie nodded. "Well, he didn't really give it to me. He told me he couldn't help the fact if someone took the list from his desk."

"Then he is on Jacob's side."

"I wouldn't say that. I was angry that he'd told me he believed Jacob and then I'd found out that he'd been stringing me along. It was more a peace-offering; *jah,* that's what he called it."

Elsa-May scratched the side of her forehead. "Don't you think that's a little dangerous if the woman was murdered? One of the people on the list could very well have killed her. Why would you put yourself in danger like that?"

Ettie shrugged. "Too late now. I was happy to stay out of the whole thing. Detective Kelly was the one who knocked on our door. Jacob and Mildred need our help. I just can't turn my back on them."

"Let's just eat our food in silence," Elsa-May said in an angry tone.

Suits me just fine, Ettie thought.

THE NEXT DAY, Elsa-May and Ettie sat in the doctor's waiting room. The receptionist had fitted them into an eleven thirty appointment slot. Ettie tried to stop thinking about Jacob, and the information Ava might be able to find out, and did her best to concentrate on her sister.

When the doctor was ready, the receptionist told Elsa-May she could go in. Ettie stood up at the same time.

Elsa-May frowned at her. "You don't need to come in with me."

"I will. I want to hear what he says."

"Please yourself, then, but I think I have to give permission for you to go in with me." Elsa-May had a word to the nurse, and then both sisters went into the examination room.

When the doctor had finished examining Elsa-May, he gave them his conclusions. "You were right to come in. It could very well be a blood clot. I'll book you straight into the hospital for tests. You'll need to have a scan and the sooner the better."

Ettie was grateful for Mildred warning her of such a thing.

"I thought people only got clots if they were still for long stretches."

Ettie kept quiet, stopping herself from pointing out to Elsa-May that she sat down without moving for hours almost every day while she knitted.

"As people get older, they're more at risk, and with your weight problem it puts you in a high-risk category."

"I don't have a weight problem. I've always been on the bigger side."

The doctor stared at her and blinked a couple times. "You could do with losing some weight. Try taking a walk every morning and cut down on your food." The doctor looked across at his computer, and then said, "I'll call an ambulance to take you in."

"That's not necessary, surely!" Elsa-May barked.

"I'd prefer that we take precautions."

Ettie leaned over close to her, and said, "Do as he says, Elsa-May."

Elsa-May looked at the doctor. "Okay, have it your way."

The doctor smiled, and then turned back to his computer and tapped on a few keys. "I'm letting the hospital know you're coming, and arranging for an ambulance."

Once they were back in the waiting room of the clinic, Elsa-May turned to Ettie who was sitting next to her. "There's no point in you coming with me. Why don't you go and see what Ava has found out?"

"*Nee,* I'll wait with you."

"Just go, Ettie. Stop being so *schtarrkeppich.*"

Elsa-May's comment made Ettie smile. It was she who was the stubborn one. "All right, then. I'll come and check on you at the hospital after I've seen Ava."

"I'll get a taxi home when they've done the test."

"I should be at the hospital before you go. You might have a long wait before they can run the test. They've probably got a long line of people in front of you."

"Just go, Ettie, and stop being a mother hen. Jacob needs your help. I'm big enough to look after myself – too big, the doctor tells me." Elsa-May chuckled. "The doctor just doesn't realize

I've got large bones."

"Okay, as long as you don't mind me going."

"Go!"

CHAPTER 9

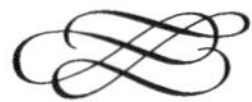

Ettie went straight to Ava's place after she left Elsa-May to wait for the ambulance.

Ava had seen her arrive and she waited at the door of her *gross-daddi haus*. "I'm glad you've come when you did. I was just about to get ready, then I was going to drive over to your *haus* to see you."

"I wouldn't have been there. I've just taken Elsa-May to the doctor, and now she's waiting to be taken to the hospital for tests."

"Nothing serious, I hope."

"The doctor thinks she might have a blood clot so she needs to have a scan."

"I hope she'll be all right."

Ettie nodded. "She's in good hands."

"Come in, and I'll tell you what I've found out."

Once they were sitting at the small kitchen table, Ava said, "I noticed something on the list you gave me; the number of conversations the people had with Camille were written on the side." Ava picked up the list and pointed out the numbers to Ettie. "Now, you can see that most of the conversations on her cell were with a woman called Judith Mackelvanner."

"Did you find out about this woman?"

Ava passed over all the printouts from her friend at the DMV, including photos of all the people on Camille's phone list.

Ava pulled out the photo of the woman and tapped on it. "That's her there; she's a doctor. I 'Googled' her and found out that she works at the hospital, and she studies neurology. I know that because she's been looking for volunteers on some trials she's running for a paper she's writing."

"Was Camille one of her volunteers?"

Ava shrugged her shoulders. "I don't know."

"Who else is on the list?"

"There was a call to a woman. Now this is interesting – her mobile phone records are in the name of Lacey Miller, but the DMV has that number down as belonging to a Leah Miller."

"Your friend traced the mobile numbers?"

"*Jah.* Now look at this photo of Leah Miller."

"That's Leah Miller who used to be in our community! She'd

have to be right around the same age as Camille. That would be one of the *Englisch* friends she had that Mildred was speaking about."

"Yep. I remember her, and she certainly looks like the Leah we know."

"Camille had also called some businesses, and a few car places. It looks as though she might have been about to buy a car. There was also a call to someone called Nick Heaton."

"Who's he?"

"I looked him up on the computer and found various articles in the paper about a Nick Heaton being arrested a couple of times, but it might not be the same man; I couldn't find photos of him to match with his driver's license photo. I also found out that there is a Nick Heaton who sells used cars. Ava continued, "But definitely most of Camille's incoming calls were from the woman doctor. There were also calls listed from the hospital to Camille's cell phone."

"Strange. I wonder who that woman was that Camille was arguing with. Would it have been the doctor, or Leah Miller, or someone else? I wonder whether Camille was sick?"

"Why would she argue with her doctor if she was sick? She could have been one of the doctor's volunteers."

"I don't know. Good work finding all that out. Be sure to thank your friend for me." Ettie took a moment to take a deep breath. "Come with me to the hospital. I've got to see what's happening with Elsa-May. I'm worried about her."

WHEN ETTIE and Ava got to the hospital, Ettie was surprised to be directed to a room on the top floor. They found the room and walked in to see that Elsa-May was sharing a room with three other women. Elsa-May was at the far wall near the window.

"Have you had the tests yet?" was the first thing Ettie asked when she stood next to Elsa-May's bed.

Elsa-May smiled at Ava. "Nice to see you, Ava."

"You feeling okay?"

Elsa-May nodded. "Fine." She looked at Ettie. "I've had an ultrasound, but they couldn't tell anything. They said the test was inconclusive and now I have to stay in while they do another test. Looks like I'll be in overnight."

"You'll need some things if you're going to be in overnight. I'll go home and bring some things to you."

"*Nee*. I'll wear the hospital gown. It doesn't bother me. I've got everything I need. Don't exhaust yourself rushing around."

"What kind of test will they do, Elsa-May?" Ava asked.

"They call it a venogram. They shoot dye into me through a catheter and then X-ray me."

Ava winced. "Sounds like it might be painful."

"I hope not," Elsa-May said. "I don't have much of a choice but to go ahead and do it."

"They can't do it today?" Ava asked.

Elsa-May shook her head. "They're doing it tomorrow. I have to fast for hours before they do the X-ray."

"Well, I guess I don't need to bring you any food, then," Ettie said.

"Take my mind off things and tell me what you've found out," Elsa-May said.

Ettie and Ava told her what they knew so far about the people on the list Ettie had gotten from Kelly.

"This Judith Mackelvanner is a neurologist?"

"Jah," Ettie and Ava said at the same time.

"Neurology is something to do with the brain, I believe," Elsa-May said. "And from what you know so far, do you think Camille might have been arguing with Judith or Leah?"

"We've no idea; it might have been neither of them," Ava said.

"What reason would she have for arguing with a neurologist?" Elsa-May asked.

Ettie was silent while she thought. "It could have been something personal. Just because this Judith Mackelvanner is a doctor doesn't mean that the argument was about something medical."

"I suppose it could've been about anything." Ava chewed on the end of her thumbnail.

"Could she have been Nehemiah's doctor?" Ettie suggested.

"I don't think so. He died from heart disease and this doctor studies the brain," Elsa-May said.

Ava turned to Ettie. "Why don't you ask Mildred if she's heard of Dr. Judith Mackelvanner?"

"That's a good idea, Ava. A good idea indeed. I'll take you to your place, and then I'll have the taxi continue to Mildred's *haus.*"

"Okay."

Ettie turned to Elsa-May. "Are you sure you don't need anything?"

"Jah, I'm sure. Don't tell anyone I'm in the hospital. I don't want anyone to worry, and I don't want visitors fussing about."

"Okay." Ettie leaned over and rubbed her sister's arm. "You'll be in my prayers."

Elsa-May breathed out heavily and closed her eyes as she said, *"Denke."*

Ettie turned to Ava. "Come on, then."

"Bye, Elsa-May," Ava said.

"Goodbye," Elsa-May said without opening her eyes.

CHAPTER 10

When Ettie and Ava approached Ava's place, Ettie was surprised to see Jeremiah's buggy. She looked closer and saw Jeremiah standing near his horse.

"My goodness. What's he doing here? I wonder if Elsa-May saw him and let him know I wanted him to do some jobs at the *haus.*"

"I think he's here to see me, Ettie."

Ettie frowned and looked at Ava only to see her face flush crimson. "He is? That's wonderful news."

Ava gave a little giggle. "It's not like that. We're just friends and that's all."

"*Jah,* that's what everyone says. That's what I told my parents when my late husband and I were secretly courting."

Ava shook her head.

When Ava got out of the taxi, Ettie said, "Say hello to Jeremiah for me and tell him I've got some work for him, when he's got some spare time." Ettie smiled and resisted teasing Ava. Ettie called after her, "That'll save me talking to him on Sunday."

Five minutes later, Ettie was at Mildred's house.

After Ettie told Mildred about Elsa-May being in the hospital and asked her to keep quiet about it, she inquired about Jacob.

Mildred answered her. "The lawyer's only just left. He asked Jacob a lot of questions. Anyway, Jacob's very tired, but he's out back now fixing fences. He's a hard worker. We've saved geld with Jacob being able to work. Camille couldn't work on the farm; all she could do was organize the workers and she didn't do that very well at all, so Nehemiah said."

"*Jah,* I suppose you would save a lot on labor now that Jacob can be so hands-on. The police haven't been back around?"

"*Nee.*"

"Tell me, Mildred, have you ever heard of a Dr. Mackelvanner?"

Mildred's eyebrows drew together. "I can't say for certain that I have, but the name does sound a little familiar. Was she one of the doctors that Nehemiah went to see?"

"I'm not sure. He saw a few different doctors?"

"*Jah,* he went to one who referred him to others; all of them tried to find out exactly what was wrong with him. His symptoms were fairly general. He went downhill so quickly."

Ettie poked a finger under her prayer *kapp* and scratched her head. "This woman, Dr. Mackelvanner, specializes in brain disorders. Do you know anyone afflicted with anything like that?"

"Only Mary."

"Mary?" Ettie hadn't figured that the doctor might have had something to do with Mary and her condition.

Mildred nodded. "Nehemiah told me that Mary had mental problems. I always thought that Camille suffered the same thing."

"So Mary would've seen a doctor."

"What's all this about, Ettie?"

"I'm following up on a few things that might be able to help Jacob. They seem unrelated at the moment, but I'm hoping they'll all piece together at the end."

"Thank you for helping. You've been *wunderbaar.* I couldn't be certain who the doctor was that Mary saw, but Nehemiah did say that Mary had some kind of mental disorder and that's all I know. He said that not long after she started having violent episodes, she was gone in a matter of months."

Ettie thought back to Mary as she'd known her many years ago, and at the time, she'd had no idea that Mary was sick. "Would Jacob know more about it?"

"*Nee,* he was only a young *bu* when Mary went home to be with *Gott.* Not unless his *vadder* told him something of it in later years, but I don't know."

"That's possible."

"Except Nehemiah wasn't much of a talker."

Ettie pushed her lips and nodded. Many of the Amish men weren't good at talking. Her own father had to be asked about his childhood and only then would he tell her stories, whereas her mother had often told her stories about how things were when she was growing up.

"Stay for lunch, Ettie. Jacob will be home and you can ask him yourself."

"*Denke,* I'll do that."

When Jacob came home, Ettie had a chance to ask him about his mother's illness.

"*Jah,* I didn't know when I was young she was sick, but I found out when I was older that my *mudder* had something called Creutzfeldt-Jakob disease. I was upset that it kind of shared my name."

Ettie frowned. "I've never heard of such a thing."

"It's a degenerative disease of the central nervous system, apparently. I looked into it."

"That sounds awful. Was she treated by a neurologist?"

"I don't know. I couldn't get much information out of *Dat* about the whole thing. He didn't like to talk about her much. It made him too upset."

"She was your *mudder;* you had a right to ask as many questions as you wanted to and have your questions answered," Mildred said.

Jacob nodded and the corners of his mouth twitched. "Why do you ask, Ettie?"

"I'm following up on a few things." Ettie figured she should tell him the truth. "In point of actual fact, I've reason to believe that your *schweschder* had many conversations with a doctor from the hospital. I found out today when I was visiting Elsa-May..."

Jacob interrupted, "Elsa-May's in the hospital?"

"Don't worry about her, she's okay, and don't let anyone know she's there. She's just having some tests. Anyway, I found out that the doctor is a woman, and she's also a neurologist. I was just wondering if she might have had anything to do with your *mudder's* treatment."

"I wouldn't be able to tell you. Is the doctor old?"

"I haven't seen her in person, but I'll find out how old she'd be. I saw a photo and she didn't look very old, maybe around forty or so."

"Anyone who treated my *mudder* would have to be around sixty I'd guess."

Ettie knew she'd slipped up. She should've had Ava check the ages of the people. Dr. Mackelvanner seemed as though she'd be too young to have treated Mary Esh. Ava's friend from the DMV would've had the birth dates recorded on the system.

Ettie turned to Mildred. "You said someone told you they saw

Camille in town arguing with a woman. Did they say what the woman looked like?"

"A woman with long dark hair, an *Englischer.* That's all they said."

"Really?"

Mildred nodded. "That's right."

"This doctor has long dark hair."

"So my *schweschder* had many conversations with this doctor and she was seen arguing with a woman who fits the doctor's description? What does any of this have to do with me? Do you think the doctor you're asking about murdered Camille?"

"I don't know. I'm trying to find out who Camille was talking to and why. That could go a long way to finding out if she'd upset anyone enough for them to want her gone."

"I'm sorry, Ettie. I don't mean to be irritable, or ungrateful. *Denke* for helping, but I don't think there's anything you can do. I'll just have to wait, hope, and trust in *Gott* that the police give me the all clear."

"And they will because you didn't do anything," Mildred said.

Jacob smiled at Mildred.

It was getting late in the day, and Ettie figured that she shouldn't press anything further since both Jacob and Mildred were under a lot of pressure. The best thing she could do was go and see Detective Kelly. He'd be able to find out about the doctor even if he had to go and ask the doctor how she knew Camille.

After Jacob went back to his farm work and Ettie finished helping Mildred with washing the dishes, Ettie made her way back to the police station.

The officer at the front desk must have recognized her; because before Ettie said a word, he said, “Detective Kelly?”

Ettie smiled. “Yes, thank you.”

“Have a seat. I’ll call him.”

Ettie did as she was instructed and sat on the wooden bench in the waiting area. She’d barely sat down when she saw Kelly walking toward her. When their eyes met he smiled and told her, with a wave of his hand, to come into his office.

Once she was sitting opposite him, he asked, “What can I do for you today? By the way, thank Elsa-May for the food, would you?”

“You ate it?”

“Of course I did. I haven’t had a good meal like that in a long time.”

Ettie smiled. “I was the one who cooked it, but it was Elsa-May’s idea when I told her about the donuts you ate for lunch.”

“I am going to make an effort, and try to eat healthier.”

“Glad to hear it.”

“Now, what can I do for you?”

"From the list of numbers you gave me, I found out that most of the incoming and outgoing calls were from the same person. She's a doctor at the hospital. Sometimes she'd call Camille from her cell phone and other times there were calls to Camille's cell phone from the number at the hospital. Then there were calls from Camille to the doctor's mobile, but Camille never called the hospital – not within the time-frame that the list you gave me was constructed."

Detective Kelly frowned. "Was Camille sick or something?"

"I don't know, but the doctor was working with volunteers so maybe Camille was one of those. The other thing I had to tell you was that two people saw Camille in town arguing with a woman who had long dark hair, and Dr. Mackelvanner has long dark hair."

Kelly rubbed his nose.

"I did have a thought," Ettie said.

"What was it?"

"The doctor is a neurologist. I thought their contact could be something to do with Camille's mother's death. Her mother died of some rare condition, and I believe a doctor who had the same qualifications as Dr. Mackelvanner would've treated her. It's a big coincidence, isn't it?"

"I'm not following you."

Ettie squirmed in her seat. She wasn't certain what it all meant, and was hoping Kelly might be able to shed some light on it for her. "I was hoping that you might be able to question this doctor and see how she knew Camille."

"I don't see that it matters." When Ettie glared at him, he said, "I'll make a note of it. I don't have the time to follow it up right now. I'm glad you came in."

"You are?"

"Yes. I've got some bad news."

Ettie braced herself, hoping it wasn't about Jacob. "You're glad I came in so you can give me bad news? I'm not glad I came in if all you have for me is bad news."

"The bullets found in Camille's apartment match one of the firearms we took from the Esh house. I'm waiting on the warrant for Jacob Esh's arrest to come through."

Ettie gasped and covered her mouth. "No! It can't be."

"I appreciate your loyalty, Mrs. Smith, but sometimes people can fool us. Just because he was born into an Amish family doesn't mean he's a saint who is not capable of murder."

"He didn't do it, and I'll prove it one way or another."

Kelly raised his eyebrows. "I suppose it's my fault for getting you involved in all this, and for that, I'm sorry."

"I dare say I would've gotten involved anyway once I found out that you arrested the wrong man."

"We've got enough evidence to arrest him."

"The gun?"

"Yes, the gun." He rose to his feet. "I don't want to appear rude, but I've got a lot on my plate."

Ettie put both hands on his desk and pushed herself to her feet. "Good day, Detective." Ettie walked out of his office, not sure what to do. Should she warn Mildred what was about to happen? Mildred would be so upset, but as Elsa-May had said to her, Mildred wasn't without people she could call on. Mildred had a telephone in her barn and she could call someone whenever she needed. Ettie got a taxi home, had the taxi wait while she collected some fresh clothes and a nightdress for Elsa-May, and then continued on to the hospital. Elsa-May had picked a bad time to get sick.

CHAPTER 11

Supported by pillows in her upright position in the hospital bed, Elsa-May smiled when Ettie came into the hospital room. "I'll be glad to get out of this place. They keep asking me what my name is. I keep telling them it's written there." She pointed to the name behind her.

Ettie giggled. "They're trying to find out if you're still in your right mind."

"They should find a better way of doing it, then. I'm not a three-year-old. And all the nurses speak loudly to me as though I'm deaf."

"I know. I remember that from when I was in hospital with pneumonia." Ettie placed Elsa-May's clothes in a drawer of the nightstand. "I've brought some things for you." Ettie then slumped on the edge of Elsa-May's bed.

"Well, what happened this afternoon when you left here? You look like you've had the wind knocked out of you."

"A lot happened. The short version of it is that Kelly's probably at this very moment arresting Jacob."

"Really?"

Ettie nodded.

"That's bad news."

"He said one of Jacob's rifles, or some type of gun, was a match with the bullets found in Camille's apartment. That's not all I found out today."

"What else?"

Ettie told Elsa-May about the doctor whom Camille had often been speaking to, and the possibility that the doctor might have been the woman Camille had been seen arguing with.

"Did you tell Kelly that?"

"I did, but he didn't seem interested. He said he'd look into it later, but I'm sure he only said that to keep me quiet or make me happy. *Nee,* not to make me happy. He wouldn't care if he made anyone happy or not. He said it just for something to say, I'm certain of that."

"I suppose he had his mind on making the arrest. Didn't he say he was up for a promotion?"

Ettie nodded. "I hope he doesn't let that cloud his judgment over whether Jacob is innocent or not."

"Looks like it's too late for that if he's gone ahead with the warrant. At least Jacob knows a lawyer now. Is he any good?"

"The lawyer?"

Elsa-May nodded.

"He's a little odd, and very young. I don't know if he's good, but he did get Jacob out of the police station pretty fast; perhaps he is good. He was questioning Jacob today so he does seem enthusiastic."

"Does that doctor you were talking about work at this hospital?"

"According to the phone records she does."

"Now, what about that man from next door to the Eshes' property, the one who wanted to buy the farm? With Camille dead, and if Jacob goes to jail, that would leave Mildred with the farm, and she'd most likely sell to him."

"That's right. He could've gone into the Eshes' home, taken one of Jacob's rifles and shot at Camille, and then put it back. He could've killed Camille, and then because of the bullet matching Jacob's gun it would have looked like Jacob made an attempt on his sister's life." Ettie tapped on her chin. "The only thing is that Mildred's at home all the time, so he wouldn't have had a chance to take the gun and then put it back."

"There's the gatherings she goes to every second Sunday, and she goes out to the knitting circle when it isn't held at her *haus*. What if he planted a gun there and it wasn't Jacob's gun after all? Did anyone think of that?"

"*Nee,* I don't think they did, and I wonder if they even checked the prints on the gun. I suppose they would've."

"Yes. I'd expect so," Elsa-May said.

Ettie continued, "Mildred wouldn't know what gun was what. She said there were quite a few guns, and some were Nehemiah's. Also Mildred did say that the neighbor keeps an eye on the place. While I was visiting Mildred he was just standing there staring at their *haus.*"

"Now what about Camille? How do you think she knows the doctor?"

"Jacob said his mother had some kind of mental illness and was treated for some disorder or other. She could very well have been seen by a neurologist."

"What illness was it?"

"I can't remember. I should've written it down. It was a strange name that I'd never come across before."

"What did Camille do when she was away from the community? I assumed she would've worked somewhere. Could she have met the doctor while she was working?"

"From what I heard, Camille worked at a winery. Something to do with making the wine."

"Stomping on grapes?" Elsa-May said with a laugh.

Ettie smiled. "Perhaps something in the office, since she told Nehemiah she had management experience."

"Should you find this doctor and talk to her?" Elsa-May asked.

"*Ach, nee.* I wouldn't like to. Detective Kelly should be the one to do that. It might not have anything to do with anything."

"Perhaps," Elsa-May said. "And it doesn't sound likely that a doctor would've killed Camille. Doctors are supposed to try to prolong lives, not cut them short."

"*Jah.* Intriguing, though, isn't it? The woman's not an ordinary doctor, and they had so many conversations."

"Perhaps Camille was sick."

"No one mentioned that might be the case. Certainly Jacob or Mildred weren't aware of any illness."

"Was Mary's illness something that might have been passed on?"

"I don't know why I didn't think of that. What was it now? It was something or other Jacob disease."

"Creutzfeldt-Jakob disease?"

"That was it. How do you know about it?"

"Yes, I think it can be passed on in some cases."

"How do you know about it?" Ettie repeated.

"It's one of the diseases that there's no cure for. I remember reading about it and I can't remember where. When people get it, I'm certain they go downhill quickly. I think, as I've already said, it might be something that could be passed on. We'd have to find out for certain."

"I wonder if Camille had the disease and didn't tell anyone. If so, why would she be arguing with her doctor?"

"Perhaps it wasn't her doctor she was arguing with. It could've been someone else," Elsa-May suggested. "Although the description did match the doctor. Anyway, you'd better go and see how Mildred is. Don't worry about me; I'm okay. I still remember who I am."

"Are you sure? I can stay with you longer. I don't want to run into Detective Kelly, and I certainly don't want to arrive there before he's been out to Mildred's *haus.*"

Elsa-May glanced at the phone on the nightstand beside her. "Why don't you call Mildred? Tell her you're going to come there. You'll soon find out if the detective's been there."

Ettie made the call and found out that Detective Kelly had arrested Jacob, and they'd just left. When Ettie hung up the receiver, she turned to Elsa-May. "She's near hysterical. I told her to phone the lawyer and that I'd be right over."

"*Jah,* I heard what you said."

"I do hate leaving you. I'd like to sit by you longer."

"*Nee,* don't be silly; you go. There'll be someone coming in soon asking me my name. I might have some fun with them this time. I'll tell them I don't know my name." Elsa-May chuckled.

Ettie wagged a finger at her sister. "Don't you do that."

"Okay, I won't." Elsa-May settled herself back into the pillow and closed her eyes. "I'll have a little sleep before the next meal comes 'round."

"*Nee,* you can't eat, remember?"

Elsa-May chuckled. "I was just testing to see if you were listening to me."

"You can't be too sick."

"Tell that to the doctor on your way out, would you?"

Ettie patted Elsa-May on her shoulder. "I'll come back and see you in the morning."

"*Denke,*" Elsa-May said, without opening her eyes.

CHAPTER 12

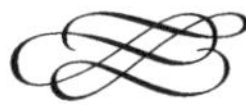

"Ettie, I'm so glad you're here."

"Did you call the lawyer?"

Mildred nodded. "*Jah,* he said he'd go straight to the police station."

"That's good of him." Ettie looked Mildred up and down. "You don't look as poorly as you sounded on the phone."

"I prayed and left things up to *Gott*. I know Jacob's innocent no matter what the police say. They'll find that out soon enough."

"That's the way," Ettie said, thinking she should've stayed with Elsa-May.

"The lawyer said Jacob would probably get bail, so if he does he'll be out in the morning just as soon as he can go before a judge."

"Very good."

"Ettie, you don't look well."

Ettie put her fingertips to her face only to feel that her cheeks were burning. "I've been busy over the last couple of days."

Mildred looped her arm through Ettie's. "Come sit down and have a cup of tea. Would you stay for dinner?"

"I'd love to stay, *denke.*" Ettie hadn't given any thought to dinner and with Elsa-May in the hospital, she most likely would've only eaten fruit when she got home.

After an early dinner, Mildred insisted on driving Ettie home rather than her getting a taxi. After Mildred hitched the horse and buggy, she said, "Why don't you just stay the night? Elsa-May's in the hospital and I'll be alone too."

"All right. I will." Ettie gave a little laugh. "Now we've hitched the buggy for nothing." Ettie patted the fine chestnut gelding on his neck. The horse turned his head and Ettie rubbed his soft nose. "You're a beauty," Ettie said to the horse.

"It doesn't hurt for me to practice hitching the buggy. If anything happens to Jacob I'll be on my own. I've never been on my own. I went straight from my *mudder* and *vadder's haus* to Nehemiah's."

"Don't talk like that. We have to stay steadfast in trusting *Gott.*"

Mildred nodded. "I'm trying, but sometimes I let the worry overtake me."

"Let's put the horse back in the paddock. Then you and I can sleep."

That night, Ettie stayed up much longer than usual while listening to Mildred tell stories of when she and Nehemiah were courting. Ettie felt a little sad for her. It didn't seem like there had been any real courtship; it wasn't a romantic time for Mildred. It sounded to Ettie like Nehemiah hadn't gotten over Mary's death. It seemed more a marriage of convenience for Nehemiah, but Mildred obviously hadn't seen things like that, or if she had she wasn't admitting it. Nehemiah had needed someone to look after his children while he worked the farm and Mildred was glad to finally be someone's wife and have an instant family.

"Camille couldn't have remembered Mary very well. Why do you think that she never truly accepted you as her *mudder?*"

Mildred heaved a deep sigh. "I don't know where I went wrong with her, what I could've done differently. Nehemiah stopped talking about Mary so the *kinner* could adjust better to me. I didn't want them to forget her or anything. I just wanted to do the job that Mary would've wanted me to do; to look after and care for them properly."

Ettie yawned and saw that it was nearly eleven. "Excuse me. I think my old body's telling me I need some sleep."

"Jah, me too. Who knows what tomorrow will bring?"

THE NEXT MORNING, Ettie heard the front door shut loudly. She opened her eyes and looked around, taking a moment to realize that she was in Mildred's house. Then she heard someone bustling around in the kitchen downstairs. Ettie poured some water into a bowl and splashed it on her face before she changed out of the borrowed nightgown and into her dress. Once she'd slipped her over-apron on, she wound her hair up on her head and placed her prayer *kapp* over the top. She made the bed and then headed downstairs.

"You awake already, Mildred?" Ettie said as she walked into the kitchen.

"It's half past nine."

Ettie opened her mouth in shock. "Is it? I never sleep this late." Ettie looked out the window to see a gray sky. "Usually the light wakes me. Looks like we might be in for rain."

"Have a seat, Ettie, and I'll make you some breakfast."

Ettie smiled, glad to have someone look after her for a change. With Elsa-May's leg being so bad for weeks, Ettie had been left to do all the cooking and all the chores.

"I was making the bread this morning when I heard the phone in the barn ringing."

"Did you make it there in time to answer?"

"*Jah.* It was the lawyer. He was saying something about them having Jacob's fingerprints somewhere."

"Where?"

"I couldn't really hear – the phone had a crackling in it. He said he'd either call me back or come here. He's hoping to get Jacob out this morning. Could you wait with me, Ettie?"

"Of course I can."

Mildred smiled at Ettie while she poured hot water into a china teapot. Ettie did want to see how Elsa-May was, but she figured Elsa-May wouldn't be ready to go home until the afternoon.

It wasn't long after they'd finished breakfast when they heard a car. Both ladies looked out the window to see the lawyer's car heading toward the house.

"He's got Jacob with him," Mildred said.

"Jah, I can see someone sitting next to the driver."

Mildred rushed to the door and waited on the porch for the car to pull up. Just as the car stopped, the rain pelted down.

Jacob got out of the car and Mildred ran and wrapped her arms around him. He put his arm around her and then they ran back to the cover of the porch.

"Everything's okay, *Mamm,"* Jacob said.

Ettie stood in the doorway. She saw the lawyer get out of the car and hurry toward them. When he stood next to Jacob, he wiped the rain off his suit and said, "The latest is..."

Mildred interrupted, "Do come inside and we can sit. I can barely hear anything with this rain."

Once they were all sitting in the living room, the lawyer said,

"They claim to have found Jacob's fingerprints in Camille's apartment."

"And I was never in her apartment," Jacob said to Mildred.

"Jacob's prints were on two glasses in her apartment, and one of the glasses, the one we know Camille had drunk out of, had remnants of poison in it."

"The poison that killed her?" Mildred asked.

Claymore nodded. "One of the poisons. She had two in her system."

Mildred gasped and clutched at her stomach.

"We don't have to talk about this now," Claymore said.

Mildred shook her head. "No, it's all right. Continue."

"Very well. Things aren't looking good for Jacob with his prints on the glasses, and the bullets."

Ettie noticed that the lawyer swallowed hard and exchanged worried glances with Jacob.

"Is there more, Mr. Cartwright?" Ettie asked.

The lawyer raised his eyebrows and then looked back at Jacob.

"You might as well tell 'em," Jacob said.

"One of the poisons that killed Camille was found in your barn, Mrs. Esh. Ethylene glycol. It's a painful death, so I'm told."

Mildred's hand flew to her mouth. "My barn? What would poison be doing in my barn?"

"Many people keep it. It's a common thing a lot of people would have for their vehicles."

"If it's common, couldn't anyone have used that poison?" Ettie asked.

"The thing is the formula has been changed in the last few years. It used to taste sweet and now they're making it taste awful." He looked at Mildred. "The one in Camille's system was the old formula, same as the one found in your barn."

"I heard she died from an overdose of some kind of sleeping pills," Mildred said to the lawyer.

The lawyer gave a nod. "They ran a second lot of tests and found she had both in her system. Traces of the sleeping pills were found in the glass – they are assuming they were dissolved in some kind of drink."

Detective Kelly must have known that, and he'd held back that information from her. Ettie decided that this would be the last time she'd help him.

"There's a lot of evidence against me," Jacob said, looking at Mildred. "I didn't do it."

Mildred nodded. "Why would we have poison here?"

"The poison in question is used in motor vehicles as a coolant," Claymore said.

"We don't have motor vehicles."

"Claymore looked it up and found that the coolant can also be used to protect some metals, or as a solvent. *Dat* probably had a bottle in the barn to preserve some metal, maybe the old buggy his *vadder* had. He was always tinkering with it."

Ettie pushed herself to her feet. "Why don't I make everyone some tea?"

"I can't stay long," Claymore said.

"Tea won't take long," Ettie said before she hurried to the kitchen. While she was there, Ettie could still hear their conversation. She turned on the stove, filled the pot and placed it on the heating plate. Then she set about placing teacups and saucers onto a tray. She knew Mildred always kept sugar cookies in a jar in the larder. Ettie found the cookies and placed them on a plate.

Claymore told Mildred that the evidence was circumstantial. It would be normal for Camille to have her brother's fingerprints in her apartment. "Anyone could have had access to some ethylene glycol. It's something many people keep."

Ettie carried the tray of cookies and teacups out to them while she waited for the pot to boil.

"What about the gun? Was the gun in question left in the house?" Ettie asked.

Jacob nodded, and Mildred said, "The guns are always left in the *haus*. Nehemiah always kept the guns in the *haus,* never in the barn."

"And did they show you the gun in question?"

Jacob nodded. "It was one of *Dat's*. They asked me if I recognized it."

"I'd better check to see if the water's boiled." Ettie hurried back to the kitchen and poured the boiling water into the teapot.

After the lawyer left Mildred's house, Ettie was tired and left for her home.

When the taxi stopped at her home, Ettie was pleased she'd be able to have a rest before going back to the hospital. Just as she opened her gate, she saw Bernie, the neighbor walking his dog.

"Hello, Ettie."

"Hello." Ettie leaned down to pat his dog. "It's a nice day for a walk."

He pushed his hat back on his head. "Where's Elsa-May? I don't often see you out and about on your own."

"Elsa-May's in the hospital. Nothing serious. She'll be home anytime."

"Ah. I see. Well, I'd better keep going."

Ettie headed toward her front door hoping Elsa-May wouldn't be mad at her for telling Bernie she was in the hospital. She had asked Ettie not to tell anyone, but Bernie asked, so what was she to do?

After a rest, Ettie headed to the hospital, hoping Elsa-May wouldn't be mad at her for leaving her alone for so long.

Ettie walked in to the hospital room and saw Elsa-May reading the bible that had been in the drawer next to her bed. Elsa-May smiled when she saw Ettie walk in.

"Are you ready to come home yet?" Ettie asked.

"I don't think I'll be able to leave until tomorrow. I've had some kind of reaction to the dye." Elsa-May lifted the sheet to reveal a very red, swollen leg.

"Agh. That doesn't look good. Does it hurt?"

"Funny thing is, it doesn't hurt anymore than it did before. The test today was uncomfortable, but at least I can eat again. They've given me the all clear."

"You don't have a clot?"

"*Nee,* I don't."

"That's *wunderbaar.* What caused your leg pain, though?"

"That, they haven't found out yet. The doctor from this hospital also said something about me having to lose weight, and that would improve circulation. Maybe that's why my leg's been hurting." Elsa-May pushed the sheet back over her leg and Ettie straightened the end of the sheet.

"Shouldn't you let the air get to your leg?" Ettie asked.

"*Nee,* the breeze of the air-conditioning irritates it. Tell me what the latest news is."

Ettie told Elsa-May all that had been said at Mildred's house.

"The only way I can figure that Jacob's gun was used was if someone had deliberately tried to make it look like Jacob did it.

They would've had to sneak into the house, use the gun, and then place the gun back in the house. Or, as I've said before, was it Jacob's gun in the first place?"

"I asked Jacob about that. He said it *was* one of his *vadder's* old guns." Ettie continued, "The lawyer says it's all circumstantial evidence. All the same, I think the lawyer's worried, and I know Jacob is dreadfully concerned to the point of being sick. He tries to be brave but I can see the worry in his face."

"Well, hello."

Both women looked in the direction of the familiar voice.

"Detective Crowley, it's so nice to see you." Ettie was overjoyed to see him and tried to contain her excitement. Now they might get someone to help them, or at least listen to them.

The detective glanced around the hospital room and moved toward Elsa-May's bed.

"How did you know I was here?" Elsa-May asked as Crowley walked further into the room.

"One of your neighbors told me where to find you."

Elsa-May glared at Ettie. "Ettie, I asked you not to tell anyone I was in the hospital."

"I was walking out the front gate and Bernie was walking his dog. He asked where you were and I couldn't lie."

Elsa-May sighed.

Crowley said, "I heard an Amish man was arrested for the

murder of his sister. I figured you would know the people involved."

Elsa-May looked at Ettie. "Pull the curtains, would you?" Ettie pulled the curtains around the bed to give them privacy from the three other patients in the room.

"We do know them," Ettie said in a low voice, hoping that he was there to help them. Now they might finally be able to help Jacob if the former detective was going to be on their side.

Crowley said, "I thought of both of you as soon as I heard."

"Thank you," Elsa-May said.

"Do you know the family well?" Crowley asked.

"Yes," Ettie said.

"Mildred, the mother – well, the stepmother – is in my knitting circle," Elsa-May said.

"Any chance of you coming out of retirement?" Ettie asked, staring at him and hoping he'd say that he'd help.

He frowned at Ettie. "Why? Is there a problem?"

Ettie and Elsa-May filled the detective in on what had happened. Ettie finished up by saying, "I'm not happy with Detective Kelly and how he tricked me in the beginning."

"I can understand how you feel about that. From what you said they've got pretty strong evidence against the young man."

"Be that as it may, he's innocent. I know he didn't do it," Ettie said.

Crowley rubbed his chin.

"Can you see what you can find out for us?" Elsa-May asked. "It's hard for Ettie with me in the hospital. She's been doing a lot of rushing here and there, and it's not easy at her age."

Normally Ettie would've taken offense at Elsa-May's reference to her age since Elsa-May was the older of the two, but she didn't mind at all if it prompted Crowley to help them.

"I'll see what I can do. I'll go straight in there. I visit everyone there every so often so it won't look like I'm there on an information-gathering expedition."

"Even though you are," Elsa-May chortled.

"Do you expect to be in here for long?" Crowley asked Elsa-May.

"I'm hoping to be out tomorrow."

"It's not possible that he can be found guilty if he didn't do it, is it?" Ettie asked before she thought the question through. She knew, of course, innocent people had been found guilty in the past.

"It does happen more often than you'd think. Some people have served long prison sentences and now, with the new DNA testing constantly evolving, they're finding out they were innocent."

Just then a nurse poked her head through the curtains. "I thought I heard voices. Visiting hours is over."

"Visiting hours are over," Elsa-May corrected her.

"Yes, that's right," the nurse grumbled while staring at the visitors, not realizing that Elsa-May had corrected her.

Crowley said, "I'm sorry. I wasn't aware there were restrictions."

Ettie took a step toward the nurse. "I'm her sister. I find it hard to get here in visiting hours."

"Well, I'll go and see some other patients and I'll be back in ten minutes to check on the patient."

"Thank you," Crowley said.

The nurse walked out.

"Can I drive you home, Ettie?"

Ettie's face lit up. "Yes, thank you. That'll save me getting a taxi."

"Off you go; don't mind me. I don't want you to get into trouble when Nurse Grisly comes back," Elsa-May said, laughing.

"Is that her real name?" Ettie asked.

Elsa-May chuckled again. "Yes, it is. I know because she signs my chart."

"You look at your chart?" Crowley asked, picking up the chart hanging on the end of the bed.

"Why not? It's my chart. I can't make head or tail of it, but I still read it. Hopefully they'll say I can go home tomorrow. The doctor will see me in the morning when he does his rounds."

CHAPTER 13

On the way home, Ettie told Crowley as many details as she knew about Camille and Jacob.

When he stopped the car, Crowley said, "From what you said, Kelly's looking at a promotion. He'll be trying to get all the help he can so he'll look good."

"I think he only wants the kind of help that'll make Jacob look more guilty. He might not like help if you're trying to find a way to prove he's innocent."

"There's only one way to find out." Crowley glanced at his wristwatch. "Hopefully he's working late."

"You're going there right now?"

Crowley nodded.

"I'm concerned that Kelly knows about the argument Camille

was seen having with a woman and yet he's done nothing to find out who she might be," Ettie said.

"And two different people told you that, you say?"

"That's right. The man next door, what was his name again? That's right, his last name was Bradshaw. I'm certain it was Ronald Bradshaw. And then someone told Camille's stepmother that they saw Camille in town arguing with a lady with long black hair."

"And you think that woman is the doctor?"

Ettie nodded. "She is a doctor." Ettie was pretty sure that she'd told him enough details, and he understood enough to find out a few things to help Jacob. Crowley believed her based solely on her word that Jacob wasn't guilty. Unless he was tricking her like Detective Kelly had. *Nee!* She shook the thought from her mind. Crowley had always been straight with them. He wasn't deceptive at all, unlike Kelly.

Once Crowley had driven away, Ettie unlocked her front door and pushed it open. She wasn't used to coming home to an empty house.

For dinner she ate a couple of pieces of fruit and then sat down on the couch to do some more needlework. A few minutes after she'd begun, she looked at the wooden chair that Elsa-May usually sat in. Without Elsa-May knitting while she sewed it seemed to be a waste of time and not as interesting. Ettie sighed and bundled the needlework up and pushed it to one end of the couch.

She closed her eyes and before long her mind drifted to Jacob and the evidence that was stacked against him. She hoped that Kelly would allow Crowley to help, just like he had last time.

A sudden knock on the door made Ettie jump. "Who could that be?" she muttered.

She opened the door to see Ava. Ettie immediately felt bad that she hadn't visited her and kept her up to date with what was going on. "Ava, come in. Can I get you something?"

"*Nee,* I'm fine. It's not been long since I had dinner."

"Come and sit down."

Once the two of them were sitting down together, Ettie told Ava everything that had happened since she'd seen her last.

"It would be interesting to know more about that doctor."

"The only way we could find out if Camille knew her because she was sick is if someone looked up Camille's medical records." Ettie clicked her fingers. "I should've mentioned that to Crowley. I told him everything I could remember, but I was trying to tell him all the facts about the evidence. I did tell him about the woman Camille was seen arguing with."

Ava's eyes glazed over.

"What is it, Ava?"

"Oh, I was just thinking how we'd be able to find out about Camille's medical history."

"I don't think we can, can we? I haven't been able to think of a way, not with the patient-privacy regulations these days."

"Hmmm, I'll give it some thought."

"Is there any way we can look up the records on the hospital computer if we both go and see Elsa-May tomorrow morning? You distract the nurse while I look on her computer."

Ettie giggled. *"Nee,* we can't do that. The patient files on the computer might not be open, anyway."

"Well, I think it'd be worth a try."

"There'll have to be another way. Anyway, we're putting a lot of store on this woman having something to do with Camille's death. She might not have anything to do with it at all. I think we'd do better to consider who would've taken a gun out of Jacob's *haus,* shot at Camille in her apartment, then placed the gun back in Jacob's *haus.*"

"Either Jacob did do it, or it looks like someone wanted it to look like he did it."

Ettie was painfully curious to know more about Camille's life. "Mildred did talk about a friend of Camille's. I can't remember exactly, but I'm fairly certain Camille still kept in contact with an *Englischer.* We should look into the girl who left the community, Leah Miller."

"Whoever did kill Camille had planned it carefully. It wasn't something they rushed into. Who has Camille's cell phone?"

Ettie's eyes opened wide. "I'm not certain, but if the police didn't take it, maybe Mildred would let us take a look at it."

"*Jah,* there could be texts and voice messages."

"Surely the police would have taken it in as evidence. Or it might be still at her apartment."

"Would they have taken it?" Ava asked. "They got her phone records."

"As soon as I see what's happening with Elsa-May in the hospital tomorrow, I'll go over and visit Mildred. They could be letting Elsa-May out tomorrow. It would've been today, only she had some kind of reaction to something they gave her."

"Do you want me to come with you?"

"*Nee,* I don't want to bother you to go to the hospital, but I would like you to come with me when I go to Mildred's *haus.*"

"I'd be happy to. What if I come here at twelve? Do you think you'd be back from the hospital by then?"

"Why don't I give you a call when I'm leaving the hospital? We have to wait until the doctor does his rounds, and that could be anytime in the morning. I wouldn't want you waiting here a long time. *Ach,* there's no phone at your place."

"That's okay. I'll go to my *mudder's haus* and you can call me there."

"*Denke,* Ava. That should work out well."

Next morning, Ettie was back at the hospital with Elsa-May.

"Have you had a good night?"

"*Nee.* My leg was hurting all night and now they say my blood pressure is up. Why wouldn't it be up, having to stay in this place for days?"

"You do look a little pale."

"That's because I've been here for days with no fresh air or sunshine. It's not a healthy place to be."

Ettie chuckled. "It is if you're sick."

"You don't like hospitals yourself, Ettie."

"That's true. I don't know if anyone would be able to make me stay in one ever again. Crowley was going to see Kelly last night, but I don't know the outcome of it. After I take you home, if I am taking you home today, I'm meeting Ava at our *haus*. From there, I'm going back to Mildred's *haus* with Ava to see if she might happen to know where Camille's phone is."

"I'd say the police would have it."

"We're hoping they don't."

Elsa-May raised her eyebrows. "I don't want you to be disappointed."

"It wouldn't be the first time. I also want to find out who Camille's friends were. I'm certain Mildred talked about her having a certain friend. Ah, yes, I know where I heard about a friend!"

"Where?"

Ettie took a deep breath while her eyes focused on the ceiling. "It was Kelly. Kelly said that Camille had told a friend of hers that she thought her brother was trying to kill her."

"*Jah,* I remember."

"So, who is this friend and how would we find her? I wonder how well she knew Camille."

"Kelly would have to know who the woman was."

Ettie scratched her head. "*Ach,* there's so much to remember."

"You're having trouble remembering things?"

Ettie glared at her sister and narrowed her eyes. "No more than usual."

Elsa-May chuckled.

Right then, the doctor walked in, followed by two younger men in white coats who, Ettie assumed, were students. The doctor murmured a 'hello' to the two ladies and barely made eye contact. He studied Elsa-May's chart.

He looked at Elsa-May and walked up to stand by her shoulder. "How are you feeling today?"

"Much better today, Doctor. I feel ready to go home."

"Your blood pressure is a little higher than it has been." He examined Elsa-May's leg. "You've got someone to look after you at home?"

"My sister." Elsa-May pointed to Ettie.

The doctor looked at Ettie and gave her a faint smile. Ettie smiled back. The doctor then spoke in low tones to the two men about Elsa-May's chart. He walked to the end of the bed and placed the chart neatly, hooking it over the end of the railing. "I'll sign the discharge papers and a nurse will be here soon to give you instructions for when you're at home."

"Very good, Doctor. Thank you."

When the nurse came and gave Elsa-May her discharge instructions, Ettie called Ava's mother's place to let Ava know that they would soon be leaving the hospital.

"Ettie, I've got something to tell you," Ava said when she got on the phone. "My *mudder* told me something very interesting and I can't wait to tell you."

"What is it?" Ettie asked.

"I'll tell you when I see you."

"What's it about? About Jacob?"

"Kind of."

"About Camille?"

"Ettie, I'll tell you when I see you."

Ettie sighed and then noticed a nurse was glaring at her while waiting for Elsa-May to get into the wheelchair. "We're just about to leave the ward. Then we'll be home as fast as the taxi can take us."

"I'll see you soon," Ava said.

"Can you just give me a little hint?" It was too late – Ava had already hung up.

CHAPTER 14

The taxi driver helped the sisters into the house. Ettie paid the driver and as soon as he drove off in his car, Ettie looked up, hearing the clip-clop of a horse's hooves.

"Here she is already," Ettie called out to her sister. "Oh, I do hate leaving you after you've just come home."

Elsa-May said, "I'll be all right. Help me into bed and I'll have a little sleep."

Ettie gave Ava a little wave to let her know she wouldn't be long.

Once Ettie got Elsa-May into bed, she walked out of the room and looked at the small bag that Elsa-May had brought back from the hospital with her. Ettie peeped in to see dirty laundry. "That'll have to be done some day, but not today." She picked up the bag and threw it in the laundry room at the back of the house. Before she left, she looked back in at Elsa-May and was pleased to see her eyes closed and her mouth opened. She noticed her chest slowly rising and falling before she gently closed the bedroom door.

Ettie climbed into the buggy to see Ava's excited face. "Well, don't keep *en aldi hutzel* waiting. What did you find out?"

Ava clicked her horse forward into a slow trot. "You won't believe it."

"What?"

"My mother also saw Camille arguing with a woman, a dark-haired woman, at the farmers' markets. And you know why she saw her there?" Ettie shook her head. "Because she was sitting at the same coffee shop nearly next to them."

"Nee!" Ettie shrieked. "Did she hear what they said?"

"Nee, but the thing is, I showed *Mamm* the picture of the doctor, you know, the one we got from my friend who works at the DMV?"

"Was it the same woman?"

"Mamm said she was certain it was the same woman. She remembers because she thought at the time that it was odd to see them together."

"What sort of argument was it? Were there raised voices, that kind of thing?"

"Mamm said they were speaking crossly to each other. From what she said, their voices weren't raised or anything of the kind, but they looked and sounded angry."

"Well, we're finally getting somewhere. The woman she was arguing with was a doctor and now we just have to find out what the two were to each other. Did they know each other as friends or was Camille a patient?" Ettie grabbed Ava's arm. *"Denke,* Ava."

Ava smiled back at Ettie, and then turned her horse down the Eshes' driveway.

"I do hope Crowley's been able to do something helpful," Ettie said. "He didn't say when he'd contact me again."

"Well, he knows where you live. He'll find you when, and if, he's got something to tell you."

Ettie nodded.

Ava stopped the horse and buggy outside Mildred's house.

Ettie rested awhile before getting out of the buggy. She'd planned to visit Mildred to find out who this friend of Camille's was, but wasn't it the police who'd mentioned that Camille had a friend she'd confided in?

"Oh, dear, I think the person I need to speak to next is Detective Kelly."

"Well, we're here now and she's probably seen us."

Ettie nodded. "Let's see how she's holding up. Then do you mind taking me into town to talk to Detective Kelly?"

"Nee, I don't mind. I don't have anywhere else I need to be."

"Denke."

"I'll follow your lead. Don't forget we were going to ask about the cell phone," Ava said.

Ettie nodded and then they both walked up to Mildred's *haus* and knocked on the front door. After a while with no answer, they knocked again.

"That's most unusual – she's not answering. She's always looking out when she hears a buggy."

"Shall we check the garden out the back?"

Ettie nodded at Ava's suggestion. Once they were around the back of the house, they walked the length of the garden. Ettie and Ava looked up when they heard a window open. They saw Mildred, with her long gray hair falling around her shoulders, looking as though she'd just woken up. "Ettie, and Ava! I'm so glad you've come. I'll be down in a minute. Let yourselves in." Then she closed the window.

Ettie and Ava smiled at each other. "She's just woken up," Ettie said.

"Seems so."

Ettie and Ava had been sitting in Mildred's living room for over five minutes before Mildred made an appearance. She came walking down the stairs fiddling with her prayer *kapp*.

"Are you feeling okay, Mildred?" Ettie asked.

"I'm okay; just couldn't find a reason to get out of bed."

"Ettie and I have got the water boiling."

"*Denke.* Have you eaten breakfast?" Mildred asked the ladies.

"We have," Ava answered.

"I've been to the hospital already and taken Elsa-May home."

"Oh good. She's better then?"

"She is. She'll just need a little bit of looking after." Ettie made a mental note to go home after their meeting with Mildred and make Elsa-May a meal before they went to see the detective. "Come on, you sit in the kitchen and Ava and I will make you some breakfast."

Mildred nodded and once they reached the kitchen, she slumped into a chair. "I didn't realize it was so late. I normally get up and cook Jacob breakfast before he starts work. I wonder why he didn't wake me."

"Most likely he wanted you to get some more sleep."

Mildred held her head in her hands. Ettie and Ava looked at each other and Ettie wondered what she could do to make Mildred feel better.

"Would you happen to have Camille's phone here?" Ettie asked.

Mildred was silent for a moment then shook her head. "*Nee.* I think she would've had that at her apartment."

Ettie nodded. She'd known it was a long shot that the phone would be there. After they sat with Mildred for a while, they said goodbye and headed out to Ava's buggy.

"Where to now?" Ava picked up the reins.

"I did want to talk to Kelly, but I think I should go and give Elsa-May some food and see if she needs anything."

After they spent some time with Elsa-May, giving her a meal and talking to her, they left her alone again and headed to see detective Kelly.

"Are you sure you're up to this, Ettie? It's a lot of running around for you."

Ettie gave a little laugh. "I've got no choice. I can't have Jacob going to jail for a crime he didn't do." It was very much on Ettie's mind that Jacob could have a much worse fate than jail, the laws being what they were. Jacob could face the death penalty, in the worst-case scenario. Ettie shook her head as if doing so would shake all the bad images of Jacob being found guilty from her head.

Ettie waited for Ava to park the buggy securely and then they walked up the road to the police station together. As they approached the station, Ettie saw Detective Crowley walking towards them.

"That's Detective Crowley right there," Ettie said to Ava in a low voice.

"I know. I met him. You introduced us when he was helping with Horace's murder investigation."

They stopped still and waited for Detective Crowley.

When he was standing in front of them, Ettie said, "We were just going to come in and tell you, well, tell Detective Kelly, something."

Crowley nodded to the coffee shop two doors up from where they were standing.

"Let's go in there and chat. I've got something to tell you as well."

Once they were seated, Ettie started out by telling Crowley that Ava's mother had said that Dr. Mackelvanner was the one she'd seen arguing with Camille. "Now that we know that, do you think Detective Kelly will look into Camille's medical records?"

"What I think is that Kelly won't see it as having any relevance to the case – not with the evidence that he's got against Jacob."

"Surely he'd have to investigate every avenue to make sure they've got the right person." Ettie ground her teeth in frustration.

"I'll tell you what," Crowley began. "I know someone in the hospital who owes me a favor. I'll have him get me the number of the doctor's private office phone, and I'll speak with her. Then we can go from there. How does that sound?"

"You'd do that? You'd go and talk to the doctor?" Ettie asked.

"Of course I would. I'll call him right now and get the number."

While they waited for their coffee, Crowley made his phone call. A minute later, Crowley was scratching down a phone number on a paper napkin.

"That was easy," Ava said.

Crowley ended his phone conversation and looked up at the two ladies in front of him. "I've got her number. I'll talk to her and then we'll know more."

"That's good of you. Thank you," Ettie said.

Crowley smiled. "How is Elsa-May today?"

"She's fine; we were just there giving her a meal. She's glad to be home."

CHAPTER 15

The next day, Ettie heard a knock on the door and hoped it was Crowley with information.

She opened the door, pleased to see it was indeed Crowley standing there with a smile on his face. She hoped that meant good news. "Do come in."

Ettie stepped aside to let the former detective into her home. He greeted Elsa-May who was lying on the couch propped up by pillows.

"You sit down and talk to Elsa-May. You're just in time for tea; I just boiled the pot."

Ettie had persuaded Elsa-May to lie on the couch instead of staying in her bed. It wasn't long before Ettie was back out in the living room pouring tea for Crowley.

"I'm anxious to know what you've learned from the doctor. Did you speak to her?" Ettie asked while she poured three cups of tea, setting one where Elsa-May could easily reach it.

"I did."

She passed Crowley a cup of tea, waiting for him to continue as she set down her own cup.

"I spoke to the doctor."

He seemed to be hesitating and Ettie wondered if the news was bad.

Ettie couldn't wait. "And what did you find out?"

"Something very interesting; something that I hadn't expected in the least."

The suspense was too much for her and Crowley wasn't helping her trembling hands with the way he was drawing things out. Ettie placed her teacup down on a table. "Go on."

Crowley rubbed his nose and his lips twitched. "Dr. Mackelvanner had been in contact with Mrs Esh, Jacob, and Camille. Nehemiah died in the hospital. Mackelvanner assisted the coroner and she wanted to run further tests but the coroner didn't agree. The coroner put his death down as heart disease, but for weeks something was nagging in the back of Mackelvanner's mind." He looked down into the teacup in his hands and slowly raised it to his lips.

Ettie looked over at Elsa-May, and when their eyes met, Elsa-May raised her eyebrows.

Once he took a sip of tea and the teacup was back on the saucer, he continued. "Her suspicions caused her to go over the coroner's head and go to the police."

"What were her suspicions, Detective?" Elsa-May asked bluntly.

"She feared he might have been poisoned."

Ettie's hand flew to her mouth.

"Then what happened?" Elsa-May asked.

"Her request for the body to be exhumed was denied. The only way to confirm or eliminate her suspicions was to get permission from the family to exhume the body, once the courts denied her request. That's when she contacted Mrs. Esh."

"Mildred did say she thought the doctor's name was familiar. I don't know how she wouldn't remember something as important as that, though," Ettie said. "The doctor really thinks Nehemiah was poisoned?"

"Correct. According to the doctor, Mrs. Esh referred her to the son, and the son didn't want to make the decision unless his sister agreed."

"And she met with Camille and they argued?" Ettie asked.

"She states that she did meet with Camille Esh on two different occasions and Camille was dead against it – pardon the pun. Dr. Mackelvanner said that Jacob agreed to it on the proviso that his sister also agreed. And there's something else I have to tell you."

Ettie took a deep breath. "Go on."

Crowley ran his tongue across the outside of his teeth as if his mouth was dry.

"Have more tea," Elsa-May suggested.

Crowley took a sip of tea, and then said, "It's nothing to be concerned about. I was at the station this morning, before I came here, to tell Kelly what I'd learned about the doctor and her suspicions. I ran into Jacob Esh at the station. I recognized him from the newspaper. I introduced myself to him and told him I was a friend of the both of you. I hope neither of you mind?"

"Not at all," Elsa May said, as Ettie waved a hand to dismiss his concern.

"And what did he say?" Ettie asked.

"I asked if he'd ever had a conversation with the doctor. He told me that the doctor first approached his stepmother and he said Mildred never made any decisions on her own. That's when the doctor spoke to Jacob. Because he never got along with his sister, he was loathe to agree alone that his father's body be touched. He referred the doctor to Camille and gave her Camille's cell phone number. And that's the last he heard from the doctor. Camille never mentioned the doctor to him and he never brought the subject up."

"Camille never mentioned that she'd met with the doctor?" Ettie asked.

"And met with the doctor more than once?" Elsa-May added.

"That's right. He said his sister never mentioned it to him and he never mentioned it to her. He admits to the fact that his sister never got along with him or he with her."

"I wonder why the authorities denied the doctor's request? Especially since the doctor had such suspicions."

"I thought about that and I spoke to a man I know at the courthouse. According to him there has to be 'good cause and exigent circumstances' for a body to be exhumed for an autopsy."

"And what does 'exigent circumstances' mean? I haven't come across that term before," Elsa-May said.

Crowley took a small notebook out of the top pocket of his shirt. "I wrote it down. Let's see now." He flipped some pages over. "Ah, here it is. It means that there must be clear evidence of probable cause."

"So, the doctor didn't have enough evidence to satisfy the court?"

"That's what it sounds like," Crowley said.

"Surely she had enough evidence to raise her suspicions. Wouldn't that have been enough?" Elsa-May asked.

Crowley shook his head. "It seems the court didn't think what evidence she had warranted such action. The state can't go digging up bodies willy-nilly."

"Does Kelly know about the doctor wanting to run more tests on Nehemiah?" Ettie asked.

"I went to tell him, but he wasn't there. He'll be back later today, after two o'clock."

"Under the circumstances, with Camille being murdered, do you think the police might be interested in exhuming the body now?"

Crowley placed his tea on the table in front of him. "It could go two ways. It might make things worse for Jacob if they find his father was poisoned. Have you considered that Kelly might think Jacob killed not only Camille but his father as well?"

Elsa-May shook her head. "I never thought of that."

Ettie glanced at the clock on the wall. "Two hours to go until two."

Crowley said, "Ettie, why don't we visit Mrs. Esh? We can ask her about the doctor."

"I've questioned her about the doctor before."

"Maybe she'll remember something she's forgotten."

CHAPTER 16

Crowley and Ettie sat in Mildred's living room. They'd said yes to tea and Mildred was busy in the kitchen preparing it.

"I'll help her. I won't be a moment," Ettie said to Crowley.

"Take your time. I don't know if I can fit another cup in anyway, just yet."

Ettie smiled, and then said, "Sip slowly."

When Ettie entered the kitchen, Mildred said, "He's a friend of yours?"

"*Jah,* he's here to help Jacob. He believes he's innocent, and he just wants to ask you some questions. It'll help Jacob." While Ettie placed cups and saucers on a tray she wondered how she'd feel if someone wanted to dig up her late husband's body.

Would she want to know if he'd been poisoned? It wouldn't bring him back.

Mildred poured boiling water into the teapot. "Okay, just a few more minutes and it'll be ready to pour. I'll carry the teapot, Ettie, and you carry the tray."

They placed the tray and the teapot on the low table between the two couches in the living room.

When Mildred sat down, she said, "You said you wanted to talk to me about a doctor?"

"That's right. Do you remember speaking to a doctor who wanted to exhume Nehemiah's body to run some tests?" Crowley asked. "Her name is Dr. Mackelvanner."

Mildred glanced at Ettie, and then looked back at the detective. "Ettie mentioned that name to me. I remember now that I did speak to her. She said she wanted to run some further tests but I said it was too late; he was buried. She wouldn't take no for an answer and kept talking at me. Eventually I told her to speak to Jacob since he's the man of the house now and probably should make all the decisions." She fiddled with the strings of her prayer *kapp*. "Why is it so important?"

"It seems the doctor has reason to believe your husband might have been murdered. And this doctor was seen arguing with your daughter on at least one, and possibly two, occasions," Crowley said.

"You mean stepdaughter," Mildred corrected him sternly.

Ettie was a little surprised; she'd never heard Mildred correct anybody from saying 'daughter' to 'stepdaughter'. She'd always called Jacob her son, so it seemed a little odd since she'd insisted recently that she treated them both the same.

"Yes, I'm sorry, stepdaughter," Crowley corrected himself.

"I'm not surprised that the doctor was arguing with Camille. Camille could send anyone crazy. You could be in a good mood and then Camille would say something hateful. She was like that. I think she liked to make people unhappy. If I didn't know any better I'd think she was the child of the devil."

Ettie nearly choked on the tea she was about to swallow. She coughed. Crowley put his tea down and patted Ettie on the back. Ettie coughed again.

"Oh dear, do you want some water?" Mildred asked.

"Jah," Ettie managed to say.

When Mildred was out of the room Ettie looked at Crowley.

"She's full of hate for an Amish person," Crowley said.

"I've never heard her say anything like that before," Ettie whispered.

Mildred hurried back. "There you go, Ettie."

Ettie took a mouthful of water. "Ah, that's better. *Denke."*

"About that doctor. I don't know why she wanted to do more tests. I didn't listen to what she had to say properly, but Nehemiah was dead and that was that. Jacob must have felt the same."

"You didn't talk to him about it?" Crowley asked. "The doctor told me that Jacob agreed, but only if his sister agreed as well."

"No. I gave him the number to call the doctor and then after he called her we never spoke of it again. He didn't tell me what he said to her and I never asked." Mildred crinkled her nose. "Everybody was scared of her and her anger; it just wasn't right."

"The doctor?" Ettie asked.

Mildred shook her head. "Camille. She was so full of bitterness and hatred toward Jacob she didn't want to – just didn't want him to have any little bit of happiness in his life. I suppose he was too scared to say 'yes' to the doctor and face Camille's anger if she'd disagreed."

Ettie nodded. "Didn't the doctor go into details when she was speaking to you of why she wanted Nehemiah's body exhumed?"

"I wasn't really listening. She said something about her not being happy with some test that she'd run and then I didn't really want to hear any more."

Crowley said, "She thinks she found evidence in the body of poisoning consistent with a substance called ethylene glycol, a common coolant used in motor vehicles."

Ettie gasped. "That's one of the poisons also found in Camille's body," Ettie said. "I didn't know that's what the doctor had found."

Crowley rubbed his jaw. "I guess I should have said so, but I didn't know that's what Camille died from."

"I thought I told you," Ettie said. "They found that poison and also another poison, which was sleeping tablets or something of the sort."

"They found that ethy… whatever it was in the barn. Jacob and I thought that Nehemiah must've used it to protect his metal tools."

Ettie rubbed her head. She jumped when she heard a loud bashing sound on Mildred's door. Seeing Mildred look so worried, Crowley jumped to his feet. "Shall I get that?"

Mildred nodded and then Ettie and Mildred followed Crowley, staying back a little way. Ettie wondered whether it was the police.

When Crowley opened the door, Ettie saw a red-faced Mr. Bradshaw from next door. "Where's Mrs. Esh?" he demanded.

"She's here. What's this about?"

"Who are you?"

"A friend of the family." Crowley put one arm up on the doorframe.

The man looked into the house. "Where is she?"

Crowley turned around to look at Mildred, and then Mildred stepped forward so Bradshaw could see her. "Yes?"

"I've just had the police come round and tell me that my fingerprints were found on the coolant you had in your barn. I told them, and now I'll tell you. I had that tin in my shed and you or your son stole it. That's why my fingerprints would've been on it. I'm not guilty of killing anyone." He stopped to take a breath. "Now, one of you stole it off my property and then killed someone with it. I want you or your son to admit to stealing it. I'm not going to prison for something I didn't do."

"Calm down. I'm sure the police just wanted to talk to you," Crowley said.

"What would you know? They said I should get a lawyer and they'll be speaking to me again."

Crowley took a step toward the man. "I think you should leave. Mrs. Esh has been through enough. Sounds like the police aren't accusing you of anything."

"Not yet they aren't." He took a step back and pointed his finger at Mildred. "Just get your coward son to admit to stealing it." He turned and strode away.

Ettie put her arm around Mildred's shoulder and felt her shaking. "Come, Mildred, sit back down," Ettie said and then steered her back to the living room.

"I'm sorry," Crowley said, following the two women. "I should've told him you weren't home."

"No. He might have come back when I was by myself."

Ettie sat next to Mildred. "Well, that explains what the poison was doing in the barn."

"No it doesn't; not really, because we still don't know who put it there," Crowley said, slumping into the couch.

"Does that mean that Jacob's prints weren't on the tin of poison?" Ettie asked.

"I'll find out." Crowley whipped his cell phone out of his pocket and walked outside.

Ettie turned to Mildred. "See? Things are looking good. If Jacob's prints weren't on the tin, then that should help his case."

Mildred swallowed hard and nodded.

When Crowley came back inside, he said, "They found two sets of prints: Bradshaw's, and... I'm afraid they found yours, Mildred."

Ettie looked at Mildred.

"I never go into the barn. How would my prints have gotten onto the thing? I hope they don't think I killed Nehemiah or Camille."

"When was the last time you went to the barn?"

"Maybe, um... I do recall I went in there a few weeks ago to fetch a stronger broom. The house broom was too soft to get some dirt off the back steps."

"The good thing is that Jacob's prints weren't found," Ettie said.

Crowley frowned. "We're going to need more than that to get him off."

Ettie and Ava stayed with Mildred until Jacob came home. When Crowley was driving Ettie home he said, "Are you still going through that list of names and addresses that Kelly gave you?"

"I am. Well, Ava is."

"Keep working through the list; there must be a clue in there somewhere. There's something we're missing."

"Will do. And while I'm doing that, can you see what else Kelly has found out?"

"I'll visit him tomorrow and come to your place in the afternoon."

CHAPTER 17

The next morning, Ettie got herself ready to go and see Ava Glick. She hoped Ava would have a free day to help her work through that phone list. Leah Miller kept coming to mind. She was someone who they could visit and she might know what was going on with Camille in those last weeks of her life.

When the taxi drew close to Ava's place, Ettie could see the horse in the paddock and she knew that Ava would be home. Ettie knocked on her door and waited. Ava opened the door. "Ettie!"

"Hello. I was hoping we could go over the phone list of Camille's again."

"I have to help my *mudder* today at the market."

Ettie nodded.

"Tell you what. I'll go there and see if she really needs me. She might not mind if I help her tomorrow instead."

"That would be good."

After they hitched the wagon, they traveled to the farmers' markets and Ettie told Ava all that had happened. "So I was thinking we should go and pay Leah Miller a visit."

"That's if it's the same Leah Miller that we know. There could be a lot of people with that name."

"*Nee,* it has to be the same one. She looked exactly the same in her photograph, only a little older."

"Yes, she did. Well, that will be our first call, if I don't have to work."

"I'll come in with you and talk to your *mudder.* I'll tell her I want to borrow you for the day."

Ava giggled. "Okay."

Their plan worked. Ava was able to have the day off if she worked the next day instead.

Once they were in the buggy again, Ava said, "You do have a way of talking people into things, Ettie."

"Do I? Now, where's that list?"

Ava pulled the list out from behind her seat and handed it to Ettie.

"Leah doesn't live far, but let's take your horse back and go by taxi. We'll cover more ground."

Ava turned the horse around and Ettie called a taxi from the shanty down the road.

ETTIE HAD the taxi wait for them while they knocked on the door of the address that was given to them. There were three small villa-apartments attached to one another. Leah's, according to their list, was number two. Ettie knocked on the door and her heart pounded heavily. What would she say to Leah? Leah hadn't gone to Camille's funeral, so had they been friends at all? Perhaps not.

"She's not home," someone yelled from the next-door property.

Ettie and Ava looked over the fence to see a young man.

"Do you know where she is?" Ava asked.

"At work, I'd say."

"Does she work close by?"

"Down at the ice-creamery."

"Sprinkles?"

"Yeah, that's the one," the young man said.

"Thank you," Ettie said.

"No problem."

As they were walking back to the taxi, Ettie asked Ava, "You know where that is?"

Ava nodded. "*Jah.* I love ice cream and they have the best in town."

"What name does Leah go by now?"

"Lacey Miller."

"That's right."

This time when the taxi pulled up at the ice-creamery, they paid the driver and let him go. "If she's not here we can have some ice cream. I won't be having ice cream for quite a while now that Elsa-May has to cut down on her food."

"You can't eat less, Ettie; you're already thin."

"I always stay the same weight no matter how much or how little I eat. I've got a good constitution. Elsa-May was always on the heavy side. I can't eat ice cream in front of her."

Ava giggled. "I suppose not. That would be cruel."

The building they were walking toward was just at the town's edge. It was a white double-story building with white tables and chairs outside, and a pink and white umbrella over every table.

"Shall we sit inside or out?" Ettie asked.

"Maybe we should sit inside. There might be more chance of seeing Leah."

"Okay, you go first."

Ava walked in through the automatic-opening glass sliding door, and Ettie followed. Ettie scanned the faces of the girls behind the counter and couldn't see Leah. They looked at the array of ice creams, sorbets, and gelatos. Ava ordered a strawberry delight, which was a scoop each of strawberry sorbet and strawberry ice cream topped with cream and strawberry slivers, all sprinkled with dark chocolate flakes.

Ettie ordered a coffee-choc surprise, which had coffee and chocolate ice cream, dark Dutch chocolate ice cream, and whipped cream with white chocolate slivers.

They were given numbers for their orders and told to take a seat.

When Ava was given her number she asked, “Is Lacey working today?”

“She’s on a break. She’ll be back in a minute.”

“Oh, good.”

Ettie and Ava found a table at the side of the room. There weren’t many people sitting inside because it was such a nice day. While they waited, Ava produced the list of names. She pointed to a man’s name. “We should look at this man next. He’s the one who had the criminal record. That is, if it’s the same man I read about in the paper.”

“A petty criminal. I wonder what Camille was doing talking to him.”

“A boyfriend perhaps? People who go on those dating websites meet all kinds of people. They could’ve gone on a date.”

“What are you talking about a dating website for? Was Camille doing that kind of thing?”

Ava shrugged. "Could've been."

They both looked up to see Leah walking toward them carrying their ice creams. Leah had a huge smile and seemed pleased to see them. She greeted them and placed their ice creams down on the table.

Ettie and Ava stood up and hugged her.

"Can you sit with us for a while?" Ettie asked.

Leah nodded. "I'm the manager so I can basically do what I want," she said with a little laugh. "How did you know I worked here? One of the girls said you asked for me."

"We heard you worked here," Ava said. "I've been here before, but I've never seen you here."

"I've not been here long, around three months. I was managing another store in town."

Ettie needed to change the subject so she wouldn't have to tell her she was on Camille's illegally-gotten phone list. Looking at her ice cream, she said, "I don't think I'll be able to get through this. It's huge."

Leah giggled. "What's been happening in the community? I heard about Jacob Esh," she said.

"That's actually what we came to talk to you about," Ava said.

"Yes, were you friends with Camille?"

"Not good friends. We knew each other." Leah breathed out heavily. "I've been bothered by something. I've even had nightmares about it, I feel so guilty. I didn't want to get into trouble so I kept quiet about it, but now seeing you two has made me feel even more guilty about it."

"What is it?" Ettie asked.

Leah leaned forward. "Camille asked me to go to the police and tell them that she thought her brother was trying to kill her."

"So it was you who told the police that?"

Leah nodded. "You heard?"

Ettie nodded. "That's the main reason the police were looking at Jacob."

"Oh no! She said it was just a prank she was playing on her brother."

"What made you do it? It doesn't sound like a prank to me," Ava said.

Leah blinked a couple times and looked away. "She gave me two thousand dollars to do it and I needed the money at the time. I changed my mind after she left, but I did need the money, so I went through with it. She told me exactly what to tell them and she wrote down the date she wanted me to go and see them."

"Do you still have that note?"

"I wouldn't think so. I don't keep anything I don't need. When I found out she'd been killed I felt really bad about going to the police, but if he's innocent he'll have nothing to worry about."

"Do you think that Camille did think her brother was trying to kill her?" Ava asked.

She shrugged. "I don't know. I felt awful when I found out what happened to Camille, and then that they'd arrested Jacob. They came around and I had to go back to the station and verify what I'd told them. I didn't tell them that she asked me - and paid me - to say it. I lied to them. I've been so worried; I don't want to get into trouble by telling them I lied to them twice. The first time I went there I didn't even know that Camille had already died."

"You must tell them, Leah," Ava said.

"Lacey. It's Lacey now," Leah said.

"Sorry, Lacey. They're heavily relying on that information and it's making Jacob look guilty. Now with everything else they're finding out, they're framing it in the reference that he was trying to kill her, if you see what I mean." Ava's voice trailed away.

Leah breathed out heavily. "Could I get charged or something?"

Ettie patted Leah's hand. "I don't think you'll get into trouble. They just want to know the truth."

Ava added, "It's possible Jacob might be charged with murder if they find him guilty."

Leah's eyes opened wide. "I'll go to the police when I finish work."

"Could you do it now?" Ettie asked.

"We'll go with you," Ava said.

"Would you?"

Ettie and Ava nodded.

"I'll take the rest of the day off, then. You wait here and I'll get my things."

When Leah left them, Ettie and Ava looked down at their ice creams.

"I'll race you," Ava said.

"*Nee,* ice cream should be eaten slowly and savored." Ettie pushed her spoon into the coffee flavored ice cream as that was her favorite flavor. She could smell the strong coffee aroma before she placed it into her mouth. The texture was smooth and creamy.

Ava had pushed the cream and the strawberries aside and was spooning the strawberry ice cream into her mouth as quickly as she could.

"We must come back here another day," Ettie said as she loaded her spoon with both coffee and chocolate ice cream.

Ava's mouth was full so she could only nod.

Leah sat down again. She had her bag over one shoulder, a sweater over one arm, and a car key in her hand hanging from a keychain.

"You've got a car?" Ettie asked.

"Yes. I'll drive us there. Don't hurry; I'll wait until you finish."

"No. I think we're ready. Aren't we, Ettie?"

"I'm good to go."

Leah led the way out to a small Honda Civic. It was only a two-door, so Ava squeezed past the front seat into the back, and Ettie sat in the front.

"I'm so glad you both came in today. This was weighing heavily on me. I'll feel so much better once I tell the truth."

"The truth sets us free," Ettie said.

"I'll have to pay back the money she gave me. I don't have it right now, but I must go and see Mrs. Esh to tell her I'll pay it back."

"Who were you speaking to at the station?" Ettie asked.

"He was a detective. I don't remember his name."

"What did he look like?"

"Hard to describe. He just looked like a detective, I guess."

"Detective Kelly's the one looking into things."

"Yes, that's it. I'm sure that was his name."

Ettie was satisfied that the police would have one less piece of evidence against Jacob. Without Leah's testimony there was no proof that Camille had feared for her life from Jacob. Now it would be known that Camille had said she was playing a prank – little did Camille know that she'd be dead when the prank played out.

CHAPTER 18

After Leah Miller made her confession to Detective Kelly about taking part in Camille's prank, Kelly wasn't at all happy and Leah was in tears. When Leah came out of his office, she told Ettie and Ava between sobs that Kelly had warned her in a nasty manner of the seriousness of what she'd done.

"Are you all right to drive, Leah?" Ava asked when the three women were standing together on the front steps of the police station.

Leah wiped her nose with a tissue. "I'm okay. Can I drive you two home?"

Ava and Ettie looked at each other, and then Ettie said, "Ava and I have some things to do in town. Thank you once again for being honest. It will help Jacob out of the mess he's in."

"Good. I can't imagine he'd do a thing like that."

Ava asked, "You wouldn't happen to know a man called Nick Heaton, would you?"

Leah thought for a moment. "No. I don't recall that I do. Why?"

"He was someone Camille knew. I was just wondering if you knew him too."

After Leah left, Ava said, "I wonder if Kelly has found out any more about the people on the list? Especially because Nick Heaton might have a criminal record if, he's the same one I found on the Internet."

"Shall we go in and ask? By the sound of things he's not in a good mood."

Just then Kelly came out of the building.

"Mrs. Smith and her side-kick."

Ava screwed up her nose.

"We were just coming in to speak to you."

"I know you think things are looking better for Jacob Esh, but we've just found out something to make our case even stronger."

"You have?"

"The will that Camille conveniently wrote just days before she died was written by Jacob."

"No. That's not possible."

"It's possible, it's probable, and it happened. We have a forensic handwriting analyst who's willing to testify that the will was not written by the hand of Camille Esh, and that it was, in fact, written by the hand of her brother, Jacob Esh."

"Jacob's fingerprints weren't found on the tin of the poison that killed her."

"He could well have used gloves."

"What about the man next door? His fingerprints were found and he wanted the farm. With Camille killed and Jacob in jail for murder, Mildred would most likely sell the farm."

"We talked to him. He claims the tin was stolen from him and that's why his prints were on it."

"And you believed him? Why don't you believe Jacob? If he shot at her while she was in her apartment, why was the gun just left with all his other guns? Wouldn't he have hidden the gun somewhere?"

"Perhaps he wasn't aware that the gun could be traced. He is Amish, after all, and like all you people he's only had a limited education."

"If you knew anything about us you'd know that some of us continue our schooling from home." Ava said bluntly, "And Jacob lived outside the Amish community for about twenty years."

Ettie could see Ava was getting upset so she put her hand on Ava's arm. "Let's go, Ava."

Ettie and Ava went home in separate taxis. Feeling completely defeated, Ettie pushed the front door open. She was pleased to see Elsa-May sitting up and looking brighter.

"I'm sorry I've hardly been here today."

"You look dreadful."

"I'll put the dinner on and then I'll sit with you and tell you all about it. Things aren't looking good for Jacob."

An hour later, Ettie had told Elsa-May all that had happened that day.

"They can tell that Camille didn't write the will?"

"Apparently so."

"It is beginning to look like he's guilty. It doesn't make sense that she would get Leah to tell the police she thought Jacob was trying to kill her."

"Perhaps she was acting out of spite since he got the farm. She might have been trying to disrupt his life by having the police come and question him, or something like that."

A knock sounded on their door.

"That might be Ava. She was very upset by what Kelly said to us. He was really quite rude when speaking about our community and the people in it."

Ettie swung the door open to see old Detective Crowley. "When are you ladies going to get a phone?"

"Crowley! Come in."

The former detective walked in and sat down. "How are you, Elsa-May?"

"I'm so much better. I feel better than I've felt in a long time."

Ettie sat down on the couch. "Do you have news?"

Crowley gave a sharp nod. "I do. I struggled with myself for a while. I know medical records are confidential and I don't have the authority anymore to look into things..."

"Yes?" Elsa-May said.

"I got my friend at the hospital to look up Camille Esh's file. Or, in fact, to see if she had a file. Both my contact at the hospital and I could get into a lot of trouble over this, so I have to be careful how I let Kelly know about it."

Ettie was now on the edge of the couch. "About what?"

"Camille had recently been diagnosed with the same fatal disease that you told me her mother died from."

"Oh my," Ettie said. "That's no good."

"And that's how she knew Dr. Mackelvanner?" Elsa-May asked.

Crowley shook his head. "No. She was under a different doctor."

"I haven't told you yet, but we found the woman who told the police that Camille feared Jacob was going to kill her. Camille had paid her to say that. We happened to know the young woman and we went with her to the police station. Kelly wasn't happy about it. She's going to look and see if she's still got the instructions Camille wrote down for her."

"That's one good thing for Jacob," Crowley said. "I'm thinking more that the stepmother, Mildred, might have had some involvement. If Camille told her that she had the disease, might Mildred have killed her to lessen her suffering? I saw Kelly earlier, and he said that Camille's will was a forgery. What if Mildred wanted Jacob to inherit the money Camille had – keep Camille's money with Jacob? Since Camille didn't get along with anyone in her family, she might have preferred her money end up elsewhere."

Ettie pulled her mouth to one side. "I don't think that Mildred is so focused on money, though, Detective. Besides, Kelly said their expert said Jacob wrote the will."

Elsa-May said, "My pick is the neighbor. He seems to have a bad temper and his prints were on the tin of poison. Also, it wouldn't have been hard for him to take the gun, drive past Camille's apartment, shoot at her, and then put the gun back in the house once Mildred had gone out."

"If that's true, the neighbor is taking a very indirect route to get the farm, don't you think? I mean, how could he have thought it all up?" Crowley asked.

"From what Ettie said, Bradshaw didn't like Camille anyway. It seems a good way to solve two problems at once; get rid of the two people who were standing in his way of buying the farm."

Ettie gasped. "It's just occurred to me. Elsa-May could be right. What if Nehemiah was killed by Bradshaw?"

"It could be possible, as they were neighbors and if they met often for a drink in the afternoon or something like that. I think the poison has to be administered over a time," Crowley said.

Ettie shook her head. "I don't think he'd drink or eat with an *Englischer.*"

"But we don't know that for certain, Ettie. He probably didn't, but he could've."

"What are you going to do?" Ettie asked Crowley. "Are you going to tell Kelly what you found out about Camille being ill?"

Crowley nodded. "I will, but I'll have to figure out how to do it without appearing to have bent the rules."

"What would you do now, if you were working the case?" Ettie asked.

"I'd have Nehemiah's body exhumed and retested."

Elsa-May said. "Who do you think might have killed him?"

Crowley raised his hands in the air. "We'd have to establish whether he was killed first. No good putting the cart before the horse."

"What else would you do?" Ettie asked.

"Then I'd go through all of Camille's phone contacts and I'd get a second opinion on the handwriting of the will. I'd also get the tin re-examined for further prints. Then I'd talk to Camille's doctor to see if he could shed light on anything."

"Then that's what you must get Kelly to do," Elsa-May said.

Crowley tilted his head and sniffed the air. "That smells delicious."

"Ah. I must turn off the stove." Ettie pushed herself to her feet. "Care to join us for dinner? I've made a pot pie."

"I'd be delighted."

EARLY THE NEXT MORNING, Ava knocked on Ettie and Elsa-May's door. When she was sitting in their living room she said why she'd come.

"I was so upset last night I couldn't settle. So I went to Nick Heaton's."

Ettie's jaw dropped. "Why? Why would you do that?"

"Don't get mad at me; he wasn't there. The man he lived with said he's in jail. We got talking, and I asked him about Camille and he didn't know if his friend knew Camille or anything."

"So it was a wasted trip and you put yourself in danger."

"*Nee*. I haven't finished."

"Go on."

"He remembers one night Nick came home and told him about some lady paying him to have him shoot into an apartment. She gave him gloves to wear, the gun she wanted him to use, and the bullets. Then she'd told him to cover the gun with a towel and leave it in the trash can at a nearby park."

Ettie gasped, "Did you hear that Elsa-May?" she yelled out to Elsa-May, who was still in bed.

"*Jah!* That's interesting, but Kelly won't believe it unless it comes from the man himself. And only Kelly can talk to him if he's in jail," Elsa-May yelled back.

Ava said, "I wanted to come and tell you last night, but I thought you could do with a good night's sleep."

"Crowley visited us last night. He told us that Camille had the same disease that her mother died from."

"That's awful. Is that why she wasn't nice to people? Doesn't it affect the brain or something?"

"It does." Ettie nodded. "Don't tell anyone that Crowley found that out; he did it by illegal means and he has to figure out a way to let Kelly know that Camille was sick. He'll have to find a way to suggest that Kelly look into Camille's medical history."

"From what we know, Camille paid someone to shoot into her apartment and then paid Leah to tell the police she feared for her life."

Ettie shook her head. "What if it was Mildred?"

"Ettie! Isn't she a good friend of yours?"

"*Ach.* I don't know what to think anymore. The more I think about it, the more I find reasons that any number of people could've killed her. Crowley said he's going to see Kelly today and he'll try to push him to do some things."

"That's good. Like what?"

"See Camille's doctor, for one. Then take a second look for more prints on the bottle of coolant, and get another handwriting expert to take a look at the will for a second opinion. I think that's all. That's all I can remember, anyway."

"That'll be good. It's good to have him on Jacob's side. Have you spoken to Jacob lately?"

"*Nee*. Not for a while, but I think I should. I just can't shake the disappointment about finding out Camille's will was written by him."

"It wouldn't hurt for us to go and visit his *haus* just in time for the midday meal, would it? We know he comes home to eat."

Ettie nodded. "I'll go fix Elsa-May something to eat before we go. Then I must come home and wait for Crowley. He's going to tell me how he got on with Kelly."

CHAPTER 19

Ettie and Ava came across Jacob before they reached Mildred's house. He was fixing some fences by the road.

He looked up and waved when he heard them approach. When Ava stopped the buggy, he walked over. "I want to thank you both for helping me. *Mamm* says you've been doing a lot of looking into things."

"We have," Ettie said, climbing down from the buggy. "I do have a question to ask you."

"Sure."

"The detective says that they found out that the will was written in your handwriting."

"Yes, it was."

Ettie frowned at him. "You wrote it yourself?"

He nodded. "Camille came to me and told me that she wanted to write a will and leave the money she had to me. I was shocked, but we were *bruder* and *schweschder* and she had no one else. She met me in the fields, just like how you came across me today, and she had a paper and a pen. She wanted me to write it out because she never had much schooling and wasn't good at writing. I wrote word for word what she asked me to write and then she signed it. She asked me to keep it secret and I never told anyone. I know the police are trying to make something of it."

Ettie shook her head. "It does sound bad."

"It makes sense the way you explain it," Ava said.

Ettie nodded. "I see how it came about."

"Anything else you want to ask me?"

Ettie shook her head. "I can't think of anything for the moment."

"Do you know a man called Nick Heaton?" Ava asked.

"I believe I looked at a used car being sold at one of his car lots. And he might be the man Camille bought her car from."

"One of his car lots?"

"*Jah,* he buys and sells used cars. I think he's got two or three places he sells used cars from."

"Would it surprise you that he's in prison?"

Jacob tipped his hat back on his head. "I suppose it does. What did he do?"

Ava and Ettie looked at each other. Ettie said, "We're not sure yet."

"Well, then I'll have someone I know in there."

"Jacob, you mustn't let those thoughts come into your head."

"I think it's best to be prepared. If I'm found innocent, well and good, and if not, I'll be prepared to face whatever they throw at me. I'm not going to live in fear."

Ettie nodded.

After they said goodbye to Jacob, Ava asked, "Do you want to visit Mildred?"

"*Nee,* not today. There are some loose ends that I wish Kelly would help us with. Someone should talk to Nick Heaton in prison and see what his dealings were with Camille. The detective talked about looking into the trust fund to see if there was money missing and I never heard any more about it."

"Most likely there was no money missing and Kelly would've put it down to the fact that Jacob knew Camille was leaving him the money anyway."

"Hmm. I wonder if Jacob's told Kelly yet that Camille had him write the will."

"'Says he.' That's what Kelly would say."

Ettie peered into Ava's face. "You're most likely right. Don't you have to work today? Or was it yesterday?"

Ava giggled. "*Mamm* gave me the week off. She could tell my mind was elsewhere and she said they've been quiet."

"Good. Now, I must go home and wait for Crowley. Care to join me?"

Ava nodded. "Let's go."

THAT AFTERNOON, Crowley walked into the house and took a seat.

"How did things go with Kelly?"

"He's put a request to the court to have Nehemiah's body exhumed."

Ettie put her fingers to her mouth. "From what you said before, I don't know if that's a good thing or a bad thing." Ettie told Crowley how Jacob said it came about that he wrote his sister's will out and she made him say he wouldn't mention it to anyone.

"There's an awful lot against him with only his say-so to defend himself. I know you've never been wrong before, Ettie, but are you really certain this time?"

"I believe in his innocence."

Crowley nodded. "We have to wait and see what Nehemiah's

autopsy brings."

"There is the matter of the other people on Camille's phone list. Ava and I found that... Well, I'll let Ava tell you."

Ava told Crowley about what she'd learned from Nick Heaton's flat mate.

"I'm sure Kelly wouldn't mind if I talk to the fellow."

"Really? That would be wonderful."

IT WAS a week later that Crowley came to tell Elsa-May and Ettie that Nehemiah's body was exhumed and re-examined and it was found that Nehemiah's death was not due to poisoning with ethylene glycol.

"Where does that leave Jacob?" Elsa-May asked.

"Have you spoken to that man in prison yet?" Ettie asked.

"Firstly, Elsa-May, I'm not sure where that leaves Jacob. And Ettie, I have spoken to Nick Heaton. We've only just gotten the information out of him. He said he'd only give me information if the courts lessened his sentence."

"What did he say?" Ettie asked.

"The courts cooperated and cut his time in prison down in exchange for him providing information. It was actually Kelly who spoke to him and got his statement."

"And?" Elsa-May asked.

"He said that some woman paid him to shoot a gun into an apartment and when he was done he had to wrap the gun in a towel and leave it in the park."

"That's exactly what his flatmate told Ava."

"He positively identified the woman as Camille Esh."

"From a photograph?" Ettie asked.

"It would have to be from a photograph, Ettie, since the woman's dead."

Ettie pressed her lips together as she stared at her sister.

Crowley added. "He got paid two thousand dollars."

"That must have been her number for everything. It was also the amount that she paid Leah Miller," Ettie said.

"Is Jacob in the clear now?"

"No. Jacob's prints were on the cup in her apartment identified as having poison in it, and Jacob forged the will."

"Yes, but Camille signed the will. Jacob told us how it all happened."

Ettie closed her eyes for a second and then glanced up at the clock on the wall.

"It's four o'clock. Would Kelly still be at the station?"

"I guess so. He probably will be there until seven tonight."

"Will you drive me to see him? I've just figured the whole thing out."

"You have?" Crowley jumped to his feet.

"I'm coming too," Elsa-May said.

"Are you well enough?" Ettie asked.

"I'm not going to miss this."

"I'll call him and tell him we're coming."

CHAPTER 20

When the four of them were settled in Detective Kelly's office, Kelly leaned back in his chair. "This will be entertaining. Go ahead, Mrs. Smith."

"We have a young girl, Camille Esh. Her mother got sick and was prone to fits of rage. She beat her young daughter, leaving internal scars that would never heal. When Mary died, Camille's father did the best he could for her and her brother. He married another woman, but Camille, even though she was young, never let herself love again."

Detective Kelly laughed. "I didn't know you were a psychiatrist, Mrs. Smith."

Ettie ignored his jab and continued, "The pain of loving and trusting someone only to be betrayed as her mother had betrayed her would be too much. Camille built invisible walls around her heart to save herself from further pain."

"Is this going to take long?" Kelly glanced at his watch.

Ettie cleared her throat, and then said, "Her inner hate of her brother was most likely spurred by the hatred she was shown by her mother. The trauma of her youth never left her. When she found she had inherited the disease her mother had, she hatched a plan. She didn't want to suffer like her mother had and die a death full of mental torture. She decided to end her life, and at the same time, she'd implicate her brother and ruin his life."

"Yes, if she had to go she'd take him with her," Elsa-May added. "Because her father, the only person she loved, had showed preference to her brother by leaving him the farm. She must've been outraged beyond belief.

"That's why she met him in the fields and had him write the will, and she signed it in front of him. He was surprised but she told him not to tell anyone. She took cups from the house after Jacob had used them, and used those same cups at her own apartment."

"So," Kelly said, "she paid Nick Heaton to shoot into her apartment and her other friend to say she thought her brother was trying to kill her. Yes, I must say I did have the same thoughts as you when I heard she had a fatal illness. I even talked to her doctor and found she had asked about the possibility of euthanasia."

"She did?"

"Yes, when she first got the diagnosis," Kelly said nodding. "I had it set in my mind that she killed herself and wanted her brother to take the blame. It's just what a spiteful woman would do and I've known a few of those in my time, believe me. She found out she didn't have long to live, so she poisons herself with the coolant, doesn't like how painful it is, so she speeds things along with a dose of pills, grinds them down into a drink and drinks them in a cup with Jacob's fingerprints that she's gotten from her stepmother's house. She dies and no one knows about her illness or the fact that she's paid people to bolster up her evil plot with evidence against her older brother."

"So you believe me?" Ettie asked.

"Like I said, I had come to the same conclusion as you, until I had the forensic team have another look at that signature on Camille Esh's will."

"And?" Crowley asked.

"We got a sample of handwriting from Mrs. Esh, and I'm afraid it's a match."

"A match to Mildred's handwriting?"

"That's right, Mrs. Smith. The signature on the will was in the handwriting of Mildred Esh. The body of the text was in Jacob's handwriting as he admits, but he was lying about Camille signing it."

A hush fell across the room.

Detective Kelly turned to Ettie. "You don't know who you can trust, Mrs. Smith. I believe I told you days ago that sometimes people can do things that surprise even themselves." He glanced at his watch. "It's too late now, but tomorrow I'm going to have Mildred Esh explain herself to me."

"You haven't spoken with her yet?" Crowley asked.

"The handwriting report only just came through." Kelly looked at Ettie. "I was beginning to listen to you and look for other possibilities, but now I know Jacob has been lying about the will. What else has he been lying about?"

Ettie didn't say anything, remembering that Mildred's prints had been found on the bottle of ethylene glycol. Could Mildred have had something to do with Camille's death?

On the way out of the station, Ettie said to Crowley, "What's the time now?"

He looked at his watch. "A little before five."

"Feel like a visit to Mildred?" Ettie whispered.

"Kelly is intending on talking to her tomorrow," Elsa-May said.

"Exactly why we should go now," Ettie said

Crowley nodded and drove the ladies to Mildred's house. Before they pulled up, Ettie said, "Let me do the talking."

"I was intending to," Crowley said. "Because I've got no idea what you're up to."

Once they were seated in Mildred's house, Ettie asked, "What time do you expect Jacob home?"

"In another hour or so."

"Mildred, I'm afraid I've got something to tell you," Ettie said.

Mildred raised her eyebrows.

"Detective Kelly is coming here tomorrow to ask you to go into the station for questioning."

"About what?"

"I think you know." Ettie stared at Mildred until Mildred looked away.

Then Mildred put her head in her hands. "I thought it was a harmless thing to do."

"What was?" Crowley asked and then he got a sharp dig in the ribs from Ettie's elbow.

"Go on. You'll feel better if you tell us," Ettie said.

Mildred looked up at them and they saw her eyes brimming with tears. "I didn't think there would be any harm. I mean, the money would most likely have gone to Jacob anyway. Camille didn't write the will, but I heard the government takes out a lot of money if someone hasn't left a will. I don't know if that's true, but that's what I've heard."

"So you and Jacob wrote that will and not Camille?" Ettie asked.

Jacob stepped into the room. "That's right."

All heads turned to look at Jacob as he loomed in the doorway of the living room. He took a few more steps into the room and sat down next to his stepmother. "I'm sorry I lied about that, but I was just trying to protect my *mudder.*"

"It was my idea, not Jacob's. The money had come from Nehemiah and he would've wanted it to go to Jacob. I forced Jacob to do it."

"Did you also make Jacob end Camille's life to prevent her suffering?" Crowley asked.

"No! We'd never do anything like that. I don't know who killed her. It wasn't me or my mother." Jacob placed his arm around his stepmother.

Ettie turned and looked at Crowley before she licked her lips and added, "Remember what Kelly said? He thought what I thought, except when he found out about the will."

A loud knock sounded on the door, causing Ettie to jump.

Jacob sprang to his feet to answer it. Loud voices were heard, and a few seconds later Kelly walked into the room.

"And here we all are," Kelly said, looking at each person in turn. "When I saw you all hurrying away from the station, I guessed this would be the place you were heading."

"Have a seat, Detective," Jacob said. "I may as well tell you what it was I just told them."

Kelly sat down in the only spare armchair. "Go ahead."

"My mother and I are responsible for writing that will. The will was the only thing I lied about to you, and for that, I'm sorry."

"So you admit to falsifying a legal document?"

"Yes," Jacob nodded.

"That's a serious crime. It's a felony in the third degree. You could both face jail time and a hefty fine."

Mildred leaned forward. "It was my idea, and I was the one who signed it, so I'm just as guilty as Jacob. No, I'm more guilty because it was all my idea."

Detective Kelly shook his head. "This is interesting. Mrs. Esh, you admit to forging your stepdaughter's will and your fingerprints are on the container - the nearly empty container - of coolant found in your barn."

"I remember now how my fingerprints would've gotten on that container. I went to find Jacob after a visit from Camille. She'd yelled at me and then said she'd wait for Jacob in the barn, and if I was to see Jacob I was to tell him she was in the barn. When I heard her drive away some time later, I went into the barn and saw some things knocked off the shelves. I didn't want Jacob to know she'd messed things up, so I tidied everything up. I could well have picked up the container while I was tidying. I didn't read the labels of the things I picked up."

"That sounds reasonable," Ettie said.

Kelly stared hard at Mildred. "You'd better be telling the truth this time, Mrs. Esh."

"Detective," said Ettie, "it occurred to me that Dr. Mackelvanner's inquiries over Nehemiah gave Camille information about coolant being so deadly. Doesn't that make you think that what you and I suspected was right – that Camille did kill herself? And, for that matter, wouldn't Jacob normally have picked things up if he'd found them knocked over in the barn? Thus getting his prints on them? Maybe that had been Camille's intention."

"Is that what you think? You think she killed herself?" Mildred looked directly at Kelly. Jacob once again put a comforting arm around his stepmother's shoulder.

Kelly raised his eyebrows at Mildred. "It's a strong possibility. Knowing that she was only going to die soon anyway and the fact that she was so bitter about her father leaving Jacob the farm." Kelly raised his hands in the air. "I guess we'll have to leave that for the courts to decide."

CHAPTER 21

Ettie groaned. Things looked bad for Jacob and Mildred since they'd lied about Camille's will. Would the courts believe Jacob was innocent of killing his sister? If so, would Jacob and Mildred go to jail over the fake will?

When Crowley and Ettie's eyes met, he said, "Are you ready to go?"

Ettie nodded. She'd done as much as she could to help Jacob, and now it seemed as though everything was out of her hands. Kelly was the first to leave Mildred's house and then Crowley, Elsa-May, Ava, and Ettie said goodbye to Mildred and Jacob.

While the four of them were driving back to Elsa-May and Ettie's house in Crowley's car, Ettie mulled the whole thing over. There were the cups with Jacob's prints in her apartment; his prints weren't even on the bottle of poison. They'd found that Camille had been lying about feeling she was in danger from her brother, and Camille had paid someone to shoot into her apartment making it look like there had been an attempt on her life. How could the police still be holding Jacob accountable? Surely it wouldn't go to trial.

"I'm certain Jacob's lawyer should be able to get him off now. They don't have much to build a case on," Crowley said.

"Yes, I was just going over everything in my head. The only thing they have against him now is some cups in Camille's house with his prints," Ettie said.

"And the will he and Mildred wrote," Elsa-May was quick to point out.

"But did she really kill herself?" Ava asked.

"That might be something we'll never know for sure," Crowley said.

"Turn the car around, Crowley!" Ettie shouted from the back seat.

Crowley hit the breaks and pulled the car off to the side of the road. "What is it?"

"Turn the car around. We're going to Camille's apartment," Ettie said.

Crowley turned his head to look at Ettie. "You know where it is?"

"Her address was on top of the paper with her phone records that Kelly gave me." After Ettie gave Crowley the address, he turned the car around.

"What do you hope to find?" Elsa-May asked.

"And how are we going to get in?" Ava added.

"Ava, don't all people around the age of forty have a tablet, computer, or a laptop computer, or something of the sort?"

"I guess if they're *Englisch* most of them do."

"Just tell us what you're getting at," Elsa-May blurted out.

"It occurred to me that if I were going to kill myself, I would find out the best way to do that."

"And you're thinking she would've used the Internet and researched ways to kill herself?" Crowley asked. "I like it."

"So, you're going to check the search history if we find a computer?" Ava said.

"Not me. One of you will have to do that," Ettie said. "I only know that there is a search history; I wouldn't know how to go about finding it."

"I'm surprised you know something like that in the first place, Ettie," Crowley said.

"I know a thing or two," Ettie said with a smile.

"How are we going to get in?" Ava asked again.

"I don't suppose you also have a key, do you, Ettie?" Crowley asked.

"We'll find a way when we get there," Ettie answered.

"Couldn't we get into trouble? Isn't it breaking and entering?" Ava asked.

Ettie shook her head. "It's hardly breaking and entering if the person who had the lease on the apartment is dead."

"I don't know what the landlord would say about that," Crowley said as he stopped the car outside Camille's apartment building.

"It's number four," Ettie said.

"I'll stay in the car. My leg needs to rest," Elsa-May said.

"Sorry, Elsa-May. We should've driven you home first," Ettie said.

"I'm okay, don't mind me. These leather seats are nice and soft. Just hurry up."

Crowley said, "There's a button on the side of your seat near the door. Push it to lay your seat back."

Elsa-May pushed the button and her seat tilted back. "Aaah, I just might go to sleep." Elsa-May closed her eyes.

When the others got out of the car, Crowley said, "You two keep your voices down. We don't want to draw attention to ourselves."

They found apartment number four just one flight up. Then they stood outside the door. Ava tried the window, but it was locked.

"You're not a detective anymore, so just pick the lock or something," Ettie said to Crowley as the three of them stood in front of the door.

"I was a detective, not a criminal," he whispered back.

"But how are we going to get in if you can't pick the lock?" Ettie asked.

"All right, I'll do it," Crowley said while reaching into his pocket. "But don't tell anybody I know how to do this."

A giggle escaped Ettie's lips. "I thought you would've learned a few skills at your age."

Crowley kneeled on one knee. "I did have a few associations with some dubious people before I got onto the Force."

The former detective poked two metal things into the keyhole. Ettie peered over his shoulder to see what he was doing. He pushed the first metal rod in and then held it steady as though it was holding a lever, while the other metal rod appeared to be pushing something down. They heard a 'click.'

"Got it," he said. He pushed the door open and looked back at them. "Don't make any loud noises and don't turn any lights on. We'll use the light from my phone, and that's all."

Once they were in, Crowley shut the door behind them, and without the light from the hallway they were in darkness until Crowley flicked a switch on his cell phone. After some minutes of looking through cupboards and drawers, Crowley found a laptop in the drawer of the nightstand.

"Don't touch it," Crowley said to them as he spread his arms to keep them back.

They stopped still and watched him.

Ettie was amazed to see Crowley remove plastic gloves from his pocket. He pulled them on and said, "Fingers crossed."

"Are you sure of what you're doing?" Ettie asked.

"Of course I know what I'm doing or I wouldn't be doing it." A few pushes of some buttons, and a long list came up on the screen. Crowley scrolled down. "And there we have it, as clear as day."

"What is it?" Ettie and Ava asked at the same time.

"Search histories on DNA evidence, what poisoning with ethylene glycol does and how to implicate someone in a murder."

"Really? It's all on there?" Ettie asked, more surprised than pleased.

Ava straightened up. "I would never have believed it."

"I'm afraid I'm going to have to call Kelly and tell him what we've found. I'll have to take this in as evidence."

"What you've found. You can keep us out of it," Ettie said. "And make sure he deputizes you first or something of the kind so you don't get into trouble."

"I think when he sees this he'll be glad to have it," Crowley said.

Ava said, "I wonder why the police didn't take the laptop with them when they came here?"

Crowley answered, "She was murdered, they thought. If she was a suspect then they would've taken all her devices with them." He raised the laptop in his hands. "And we'll easily be able to verify whether or not this was in her possession on the dates she looked up all those sites, judging by the times she accessed her emails or other things like that. The tech people can verify things like that."

"That looks like the power cord," Ava said, pointing to the cord on the floor.

"I'll take that too," Crowley said.

Ava picked it up and handed it to him.

Crowley said, "I'll take this directly to the station, and then I'll take you ladies home."

THE FOLLOWING WEEK, Elsa-May and Ettie went to visit Mildred after they heard the news that all charges against Jacob had been dropped.

"You must feel relieved now that Jacob's free," Elsa-May said.

Mildred smiled. "I do. And he's so relieved now. I'm grateful to the both of you, and your detective friend, for looking into things. Without your help Jacob would be facing trial for murder. And the nice detective said he was going to recommend that our offense be classed a misdemeanor, which he tells me is a good thing. We might have to pay a large fine, but I don't care. It seems such a little thing now that Jacob has been let off a murder charge."

"Nice detective? You're talking about Detective Kelly?" Elsa-May asked.

"Jah," Mildred answered.

"All's well that ends well," Ettie said. "Who would've even imagined that Camille would've killed herself and deliberately made it look like Jacob did it?" Ettie turned to Elsa-May. "Well, I'd better get you home so you can rest."

While the two elderly sisters waited down at the end of the driveway for the taxi, Ettie noticed the man next door, Bradshaw. From the distance she was to him, he looked to be the size of her thumb, but she could still see him standing with his feet apart and his hands on his hips, glaring at them.

Elsa-May turned to see what Ettie was staring at. "Ah, the neighbor you were telling me about?"

"Jah, that's the one."

"He doesn't look happy."

"He wouldn't be happy now that he knows they're not selling the farm," Ettie said.

After Ettie was silent for a while, Elsa-May asked, "What are you thinking about?"

"Do you think that Camille would buy a car if she was about to kill herself?"

"*Jah.* She had to live like killing herself was the last thing on her mind if her plan was going to work."

"I suppose you're right."

THE TWO ELDERLY sisters weren't home long when they heard a man's voice call out through their open front door.

Ettie knew right away that it was Detective Kelly. She let Elsa-May stay knitting while she walked to the door. "Come in, Detective."

She showed him to the living room and once he'd said hello to Elsa-May, he sat down and faced Ettie. "Mrs. Smith, I want to firstly congratulate you, and secondly apologize to you. I'm sorry for how I've acted toward you. The stress of the job makes me go a little crazy sometimes."

Ettie gave a little laugh.

He shook his head. "I didn't listen to you, and I should've. I would've been able to solve this thing a lot quicker if I hadn't been so focused on Jacob being guilty. I'm afraid my team is overworked and we immediately head to the most obvious leads. Anyway, my behavior toward you was unforgivable."

"Nothing's unforgiveable," Elsa-May said, looking over the top of her glasses at him.

"That's right." Ettie nodded. "I accept your apology."

"In a way, I regret getting you involved, and in another, I ask myself what would have happened if I hadn't," Kelly said.

Ettie swiped a hand in the air. "You would've figured it out. Anyway, we ended up thinking along the same lines about Camille."

He breathed out heavily. "It seemed too far fetched. Who would've thought the woman would've set her brother up like that and then killed herself?"

"She was a tortured girl," Elsa-May said.

Ettie nodded. "Yes, it's very sad."

Detective Kelly nodded. "Some criminals are born and others are made. Seems Camille's early history set her up for a life of violence against herself."

After everyone was silent for a while, Elsa-May suddenly spoke. "Ettie, make the detective some tea."

"Do you have coffee?" he asked.

Ettie frowned at him. "I've got green tea or lemon tea, Detective."

"Tea will be fine. You choose which one. I suppose I've had enough coffee today."

Ettie pushed herself to her feet. "I made some lovely brownies today, too."

The detective patted his stomach. "Just the tea thanks, Mrs. Smith."

When Ettie brought the tea items back on the tray, she set them on a low table in front of the detective. "How did your promotion go?"

He shook his head. "No good, but I do pride myself on the fact that I guessed that the mother cooked up the scheme about the will." He picked up some sugar and poured it into his tea. Once he stirred the tea, he brought it to his lips and took a sip. "Now, I hope you might consider being my contact in your Amish community."

Ettie frowned. "What do you mean? Nothing ever happens in our community."

He set his tea down on the table. "According to our records, quite a bit happens with you Amish people."

Ettie pulled her mouth to one side; she was caught in a hard place. She couldn't trust him like she'd trusted Crowley, but she did want to help people when they were in trouble.

He leaned forward. "Would you consider helping me in whatever way I ask?"

Ettie thought her answer through carefully. "Well, if you need me, and I'm still around, let me know."

"Good. I was hoping you'd say that, because I've got a little matter that I was hoping you'd help me with, but it's not exactly police business this time. It will please me enormously if you agree."

Elsa-May leaned forward. "What is it, Detective?"

A grin broke out on the detective's face. "Mrs. Smith, would you make me more of your sausage and egg casserole? Perhaps a muffin or two?"

Ettie heaved a sigh of relief and held her hand over her heart while Elsa-May giggled. "You had me worried for a minute," Ettie said.

"I'll make you that casserole – mine's much tastier than Ettie's," Elsa-May said.

Ettie opened her mouth at her sister. "Elsa-May!" Ettie then giggled and said, "That's most likely true, but I'll bake you some bread and it'll be the best you've ever tasted."

"Not that you're boastful or anything like that, Ettie," Elsa-May said with a crooked grin.

"Exactly. I'm not being boastful, just factual," Ettie said with a nod of her head.

"Thank you, and since you're my inspiration to eat healthier, Mrs. Smith, I'd be delighted to taste your bread." He looked at Elsa-May. "And your casserole." The detective picked up his tea and took another sip.

Ettie pushed herself to her feet.

The detective screwed up his nose. "Are you sure you don't have coffee?"

Ettie chortled. "I was just getting up to get you some."

While Ettie was in the kitchen listening to the low buzz of conversation coming from Elsa-May and Detective Kelly, she reflected on how blessed her life had been. She'd been married for years to a wonderful man before *Gott* had called him home, and she had many children and grandchildren. Then there was Mildred who'd had so many problems in her life. Camille really had lived a tortured life, which seemed unfair.

Sometimes Ettie got dissatisfied living with Elsa-May and her annoying ways, but now Ettie realized how blessed she really was. *Denke, Gott,* she said under her breath. There are always others worse off, she thought. Why do some people have it easier than others? *Ach, the mind of Gott, who knows it?*

Ettie carried a mug of coffee out to Detective Kelly, wondering what kind of inquiries he'd have her make next.

MURDER IN THE AMISH BAKERY

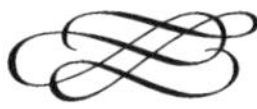

ETTIE SMITH AMISH MYSTERIES BOOK 3

CHAPTER 1

"It happened again, Elsa-May," Ettie yelled from the kitchen.

"Who's coming over?" Elsa-May called back from the living room.

Ettie threw down the tea towel onto the kitchen counter and walked into the living room with her hands on her hips. "I didn't say anyone was coming over. You need to get your hearing checked. I said that the bread sank in the middle again."

"You don't have to shout at me," Elsa-May said setting her knitting in her lap.

Ettie sighed and fell onto the couch. "I don't mean to be cranky. It's just that the bread has sunk again, and that's another batch of wasted ingredients."

"What do you think is causing it?"

Ettie shrugged. "I don't know. I've gone through everything I can think of. I haven't done anything different and you know how good my bread usually is."

"*Jah*, your bread is *wunderbaar* normally."

"Just when I was going to take a loaf over to Detective Kelly. I told him how good my bread is, and I don't think he's ever tasted it before. Has he?" Ettie stared at Elsa-May waiting for an answer.

"Not that I'm aware of. Are you sure you're not doing anything differently? There must be something that's affecting it."

Ettie shook her head. "I just wish I knew what it was. There must be something, but what?"

Elsa-May picked up her knitting again. "I'm not going to be much help to you. I haven't made bread in years. Not since we moved in together."

The two elderly sisters had begun living together after both their husbands died.

Elsa-May looked over the top of her glasses at Ettie. "Perhaps it's the ingredients. Have you bought new ingredients lately?"

"I buy everything in bulk, and I'm working my way down. I'm nearly due to buy more. I haven't bought anything new at all."

"Perhaps there's something wrong with the yeast."

"*Nee*. It's worked for me before."

"Do we have something wrong with the oven?"

Ettie shook her head again. "The oven is working perfectly." Ettie bit the inside of her lip while wondering what to do.

"Why don't you ask Ruth Fuller? See if she's got any idea."

"I couldn't possibly ask Ruth. She's so busy, and besides, everybody's always after her bread secrets."

Elsa-May chuckled. "You wouldn't be asking her for secrets. You'll be asking her what you might be doing wrong."

Ettie raised her eyebrows and considered what her sister had said. She waved a bony finger in the air. "You know, you just might be right."

Elsa-May smiled while she continued clicking her knitting needles together.

After a moment of silence, Ettie said, "You know what?"

"What?"

"I'm going to call her right now."

"Good. Why don't you do just that?"

Ettie took some money out of her bedroom, and then hurried to the shanty that held the telephone down at the end of her street. She placed the money in the tin can, and then dialed the number she had written in her notebook.

Her friend, Ruth, owned the biggest Amish bakery in town and her bread was famous. Everyone wanted to know how she made her bread so tasty and special. Ettie would have to be careful what she said to Ruth; she didn't want to make it sound like she was after any of Ruth's bread secrets.

After a few rings, someone answered the phone. "Hello," a man said.

"Hello. Is this the bakery where Ruth works?"

"Ruth owns the bakery."

"Yes, that's what I meant. Is she there at the moment?" Ettie heard a click. Either the person had just hung up on her, or he was heading to find Ruth. Ettie stayed on the line to find out which one.

"Hello, this is Ruth."

"Ruth this is Ettie, Ettie Smith."

"Ettie, it's lovely to hear from you."

"*Denke,* Ruth. I have a favor to ask. I have a question about bread."

"*Jah,* go on. What is it?"

"I've been baking bread exactly the same way for years, and for the last few days, it's been falling in the center."

"Sounds like too much yeast or the temperature is too high."

"*Nee.* I'm just doing everything the same as I've always done it. I haven't been doing anything differently."

"Think about it, Ettie, you must be doing something differently if it's falling in the center now, and it hasn't been before."

"I suppose that's true, but I can't think what it would be." There was silence on the other end of the phone for a moment.

"Meet me here tomorrow morning and we can talk about it then. I've just got to get this last order out and I'm running behind time."

"Denke. That would be *wunderbaar.* I don't want to keep you from your work. I'd love to come and meet you tomorrow morning. What time would you like me to be there?"

"Three."

"In the morning?"

"Jah that's what time I always start. The workers get here at four."

"I'll be there and thank you again, Ruth. I really appreciate you helping me with all of this."

"I'll look forward to seeing you at three in the morning, Ettie. Bye-bye now."

Ettie hung up the phone and wandered back to her house. How was she going to wake up at three in the morning? She and Elsa-May normally woke up around seven to seven thirty. Even when she'd been married and had to get her husband breakfast before he worked on the farm she only woke at five.

Before she reached her house, she saw her neighbor, Bernie, walking toward her leading his dog.

"Good morning, Ettie. How are you?"

"I'm fine, and you?" Ettie reached down to pat the small dog.

"Good, good. How's Elsa-May doing since she got out of hospital?"

"Fine. As you know she didn't have a clot at all, but the doctor did tell her to lose weight. He suggested she walk every morning."

"I haven't seen her about."

Ettie shook her head. "I'm afraid she always seems to have an excuse. It's too cold, it's too hot, and so forth."

"She needs a dog. That'll make her walk. She'll have to take the dog for a walk."

Ettie's dear old dog, Ginger, had died some time ago and another dog had been out of the question ever since. They did have a small back-yard and a dog door. "Interesting idea. I'll give it some thought. That could be the very thing she needs."

"I've got a friend who works at the dog shelter and he said they just got a lovely Maltese Terrier puppy."

"Maltese Terrier? What do they look like? Are they the white fluffy ones?"

"Yes. They're lovely dogs."

"I don't think that will do. Elsa-May and I are used to much bigger dogs, farm dogs."

"Smaller dogs are a lot less trouble. They cost less to feed and their business is a lot smaller. Trust me, they're a lot less trouble. And it will give your sister a reason to walk and a big dog might be too strong for her."

"You could be right about that. I'll give it some serious thought," Ettie said. "You've given me something to think about."

"Very good. Say hello to Elsa-May for me."

"Will do," Ettie called over her shoulder as she opened her front gate. She wouldn't mention the dog to Elsa-May because she would give a flat 'no' regarding having another dog in the house. If she did decide to go ahead with getting another one, it would have to be a surprise. Once Elsa-May saw it, she'd surely fall in love with it.

Elsa-May looked up from her knitting when Ettie walked into the house. "You were a long time."

"I've got some exciting news. Ruth said to meet her at the bakery tomorrow."

Elsa-May sat up straight in her chair. "What? At the bakery?"

Ettie nodded. "*Jah,* that's right. I told her the problem I was having and she said to meet her there tomorrow morning."

"Why go there? Couldn't she tell you over the phone what you're doing wrong?"

Ettie shrugged her shoulders. "I don't know why she wants me to go there; I just agreed."

"Good for you. You might be able to pick up some secret tips."

"I just hope she solves the problem of what's going on with my bread.She said she thought it might be that I've got the kitchen too hot, or the bread too hot or something."

"The weather hasn't been any hotter, and neither has the kitchen. You're using the same amount of things that you're always using, aren't you?"

"That's right."

Just then they heard a knock, and both turned to look toward the front door. Ettie got up to answer it and saw her young friend, Ava Glick.

"Ava, come in. It's lovely to see you."

Ava walked inside. "*Denke,* Ettie." Ava gave a little laugh as she walked toward Elsa-May. "Hi, Elsa-May."

"Hello, Ava. Come and sit with us."

Ava took a deep breath. "Have you just baked bread? It smells *wunderbaar.*"

Ettie grunted. "It smells all right, but that's where it ends."

Ava turned her attention to Elsa-May. "What are you knitting?"

"I'm always knitting. Lately I've been knitting *boppli* clothes. If I don't know people having *bopplis,* I give them to charity."

"That's good of you," Ava said.

"I might as well do something useful with myself."

"Would you like some tea or *kaffe,* Ava?" Ettie asked.

"*Kaffe denke,* Ettie."

Ettie hurried into the kitchen to make the coffee. She threw the bread in the trash basket in disgust. Once she poured the coffee into the coffee pot, she cut some apple cake and put some gingersnaps on a plate. She took everything in on a tray and placed it in the living room. By the look on Ava's face, Ettie knew she was there to tell them something.

"There you go," Ettie said as she passed a cup to Ava. Once she had a cup for herself, she sat down on the couch.

"Well what is it that you've been doing with yourselves?" Ava asked the elderly sisters.

"I've been having bread problems," Ettie said, still fuming about her failed bread. "My bread is falling in the middle and I've no idea why and it's been distressing."

Ava looked concerned as she took a sip of coffee. "That's no good."

"*Nee,* it's no good at all. I called Ruth, and she told me to go to her bakery tomorrow morning."

"Ruth Fuller?"

Ettie nodded.

"Is she going to tell you how she makes her bread?"

Elsa-May interrupted. "She'll never tell anybody. People come from miles around to have her bread. And people have been asking her for years to reveal her secrets."

Ava frowned. "It can't be *that* secret; its only bread."

"It's not just any bread," Elsa-May said.

"Have you never tasted Ruth's bread, Ava?"

"*Nee,* I haven't."

Elsa-May and Ettie looked at each other. That would explain Ava's attitude.

"Bread is the staff of life, Ava. Haven't you heard that?" Elsa-May said bluntly.

"*Jah,* I know, but…"

"There's no buts about it, Ava. Our whole diet is based around bread. If you take away bread, what are we left with?" Elsa-May smiled when Ava chuckled.

"And she'll solve your problem with your bread, Ettie?" Ava asked.

"I hope so. If she can't help me, I doubt anyone can."

"She'll know what you're doing wrong, Ettie," Elsa-May said.

"I hope so, but I don't know how she's going to help me with what I'm doing wrong if she doesn't come here and see it for herself. She needs to be in my kitchen. It's not the same me just telling her about it."

"Ettie, she's just invited you to the place where they make the best bread in the world. You should be able to figure out what you're doing wrong just by being there."

Ettie stared at Elsa-May. "I hope so."

"Besides, I'd rather not have her see how small our kitchen is." Elsa-May looked down at her knitting.

Ettie pursed her lips. "There's nothing wrong with our kitchen. It's just the two of us, and it's all we need."

Elsa-May's eyes narrowed. "Don't think of asking her to come here to watch you make bread. She might say she will to be polite."

Ettie wasn't happy with what her sister said, but remained silent.

"Would you like me to drive you there tomorrow, Ettie? I won't come in; I could drive you there and fill in time around town, and take you home when you're ready."

"That's very kind of you, but she wants me to meet her at three in the morning."

"That's early," Ava said.

"That's what time she starts. I didn't like to say it was too early for me since she's doing me a huge favor."

"Well I could take you, and I could just wait in the buggy until you've finished."

Ettie shook her head. "*Nee* it's far too early. I'll call and book a taxi tonight for the morning."

"Are you certain?" Ava asked before she took another sip of coffee.

"I'm certain."

When Ava left fifteen minutes later, Ettie and Elsa-May waved as her buggy drove away from the house.

"She doesn't come to visit very often for no reason at all," Elsa-May said.

"When she first arrived, I thought she was going to tell us something. It seemed to me that she had some news."

"Jah, I wonder if she had something to tell us. Do you think there's something wrong in her *grossdaddi haus?* She could need you to repair something, Ettie."

"Then why didn't she ask?"

Both sisters walked back into their house.

"She might have felt awkward about you spending money when the main *haus* is sitting vacant."

Ettie raised her eyebrows. "Perhaps the oven or something has stopped working and she needs it repaired. I'll visit her tomorrow after I see Ruth and I'll ask Ava if everything's all right."

CHAPTER 2

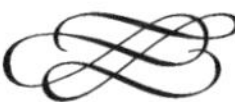

Ettie had her alarm clock wake her so she would have enough time to get ready for the taxi to drive her into town at three. She changed out of her nightgown and into her dress. Once she placed her black over-bonnet on top of her white prayer *kapp,* she went into the kitchen to have her morning glass of water with a squeeze of lemon juice. It was far too early to think about breakfast.

Once she laced up her black boots, she pulled her black cape from the peg behind the front door, swung it over her shoulders, and waited by the door for the taxi.

The taxi appeared right on time at two forty-five. She opened the front passenger-side door and sat in the front seat.

"Good morning."

"Good morning," Ettie said back to the man. Ettie was glad that the driver wasn't a talker, as she was still trying to wake up. The last thing she had wanted was to have to think about making conversation. It normally took her brain some time to catch up with her body of a morning.

The taxi took her right to the front door of the bakery. As the taxi zoomed off down the gray road, Ettie saw that the street was deserted, and she wasn't surprised. A few minutes later, she saw a small figure in the distance. As the figure drew closer, she saw that it was Ruth. Ruth gave a wave and Ettie waved back.

"Ettie, I didn't know if you'd make it this early in the morning."

"I said I'd be here." Ettie smiled. "*Denke* for sparing me the time."

"I'm happy you've come. I don't often take time to see friends. I'm so busy in the bakery every day. I'm here six days a week, you know."

"Are you? That's a lot to work, isn't it?"

"It is and it's hard work too. I try not to work Sundays, since it's our day of rest, but I do have to be here early to let the workers in."

"Can't you give one of them a key?"

"I'm the only one with the key and that's the way it shall stay." Ruth opened her hand to reveal a key, and then she held it up in the air. "This is the only key, besides my spare key at home." She nodded her head to the alley. "I always enter through the back."

Ettie followed her around the back. Ruth pushed the key into the lock and then slowly turned it until they heard a click.

When they walked in, Ruth flicked on some lights and the place lit up. Ettie was reminded how the members of the community were permitted to have electricity in their places of business, but not their homes. Electricity in their homes was bringing 'the world' in.

"You've been here before, haven't you?" Ruth asked.

"I haven't been back here, *nee*. I've been to the store section out in the front to buy bread and the other goodies that you make so well." Ettie looked up at the wooden vaulted ceilings and her gaze lowered to the rows of stainless steel ovens and steel countertops. "It all looks modern and so shiny."

"I've got the latest equipment. I have to have it, with the volume of bread we put out."

Is having the latest technology the key to making her bread? Nee! She's been making the same bread for years. "You can still produce the same bread with all this new equipment?"

"*Jah,* of course, I can."

Ettie was hoping that Ruth would take her on a tour to show her what all the equipment was used for.

"Tea, Ettie?"

"*Jah, denke.* I'd love some. It was too early to have some when I left. Tea would go down quite nicely."

Ruth smiled and beckoned her to follow. "Come with me into

the lunchroom." After Ruth put the kettle on to boil, she sat down at the small table with Ettie.

"How many workers do you have?"

"I have thirty employees. Not all of them are full-time; some are part-time. I'm branching into other things. I make chocolate chip cookies, brandy snaps pinwheels, cheese torts, cheese tarts, cream sticks, and lots of other things. Bread is still my main seller."

"Jah, that's what you're best known for."

"So tell me the problem you're having with your bread, Ettie. I didn't have time to listen on the phone yesterday."

"I'm making the bread in the same way that I always do. The temperature of the kitchen and the temperature the oven are exactly the same, and I've been using the same amount of ingredients."

"Do you measure exactly, or do you just measured by sight? A bit of this and a bit of that?" Ruth made pouring motions with her hands.

"I measure by sight. I know the measures. I've been making bread since I was a *maidel.* I've always done it that way, as my *mudder* before me did."

"Tell me what you do exactly. Wait a minute, I'll make the tea." Ruth rose to her feet, and then placed a tea-bag into each cup before she poured hot water into the cups. "Milk, Ettie?"

"No milk for me."

"I have it that way too." Ruth placed the cups on the table in front of them. When she took a sip of tea, Ruth leaned back in her chair and closed her eyes. "Go on, Ettie. You were telling me exactly what you've been doing,"

Ettie launched into explaining exactly what ingredients she used and what she did with them. She finished by saying, "And then I knead it on a floured surface, by pushing with the heels of my hands, away from me as I'm adding in the rest of the flour." Ettie hoped Ruth hadn't fallen asleep, but who could blame her if she had? It was time for sleeping not time for baking. Even the cows weren't awake at this time.

Ruth opened her eyes. "That sounds about right, but unless I'm there watching what you do I simply can't say what's going wrong."

Normally, Ettie would've invited Ruth over to her house, but by the sounds of things Ruth was too busy. Ettie didn't want to be a bother and neither did she want to upset Elsa-May, so she simply nodded at what Ruth said.

"The only thing I can say is that it must be too hot in your kitchen. The yeast consumes the starches in the flour and converts them into carbon dioxide and alcohol, which is what causes the bread to rise. The activity level of the yeast is dependent upon the temperature in the room, so if it's too hot the yeast will become overactive."

Ettie sighed. "I don't think the temperature's any different to normal."

"Why not try a pinch of salt in your mixture next time? See if that works. It'll slow down the fermentation and enzyme activity in your mixture."

"*Denke,* Ruth, I'll try that." Ettie looked out the door of the tea room into the bakery. "You certainly must keep busy, especially when you're got all the other goods to make now too."

"It does keep me busy, and I love working in the store and meeting people. I've made such good friends over the years. If I didn't have the bakery, I don't know what I'd do. I guess I would just waste away sitting in a chair all day. That's what I saw my *mudder* do when she got older and I don't want to turn out like her. She had nothing to be excited or happy about."

Ettie's thoughts turned to Elsa-May who sat in a chair all day knitting despite the doctor telling her to get some exercise. Perhaps she should get Elsa-May a dog as the neighbor had suggested.

"I'm seventy seven now, Ettie. People keep telling me to retire but why would I do that? I feel the same now as what I did when I was forty. I might look different, but I feel young. I really don't feel old."

Ettie said, "I know what you mean. We don't look the same on the outside, but we're the same on the inside." Ettie took a mouthful of tea. "Am I keeping you from your work?"

Ruth shook her head. "I always come in at this time to have a quiet time by myself. I make a cup of tea, and sometimes I'll look over the books or do paperwork. When the others get here, it's so noisy I can't even hear myself think."

"And what time did you say the others arrive?"

"The bakery staff arrive at four and the staff who run the store come in at seven. This place will soon be buzzing."

"I imagine it will."

"So what have you been doing with yourself, Ettie?"

"Besides trying to make a decent loaf of bread, not a lot."

"Have you decided what to do with Agatha's *haus* yet?"

"I'm nearly through with repairs, then I'll lease it. Ava Glick's already leasing the attached *grossdaddi haus*. She's a lovely girl."

"She seems to be. I don't know her very well. Couldn't you and Elsa-May move into it and lease out the one you're living in now? From what I can remember, Agatha's *haus* is a lot bigger than yours."

"I was thinking of moving into it at one stage, but the dreadful business with Horace being murdered and his body hidden under the floor for so many years made me rethink the idea."

"I can understand that. There's no one living in it now?"

"*Nee* not in the main house. Elsa-May's grandson, Jeremiah, is finishing the repairs and then I'll lease it out to a nice *familye*."

"Good idea."

"I would sell, but in her will, Agatha requested that I leave Ava in the *grossdaddi haus* for as long as she wanted. Besides, I don't need to sell."

When they finished their tea, Ruth said, "I'll show you the place."

"I'd love to have a look around. I'd like to know what all those big machines are for."

"Come on, then."

Ettie said, "It's gleaming and clean, not a speck of dust anywhere."

"It takes a good hour to clean up every night. I insist on the place being spotless and we have to abide by all the health regulations. We have inspectors over here all the time."

"*Jah,* of course, you would have to stick to all the rules."

Once they'd had a look around the bakery, Ruth said, "Now I'll take you through to the older section where my office is." As they walked to the front of the bakery, Ruth pointed to a door. "That leads to the store, and this one here is my office." She pushed open another door. "This is where I do all my paperwork."

"Don't you have someone to do that for you? With a business this size I'd imagine there's a lot of paperwork."

Ruth laughed. "I do have a bookkeeper, but it's quite a job to arrange the paperwork to send off to him."

Ettie followed her into the office.

"That's strange. I always turn the light off and I was the last one out." Ruth took two steps into the room and screamed.

Ettie froze in place and then looked to where Ruth was staring. She stepped next to Ruth and it was then that she saw the body. A man who looked to be quite dead lay on the floor behind Ruth's desk.

"Is he...?" Ruth asked.

Ettie stepped over to have a closer look. The man was face down on the floor in a puddle of darkened blood. There was a large knife in his back, and he had a large Bible clutched in one hand. "I'll see if he's breathing. You call 911."

CHAPTER 3

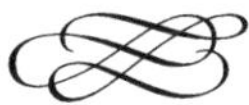

While Ruth picked up the phone, Ettie crouched down beside the man and put two fingers on his neck to feel for a pulse. Ettie was familiar with the stale stench of death that hung in the air, so she knew that the soul of the man stretched out before her had gone to meet his maker. There was no pulse, not even a faint one. "He's dead," Ettie announced so Ruth could relay that to the operator.

Ettie touched the lifeless wrist beside her foot, knowing that the neck was the better place to find a pulse but hoping for a sign of life none-the-less. Ettie put her hands on the desk, and pulled herself to her feet and waited for Ruth to get off the phone.

When Ruth hung up the phone she walked closer to take another look at the man.

"Nasty way to go," Ettie said. When Ruth remained silent, Ettie looked at her to see that her mouth had fallen open. "Did you know him?"

Ruth slowly nodded.

"Who is he?"

Ruth sat down. "He's a customer. He had a permanent order for bread. His name is Alan Avery and he's got a busy café not far from here." She looked up at Ettie. "What was he doing here and why is he dead?"

Ettie shook her head. "I've no idea, but we know he wasn't here alone."

Ettie looked down at the knife sticking out of Alan Avery's back. "Is that one of your knives?"

Ruth raised herself a little in her chair. "*Nee.* We don't have knives like that. It looks like a butcher's knife."

"Is that your Bible?" Ettie asked.

Ruth looked at the Bible and covered her face with her hands. "It is. It's my Bible. Why is he holding it? Take it out of his hands, would you, Ettie?"

Ettie frowned. "I can't. The police will need to have things just as we found them. Where had you left your Bible?"

She pointed to a bureau. "I always leave it in that."

Ettie nodded. "Does he pick up the bread? Could he have come to collect his order?"

Ruth shook her head. "He always comes at seven-thirty. It's

either him or one of his workers, but recently I refused to supply him."

Ettie raised her eyebrows. "Really? Go on."

"We had a falling out when I found out he was opening a bakery right down the road. He was calling it 'The Amish Bakery.' What do you think of that? He's not even Amish."

Ettie rubbed her chin.

"Of course, I stopped supplying him after that."

"Jah, I suppose it was only a matter of time before he'd be making his own. It would never be as good as yours, of course."

"Nee, it wouldn't and that's why he's been trying to buy me out for the past three years."

A loud buzzer sounded.

"That'll be the staff at the back door. I'll have to go and let them in."

While Ruth hurried away, Ettie wondered what was keeping the police. Right at that moment, Ettie heard a loud pounding coming from somewhere. She opened the door to the retail store attached to the bakery and looked through the store windows to see the police and the paramedics out on the street. She hurried through and unlatched the deadbolts on the door.

"He's through this way," Ettie said as she hurried back to Ruth's office.

Ettie stayed out of the room to let the paramedics and the police do their jobs.

"Mrs. Smith?"

Ettie turned around to see Detective Kelly.

"Detective Kelly, I wondered if I'd see you today."

"The 911 call came from a Ruth Fuller. Is she here?"

"That's my friend. She owns the bakery and she's just gone to let her staff in through the back." Ruth walking toward her distracted Ettie. "Detective Kelly, this is Ruth Fuller."

"Hello. You made the call?" The detective flipped a notebook open and drew a pen out of his inner coat pocket.

Ruth nodded. "I did."

"She knows him, the dead man," Ettie interrupted.

"And who is he?"

Someone came up to the detective, and said, "I'd estimate he's been dead for roughly four hours."

When the man who'd been talking to the detective went back into the office, Ruth said, "His name is Alan Avery. He's got a café where he sells sandwiches not far from here."

"And you were the one to find the body, Mrs. Fuller?"

"I did. I was showing Ettie around, and then we saw him right there on the floor. He's holding my Bible. Do you think I could have it back? And, I've got policemen in my bakery. I can't make the bread when they're around."

Detective Kelly shook his head. "I'll need both of you to come down to the station. We'll need your prints for elimination." He looked directly at Ruth. "You'll have to tell your staff to go home. We'll need to shut the whole place down while we have a good look around."

A policeman stood very close to the detective, and said in a quiet voice, "There's no immediate sign of forced entry." When Kelly nodded, the policeman walked away.

Ruth wrung her hands. "I don't like losing a day."

"See if your insurance will cover it. Call them, tell them what happened, and they'll send someone to clean up the blood. When we're finished here, of course. Now who had access to the place? How many people have a key?"

"Just me. I was telling Ettie when we came in that I have the only two keys. One is hidden at home and the other one is here with me now."

"I want you to call me if that hidden key is missing."

"Yes, I will."

"Do you have any idea what the man might have been doing here?"

"It's obvious he was after my bread recipe." Ruth stared at the detective and looked away when deep furrows appeared in his forehead. "I'll have to tell my staff to leave now before they begin. I hope they haven't started already." Ruth hurried away.

"What do you make of it, Detective?" Ettie asked.

"All I can make of it so far is that at least two men made it in, and one man - or more - made it out after killing Mr. Avery. It's not a suicide, we know that much from the knife in his back."

Ettie tapped a finger on her chin. "I wonder why he had Ruth's Bible in his hand."

"He could've been stabbed and knew he was going to die, saw the Bible and thought he'd make amends with the man upstairs before it was too late."

"Perhaps, but it wasn't left out on the desk or anything. Ruth said she always kept it in the bureau, so unless he had been through it and opened the cupboard, he wouldn't have known where it was."

"Funny you should be here, Mrs. Smith. Almost like you knew there was going to be a murder."

Ettie frowned. "I was having bread problems and Ruth offered to help."

"If you'll excuse me, I'll need to go in and see him for myself."

Ettie stood and watched the detective walk into Ruth's office. Ruth returned to stand next to Ettie while yellow crime scene tape was crisscrossed over her doorway.

When Ruth saw one of the evidence technicians pop her Bible

into a plastic bag, she called out, "That's my Bible. Don't touch it."

Kelly came to the doorway. "I'm going to need it for a while. Once the technicians are finished in here, they'll make their way through the rest of the building. You could wait here, Mrs. Fuller, or I can take your key, lock up when we're finished, and drop the key back to you."

Ettie looked at Ruth when she didn't answer. "Come on, Ruth, we shouldn't stay here. I'll walk you home."

"Don't we have to go to the station and have our fingerprints taken?"

Kelly glanced at his watch. "After nine; there's no immediate hurry."

Ruth nodded, and handed Kelly the key. She told him where she lived and the detective said he'd deliver it to her when they were through.

Before she left, Ruth asked the detective, "Will we be open for business tomorrow?"

"Hopefully."

"I must call all the cafes and restaurants I supply bread to and tell them that there'll be no bread today."

Kelly said, "Don't you have someone else who could do that for you?"

"I did have but I just sent everybody home. All the phone

numbers of my customers are in the office there. Can I get them?"

Kelly shook his head. "No. You can't go in there now, I'm afraid."

"People will be coming to get their orders and there won't be any."

"Let's make a sign to put on the door, Ruth," Ettie suggested.

"I suppose that will have to do." She turned to Ettie. "I'll put a sign on the front door and another on the back door. People often go to the back door to pick up the deliveries. And the people who just want one or two loaves come to the store."

Ettie and Ruth entered the store where they found paper and pens to write the signs. Once they'd taped one to the front and one to the back door, they set off to Ruth's house.

When Ruth pushed her front door open, Ettie said, "You should check to see if that spare key is still here."

"*Jah.* I hope someone hasn't been in here and taken it. I wouldn't feel safe in my own home if someone's been here without me knowing."

Ettie followed Ruth into the kitchen and watched her open the canister that was on the kitchen counter. She reached her hand in and pulled out the key. "It's still here."

"Well we know they didn't get in that way," Ettie said.

"I wonder whether the police will find out how they got in. I hope so anyway. I've got eggs. How would you like them, Ettie?"

"Anyway you cook them will be fine with me."

Just as Ruth had dished out poached eggs onto two plates, someone knocked on the door. Ruth peeped through the window. "It's that detective friend of yours."

"I didn't think they'd be finished with the place already."

Ruth hurried to let the detective through the door. "Good morning again. Come through to the kitchen."

The detective sat at the kitchen table.

"Would you like some breakfast?" Ruth asked.

"I'm fine thank you. I'll have something at the station later."

"Like what?" Ettie asked. "Pink iced doughnuts? It would be better if you had something decent in your stomach, Detective."

He smiled. "My dietary habits have improved since you saw me eat those doughnuts." He looked at Ruth. "I would appreciate a little something."

Ettie poured the detective a cup of coffee from the pot on the table, and then pushed it toward him. "Did you find out what he was doing in Ruth's office?"

"Thank you, Mrs. Smith. No, we didn't find that out." He took a mouthful of coffee.

Ruth handed him a plate of eggs and toast.

"Is this your famous bread?"

Ruth smiled as she sat back down at the table. "Yes, it is."

"You've heard about Ruth's bread?" Ettie asked.

"I heard the evidence technicians talking about it today. They said it's the best bread around."

"Yes that's what everyone says about it. My bread's the best." Ruth gave a nod.

Ettie looked at her friend and smiled. She displayed no pride when she admitted her bread was the best, it was simply said as a fact. Ettie looked back at the detective. "I was having problems with my bread and that's why I was there this morning, talking to Ruth about it."

He put a forkful of food in his mouth and nodded. "Yes, you told me that. He was Alan Avery, we found the ID in his wallet."

"That's right; he was a good customer of mine up until recently."

"What happened?" the detective asked.

"He and his daughter run a café, well a sandwich bar I suppose you'd call it, and anyway, he had a permanent order of bread with me. He said my bread is what kept his customers coming back. Alan wanted to buy me out, and kept offering me more and more money. I kept saying 'no' and told him that I wasn't selling. Then, one day, I found out that he was opening a bakery right near me, just a short distance away on the same road."

Detective Kelly nodded. "He's got every right to do so; it is a free country."

"Be that as it may, as soon as I found that out, I cancelled his order and said to him, 'you can make your own bread.'"

"And how long ago was that?"

"I'd have to see when we stopped supplying him. I could have a look at my records, which are in the office that I can't go into. I would guess it was about three or four weeks now. Yes, I think that's right. Four weeks at the most."

The detective pulled out his notepad and wrote something down. He suddenly looked up. "Was your spare key here?"

"Yes it was. I knew it would be. No one's been in my house."

"Try the toast detective," Ettie said.

Ruth said, "It's not today's bread. It was made yesterday, but it's still good for toast."

The detective picked up the toast and bit into it. After he ate the mouthful, he said, "This is good toast. The nicest I've tasted in fact."

"Why haven't you bought bread from Ruth's place before?" Ettie asked.

"I would have if it was closer to the station. So Allen Avery runs a local sandwich establishment?"

"That's right, only about two blocks from my bakery. He works with his daughter and I heard that he was intending to put his daughter in charge of the new bakery."

"Would you happen to know his daughter's name?"

"Melissa."

"Do you know Melissa very well?"

"Just about as well as I know my other regular customers."

"Seems the man was killed between midnight and one o'clock this morning. Where were you, Mrs. Fuller, at that time?"

"I was asleep in my bed. Right here in the house."

Kelly looked around. "And you live on your own?"

"I do. I've never married."

"So, you're Miss Fuller?"

"I am, but I allow people to call me Mrs. Fuller seeing most women my age have been, or are, married."

Detective Kelly turned to Ettie. "And you, Mrs. Smith?"

"I was married, but Mr. Smith died."

Kelly took a deep breath. "I meant, where were you between midnight and one?"

"Let me see, around midnight and one? I was asleep, of course. Elsa-May can tell you that."

"Neither of you are under suspicion. I just need to know where you were."

"So that means we *are* under suspicion, otherwise you wouldn't have asked us where we were."

Kelly frowned. "The man had a knife driven into his back. I think the force required for that suggests a man did the stabbing. I'll have to wait until the forensic report comes back."

"Fortunate for us," Ettie said.

"That's why I need you to come in to have your fingerprints taken."

Ettie still didn't trust Detective Kelly, not like she'd trusted Detective Crowley. Kelly had put one over on her before, and she was not going to fall for his lies again.

Kelly cleared his throat and looked across the table at Ruth. "Would you happen to know if Alan Avery had any enemies, Miss Fuller?"

Ruth shook her head. "You can call me Ruth. I wouldn't know at all if he had enemies. I didn't know him that well. I didn't see him every day. Sometimes he'd pick up the bread, or it was his daughter, and sometimes one of his workers would pick up the order."

Kelly said, "Well, I better get back to the station. By now Alan Avery's family will know what's happened to him."

"His wife died years ago. He's only got his daughter," Ruth said.

"Oh, I see."

Ettie asked, "Don't you feel better with something in your stomach, Detective?"

"Yes, I do. Thank you, Ruth, for making me such a lovely breakfast. And I feel honored to have finally tasted your bread. And I'll buy my bread from you in the future."

"It was a pleasure, Detective. Do you have the key to give back to me?"

"They're still working there. Someone will bring it to you. If you're not here they'll bring the key to me, and I'll personally bring it to you later today. It could possibly be this evening before they're through."

"What about my Bible? I need it back."

"I'll let you know when we're through with it. We might have to keep it as evidence at least until we find the person who killed Avery. After you ladies have had your prints taken, I'll have some more questions for you."

CHAPTER 4

After the detective left Ruth's house, she turned to Ettie. "What did he mean, Ettie? What evidence could my Bible be?"

"I guess it could have a fingerprint on it, or something like that."

"I wonder what Alan Avery was doing in the bakery. Do you have any idea at all, Ruth?"

"I told the detective that the man was there to steal my bread recipe. It's the only thing that makes sense."

"Where do you keep the recipe?"

"Out of sight."

Ettie nodded and didn't want to press her further. "Did you check to see if it was still there?"

"*Jah* it was."

"Did he come close to it?"

Ruth gasped and covered her mouth. "Ettie, I've just thought of something. Last time Alan Avery came into my office to pay his bill, he admired my old bureau and I told him it held my most prized possession. I meant my Bible, but he would've thought I meant my bread recipe."

"And you said that to Alan Avery recently?"

Ruth nodded. "I remember I did and it could've been that last time he was in my office before I heard he was opening a bakery."

"And he thought that's where you hid your bread recipe, and that's why he was holding your Bible? We know there were two people there. When the second person found out there was no bread recipe, he must have killed Alan Avery."

"Ettie, we must tell your detective."

'We must, but he's not my detective. I'll go look at the time." Ettie walked to look at the clock over the fireplace and then went back into the kitchen. "It's not even nine yet. We've some time to fill in before we go to the police station." Ettie sat down at the kitchen table with Ruth.

"Do you have any idea who that second man could be? Who else has shown interest in your bread recipe?"

"There have been a few people who have wanted to buy it."

"Tell me their names."

"There's a man called Hugh Dwyer; he runs a small goods store with an Amish café attached. He's just started franchising it. He's offered to buy me out, even sent me over a contract for me to write my own price on."

"And you were never tempted?"

"He had a 'no compete clause,' which means I'd never be able to make my bread anymore, not even for myself."

"That seems harsh, but I suppose he thought it reasonable to ask since he was willing to pay a large sum."

"I'm not ready to retire. My whole life has been wrapped up in the place for so many years."

"So this man, Hugh, wanted to buy your bread recipe, offered you a lot of money, and you'd have to close your bakery?"

"That's right. I'd have to sell it to someone else without my recipe."

"Who else wanted your recipe?"

"Rupert Bird. He has a bakery in Harrisburg."

"Amish bakery?"

"*Jah.* I've been there. He invited me to go and see it. Of course, he was all friendly at the time and made out it would be to my benefit if I saw his successful operation. When I got there, it wasn't as big as he'd said."

"Go on," Ettie said.

"He asked me again to sell, and again, I said 'no' and his face went as red as a beetroot and even the tops of his ears went red. He said I'd be very sorry if I didn't sell to him. I got out of there quick and came back home."

"Were you scared?"

"*Nee,* not really. I didn't take him too seriously. They were just words spoken in anger and frustration."

"Did he offer you as much money as Alan Avery?"

"*Nee.* Alan Avery offered the most money, a ridiculous amount of money. I don't know if that other man, Mr. Dwyer, was serious about me writing my own price on the contract."

Ettie fiddled with the strings of her prayer *kapp*. "So it sounds like Alan Avery really wanted your bread recipe and he was prepared to engage in criminal activity to get it."

"I can't think of why else he'd be in the bakery. Nothing else makes sense."

"Particularly since he had hold of your Bible. He would have gone to your bureau expecting to find your bread recipe or your bread starters and he pulled out your Bible." Ettie stared at Ruth. "Some don't use a bread starter anymore. Do you use a bread starter?"

Ruth shook her head. "I can't tell you what I do, Ettie."

"Just curious. You'll have to let Detective Kelly know all that you told me when we go in. Was there anyone else who wanted your recipe?"

"No one else with a serious offer. I get asked for the recipe and for my secrets all the time; most of the people are customers who buy three to four loaves of bread a week."

TWO HOURS LATER, Ettie and Ruth were sitting in the police station waiting to have their fingerprints taken.

Ettie groaned.

"What, Ettie?"

"I'm just thinking about Elsa-May at home. She's got no idea I'm sitting in a police station about to have my fingerprints taken. Neither has she got any idea what's happened in your bakery this morning."

"You'll have a lot to tell her when you get home. Do you think she'll be worried about you?"

"*Nee.* I told her that after I saw you, I was going to drop by Ava Glick's, so she won't be expecting me back until later this afternoon."

"You ladies here to be fingerprinted?" a gruff voice said.

They looked up at the officer.

"Yes," Ettie said.

"One at a time, please."

Ettie went first and followed the man into a room.

"Wash your hands thoroughly please." He pointed to a sink with antibacterial soap in a pump bottle.

After Ettie washed her hands, the officer handed her two paper towels. She dried her hands thoroughly and threw the paper towels in the bin.

The officer took hold of Ettie's hand while saying, "I'm going to roll your thumb from side to side, so just relax as best you can." He told Ettie how to spread her hand, and then he took a rolled impression of each thumb and finger, after inking each one. "All done. Now you can wash the ink off."

Ettie looked down at the ink on her hands. "I hope it comes off."

"Most of it will. When you go out, can you send your friend in?"

Ettie scrubbed her hands, and then it was Ruth's turn.

After they'd both had their prints taken, they made their way back to the front of the station to wait for detective Kelly. It wasn't long before the detective stuck his head into the waiting area, and beckoned for them to follow him.

When they were all seated, Ettie began, "Has Alan Avery's daughter been told about his death?"

"Yes. His daughter has been informed, and you were right, Ruth, his wife died some years ago."

"We've figured out why he was in there," Ettie said.

The detective frowned. "Who was where?"

"Alan Avery; why he was in Ruth's office."

The detective pushed himself back in his chair. "Why was he there?"

"The man had offered Ruth an extremely large sum of money to buy her bread recipe. Apparently other people wanted it too."

"I can believe it. Bread's big business."

Ettie continued, "Ruth has an antique bureau in her office and she had often told people, when they admired it, that it held her most prized possession. Which, of course, was her Bible. What if someone thought that bureau held her bread starters or bread recipes?"

Ruth frowned. "I don't know if I told everyone that, but I do remember telling Alan Avery that not too long ago."

"Let's wind back a little. You're losing me. What's a bread starter? Is that like an entrée?" the detective asked.

Ettie raised her eyebrows when she looked at Ruth figuring she'd be the one to best explain what a bread starter was.

"A bread starter is a leavening agent," Ruth said.

"Like yeast?" Kelly asked.

"Yes exactly. And some bread starters are passed down from one generation to the next. The old starters are the best because they often will contain wild yeast that has a distinctly different flavor than today's harvested yeast."

"Can starters be used in all the different varieties of bread?" Kelly asked.

"The starters are mostly used in Amish friendship bread and sourdough."

Ettie wondered if that was Ruth's secret; maybe she had particularly wonderful bread starters.

"So you see, there was something tangible to steal. I should say they thought that there was something there in that bureau to steal," Ettie said.

Ettie and Ruth went on to tell Detective Kelly about Hugh Dwyer, the man with the Amish small goods stores, and Rupert Bird, the man who lived in Harrisburg and who had the Amish Bakery.

The detective looked at Ruth. "Do you really think that Alan Avery might have thought the bureau contained your bread recipe?"

Ruth nodded. "It's very possible."

"It does give him a reason to be there. Why else would someone break into an empty bakery at night unless you keep large sums of cash? Did you keep a lot of cash on your premises?" He stared at Ruth.

"I only bank once a week. Joe, my bakery manager is always insisting we should bank at the end of every day. I tell him 'no.' I've always banked once a week."

"So you regularly had large sums of cash on hand?"

Ruth said, “Sometimes. But we banked yesterday.”

“If they were after money, wouldn't they be watching the place to see how often they banked and what day?” Ettie asked.

“They might not be efficient thieves, Mrs. Smith.”

“I was starting to think you ladies might be right, up until I found out about the cash. How much money are we talking about, Ruth? What would you normally bank every week?”

“Usually just under twenty thousand dollars.”

The detective gasped. “The bread business must be good.”

“I do have rates, taxes, the accountant, and the staff bill to pay,” Ruth said defensively. “And I insist on being paid in cash.”

“Ruth, I wasn't being disrespectful. I'm sorry for my comment.”

Ruth nodded.

“Now that I know how much cash you regularly keep on your premises, that changes everything. He very well might have been after your recipe, but he's more likely to have been after the cash. You might be right, he could've thought while he was there he'd see if he could find your recipe.” He placed his hands on his desk and laced his fingers together. “Then that could explain why the Bible was in his hands. And when there was no cash, and no bread recipe, his accomplice did away with him in a fit of rage.”

“You believe us? You believe he might have been after the bread recipe?” Ruth asked.

"I'm not ruling anything out at this stage. We've got two and possibly three reasons for someone to break in. We have the cash, and the recipe, or the bread starters." He took a pad and a pen out of his top drawer. "Now, Ruth, can you give me the names of all the people who wanted to buy your recipe?"

Ruth repeated all the names she'd previously given the detective, while Ettie stared at the faint ink smudges on her fingers.

When the detective finished writing he looked up. "I'm sorry about the ink stains, Mrs. Smith, they should fade soon."

"Has your team at my bakery found out anything yet, Detective?" Ruth asked.

"They're collecting evidence, and then it has to be processed. It's not a quick process, I'm afraid. Hopefully you'll have your key back later today."

"I hope so. I don't like letting my customers down."

"I'll personally bring your key back to you."

Ruth nodded. "Thank you."

The detective rose to his feet. "Thank you, ladies, for coming in and giving us your prints. And I'll look into the information you've given me."

"You will?" Ettie asked.

He nodded. "I will."

"When can I get my Bible back?" Ruth asked.

"All in due time," the detective said.

Ettie and Ruth left the police station and headed back to Ruth's house.

Before they had gone far, Ettie stopped walking. "Why don't you come back to my *haus,* Ruth? It's not nice to be on your own after all that's happened. We can go back to the station and let Kelly know you'll be at my place. He knows where I live."

"I'd like that, Ettie. And you're right, I don't feel like being on my own."

WHEN RUTH and Ettie walked into the house, Elsa-May stared at them open-mouthed. She placed her knitting down and pushed herself to her feet. "Ruth, I wasn't expecting you. Come in and sit."

When the three of them sat down, Elsa-May looked at Ettie. "What's happened?"

Ruth and Ettie told Elsa-May the whole thing about the murdered man, and the people who had wanted to buy Ruth's bread recipe.

"What do you think, Elsa-May?" Ettie asked.

"I agree with you, Ettie. If they were after the money, they would have kept a watch on when the banking was done. It doesn't make sense for them to go to all the trouble to break in and then have no money to steal. They must have been after the recipe."

"I hope the police find out how they got in. I have the only two keys," Ruth said.

Ettie continued, "I'm certain Detective Kelly thinks they were after money. He thought they were after Ruth's recipe until he asked about the amount of cash that gets banked once a week."

"Well, didn't you tell him how much Ruth's recipe must be worth, Ettie?"

Ettie looked at Ruth. "We tried to, didn't we, Ruth?"

Ruth nodded. "I told him how many people wanted to buy it."

"I can't recall if Ruth told him how much she'd been offered. In fact, I'm certain that no figure was mentioned."

"Then you should go back and tell him that it'd be worth a lot of money," Elsa-May said with a sharp nod of her head.

"He'll be here later. He's dropping the key off to Ruth."

Ruth added, *"Jah,* the police are still looking through the bakery for evidence."

Ettie nibbled on the end of her fingernail. "So much was happening so fast. We should've thought to tell him that, Ruth."

"You can tell him soon," Elsa-May said.

"Now that I'm here, Ettie, do you want to make some bread and I'll watch what you do so I can try to spot where you're going wrong?"

"*Denke,* Ruth, but I'm too shaken up after everything that's happened."

"You both sit there, I'll make everyone a nice cup of tea," Elsa-May said.

Ruth stayed the rest of the day at Ettie and Elsa-May's house and when Detective Kelly arrived, Ettie ushered him into the living room.

"What have you found out so far?" Elsa-May asked before the detective had a chance to sit down.

The detective looked at Elsa-May and then lowered himself carefully into the rickety wooden chair. "We've found out that the deceased had gotten himself into a large amount of debt." He looked at Ruth. "It does sound like he was after the cash and not your recipe, Mrs. Fuller. Excuse me, I meant to say Ruth."

"That doesn't make sense," Ettie said. "He was offering Ruth a lot of money for her bread recipe. We forgot to tell you this morning just how much money he was willing to pay her."

"And he'd just bought a large building not far from me; he was going to turn the building into an Amish bakery," Ruth said. "That conversion would've cost a lot of money to do."

The detective rubbed his chin. "And that's the problem. You see he was spending far more money than he was making. That's why people in this country today are having a lot of problems; too many people are spending at a rate faster than they're earning."

"If he was in a lot of debt, surely Ruth's weekly takings wouldn't go far to solving his problems," Elsa-May said.

The detective answered, "When people are desperate, some money is better than no money at all. Ruth's weekly takings were quite a tidy sum."

Ettie cleared her throat. "If what you're saying is correct, Detective, who do you think the second person was in the bakery with him? Do you think they went in together, or had they both broken in and they surprised each other?"

"Hopefully the evidence we've collected will help us come up with the answer to that, Mrs. Smith." He reached into his pocket. "Here's your key, Ruth. The insurance company had the cleaners in already."

"That was fast." She reached over and took hold of her key. "Thank you. Now I can open for business tomorrow. How did they get into the building? Have you found out that yet?"

He shook his head. "Not as yet, but we'll know more, hopefully, over the next few days."

"Are you going to look into those names Ruth gave you?" Ettie asked.

"At this time, we're going over the leads that Alan's daughter, Melissa, gave us."

"Which are?" Elsa-May leaned forward.

"I can't disclose that, I'm sorry. They are to do with certain debts Mr. Avery had, and that's all I can say. If nothing comes from our assumptions that he was after the cash, of course, we'll look into the option that he, and the person with him, might have been after your recipe, Ruth."

"But if Ruth is right about that, don't you need to act fast, so whoever killed him doesn't have time to cover his tracks and perhaps concoct some sort of alibi?" Elsa-May asked sternly.

"I don't have enough men to send all over the countryside. Where one of the men who wanted Ruth's recipe lives is out of my jurisdiction. All kinds of red tape are involved, not to mention the extra paperwork. Not that I'd mind doing all of that if I believed one of these men might be involved, but it's too much of a long shot. There's zero evidence at this stage to connect either of those men to Alan Avery." He pulled a notepad out of his pocket and looked at it. "The fact that Hugh Dwyer and Rupert Bird wanted to buy Ruth's recipe, just the same as the deceased, doesn't mean that one of those men killed him." The detective shook his head. "We need some solid evidence before we head down that track."

"Won't you just talk to these men?" Ettie asked. "It couldn't do any harm. Just talk to them and you might get a lead."

"We might, and we might not. It depends on what the forensic evidence and our other inquiries turn up. We do need to follow certain procedures. After we exhaust one line of inquiry we go down another. If we followed all the leads at once, we wouldn't be working efficiently."

Ettie nodded. "I'm sorry, Detective, we haven't offered you anything. Would you like some tea, or perhaps some coffee?"

He stood. “No, but thank you. I’ll have to get going.”

“Thank you for bringing the key over,” Ettie said.

“Yes, thank you,” Ruth added.

When the detective left, the ladies sat back down. Just as Ettie was about to speak, they heard hoofbeats.

“Who could that be?” Ettie asked as she pushed herself up off the couch.

CHAPTER 5

Ettie opened the door enough to see Ava's buggy coming toward the house. "It's Ava," she said to the others who were still in the living room.

Ettie leaned against the doorpost and waited for Ava. "It's nice to see you again, Ava. Everything all right, is it?"

"*Jah,* Ettie, everything's fine."

"Well, come in. We've got Ruth Fuller visiting us too."

After Ava greeted everyone, she sat down with them.

Elsa-May said, "Ettie and Ruth had a nasty shock this morning."

Ava whipped her head around to look at Ruth and Ettie, "Why? What happened?"

Ettie leaned forward. "I was over with Ruth today at the bakery — very early, as I told you yesterday when you offered to drive me there — and we found a dead man in her office. He was dead on the floor with a knife in his back."

Ava gasped and covered her mouth with her hand. "That's awful! Who was he?"

Elsa-May answered Ava's question. "He was a customer of Ruth's." Elsa-May went on to tell Ava everything that Ettie and Ruth had told her.

"And the police think he was after the weekly take?" Ava asked Ruth.

Ruth nodded. "Seems so."

"You don't take that money to the bank all by yourself, do you?" Ava asked.

"I have two young men go to the bank with the money. One carries the money and the other walks beside him. I feel safer with two going to the bank and it's not that far from us."

"Wouldn't it be better to bank more often than once a week? It is dangerous to have too much cash about," Ava said.

"You're right. I suppose some habits are hard to break. I've always banked once a week, but I guess I might have to change the way I've always done things."

"Is there anything special that brings you by today, Ava, or did you just want to come visit a couple of old ladies?"

Ava giggled. "I do have something to tell you. I was supposed to tell you yesterday, and I didn't. Now I have to tell you today, but I don't like to tell you after what you've just told me."

"Not more bad news, is it?" Ettie asked. "I don't know if we can take another shock."

Ava shook her head and laughed. "*Nee.* It's *gut* news. Well, I think it is."

"We could all do with some news like that. What is it?" Ettie said.

"It's about me and Jeremiah."

"Jah?" Elsa-May and Ettie said at the same time as they leaned forward.

Ava giggled. "We're getting married."

Ettie clapped her hands. "I knew it, I knew it."

Elsa-May pushed herself to her feet and gave Ava a hug. "That's *wunderbaar.* Now we'll be related. You'll be my grand-*dochder*-in-law."

"And my great-niece," Ettie added.

"I'm happy for you, Ava," Ruth said.

"Denke." Ava's face beamed.

"It's certainly good news. Where is Jeremiah? Why didn't he come with you?" Elsa-May asked.

"He's got a job that he's finishing off. Otherwise he would've come with me. I tried to tell you yesterday but the words wouldn't come out. Now that we've told both sets of parents, it's only a matter of time before everyone knows. Jeremiah didn't want you finding out from other people."

"And when is the wedding?" Ruth asked

"Not until the end of the year."

"I had an idea you had something to tell us yesterday," Ettie said.

Ava put her hand on her chest. "My heart was beating too fast to tell you. I thought I'd explode."

"And where will the two of you live after you get married?" Elsa-May asked.

"In the house he's been building on his parents' land."

"He's been building that for a while. He'd better get a hurry on," Elsa-May said.

"He has done a fair amount of work on it these past few months." Ava turned to Ettie. "I hope you don't mind me leaving the *grossdaddi haus*. Do you want me to find someone else to lease it from you?"

"I think I might sell it, rather than lease it. I've got plenty of time to think about that anyway."

"You could get someone over to tell you how much you should expect to get for it if you do decide to sell," Ruth said.

"It's far too early for that, Ruth."

"I have a very good customer who's a realtor. She's a very nice lady. Some would call her 'pushy,' but I guess that's why she's successful. Why don't I see if she'll come out to tell you how much the house is worth? It won't cost you anything."

Ettie scratched her neck. "I've been waiting on Jeremiah to do a few things around the place."

"He's almost finished, Ettie," Ava said. "He's only got those boards on the porch to replace now."

Ettie chuckled. "I suppose he's been using my house as an excuse to go talk to you, has he?"

Ava's face lit up. "It was a good way for us to see more of each other."

Elsa-May clapped her hands together. "Now, about this wedding. Have you chosen your attendants?"

Ettie said, "I think you're too old to be an attendant, Elsa-May."

Everyone sniggered.

"I wasn't thinking of myself, Ettie," Elsa-May said with a laugh.

"Two of my cousins are going to be my attendants, I hope. I haven't even asked them yet. They're going to be my next stop, and then, later today, my *mudder* and I are going to choose the material for the dresses."

"Let me know if you want any help with anything." Elsa-May stopped knitting and stretched out one of her hands. "I think I'm getting a bit of arthritis in one of my hands but it hasn't stopped me knitting, so it won't stop me sewing, if you need an extra pair of hands."

"Denke, Elsa-May. We've got a lot of time, and I think that's something my mother would like to do by herself. I hope I haven't intruded, but I really had to tell you today because

we're running out of time before everyone finds out. I didn't want you to be the last to hear the news."

Ettie said, "That's quite all right. We appreciate you coming over and telling us. We're always happy to have news of weddings."

Ava rose to her feet. "Well I better be going; I have to meet my *mudder* at home so we can go to her *schweschder's haus."*

After Ava left, Ettie noticed that Elsa-May couldn't stop smiling.

"I can't help feeling we're partly responsible for their union," Ettie said.

"I think so too, Ettie. It all started from the time we had them for dinner that very first time. They're a *gut* match."

"Jah, they are. Both are in their late twenties and never seemed interested in anyone else. I thought Ava might never marry," Ettie said.

Ruth chuckled. "Just like me. It's not so bad being on your own, but in the bad times I've always felt it would've been nice to have someone by my side. There haven't been too many bad times, and I've got my friends. Like today; I don't know what I would've done if you hadn't been there to help me, Ettie."

Ettie leaned over and patted Ruth on her arm. "I'm glad I was there to help, and to be of comfort."

Elsa-May pushed herself to her feet. "I'll go and make us something to eat."

When Elsa-May was out of the room, Ruth turned to Ettie.

"What is it?" Ettie said when she saw the look on Ruth's face.

"There's something I haven't told you yet."

"Well, tell me now."

"When I wouldn't sell to Rupert Bird, he said I'd be very sorry. What do you think he meant by that, Ettie?"

Ettie grimaced. *"Jah,* I remember you did tell me something like that. We should've told the detective."

"He didn't seem very interested in finding out more about Rupert Bird. And he might be right, Rupert might not have anything to do with anything."

"He threatened you, Ruth. He can't go around making threats to people."

"Well, he did. And I told you I wasn't scared by what he said, but I really was."

"Where'd you say his bakery is?"

"He's an hour's drive away at Harrisburg. It's quicker in the car, but the bus would probably take an hour."

"Would you be willing to pay him a visit? I'd go with you and we could ask him questions."

"What about, Ettie?"

"You could make an appointment with him; maybe say you're considering selling after all. Then, when you're face-to-face, tell him about the terrible thing that's just happened and that's the reason you're thinking about retiring. Tell him you're reconsidering his offer. Then say the name of Alan Avery and watch his face."

"I'd be willing to go if you're certain you don't mind coming with me"

"Jah, of course, I will. When you mention Alan's name, we'll see what he does. Maybe he knows him and if he does he might say something."

"What if he's got nothing to do with it all?"

"Well then we would've gone on a nice trip. Let's do it tomorrow. It'll do us both good to get away for a day."

"Get away where?" Elsa-May asked when she came back in with a tray of sandwiches.

Ettie told Elsa-May what they were planning.

Elsa-May sat down in her chair. "Be careful. If he did have some involvement, you're likely to be putting yourselves in danger."

"We can't sit around and do nothing, Elsa-May," Ettie said.

"I certainly don't feel safe going into the bakery before the staff get there now."

"Nee, you shouldn't do that." Ettie explained to Elsa-May that Ruth used to go in early, an hour before her staff.

"Do you have enough staff so you can go to Harrisburg with Ettie?"

"I've got plenty of staff," Ruth said. "I don't need to be there.

I'll call my manager tonight and tell him I won't be in tomorrow."

"You've been given the 'all clear' to open tomorrow, then?" Elsa-May asked.

"The detective didn't say I couldn't. He gave me the key back."

"Well, I hope they haven't left a mess." Elsa-May leaned down and picked up her knitting out of the bag at her feet.

"He did say that the insurance company found cleaners and they've already done their job. My manager will have to collect a key from me tonight. He doesn't live far from me. I don't like trusting anyone with a key or certain other things, but I suppose I'll have to."

"Will we go by bus tomorrow?" Ettie asked.

"That's how I got there last time."

"Then that's exactly what we'll do."

"I don't have Rupert Bird's phone number; it's in my office."

"Well, we'll have to surprise him, then," Ettie said. "And that might be even better!"

CHAPTER 6

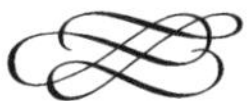

Early the next morning, Ettie took a taxi to Ruth's house. The bus stop where they'd board the bus to Harrisburg was walking distance from Ruth's house. Ruth stepped out her front door as soon as Ettie stepped on her porch.

"All ready?" Ettie asked.

"I think so," Ruth said. "I've got the bakery organized for me not being there. I think they'll manage, seeing I'm not really there on a Sunday either."

"I'm sure they'll manage."

As they waited for the bus, Ruth said, "I hope this isn't going to be a wasted trip."

"If nothing else, it might eliminate him from our list of suspects. We know Alan Avery was murdered, and if he wasn't there looking for cash, he was there for your bread recipe. There was someone else in your bakery with him, but who was it?"

"*Jah,* and Elsa-May was right about the weekly takings not making a dent in his debts. The big building he bought must have cost over three hundred thousand, and I'd dare say it would cost another two hundred at least to fit it out properly."

Ettie nodded. "That is a big investment. And why would he do all that when he knows that you make the best bread in town?"

"You think he planned to steal the recipe from me all along?"

"It makes sense seeing that you refused to sell it to him."

It was mid morning when they arrived in Harrisburg. When they stepped off the bus, Ruth said, "If my memory is correct, the bakery is not too far up this street." They continued along the main road, and then Ruth pointed. "There it is. See that brown awning?"

Ettie stopped still, and squinted. "*Jah.* That's it?"

"*Jah,* it is," Ruth tugged on Ettie's sleeve. "Come on."

When they arrived at the bakery, Ruth asked one of the staff if Rupert Bird was in. Minutes later, a tall lanky man in his forties with a receding hairline hurried toward them. He held out his hands to Ruth. Then he pulled her in close and kissed her on both cheeks. "Ruth, I never thought I'd see you in my bakery again."

"Hello, Rupert. I never thought I'd be here either."

Rupert looked at Ettie.

"This is my friend, Ettie Smith. Ettie, this is Rupert Bird."

Ettie quickly stuck out her hand so he wouldn't kiss her. She was grateful that he shook it and made no attempt to lean in and kiss her.

"Morning, Mrs. Smith."

"Everyone calls me Ettie."

"Fine, call me Rupert. Please, come through to my office." As they walked through the bakery out the back, he explained, "I've got new equipment that's just been installed." He pointed to the ovens.

"Looks good," Ruth said.

Ettie thought it best to remain silent. She knew nothing of making bread in large quantities and lately had been experiencing problems making just one decent loaf.

All the way down, at the very back of the building, was Rupert Bird's office.

"Have a seat," Rupert said.

Ettie looked around at the couch and the two blue velvet chairs. She sat in a chair while Rupert sat on the couch. Ruth sat in the other chair facing Rupert.

"I take it you're visiting me for a reason?" he asked Ruth as he leaned forward.

"I am. I'm considering retiring."

A huge smile appeared on Rupert's face. "Excellent. I never thought I'd see the day when you'd actually agree to sell."

"I haven't agreed to sell."

Rupert frowned and tipped his head to one side. "Then why are you here?"

"I'm here because I'm thinking of retiring, but I haven't fully made up my mind. A dreadful thing happened yesterday. A man was found murdered in my office."

Rupert's eyes grew wide. "That's dreadful. Who was it? Was it someone you knew?"

"It was a customer of mine, a very big customer. He was a local man by the name of Alan Avery."

Ettie stared at the man to see what he would do on hearing the dead man's name. He merely blinked a couple times and stared at Ruth.

"I'm very sorry to hear that. I'm sorry that your decision to retire was prompted by such a dreadful and violent thing. Do the police know who did it?"

Ruth shook her head. "Not at this stage. They do have evidence coming through, and then they'll find out who did it."

"How did he come to be in your bakery?"

"We don't know. The police believe he was after the weekly cash. Although, he didn't know we'd banked the day before."

Rupert nodded. "Times are tough for a lot of people these days."

"It appears so."

Rupert stood, walked over to his filing cabinet and opened the top drawer. "I'll just go over some details with you. Most of them we've discussed before."

"I don't recall discussing any details with you before."

"Well I've had a contract drawn up. It's not the final contract; it's just a mock up at this stage. I had it drawn up some time ago. It'll have to have some things changed, but it's something we can work on together if you decide that you do want to go ahead and sell."

He handed Ruth what looked like a five page contract.

"Thank you, I'll look through it."

He sat back down. "Are you talking to other people?"

"I do have others who've offered to buy me out. I thought I should talk to everyone before I make a final decision. There's one man who lives in Lancaster County who's got an Amish small goods store and he plans to roll out a hundred more stores across the country over the next five years."

"That is a lot."

"Yes. It is."

"He's obviously got more money to offer you than I do, but something tells me that money isn't the most important thing to you. Something in my heart is telling me you want to sell to me."

Ettie could see Ruth was struggling with what to say. "Ruth must make a business decision with her head and her heart."

"I can tell you, Ruth, that I'll give you all the credit for your bread. I'll even name it after you and have your face on the packaging."

Ruth shook her head. "No. I wouldn't like my likeness on a bread bag, or anywhere else for that matter. I've never had my photograph taken."

"I'm sorry. I didn't mean to offend. I forgot many of the Amish don't like to have their photos taken."

"Some don't mind, but that's not the way I was raised."

"Ruth, is there anything I can do or say to convince you to sell to me? What do I have to do to have you sell to me?"

"I don't think there's anything. I wanted to come here again to see what your operation is like now. We didn't leave on very good terms last time."

"You're right and I apologize for that. I'm too hot headed for my own good sometimes. My wife tells me that all the time."

"Well, thank you. Now that we've had another meeting, I've got something to think about."

"Thank you for coming out all this way to see me. Do you have to head off right now? Can I take you ladies out to lunch somewhere?"

Ettie and Ruth looked at each other. "Yes, we do have time before the bus returns don't we, Ruth?

"If you can spare the time, we'd like that," Ruth said.

"Excellent. I'll just tell my staff where I'm going." He rushed out of the office and Ettie noticed an open laptop computer on his desk.

She headed over to it.

"What are you doing?" Ruth hissed.

"Shh. Watch the door. Tell me when he's coming back." Ettie pushed a couple of buttons and the Internet browser was activated. "Where's Ava when you need her?" Ettie muttered. "This is different from the last computer I tried."

"He's coming, Ettie."

Ettie managed to sit back down just before Rupert saw that she'd been standing up.

"Okay. I'm all ready to go. I know a nice restaurant not far from here. I've been looking for an excuse to go back there."

CHAPTER 7

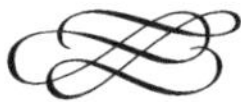

After they'd put their meal orders in, Rupert Bird said, "It must have been awful to have someone murdered in your bakery."

"Yes, it was. He was murdered right in my office. I found him in the morning when I went in."

Ettie said, "We've got very good detectives in our town; they always find the guilty ones."

"Always get their man, do they? Like the Canadian Mounties?"

"Like the what?" Ruth asked.

"Canadian Mounties they're the police in Canada. That's their slogan, they always get their man."

Ruth nodded.

The waitress set thick slices of sourdough bread on the table.

"No bread is as good as yours, Ruth. That's why I'm desperate to get my hands on your recipe."

Ettie stared at him while he was talking to Ruth and wondered just how desperate he was. Was he desperate enough to kill for it? What if he'd been in an arrangement with Avery? Avery could have misunderstood what Ruth had said about her prized possession being in the bureau. He might have told Rupert he knew where the recipe was hidden. When they opened the bureau, all that they found was a big old Bible. That brought Ettie to consider the knife. *If the knife wasn't one of Ruth's, that meant that the second man had to have brought it in with him, although it was possible it had been Alan's. That could make it a pre-meditated murder.*

"What do you think, Ettie?" Ruth asked.

"Excuse me? I didn't hear that, I'm sorry."

The waitress bought their meals. Rupert had ordered a steak, and Ruth and Ettie had ordered salads.

Ruth continued, "Rupert was just saying we should stay overnight and watch his bakery in operation tomorrow morning."

Ettie knew that Ruth was looking for her to come up with an excuse. "I'm afraid we can't. I've got my sister ill at home. She's not long out of the hospital and I'll have to get back in time to make her a meal."

"Sorry to hear that. Nothing serious, I hope?"

"They thought that it might be, but it wasn't. She still has to be watched carefully, though."

"Maybe some other time," Ruth said, smiling at Rupert.

"I'm glad we've been able to talk on friendly terms again, Ruth. Especially after my outburst last time you were here."

"No one's perfect, Rupert. It just shows you're very passionate about bread."

Rupert tossed his head back and laughed. "And do you know when it started?"

Ruth nodded. "I know."

Rupert said to Ettie, "I had a taste of Ruth's bread when I was a child. Ruth's bread changed the direction of my life. I might have become an accountant like my father if it weren't for Ruth. I just don't know why I can't get my bread to taste anywhere near as good as hers."

"I'm sure it tastes nice," Ettie said.

"I do get compliments, but I know it could be better," Rupert said.

Ettie sighed. "Well, at least your bread doesn't fall in the center like mine's been doing lately."

"Are you a baker too, Ettie?"

"No. I bake bread for me and my sister four times a week, well, up until I've had this problem with the bread."

"When you bring it out of the oven, are you putting it back on top of the oven?" Rupert asked.

"No. I'm putting it on a wooden tray as I always do."

"What about the quantities? Are you perhaps using more yeast than before?"

"Ettie has never measured her quantities. She knows to put a bit of this and a bit of that. She's doing the same quantities as always."

Ettie nodded. "Yes, and I've never had this problem before."

"If I were you, I'd start measuring. That's the only way you'll find what you're doing wrong. And if that doesn't work, you'll have to use a thermometer."

"I'll have to try that I suppose. Rupert, you mentioned that your parents took you to Ruth's bakery when you were a child?"

"That's right."

"Did you once live near Ruth's bakery?"

Rupert immediately looked away from Ettie. "We were passing through." He looked over at Ruth. "I hope you'll consider my offer. The figure I mentioned to you last time you were here is negotiable. Will you speak to me before you make your final decision?"

Ruth nodded. "I will."

Rupert's face beamed. "Thank you, Ruth."

A waitress came over to ask if they wanted anything else.

"Just the bill please," Rupert said.

"Thank you for a lovely lunch, Rupert, and I will start measuring. I have to try something different."

When the waitress brought the bill back, Rupert took out a wad of rolled-up notes out of his pocket. He peeled off a couple of notes and placed them under the bill. "I'll drive you ladies to the bus stop."

"We can walk," Ruth said. "It's not far from here at all."

Ruth and Ettie said goodbye to Rupert Bird, and then left the restaurant.

"He doesn't seem to be short of money. Did you see all that money he had in his pocket?" Ettie said.

"I certainly did."

"And did you notice he looked funny when I asked if he once lived close to your bakery?"

"*Nee,* I didn't."

"He couldn't look me in the eye, and then he changed the subject."

When they reached the bus stop, they had twenty minutes to wait before their bus left for home.

"Would Rupert be the same age as Alan Avery?"

"They could be around the same age," Ruth answered.

"I'll get Ava to look into things for me. She's very good at doing computer searches, and she's got a close friend who works in the Motor Vehicles Department."

"Should we let the detective know we've met with Rupert?" Ruth asked.

"He didn't seem interested at all. He already said he wasn't going to question him or the other man who wanted your bread."

"Hugh Dwyer?"

"That's right, Hugh Dwyer. He might talk to them eventually but only when he comes to the conclusion that it wasn't a robbery."

"We won't mention anything, then."

"Jah, I think that's best."

AFTER ETTIE WALKED Ruth safely home from the bus stop, she had a taxi take her home. She turned the door handle and before she could step into the house, she heard Elsa-May shriek.

"Shut the door, Ettie."

Ettie stepped in and quickly closed the door behind her. Her attention was drawn to a white streak heading for her feet. She looked down to see a small puppy. "He's adorable. Where did he come from?" Ettie leaned down to pat the pup.

"Your friend next door."

Ettie bit her lip. She hadn't meant that they'd take the dog Bernie had mentioned. "He did say something to me about a pup, and I said we'd think about it."

"Seems you told him I needed a dog to get me to go for a walk."

"I did say something to him, and he suggested that you should get a dog."

"Well now you've got one, Ettie. And he's left a present for you on the floor over there."

Ettie stood up and looked over at the 'present' the dog had left, and giggled. She looked back at the dog. "Did you do that?"

"That's why I've never liked dogs in the house, they're dirty and messy. They also encourage mice."

"Elsa-May, they do not encourage mice. He'll learn to go outside. We've already got the dog door." Ettie leaned down and patted the dog once again. "What's your name? Did Bernie say what his name was?"

"We're not keeping him, Ettie."

"Not *we,* he's *your* dog. I said I'd never have another dog after Ginger died. I don't mind helping you look after him. I'll even get rid of his first accident."

Elsa-May looked over at the dog. "He is a little bit cute, but dogs are a lot of trouble."

Ettie stood up. "What trouble? We've got a yard big enough for a small dog, we've got the dog door, and we can take him for walks. That's what the doctor told you to do. Maybe this little fellow will talk you into taking him for a walk."

"Do you think we should keep him?" Elsa-May asked.

"I do, now that he's already here." Ettie picked the dog up and walked over to her sister. "You hold him while I clean up his mess." Ettie knew that the longer Elsa-May had him around, the more she'd want to keep him.

When Ettie finished cleaning up, she washed her hands and went back to Elsa-May, intending to talk her into keeping the pup. "Where is he?" Ettie asked when she saw that her sister wasn't holding him.

Elsa-May pointed to the corner of the room. "I've made him a little bed."

The pup was curled up on a mattress made out of one of Elsa-May's good blankets.

"Your gold blankets are your good ones, aren't they?"

Elsa-May nodded. "I couldn't use the blue ones. They're not soft enough."

Ettie smiled. That's when she knew they were keeping the dog. She stepped closer to see that the dog was fast asleep with his head between his front paws. "He's asleep."

"He won't be much longer if you keep talking that loud."

Ettie tiptoed to the couch and sat down. "I've had a long day."

"Tell me all about it. Start at the beginning."

Ettie told Elsa-May every detail of their trip to Harrisburg to see Rupert Bird. "And then I got to thinking while we were out today, about the knife. It wasn't Ruth's knife, so either the other man in the bakery with Alan brought the knife with him, or Alan Avery had the knife. Why would someone carry a knife around like that if they weren't intending to use it?"

"Hmm. Detective Kelly thinks that the people were after cash. Would they have carried a knife in case they ran into any trouble? For self defense purposes?"

"It makes no sense," Ettie said. "Unless the second man brought the knife with him intending to kill Alan Avery as soon as they'd found the bread recipe, or the starters."

"So, Ruth's admitted to using starters?" Elsa-May said.

Ettie shook her head. "She's keeping quiet on the whole thing. I'm assuming she would, though. Anyway, when the recipe and nothing else was found, the accomplice might have killed Alan in anger."

"And you think that he had intended to kill Alan anyway, once the recipe was found? Leaving Alan's body in the bakery and Ruth's bread recipe missing?"

Ettie thought for a while. "I guess so. What are your thoughts?"

"I suppose if he'd been successful in stealing her bread recipe, there'd be no way to prove that someone was using Ruth's starters or recipes. In that way, the thief would be hard to track down."

CHAPTER 8

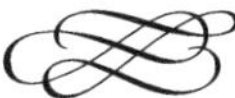

Ettie got herself ready to go to Alan Avery's funeral. She and Elsa-May picked up Ruth in the taxi and headed to the chapel where the funeral service was to be held.

They sat in the back row of the church and waited for the service to begin. Ettie looked up at the stained glass windows with scenes of the resurrection. Then she stared at the statues and the cross that took a prominent position at the front of the room. Ettie was reminded how the *Englisch* believed different things.

To some of the *Englisch,* a church was a building where they went on Sundays, but to the Amish, the church was the people who belonged to the body of Christ. Their church wasn't a building, and that's why they held their meetings in the houses of different members of the community. For convenience, in communities where members lived too far apart, they had erected buildings for their meetings, but these buildings were never referred to as churches.

When the seats were filled, a man in white robes entered and everyone stood. After a hymn was sung, everyone sat down again. The minister said a prayer and then a man got up to say something about Alan Avery. When he finished, another man got up to speak.

Ettie noticed a young woman crying in the front row. "Is that the daughter?" she whispered to Ruth.

"Yes, it is. That's Melissa."

Ettie had suggested they go to the funeral. Detective Crowley had always told Ettie that you find out a lot of things out at funerals by keeping eyes and ears open. Right now, they were keeping theirs open to find someone who might have profited from Alan Avery's death.

After the speeches, another hymn was sung before the minster read a few passages of Scripture. After the minister closed in prayer, everyone made their way out of the church and walked a little distance behind the church to the plot where Alan Avery would be buried.

As everyone gathered around the coffin that was placed over the grave, more words were said. It wasn't long before the coffin was lowered into the ground.

Ettie noticed that the daughter was making her way around, talking to everyone. When Ruth and Melissa's eyes met, Ruth waved, and then Melissa made her way over.

"Ruth, it was so good of you to come. I've been meaning to come by and see you. It must have come as an awful shock to find my father on your floor like that."

Ruth introduced Melissa to Ettie and Elsa-May.

"Will you all come to the wake?" Melissa asked.

"We'd love to, Melissa," Ruth said.

"Do you know what my father was doing in your bakery?"

"We weren't talking to each other at the time. As you know, I cancelled his standing order."

"Yes I know. I thought you might have asked him to meet you there, or something."

Ruth shook her head. "No. I haven't heard from him since he told me he was opening a bakery down the road."

"Believe me, Ruth, I knew nothing about that, or I would've told him not to do it. That was his dream for me, not mine. He wanted me to run it, but I was happy with my little café."

"I hope he hasn't left you in financial difficulties," Ruth said.

Ettie and Elsa-May stayed a distance away so they wouldn't appear to be listening in, but they were.

"He has, Ruth. I found out that he'd borrowed an awful lot of money. Now the people he borrowed money from are demanding that I pay them." Melissa put her hand to her head. "It's all too much. Dad being killed, and now people are harassing me for money. He didn't owe you money too, did he, Ruth?"

Ruth shook her head. "He always paid in cash at the end of every week. Just tell these people you don't have the money."

"And end up like my father?"

"Do you think they had something to do with his death?"

"I don't know what I think anymore, but somehow those people found out I was due to get an insurance payout from dad's life insurance policy, and now they want me to give them that. The insurance company won't even release the money until the police find out more about his death, though. So I don't even have the money yet."

"How much did he owe them?"

"More money than I can say out loud. I don't want to hear myself say it."

"Who are these people? You should go to the police."

Melissa nodded. "Anyway, today is about my father. Come and have something to drink. I've got to get around and talk to everyone." Melissa leaned closer to Ruth, and said, "Even though that's the last thing I feel like doing."

They followed Melissa into a room at the back of the chapel where the wake was being held. Ettie got herself, Elsa-May, and Ruth some sodas.

"Did you hear what she said, Ettie?" Ruth asked.

"*Jah,* I did. She was certainly giving you a lot of private information. I didn't know you knew her that well."

"I've known her for a few years, but we never talked about personal things."

Ettie said, "Sounds like he borrowed money from private lenders – loan sharks."

"See if she can tell you more about them, Ruth," Elsa-May said.

Ruth nodded. "Okay, I'll wait until she's made her way around and talked to everyone, and then I'll see what else she can tell me about these moneylenders."

"And ask her if her father knew Rupert Bird, or Hugh Dwyer," Ettie added.

Half an hour later, Ruth decided she couldn't wait any longer. She saw that Melissa was now by herself so she walked over to her.

After they'd been talking for a while, Ruth came back to Ettie and Elsa-May.

"Well, what did she say?" Elsa-May asked.

"I'll tell you after we leave here," Ruth said.

CHAPTER 9

When they were back at Ruth's house after Alan Avery's funeral, Ruth sat Elsa-May and Ettie down in the living room and then told them what Melissa had said.

"I didn't want to tell you where anyone could overhear. Melissa Avery told me that the first thing she knew about her father borrowing the money was when he hid in the back of the shop when he saw two men walking toward the café. The men came in and asked for him, and she told them he wasn't in and she didn't know when he'd be back."

"Did she say what they looked like?" Ettie asked.

"They were big and muscled. She called them 'thugs.' When they left, she confronted her father and he admitted he owed them money. He'd borrowed from them to remodel the bakery."

"Did her father know the other two men that Ettie mentioned?" Elsa-May asked.

"She wasn't certain about Rupert Bird, but she did know that her father knew Hugh Dwyer."

Ettie explained to Elsa-May. "He's the local man with the Amish small goods store."

Elsa-May nodded.

"She said they met a long time ago when they were in chef's school. You see they have their apprenticeships when they're assigned to different firms, and then they also had to go to school sessions. She said they'd always been rivals, but she was sure they'd been friendly rivals. Years ago, Hugh once worked as a head chef and he got Alan a job where he worked."

"Sounds like they knew each other well," Ettie said. "Did you tell Melissa that Hugh was also trying to buy you out?"

"I told her that, and she said that her father would have been livid with rage if he'd known. He hadn't mentioned anything to her, so chances are that he didn't know."

"I wonder if he did know, and just hadn't mentioned anything to his daughter," Ettie said.

"Are you thinking they were in it together, Ettie?" Elsa-May asked. "Both Hugh and Alan had broken in and were trying to steal Ruth's recipe?"

Ettie shrugged. "I don't know what to think. It sounds likely that Hugh might have been in that room. Could they both have been intending to double-cross the other? Ruth, I think we need to go and visit Hugh Dwyer," Ettie said.

"Do you think so?" Ruth asked.

Ettie nodded. "I think we should go there tomorrow."

"Was he at the funeral?" Elsa-May asked.

"*Nee,* I know what he looks like. He wasn't there. All right, Ettie, I'll visit him tomorrow if you come with me," Ruth said.

IT WAS JUST after nine the next morning when they arrived at Hugh Dwyer's Amish small goods store.

"Ruth!" Hugh rushed over to Ruth.

He was a tall thin man with pale skin, dark hair, and a narrow moustache.

"Hello, Hugh. My friend and I thought we'd pay you a visit. This is my friend, Ettie Smith."

He tipped his head to Ettie. "Nice to meet you."

"And you as well," Ettie said.

"I was just about to have my second morning cup of coffee. Care to join me?" he asked.

"We'd love to," Ruth said.

They followed Hugh to a table in his café, which was attached to his store. After he gave one of his employees their drinks order, he said, "Now tell me, Ruth, what brings you here today?"

"Have you heard what happened to Alan Avery?"

He nodded. "I did. I've been meaning to call you. It must have come as a shock. I read in the paper that you found him."

"Yes, I did. And Ettie was with me at the time. You knew him, didn't you?"

"I've known him for many years. We worked together at one point in time."

"When did you see him last?"

"I honestly can't remember. It would've been a good six months ago. We knew each other, but we were never close friends."

"I'm considering retiring, and I'm wondering if you're still interested in buying my recipe?"

"Always. I'm interested under the conditions on the contract I sent you."

Ruth nodded. "I still have the contract. I think it's a little extreme. Surely I should be able to make my own bread just for myself."

He shook his head. "I can't have any gray areas in the contract. It might start off being just for you, but then you'll have visitors, and if you've got a starter, they might take some of that, and then my exclusive bread is not so exclusive any more."

"I suppose I just have to make my decision, and then we can sort out the finer details later."

He ran a finger along his narrow moustache. "Are you considering other offers?"

"I do have a couple of other people interested, but that's no different from when we first started talking."

The waiter brought their coffees over.

"When we finish these, I'll show you around."

"I'd like to have a good look over your shelves, you seem to have an interesting variety here. I haven't been in here before," Ettie said.

"Everything on our shelves is authentic Amish food. I don't know if Ruth told you, but we've got big plans for many more stores."

"Yes, Ruth mentioned you were expanding."

When they were finished with their coffees, Hugh took them to the front of the store and worked through to the back, explaining all the goods and where he'd sourced them. "Now you can look over my kitchen."

"We'd love to," Ruth said.

"It's not busy now, but we're packed out at lunch time."

Ruth and Ettie followed Hugh into his kitchen and looked around. "There's no room to make the bread."

"No. I wouldn't make the bread in here. I'd need your bakery. Didn't you read the contract?"

"I didn't see that in it. I'll have to look over it again. I've had a few offers and I get a little confused."

Ettie followed close behind Hugh and Ruth. When Ettie looked up, she saw a rack of knives on the wall. They were graded in size from smallest to largest. Ettie noticed that the largest size was missing. And not only that, the knives looked exactly the same as the knife that had been sticking out of Alan Avery's back. Ettie hadn't realized she'd been staring at the knives until Hugh came to stand beside her.

"They are a lovely set of knives," Ettie said. "Are they commonly available? I've been looking for a better set of knives." Since Ettie was so close she could see a bruise across the left cheekbone of Hugh's pale face.

"Many people throw knives away without realizing they just need sharpening. I brought these knives back from an overseas trip. You can't get them in this country." Hugh continued showing them the rest of his kitchen, but Ettie couldn't stop thinking about the missing knife.

At the end of their visit, Ruth said, "Thank you for showing us around. I will have another look at your contract and give it some serious thought."

"You do that, Ruth. And I'll be in touch with you soon."

When they were a distance away from the store, Ettie said, "Did you see that, Ruth?"

"The missing knife?"

"*Jah.* We definitely have to tell Detective Kelly what we found. It looks like an exact match. It had the same grooves in the handle and the same inscription on the base of the blade near the handle. It seemed to be the same inscription anyway, from a distance."

"And did you see he had a bruise on his face?"

Ettie nodded.

Just as they were walking up the steps of the police station, they came face to face with Detective Kelly who was walking out of the building.

"Hello, ladies, are you coming to see me?"

"We are."

"Were you going somewhere?" Ruth said.

"It can wait. Come into my office, we can talk there."

Ruth and Ettie followed Kelly into his office, and then sat down.

When Kelly sat opposite, he said, "What can I do for you ladies today?"

"We have some things to tell you," Ruth said.

Ettie began, "We went to see Hugh Dwyer today. He's the man who runs the Amish small goods store. Actually, he owns the store."

The detective lifted both hands to his head. "And why would

you do that? Didn't I tell you ladies I would follow that up after my other inquiries?"

"We went there to find some things out," Ruth said.

"And I'm guessing you found something out, and that's why you're here?"

Ruth and Ettie both looked at each other, and then nodded.

"He took us to have a look over his store and his café. When we went into his kitchen, we saw he had knives that looked identical to the knife sticking out of the back of Alan Avery," Ettie said. "There were around eight knives on the rack, all of different sizes."

"And his largest knife was missing," Ruth added.

"And not only that, he had a bruise on his cheekbone."

The detective pulled out a pad and made some notes.

Ettie said, "He said that the knives weren't available in this country and he brought them in from an overseas trip."

"Okay. I'll check on how we're doing with the identity of the knife. As far as the bruise on his face is concerned, there was no sign of a struggle. It seems as though the knife in Avery's back had come as a complete surprise to him." The detective winced. "Looks like I have to pay Hugh Dwyer a visit sooner than I'd planned."

"There's one more thing, Detective," Ettie said. "Hugh Dwyer has known Alan Avery for many years."

"But he didn't go to his funeral," Ruth added.

"You ladies don't know how to stay out of trouble. You went to Alan Avery's funeral?"

"Yes, I went out of respect. As you know, I've known him for many years. He was murdered in my bakery, so the least I could do was go to his funeral, Detective."

"And you think this Hugh Dwyer fellow knew him well enough to go to his funeral?" The detective asked.

"They used to work together. He said that they'd known each other for many years, but they weren't good friends. So I suppose it wasn't unusual for him not to go to the funeral," Ruth said.

Without saying anything, the detective turned to his computer and tapped some keys on the keyboard. He turned the computer screen to face Ruth. "Would this be Hugh Dwyer?"

"Yes, that's him."

He turned the screen to face himself. "He's got a record. Petty theft. At least we've got his prints on record." The detective raised his eyebrows as he read more of what was on the screen. He turned back to the ladies. "You ladies best steer clear of him."

"We will," Ruth said.

"I will check out what you just told me, and then I want you ladies to go back and live your lives as normal. Leave the investigations to us."

Ettie nodded. "Yes, we'd like to do that, wouldn't we, Ruth?"

"I'd like to rid myself of the awful memory of finding Mr. Avery dead in my office, then I could go back to how things used to be."

"You said you didn't know Alan Avery's daughter, Melissa, well?" the detective asked.

Ruth answered, "Not very well at all. We did have quite a chat, though, after the funeral."

"Did she happen to mention she's going to do quite well out of her father's life insurance policy?" The detective looked smug.

Ettie and Ruth looked at each other. They knew Melissa was being harassed by loan sharks, but was it their place to tell the detective that all the money coming from the policy was going to go to pay off her father's loans?

"I wasn't going to mention anything," Ruth said, "but Melissa told me that the men her father had borrowed money from are coming after her. They found out about the life insurance, and they want her to pay back the money her father borrowed."

The detective raised his eyebrows and wrote something else down on his note pad, while muttering, "I guess I'll have to talk with her again, as well." The detective rose from his chair. "Thank you ladies for coming in. You've given me a few leads to follow up, and I appreciate that."

When Ettie and Ruth had left the building, Ettie said, "I'd like nothing more than to forget about things. It's hard to forget about it when I think of that poor man with the knife sticking out of his back."

"Yes, Ettie, I also find it hard to forget. I ran into my realtor friend this morning. The one I was telling you about, Brandy Winnie. She said she'd be pleased to come and take a look at your house."

"I suppose that would take my mind off things."

"That's what I hoped you'd say because I did make an appointment for you to meet her at your house tomorrow."

Ettie frowned. "You didn't, did you?"

"I did; at eleven in the morning. I know it's hard for you to make appointments and things with you not having a phone. I've got one at the bakery, but I remember how hard it was to get in touch with people when I didn't have a phone."

"Denke, Ruth. Eleven you said?"

Ruth nodded.

CHAPTER 10

"Jah, you have to come to the *haus* with me today, Elsa-May. I don't want to be talked into anything that I'm not ready for. Ruth said the realtor's pushy. I don't know why Ruth made this appointment without asking me."

"She would only have thought she was doing the right thing for you." Elsa-May stroked the fluffy white puppy in her lap.

Ettie breathed out heavily. "I suppose so."

"I don't like to leave Snowy alone. Look, he's going to sleep."

"Is that his name, Snowy?"

Elsa-May nodded. "It came to me this morning."

"You could bring him, but it might be distracting when we're trying to talk to the realtor. He'll be all right. He sleeps most of the day anyway."

"Okay. We'll be right back, Snowy," Elsa-May whispered to her dog.

"He'll have the run of the place, or he can go out the dog door into the backyard."

Elsa-May stood up and then placed Snowy on his dog bed in the corner.

"Finally," Ettie said when she saw Elsa-May put the dog on his bed.

Elsa-May chuckled. "You were the one who wanted me to get a dog."

"I wanted you to walk. Have you taken him for a walk yet?"

"I might do that later today."

"Gut. I might go with you. Now let's go and wait outside. The taxi will be here any minute."

The two sisters placed their black over-bonnets over their prayer *kapps,* and put their capes over their shoulders before they stepped outside. The wind was chilly, but it wasn't long before the taxi arrived.

When they stepped out of the taxi at the end of their journey, Elsa-May looked up at the house. "Jeremiah's certainly made it look better."

"Jah, it's taken a bit to get it into proper shape. Let's get out of the cold and wait inside." Ettie had noticed that Ava's horse was not in the yard, so she knew that her young friend was out somewhere.

Minutes later, a shiny blue car pulled up in the driveway. A tall slim blonde-haired woman stepped out. She opened the back door to retrieve a briefcase and headed to the house.

When Ettie looked through the window and saw her approach, she opened the door.

"Mrs. Smith?"

Ettie nodded.

"Lovely to meet you." The tall blonde woman put out her hand.

Ettie shook her hand. "It's lovely to meet you, Ms. Winnie."

"Please call me Brandy." She looked over Ettie's shoulder at Elsa-May.

"And this is my sister, Elsa-May."

"Nice to meet you too." She shook Elsa-May's hand and then flicked her long hair over her shoulder. "Ruth tells me you're thinking of selling?"

"I will be selling later on. I've got a young friend living in the *grossdaddi haus* until she gets married, and then I'll sell."

"Perfect. Would you like to show me through?"

"Before I do that, I must tell you that a man was murdered and hidden under the floor for forty years."

Brandy's mouth turned down at the corners. "I heard about that. So that was this house?"

Ettie nodded.

"That will affect the price. By law, I do have to let people know if anyone's been murdered at a property they're viewing. The other thing is, it might take some time to find a buyer. The price will have to be drastically reduced, too. Ruth's just had someone murdered in her bakery, Alan Avery."

Ettie nodded. "Did you know him?"

"I know everyone. I know all the gossip – who's having affairs with who, that type of thing. I knew both Alan and his daughter, Melissa. Of course, what happened to him was no surprise." She shook her head.

"What do you mean?" Ettie asked.

"He'd borrowed money from Big Freddy. Big Freddy isn't just any loan shark; if you don't pay him back, you'll end up at the bottom of the harbor with no questions asked."

"Did you sell Alan Avery the building he recently bought? I believe he was going to turn it into a bakery," Ettie said.

"Yes, I did. And I happen to know he used the money from his wife's insurance settlement to pay for it. And the money for the remodeling was Big Freddy's money."

"How did his wife die?" Elsa-May asked.

"You didn't hear about it?" She looked at both of the sisters in turn, and when they shook their heads, she continued, "She died many years ago. She'd disappeared for around five months, and then she was found murdered."

Ettie and Elsa-May looked at each other.

"Murdered?" Ettie asked.

"Yes, and they never found out who did it."

"I had no idea. Ruth didn't mention that."

Brandy pushed her hair back from her face. "It said in the paper that Alan was found in Ruth's bakery holding a Bible. I didn't like to ask Ruth, but does anyone know why he was holding a Bible? It seems as though it must've held some significance to him."

"I'm not sure," Ettie said.

"Oh, that's disappointing. Now, back to your house. Show me around."

Ettie showed her through the house with Elsa-May following along behind.

When they came to the end of their tour, Ettie said, "As you can see I've had some work done. There's just a little work still needed on the porch, and then all the work will be finished."

"It's good that you've had the house freshly painted inside. That always helps. I suggest having an open house and seeing what kind of offers we get. I've got a few people looking for low-priced homes; I'll call a few of them and get them through."

Ettie wasn't sure she liked the idea of Agatha's house having to go for a low price. "I'm not ready yet," Ettie said.

"Ettie, it's not going to sell quickly even at a reduced price. No one wants to live in a house where someone was murdered." She reached out a hand to rub Ettie on her shoulder. "Oh, don't look so sad. I'll get you the very best price possible." Brandy went back to her briefcase she'd left by the door. After she pulled out some paperwork, she said, "Just sign this. I'll cover the cost of the advertising."

"What am I signing?" Ettie asked.

"An exclusive property listing for six months."

"I've still got the lady in the *grossdaddi haus.*"

"Very good," Brandy said. "I should have a look at that accommodation too, then."

Ettie shook her head. "I don't think Ava would like that. She's not home at the moment. It's much the same condition as this place. It's got one bedroom, a living room half the size of this one, the kitchen's half the size as well, and there's a tiny bathroom with shower and toilet."

"My grandson has to finish off the repairs at the front of the house too," Elsa-May said.

Ettie nodded. "Yes, he's got to finish replacing some of the boards on the porch."

The realtor folded her arms. "It's not going to be an easy sale. Best we start sooner rather than later. We could have a delayed possession date for the buyers, which will give your friend plenty of time to move out. We can date it at a time to suit her."

"I didn't know you could do that," Ettie said.

Brandy nodded. "Of course you can."

"Brandy, since you know everything. I'm wondering if you know a man called Hugh Dwyer or a man called Rupert Bird?" Elsa-May asked.

"I've never heard of a man by the name of Rupert Bird, but I do know Hugh Dwyer. No one in my office will deal with him anymore. He's unscrupulous. A few years ago, he was always trying to put shady deals together. He was trying to be tricky, buying property with no loan and no money down, and flipping them before he had to pay for them. Technically what he was doing wasn't illegal, but we realtors have to be careful with deals like that because if anything blows up, we'll get the blame and be the ones to suffer the consequences."

"That's interesting," Elsa-May said.

Brandy went on, "I also heard he was caught shoplifting more than once."

Ettie recalled the detective mentioning Hugh had a record of petty theft. Ettie's gaze fell to the listing agreement in her hands. "Will you give me a day to read through this?"

"Yes. How about I meet you back here at the same time next week?"

"Okay."

"Perfect. Here's my card with all my numbers."

Elsa-May looked over Ettie's shoulder at the card. "Winnie. That's an unusual surname."

Brandy giggled. "I don't tell too many people, but that's not my real name. My name was Winchester, but it was too long for the business card. I changed it to Winnie."

"I thought I could use it for slogans as well. 'Win a better price for your house when you sell with Winnie.' 'Win with Winnie.' Winning agent, Brandy Winnie.'"

"They are catchy," Elsa-May said.

"And it does fit nicely on the card too," Ettie said with a smile.

"So is Brandy your real name?" Elsa-May asked.

Brandy shook her hand. "No it's not."

"Do you mind me asking what your name used to be?" Elsa-May asked.

"It started with a B. It's a dreadful name. It's Boadicea."

"Ah, I see why you changed it," Elsa-May said.

"I think Boadicea is a lovely name. I know many people who don't like their names," Ettie said.

When Brandy left the house, Elsa-May said, "I never knew it was so easy to change one's name. She's right about Winchester being too long on the business card."

Ettie and Elsa-May chuckled.

"Well, she was a whirlwind," Ettie said.

"Ruth did say she was pushy," Elsa-May reminded her.

"What do you think about what she said about Big Freddy?"

"Seems as though Alan Avery got himself into a lot of trouble."

"I think we should tell Kelly. That's something he should know about."

"He knows already. Didn't you tell me Kelly knows that he was having money problems?"

"Didn't you hear what Brandy said, Elsa-May? It was Big Freddy, not just any private lender, or loan shark. Sounds like this man kills people who don't pay up."

"We should go straight to Detective Kelly, then, and tell him."

Ettie nodded.

"Will he listen to us?" Elsa-May asked.

"He might."

CHAPTER 11

"Come in, ladies. You know the way by now," the detective said when he greeted Elsa-May and Ettie at the front of the police station.

They followed him into his office and sat down.

When Kelly had taken his seat opposite them, he asked, "Have you come to tell me something?"

Ettie was the first to speak. "We've come to tell you that we've heard that Alan Avery owed money to someone called Big Freddy."

"Big Freddy? Are you certain?"

Elsa-May said, "That's what we were told."

"Who told you?"

"The realtor who came to look at Ettie's house. Her name is

Brandy Winnie, and she says she knows everything that goes on."

"We've never been able to pin anything on Big Freddy. Interesting information, but it's unlikely he killed Avery. Besides, how would Big Freddy get his money back if he killed him?"

Ettie said, "You mentioned Melissa Avery having a payout from her father's death. Melissa said they want her to pay. That's what she told Ruth at the funeral."

"Yes, I remember Ruth mentioning that, but I didn't know that it had anything to do with Big Freddy. This does shed light on things."

"Do you know about Avery's wife disappearing and then being found dead?" Ettie asked.

"I've only just found that out. How did you find out?"

"The same realtor."

"I wasn't working in this area around that time. It's a wonder your friend, Ruth, didn't mention anything about it to you. She would've known; it was big news a few years back."

Ettie and Elsa-May looked at each other. It was strange that Ruth had never mentioned anything of the kind to them.

Elsa-May pushed herself up from the chair. "I'll have to get home to my dog."

"Would you happen to have the realtor's number?" the detective asked Ettie.

Ettie shook her head. "I didn't bring her card with me; I left it in my house. Her name is Brandy Winnie; she'll be listed in the phone book."

"Yes, she'll help you *win* some information," Elsa-May said. "You might even *win* the case."

The detective lifted an eyebrow.

Ettie stood up and poked Elsa-May in the ribs. "Stop it."

Kelly frowned at them.

Ettie felt the need to explain Elsa-May's odd behavior. "Elsa-May's trying to put a 'win' into every sentence. She was doing it all the way here in the taxi. It gets quite annoying after a while."

"I'm not going to *win* with you, am I, Ettie?" Elsa-May said.

Ettie grunted and looked at the detective. "I'll get her out of here for you."

The detective blinked and nodded. "Please."

After Ettie managed to steer Elsa-May out of the office, she stepped back in, and said, "Is Melissa in any danger from Big Freddy?"

"She could well be. I'm on my way to talk to her now." He grabbed his coat that was draped over his chair.

As the detective rushed past the two sisters, Ettie said to Elsa-May, "We forgot to mention what Brandy said about Hugh Dwyer being unscrupulous."

"You won't *win* by forgetting things, Ettie."

"Stop it!" Ettie stamped her foot, which caused Elsa-May to snigger.

"Don't worry. It sounds like he's going to talk to Brandy himself."

"I hope so. I'll have the policeman at the front desk call us a taxi."

When they arrived home, Snowy ran up to them. "I'll take him outside, Ettie, you check to see if he's left any surprises."

They'd shut the bedroom doors before they'd left that morning, so Ettie looked over the kitchen and the living room floors. "All's clear in here," she yelled to Elsa-May.

While Elsa-May was outside with the dog, Ettie put the pot on to boil. She then sat at the kitchen table wondering why Ruth hadn't mentioned the fact that Alan Avery's wife had been murdered. *Surely that would have been something to mention?*

"Ettie, we need to make pies."

Ettie looked up at her sister who was holding Snowy in the doorway of the kitchen. "That's right. I completely forgot about the pie drive. I'll make us cups of tea while we figure out what kind of pies to make."

The charity pie drive was on the day after tomorrow. In the past, the sisters normally made ten pies between them to take to the drive. That was the most they could manage in their small kitchen.

Elsa-May put Snowy on the floor and sat down at the kitchen table. "We've got lots of apples. We've enough to make three apple pies."

"We've got pumpkin from Bernie next door. What else do we have? I really don't want to go out again. I've been out nearly every day for the past week."

"We got plenty of jam. We could make some jam cakes."

"Not exactly pies, but people do like jam cakes."

CHAPTER 12

On the morning of the pie drive, Ava arrived in her buggy to pick up Ettie and Elsa-May, and the goods they were taking to sell.

"*Denke* for collecting us, Ava," Ettie said, as Ava helped them into the buggy with their baked goods.

"Any time, you know that."

Once they were all in the buggy, Ava drove the horse forward.

"I see you've done some baking too, Ava," Elsa-May said.

"I have, but not as much as I'd hoped. I've been busy helping *Mamm* with the dresses for the wedding."

"Are your cousins going to be your attendants?" Ettie asked.

Ava rolled her eyes. "When I asked them, they had their neighbor, Trudy, there. And she asked if she could be an attendant as well. I only wanted two and now it looks like I've got three."

"Couldn't you just have said 'no?'" Elsa-May asked.

Ava shook her head. "She looked so excited I didn't like to tell her 'no.' I really wasn't expecting her to ask me. Now we've got three attendants' dresses to make."

"Well, you have plenty of time," Ettie said.

"That's true. *Mamm* is one of the ladies setting out the tables today."

When Ettie, Elsa-May, and Ava arrived, they set up their baked goods on the table closest to the refreshment tent. Ava went back to her buggy and brought out two fold-up chairs for Ettie and Elsa-May.

"That's very thoughtful of you, Ava," Ettie said.

"Hopefully we'll be selling so many pies we don't have time to sit in them," Elsa-May said.

It was an hour after the pie drive started before the park's grounds filled with people.

Ettie suddenly dug Elsa-May in the ribs. "Look over there, that's Hugh Dwyer."

"The man who owns the Amish small goods store?"

"*Jah,* that's the one. I've visited him with Ruth."

"Looks like he's heading this way. I think he's seen you." Elsa-

May walked down to the other end of the table to serve some customers, leaving Ettie alone.

Elsa-May was right. Hugh Dwyer was heading straight for her. She gave a little smile and waved to him.

"Mrs. Smith, isn't it?"

"Yes it is, but you can call me Ettie."

"I remember that, and I never forget a face."

"What brings you here today?" Ettie asked.

"I'm always looking for new goods to add to my inventory. I might find my next pie supplier here."

Ettie nodded.

Hugh continued, "Is Ruth here today by any chance?"

"No, she should be back at her bakery today."

"She's back in business already?"

"Yes the bakery was only closed down for a little over a day."

"Are you particularly good friends with Ruth?"

"Yes, I'd say that I am. Why do you ask?"

He rubbed his jaw. "I just can't stop thinking about poor Alan. Do the police have any idea why he was holding a Bible when they found him?"

"I have no idea what the police think," Ettie answered.

“Well what does Ruth think? I’m only asking because it seems strange.”

“It is, and it’s also strange that he was in the bakery after closing. What would he have been doing there?”

Hugh chuckled. “It’s obvious, isn’t it?”

“Is it?” Ettie asked.

“He would only have been there to find Ruth’s bread recipe. Everyone knew he was trying to buy it from her and she wouldn’t sell it to him.” His eyes fell to one of her pies on the table in front of him. “That looks like a nice pie.”

“These are my pies and my sisters, and a couple of them were baked by a young friend. Our pies aren’t very good. Not like Clara Yoder’s.”

“And would Clara Yoder be here today?”

“Yes. She's directly across there, in the purple dress. She's talking to that man who's wearing the black hat.”

“Thank you, Ettie. I think I shall go over there and sample one of her pies.”

When Hugh Dwyer left, Elsa-May walked back and stood by Ettie’s side. “And what did he want?” Elsa-May asked.

“He asked why I thought Alan Avery was found with a Bible in his hands.”

“That’s ridiculous. How would you know something like that?”

Ettie shrugged. “Hugh seemed to think that it was no secret

that Alan Avery was there to get Ruth's bread recipe. The only thing he seemed confused about was the Bible. I wonder if the police have been to see him yet to ask about that knife?"

"Yes, the knife that was missing from his kitchen when you and Ruth went to visit him. Well, it might not have been missing. It could have been placed somewhere else," Elsa-May said. "You should've asked him to tell you how he got that bruise on his face."

"I mentioned that to the police and they didn't think it was important. They said there was no sign of a struggle in Ruth's office. It's only a faint bruise, so it was probably an old one. That reminds me, we must find out why Ruth hasn't mentioned that Alan Avery's wife was murdered."

Elsa-May shook her head. "Not 'we,' you can do that by yourself."

"Won't you come with me? I thought Ava could take us around to see her when we finish here."

"You're forgetting about Snowy." Elsa-May said.

"What about him? He's just a dog. He'll be alright by himself a little while longer."

Elsa-May snapped, "He's not a dog, Ettie, he's a little pup. He's not used to being on his own. He's used to being with a litter of pups and a mother dog. I'm sure right now he'll be crying, wondering where we are."

"Very well, then. I'll see if Ava will drive you home and then drive me to Ruth's. Will that make you happy?"

"Jah."

Ettie wagged a finger at her sister. "But only if you take him for a walk."

"I will take him for a walk, but not if it's too cold."

Ettie shook her head knowing that it would probably be colder by the time they got home. "Speaking of Ava, where is she?"

"Over there." Elsa-May pointed to the refreshment tent where she was sitting down having a cup of coffee with Jeremiah.

"Ah," Ettie said. "Young love. Do you remember what it was like, Elsa-May?"

Elsa-May chuckled. "I've got a dim memory of it."

"They do look good together, don't they?"

"They certainly do."

Ava looked over and saw them looking at her and gave a wave. And then Jeremiah turned his head and smiled at them.

"They're probably saying what a couple of old fools we are, Ettie."

"I think you're most probably right. And isn't that what we thought about the old people when we were young?"

Elsa-May nodded, and then customers approaching their table took the elderly sisters' attention.

CHAPTER 13

Ava delivered Elsa-May and Ettie back to their home when the pie drive was over. In total, the pie drive had raised just over twelve hundred dollars for charity.

"Ava, you must come in and meet Snowy."

"I'd love to. Are you in a hurry to go to Ruth's, Ettie?"

"I'm in no particular hurry. A few more minutes will give Ruth time to get home from the bakery."

As soon as Elsa-May pushed the door open, the pup came scampering towards her, and then danced on his hind legs for Elsa-May to pick him up. Elsa-May crouched down and picked him up before she moved into the house to let the others in.

She turned around for Ava to see Snowy.

Ava stroked his head. "He's lovely, he makes me want a puppy."

"Take him, if you want him," Elsa-May said.

"I can't. He's your dog."

"I don't want him."

"I couldn't.

Ettie giggled. "You'd have to run it by Jeremiah anyway, Ava, because you'll soon be living with him."

"He's already got two dogs," Ava said.

Ettie walked further into the house. "Look at this Elsa-May." Ettie picked up a chewed boot.

"Nee!" Elsa-May screamed. "That's my best pair of boots."

"They *were* your best pair of boots," Ettie corrected her. "Looks like he's only chewed one of them."

Elsa-May snapped, "Well one boot's not much good to me, is it?"

At that moment, Ettie was pleased that the pup was Elsa-May's dog and not hers.

Ava looked over Ettie's shoulder. "It's not too bad; it might be able to be fixed up."

Elsa-May sighed and said to the dog. "Why did you have to go and do that? Just when I was starting to like you."

Ava and Ettie laughed.

Ettie said, "I'll put it in a bag ready for the next time we go to the boot maker."

"*Denke,* Ettie."

"Can I hold him?" Ava asked.

"Take him with you if you want," Elsa-May said.

"She's not serious," Ettie said to Ava.

Ava took hold of the dog. "She sounds serious."

"I never said I wanted a dog. The man next door forced him on me before I had a chance to say anything. It seems Ettie opened her big mouth once again, and told our neighbor that I needed to walk."

"It's not what I said, Elsa-May, it's your doctor who said you need to walk. I was just telling Bernie that you needed exercise and that's what the doctor had said."

"*Wunderbaar!* Now everybody knows my private medical information."

"Not everybody, just Bernie," Ettie said. "It's not as though he's going to tell everyone."

"Thanks to your big mouth, now Ava knows. And she'll likely tell Jeremiah, and then he'll tell his *mudder* and *vadder.* The last thing I need is them fussing about."

"Give the dog back to Elsa-May, Ava, we'd better get going."

Ava handed the dog back. "*Jah,* it's time we headed off."

Elsa-May took hold of the dog. "You're a bad, bad dog for chewing my boot. Couldn't you have chewed Ettie's boot? It was right beside mine, and I'm sure it was tastier." The pup licked Elsa-May's hand. "I suppose you think being cute will keep you out of trouble? Are you sorry? I suppose I can forgive you just this one time." Elsa-May looked up at Ava. "Are you sure you don't want him?"

Ava smiled. *"Nee denke;* I don't."

Ettie pulled Ava out the door and closed it behind them.

"Bye," Ettie called to Elsa-May through the closed door. They didn't hear a reply.

"Does she like the dog, or not, Ettie?"

"She loves him."

"She kept trying to give him to me."

Ettie shook her head. "She loves him. She just doesn't want to admit it. And now instead of knitting all the time she has him in her lap. Which I suppose is good because she's getting arthritis in her fingers and probably can't knit for too many more years."

They climbed up into the buggy, and then headed to Ruth's house.

Ava asked, "So why exactly are we going to Ruth's *haus?"*

"I've got a couple of things to ask her. I need to know why she didn't mention anything about Alan Avery's wife being murdered years ago. You'd think that would've been an important thing that she should have told me."

"She might not know about it."

"She's known the Averys for a long time. She told me she's known them for many years. She would've heard about it at the time it happened."

"Do you think the two murders are linked? Do you think that the same person who killed Alan might have killed his wife as well?" Ava asked.

"Hard to say since they never found out who killed Alan's wife. That's what Brandy told me. Brandy said Georgina, Alan's wife, disappeared, and then she was found months later, murdered."

"So she just disappeared and no one could find her?"

Ettie nodded. *"Jah."*

When they got to Ruth's house, they saw Ruth at the front door just about to enter her house. She stepped back, and waved to them.

"This is a nice surprise," Ruth said. "Come inside and I'll put a pot of tea on."

They followed Ruth through to her kitchen and sat down at the table. After Ruth put the pot on to boil, she sat down with them.

"We've been to the pie drive this morning," Ettie said.

"I totally forgot that was on. I usually go to all the pie drives. How did it go?"

"*Wunderbaar*. Together we raised over twelve hundred dollars for charity."

"That's very good. That's better than last year, isn't it?" Ruth asked.

"I think so. The reason I've come here, Ruth, is that I've just found out something interesting and I have to wonder why you hadn't told me about it before now."

Ruth tilted her head to one side. "What is it, Ettie?"

Ettie took a deep breath and exhaled slowly. "I heard that Alan Avery's wife disappeared years ago, and then months later, she was found murdered."

"That's right. That did happen many years ago."

"You knew?"

Ruth nodded. "I wasn't keeping it a secret. I didn't think to mention it. It didn't come to mind."

"Don't you think it's strange that a man was found murdered and a few years before that his wife was also murdered? What are the chances of that happening?"

"*Jah.* I see what you mean. It does seem odd. And if it was the same person who killed both of them, that means that Alan Avery might not have been after my bread recipe. When Georgina was murdered, no one was after my recipe back then. Although there were plenty of people asking for it, no one was offering to pay for it."

Ettie thought about what Ruth had just said. It still left her wondering why Alan Avery was in Ruth's bakery after closing hours. "Tell me everything you remember about Georgina's murder, Ruth."

Ruth screwed up her face. "It was a long time ago. Hmm, let me think." Ruth's gaze shifted to the ceiling. "I remember that she vanished, and everybody was searching for her. When she didn't turn up for many months, everyone feared the worst, and then she was found dead."

"How did she die?" Ava asked.

"She drowned. To my knowledge, the police never found out whether she disappeared of her own accord, and then accidentally drowned, or whether she was abducted against her will and drowned on purpose. That's if my memory serves me correctly."

Ettie looked across the table. "You'll be able to find all that out on the library computer, won't you, Ava?"

"*Jah,* I should be able to. If nothing else, there should be some old newspaper records of the murder. How long ago was it, Ruth?"

"It could've have been as long ago as eight or nine years." Ruth stood up. "Tea or *kaffe?*"

"I'll have tea *denke,*" Ettie said.

"Me too," Ava said.

As she made the tea, Ruth asked, "How did it go with the realtor, Ettie?"

"Very good. I'm meeting her back at the house in a few days."

"You're selling Agatha's *haus,* Ettie?"

Suddenly Ettie realized she hadn't told Ava what she'd found out from the realtor, or even that she'd had the realtor come to look at Agatha's old house. *"Jah,* well only after you're married, of course. You weren't there the other day when I had a realtor give me an idea of what the house is worth. It was disappointing news, I'm afraid, because of the murder. She said that I would get a very low price for it. Also, it would take a long time to sell."

"That's a shame," Ava said. "It's such a nice house and I've loved living in the *grossdaddi haus."*

Why don't you and your Jeremiah buy Ettie's *haus,* Ava? You're used to living in the spot already." Ruth placed the teapot down and sat back down at the table.

"Jeremiah has got a *haus* for us already."

"The one he's been working on for years?" Ruth asked.

"That's the one. He's nearly finished."

"Brandy certainly knows a lot of people in town," Ettie said changing the subject.

"Jah, that's her business to know everybody and everything that's going on around the place," Ruth said.

Ava turned to Ettie. "Ettie, before I forget, will you come with me tomorrow to get some material for the men's suits for the wedding. I'm making a suit for Jeremiah and he's got three friends who'll need suits. We can go to the library after that and use the computer."

"I'd love to. I'm sure Elsa-May would too. What about your *mudder?*"

"*Nee,* she's too busy with too many things."

"That is something I would really like to do, Ava. *Denke.*"

While Ettie and Ava had been talking, Ruth had poured their tea.

Ruth said, "That's something I've missed out on by never marrying. I've had no wedding of my own and don't have any *kinner* to look forward to their weddings."

"I remember you had an admirer or two."

"There was only ever one, Ettie."

"William Yoder?"

Ruth nodded. "He asked me to marry him, and I wouldn't give him an answer. I wasn't sure. How do you know what love is if you've never been in love?"

"You don't," Ettie said. "It's a leap of faith. You have to trust *Gott* to bring you the right man, and to help you make a good marriage."

"When I decided I'd tell him yes," Ruth's head sank, "I found out that he'd asked Iris to marry him."

"That's awful," Ava said.

"I heard a whisper that he and Iris moved very quickly to marry," Ettie said. "It was a surprise at the time for me because I knew he liked you."

"And that was the only man you've been interested in, Ruth?" Ava asked.

"Jah, I left things too long. Anyway, he married Iris, and he died five years ago."

Ava nodded and the three ladies were silent for a while. Ettie patted Ruth on her arm when she saw that Ruth looked sad.

Ava said, "My *mudder* kept telling me I'd better find a man before I was twenty, but I was interested in other things when I was younger."

Ettie added, *"Jah,* and Jeremiah's parents were worried about him."

CHAPTER 14

The next morning, Snowy barked and scampered to the door as Ettie opened it for Ava to enter.

"No! Bad dog," Elsa-May said firmly taking the dog away from the door.

Ettie walked up behind her sister. "Oh, Snowy looks all sad now."

"I don't want a barking little dog. There's nothing worse than a yapping irritating dog."

"Come in, Ava. Are you early, or am I late?" Ettie asked.

"I'm a little earlier than I said I'd be."

"Well, I'm already to go. Elsa-May has decided to stay home." Ettie reached behind the door to lift her black cape off the peg. As she wrapped it around her shoulders, she said, "Bye, Elsa-May. Bye, Snowy."

Elsa-May picked up Snowy's paw and waved it at them.

Ava closed the door behind them. "She's really attached to that dog, isn't she."

"*Jah,* she'll never admit to it, though. Since it's on the way, Ava, do you mind driving me to the police station? There are just a couple of things I'd like to ask Detective Kelly."

"Of course, that will be okay."

"Denke."

Half an hour later, Ettie and Ava were waiting at the police station for Detective Kelly to see them. He suddenly appeared and beckoned for them to follow.

When they sat down in his office, he asked, "Now what can I do for you today, Mrs. Smith?"

"I have a question for you, Detective."

"Yes? Go ahead."

"I was wondering if you've questioned Hugh Dwyer yet about the knife?"

"Mrs. Smith, I know you've been helpful to me in the past, but that doesn't mean I can let you in on my entire investigations."

Ettie frowned. "It was a simple question, Detective, and you're right about me being helpful to you. And I'd like to be helpful to you again in the future. Remember how hard you found it when no one in my community would talk to you? That wasn't so long ago."

Detective Kelly drew his lips together as if he'd sucked on a lemon. "What is it in particular that you want to know?"

Ettie licked her lips. "I just had a question about the knives in Hugh Dwyer's kitchen. Did you see that the largest knife was missing? And, if I'm right, isn't it exactly the same as the knife that was sticking out of Alan Avery's back? I did have a good look at the handle, and the inscription in the metal part of it just above the handle, when I was checking for a pulse."

"You're correct. The knives you saw in Dwyer's kitchen are the same brand and model of the knife that killed Alan Avery. When we checked his set of knives, they were all present and accounted for."

"They were? Well when we went there, the largest knife was not on the rack."

"Normally I'd say it could've been elsewhere, in the dishwasher or somewhere like that. I had a good look at the knives and noticed that the largest one seemed to be newer than the rest of them. I questioned Mr. Dwyer about it and asked him if the larger one had been more recently acquired. He denied it and said he purchased the set overseas, and said he'd find the receipt, and then he'd scan and email it it to me."

"Isn't that reason enough to look more closely at Hugh Dwyer? Both Hugh and Alan Avery wanted Ruth's bread recipe, and you said yourself it looked like his knife had been replaced."

"If I took those two pieces of information to a judge to get a warrant for his arrest, or even a search warrant, I'd be laughed at. I do want to be taken seriously in this town. I'm not saying that you're wrong; I need more evidence than Dwyer using the same brand of knife as the one that killed Alan Avery. I did do some research and found out that the knife is not commonly available, so I'm following up on suppliers."

"Hugh made it sound as though the knives were rare."

Kelly's lip curled. "You questioned him?" When Ettie nodded, Kelly shook his head in disgust. "Mrs. Smith, go home and forget the whole thing, would you?"

"Detective Kelly, my friend and I found a dead body in her office. It's not something I'll ever forget."

Kelly blew out a breath. "I found out there is one supplier of those knives here in the US. I'm waiting for a call back from them regarding who they've supplied around this area."

Ettie was a little pleased that he was starting to follow some leads.

The detective continued, "It's a good thing you've come by today because I want to show you some photos to see if you recognize anyone." The detective opened a folder on his desk, pulled four photos out, and placed them in front of Ettie. "I want you to have a close look and tell me if you've seen any of these men in or around the bakery."

Ettie picked up the photos of each of the four men and studied them in turn. "No. I can't say that I've ever seen them before. These faces, I *would* remember."

"Yes you'd remember their faces, but you wouldn't *want* to remember them.They're hardened criminals."

"Who are they?" Ettie asked.

"These are the loan sharks Alan Avery borrowed money from." Detective Kelly tapped a finger on one of the photos. "This one is known as 'Big Freddy.' He's the head of the criminal organization, but we've never been able to pin anything on him."

"They all look rather intimidating," Ava said.

"You wouldn't want to meet any of them in a dark alley," Kelly said.

"And the other three work for Big Freddy?"

"Yes. As far as we've been able to tell. Seems as though Big Freddy sits back and calls the shots and the other three do his bidding." The detective put the photos back in the folder.

"Can I have one more look at them?" Ettie asked.

He retrieved the photos and pushed them toward Ettie once again.

Ettie picked each one up and had a closer look. "Has Ruth seen these photos?"

"Yes. I was down at the bakery this morning speaking to Ruth. She claims to have never seen these men before in her life."

Ettie's gaze fixed onto the detective's face. "And you don't believe her?"

"That's not true. I've got no reason not to believe her." Detective Kelly leaned forward. "Do you know something that I don't, Mrs. Smith?"

"No. It's just when you said 'she claims never to have seen the men before' it sounded like you didn't believe her."

The detective sighed, and then rose from his chair. "Is that all I can do for you today, Mrs. Smith?"

Ettie raised her eyebrows. "I just came here to find out what you'd learned about the knife at Hugh Dwyer's place."

"Very good; call and see me again if you wish. I enjoy our chats."

Ettie rose to her feet. "Yes, I'm sure that you do. Come on, Ava, let's go." Ettie hurried out of the police station with Ava following her.

"Ettie wait! I've never seen you walk so quickly."

When she got to the door of the station, Ettie turned around. "Well the man infuriates me. I couldn't wait to get out of his office. Sometimes he's just downright rude, and after all the help I've given him in the past it's unacceptable."

"Are you sure you want to come with me today?" Ava asked.

Ettie forced a smile. "It's all right. I'll calm down in a minute. How far is Coatesville again?"

"I'm leaving the buggy at the farmers' market where *Mamm* parks her buggy when she's at work, and then we can catch a bus from there. It'll be less than an hour's bus ride."

CHAPTER 15

Later that day, Ettie and Ava arrived at Healey's Fabrics in Coatesville. As soon as they walked in, Ettie smelled freshly cut material. It reminded her of how her mother sewed constantly for Ettie and her brood of siblings.

"Do you know exactly what you're looking for, Ava?"

"*Jah*. I'm looking for charcoal-colored wool, or some kind of wool blend. *Mamm* said I'd need five yards for each suit. So that means I'll need twenty yards. There'll be Jeremiah, and his three friends will want the same suits. Charcoal isn't gray and it's not black either."

"*Jah*. I know what a charcoal color is."

A male sales assistant approached Ava, and when she explained what she wanted, he pointed her toward the fabrics at the back of the store. The sales assistant said that he'd let them browse.

"Come on, Ettie. It's down this way."

"*Jah*. I'm coming." Ettie's attention was taken by the intricate patterns in the samples of lace by the window. Just as she was about to turn and join Ava, something caught her eye. She looked out the window to see a familiar woman walking past. Ettie looked again to make sure she wasn't mistaken. There was no mistake about it; the woman walking past the window was Melissa Avery. Melissa was with a man. Ettie had a good angle to see who the man was. She was certain it was one of the men in the photographs that Detective Kelly showed her earlier that day. Ettie quickly turned around so she wouldn't be seen if either of them if they happened to glance into the store.

Ava came up to her. "What is it, Ettie?"

"It's Melissa Avery, and she's with one of those men in the photos."

"The girl's whose father was killed?"

Ettie nodded.

Ava peered out the window at the couple who were just past the store. "Are you certain?"

"Yes, I got a clear look at him. It's definitely one of those men in the photos."

Ava gasped and covered her mouth with her hand. "Not Big Freddy?"

"*Nee*. One of the others."

"Are you sure you're not mistaken?"

Ettie grabbed Ava's hand and pulled her out the door. Melissa and the man were now some ten yards in front of them. "Let's follow them and see where they go," Ettie whispered.

"We can't do that, Ettie."

"Why not? Detective Kelly says it's a free country."

"They might see us."

"And?"

"If you're right, then he's a bad criminal."

"Has a criminal history," Ettie corrected her.

"Okay. We'll have to stay back so they don't see us."

As they followed the pair, they saw the man put his arm around Melissa's waist. Ettie and Ava looked at each other with raised eyebrows. It seemed they were a couple. They followed them until they walked into a café a few doors up and across the road from the fabric store.

"We'll give them a few minutes and you can go in and see what they're doing," Ettie said.

"Me? Why me?"

"Melissa might recognize me from the funeral, and you weren't at the funeral, so she won't recognize you. Go in and order a take-out coffee. While you're waiting for it to be made, see if you can sit close to them and hear what they're saying."

"It's not very likely that I'll be able to do that."

Ettie shrugged. "Less talking and more action." Ettie made shooing motions with her hands. "Go on, go in now. I'll wait back in the store."

Ettie went back into the fabric store and stayed by the window. If she stood in just the right place, she had a good view of the door of the café.

Fifteen minutes later, Ettie saw Ava heading back with two take-out coffees. "I didn't tell her to get two coffees, I only told her to get one," Ettie muttered to herself as she stepped outside the store. "Well, did you hear anything?"

Ava handed Ettie a cup of coffee. "Nothing. I didn't hear anything. I couldn't get close enough. They were snuggled in a corner, holding hands and smooching."

"What? They were kissing?"

Ava nodded, and then took a sip of coffee. "Ahh. This is hot. Anyway, I did get a good look at him and you were right. He is one of those men from the photos this morning."

Ettie nodded and then looked at her cup. "Well we can't drink this in the store. We'll have to sit down and drink it before we go back in. I don't think they'd like us spilling coffee all over their fabrics." Ava followed Ettie to a nearby seat, and when they sat down, Ettie said, "I'm glad you've seen him too. This does put an entirely different slant on things."

"What are you thinking, Ettie?"

"It seems to suggest that the daughter is somehow involved in her father's death. She lied about the loan sharks coming after her."

"Are you sure? How could she have something to do with her own father's death?"

"Many people kill for money and her father's life was insured." Ettie took the lid off her coffee and took a sip. "Ah, it *is* hot."

"I wonder what they're doing here?"

"He might live here for all we know. It's too risky to keep following them. We might be seen and we could end up in danger. I don't think there's anything more we can do except tell Kelly that we've seen Melissa with one of those men in the photographs this morning."

Ava and Ettie sat in silence for a while. Ettie had one eye on the entrance of the café. The couple hadn't come out.

"When we finish here, Ava, do you mind taking me back to the Police Station?

"*Jah,* of course, I will, Ettie."

Ettie took another mouthful of coffee. "I don't think I can drink any more of this."

"It's not very good."

"*Nee* it's not. I'm going to throw mine out." Ettie stood up and put her hand out for Ava's cup. Then she threw both containers of coffee in the trashcan.

"Ettie, do you think we should call the detective instead? Maybe he'll want to know right away."

"*Jah.* I don't know why I didn't think about that. Let's find a phone and call him before we do anything else."

When they found a public phone, Ettie made a call only to find out that detective Kelly wouldn't be back until much later in the day. The officer on the other end of the call offered to take a message, but Ettie declined to leave one.

"He's not there?" Ava asked.

Ettie shook her head. "He's out and won't be back until late today."

"That's okay, we'll call in and see him on the way home."

"Let's go and have a look at that fabric, shall we?" Ettie said.

Ettie and Ava walked back into the fabric store. Ava found the exact charcoal-colored wool blend material she was looking for and the store was able to supply the quantity she needed.

As they stepped out of the store, Ettie said, "I wonder if they're still in the café."

"They might be. Do you want me to go and have a look?" Ava asked.

Ettie shook her head. "*Nee.* It won't do any good since you won't be able to get close enough to hear anything."

They caught the bus back to the farmers' market and continued by buggy to the police station.

When Ava stopped the buggy close to the station, she said, "You go in and I'll wait here."

"Okay. I shouldn't be too long." Ettie hurried into the station only to be told that Detective Kelly still wasn't back.

Ettie stepped up into the buggy.

"He's still not there?" Ava asked.

"*Nee*. I'll have to call him tonight."

"How long does he work for?"

"Detective Crowley used to work all hours. I'm guessing Detective Kelly is the same."

When they were just about at Ettie's house, they came across Elsa-May carrying her pup. Ava stopped the buggy when it drew level to Elsa-May.

Ettie yelled out, "Isn't the dog supposed to walk too?"

"He was walking, and now he's tired. He sat and refused to go any further. I'm just going a little farther and then I'll turn around and come back. Are you pleased about that?"

"*Gut!* I'll see you at home."

Ava continued the buggy onward, and stopped outside Ettie's house.

"Come inside and show Elsa-May the fabric. Do you have time?" Ettie asked.

"*Jah,* I do."

"*Gut*. Elsa-May will be pleased to be the first to see it, besides me, of course." When they walked into the house, they saw chewed up pieces of wood and small stuffed animals on the floor."

"Looks like a storm hit the place," Ava said.

"*Jah*, a Snowy storm." Ettie kicked the toys out of the way as she walked to the kitchen with Ava close behind.

Just as they sat down at the kitchen table, they heard Elsa-May close the front door. She joined them at the kitchen table, sitting down with the dog in her arms.

"I don't know why everyone keeps telling me walking is good for me. I feel like it's going to kill me," Elsa-May said.

"I'm sure you'll get used to it. Now have a look at this." Ava unwrapped a corner of the package in front of her to reveal the fabric.

"That looks lovely, Ava. I want to touch it but my hands aren't clean. That'll make beautiful suits."

"It should, for the price of it," Ettie said.

"I'll only have one wedding, Ettie."

Ettie pulled a face. "And that's all you'd be able to afford."

Ava giggled. "I don't care. I just want everything to be perfect."

"Where did all those toys come from?" Ettie asked Elsa-May.

"Your new best friend from next door brought them over. His

dog grew out of the toys, he told me. Anyway, I hope it keeps Snowy away from my boots."

Ettie grasped Elsa-May's arm. "Elsa-May, you'll never guess what we saw today."

"Get me a glass of water first, and then tell me," Elsa-May said.

Ava jumped up. "I'll get it"

While Ava was getting the water, Ettie told Elsa-May about the photos that Detective Kelly had shown her, and then told her that they saw Melissa Avery with one of those men.

After Elsa-May took a mouthful of water, she said, "Are you certain your eyes weren't playing tricks on you, Ettie? It's an easy thing to do, especially since you just saw the photos this morning."

"*Nee,* Ava saw him too."

"That's right, and I'm positive, too, that it was one of those men."

"Really? Well that doesn't look too good for Melissa Avery. Have you told Kelly what you saw?"

Ettie shook her head. "We tried to call him as soon as we saw the man, but he was out of the station. Then we stopped in on our way here, but he still wasn't back."

Elsa-May said, "Give him an hour, or so, and then try him again."

Ettie nodded. "*Jah.* That's what I was going to do." Ettie hit her head. “Ava, we forgot about looking up to find out more about Georgina Avery’s death.”

“I totally forgot about it. I’ve had my mind on the wedding. I’ll go to the library tomorrow and look it up on the computer.”

“Would you?” Ettie asked.

Ava nodded.

Later that evening, Ettie got through to Detective Kelly and told him that they had seen Melissa Avery and one of those men who were in the photos he’d showed her earlier that day. He asked her which one, but she wasn’t able to describe him well enough for him to determine the man’s name. Detective Kelly asked her to come in at twelve the next day.

CHAPTER 16

When Ettie woke the next morning, she remembered she had that second appointment with Brandy Winnie, the realtor, at the house.

Ettie sat up and yawned, and then she swung her feet over the side of the bed and attempted to slide them into her slippers. When she could only feel one, she looked over the side of the bed for the other. She stood up after placing her foot in the sole slipper, and looked under the bed. Ettie always wore soft slippers in the house rather than going barefoot on the floorboards.

There was only one place her slipper could be. She walked out to the living room wearing one slipper and saw Snowy munching on her other fluffy slipper. Elsa-May was knitting beside him.

"Elsa-May, can't you see he's chewing on my slipper?"

Elsa-May glanced down. "*Jah*. Sorry about that."

"Well, why didn't you stop him?"

Elsa-May looked at Ettie over the top of her glasses. "It was too late. When I came out this morning, he'd already ruined it. I figured if I let him keep chewing on it, that would save something else in the *haus* from being ruined."

Ettie groaned and put her hands on her hips.

Elsa-May smiled, seemingly calm about Ettie's slipper being torn to shreds. "I've got a spare pair in my cupboard you can have."

"Denke." Ettie went to her sister's cupboard and pulled out the slippers and stuck her feet into them, after kicking off her now-partnerless slipper. "These will do."

The two sisters went into the kitchen for breakfast.

"I've got that second appointment with Brandy today at the *haus*. Do you want to come?"

Elsa-May shook her head.

"Then after that, I'm going to see Detective Kelly to tell him which one of those men I saw with Melissa Avery."

"Okay, then I'll cook the evening meal."

"Only if you feel up to it."

"I'm better, nothing wrong with me. I'm getting exercise like the doctor said, so no need to worry."

"Hello again, Ettie." Brandy Winnie was as bubbly as ever.

Ettie waited for her at the front door. "Hello. Come in, Brandy."

"Lovely day, isn't it?"

"It's a bit chilly, so I suppose if you like the chilly weather, it's a lovely day."

"Oh yes. I love the cold; I love sitting cozy in front of an open fire sipping hot chocolate with marshmallows."

"Yes that does sound good," Ettie said.

As soon as Brandy walked in, she said, "Have you decided to go ahead and sell?"

"Yes I will sell it, but I don't want anything to be finalized until after my young friend moves out. I've only bought one house in my life and that was with my sister, Elsa-May. I lived in my parents' home, and then I went straight into my husband's house."

"That's exactly why you have me. I'll fix up all those details and handle everything for you." Brandy pulled paperwork from her briefcase. "I'll just explain the listing procedure, and then, if you're happy with that you can sign the paperwork."

"We better go sit down at the table," Ettie said.

"That brings up a question. Are you planning to sell the furniture with the house?"

"No," Ettie answered. "There are pieces I think I'd like to keep, and I might give others to my friend when she gets married."

Fifteen minutes of explaining later, Ettie signed the paperwork. "That's a relief. But I hope you do get a good price for it. Not for myself; it was my dear friend's house and it seems such a waste if I don't get a good price for it just because someone was murdered here."

"Yes, I quite understand. I'll get you the best price possible, and that's a promise I make to you."

"Thank you, Brandy. I appreciate that. Now, I have a question to ask you on quite a separate subject from real estate."

"Yes what's that?"

"What do you know about Melissa Avery?"

Brandy batted her long false eyelashes a couple of times. "She had a very strange relationship with both of her parents. I should say with her mother, and her stepfather."

"Stepfather? Alan Avery? Was he her stepfather?"

"Yes. Alan Avery wasn't her real father. Her father died when she was just a young girl. In no time at all her mother married Alan Avery. I've been told that set a few tongues wagging."

"Why was that?"

Brandy looked away from Ettie for a moment, before she said, "There should be a waiting period after someone dies before someone remarries."

"And why did Melissa have a bad relationship with her mother?"

"She didn't want her mother to marry Alan. What made things worse was that Alan was never at home. He was always out working. Georgina, Melissa's mother, became very lonely and turned to drink. She became an alcoholic and some say she drank herself to death. It was really quite sad."

"I had no idea."

"I think that's why Alan Avery tried to make things up to Melissa. With the money from his wife's life insurance settlement he bought Melissa the café. When that didn't make her happy, he went ahead and bought that big warehouse he intended turning into a bakery."

Ettie was certain that Melissa had told Ruth she wasn't interested in having a bakery. Had Melissa lied to Ruth? "Do you know how much Georgina Avery's life was insured for?"

"Not a lot. I believe it was about seven hundred and fifty thousand."

Ettie's eyes grew wide. That certainly sounded like a lot of money to her. "I had no idea."

"Didn't Ruth mention it to you?"

"Ruth knew?"

"It was common knowledge amongst people who knew the family."

Ettie shook her head. "*Nee,* she never mentioned it." Ettie's mind ticked over. Melissa's mother, Georgina, was found dead and happened to have life insurance. A few years later, Melissa's stepfather was murdered and he also had life insurance. Melissa had made out that she was going to see very little of the money, due to her father owing money to one of those thugs. Seeing that she'd been kissing one of those thugs, Ettie doubted he would be demanding money.

"Oh dear, have I upset you, Ettie? I'm certain Ruth wasn't keeping that information from you deliberately. She might have even forgotten it."

"I'm not upset. I'm just thinking about something. Last time you were here, you mentioned Big Freddy. Do you know if Melissa had any connections to Big Freddy or any of his men?"

Brandy shook her head. "The only thing I can think of is that her father owed him money." Brandy leaned forward. "Why? Have you heard anything different?"

"No, I was just wondering, that's all." Ettie had no intention of telling Brandy she'd seen Melissa with the thug.

"Have the police found out who murdered Alan Avery yet? There hasn't been anything on the news about it and no one seems to know. I haven't heard a thing."

"They don't know anything yet. Brandy, would you mind taking me to Ruth's bakery if you're heading that way?"

"Of course I can. I'm going back to my office, and it's just a few doors from there."

Ettie couldn't wait to see if Ruth knew that Alan Avery was

Melissa's stepfather.Brandy dropped Ettie right outside the door of the bakery. Ettie hoped that Ruth was still there.

She walked through the door of the retail area of the bakery and asked one of the workers if Ruth was there. The worker led her to Ruth's office.

Ruth looked up. "Ettie! This is a surprise."

"I just had another meeting with Brandy and she brought me into town. I've found out something interesting."

"Sit down and tell me."

Ettie pulled out a chair and sat across the desk from Ruth. "Did you know that Alan Avery was Melissa's stepfather?"

"*Nee*. Did Brandy tell you that?"

Ettie nodded.

"She said that he married Melissa's mother not long after her father died, and the marriage was an unhappy one. Brandy said Melissa's mother had turned to drink."

Ruth said, "There was talk that Georgina was a drinker. That's why Alan wasn't too concerned when she disappeared. Apparently she'd done that a couple of times before. She'd be gone for a couple of days here and there without telling anyone where she was going. The last time she'd left without telling anyone, Alan got concerned when it got to day four. I knew that much but I never knew that he was Melissa's stepfather."

"According to Brandy, Melissa blames Alan for her mother's death, or at least blames him for her mother's drinking. Brandy said Alan bought her the café to make it up to her – get on her good side, and when that didn't work he bought the building he was going to turn into a bakery. Why would Alan do that if his daughter didn't really want a bakery?"

"Maybe she did, then. She might have been embarrassed to admit it to my face."

Ettie nodded. "*Jah,* could be. That would make sense."

Ruth leaned back in her chair. "Kelly visited me today."

"He did? What did he want?"

"He's been following up the information about the knives. The only firm that supplies them in the US gave Kelly their list of customers who've purchased the whole set, or knives belonging to the set. He found out that Hugh Dwyer had ordered that exact same knife, the same as the one that killed Alan Avery."

"The large one that we saw was missing?"

"*Jah*. And do you know when it was ordered?"

"*Nee,* tell me quick."

"Two days before the murder."

"Two days before? That's odd. He's got something to hide. He told Kelly that the large knife wasn't a replacement."

"And that's not all," Ruth said. "Rupert Bird also bought that exact same set six months ago. Detective Kelly is on his way right now to talk to Rupert Bird."

CHAPTER 17

Since he was most likely already in Harrisburg talking to Rupert Bird, Ettie would have to wait to tell the detective about Melissa's grudge against her stepfather.

Ruth who'd been sitting down talking to Ettie suddenly covered her face with her hands and began to cry.

Ettie ran over to her and placed her arm around her shoulders. "What is it, Ruth? What has upset you?"

"I've decided that I'm going to sell up. I've had enough! I just can't do this any more. Everything's against me."

"*Nee.* Nothing is against you. Sometimes we get trials thrown at us. All the things that come against us make us stronger."

Ruth sniffed. "Everyone thinks I'm a strong person, but I'm not at all. Just because I've always been on my own they think I'm tough."

Ettie saw a box of tissues on the filing cabinet. She plucked two out, and handed them to Ruth. Ruth took the tissues, wiped her eyes, and then blew her nose.

"I can't do everything anymore. All the strength I had is gone."

"Why don't you take a few days off?"

Ruth opened her mouth and stared at Ettie as if she'd just sworn or said a bad word. "I can't take any time off."

"Of course, you can. You must be under a lot of pressure running a business of this size on your own for so many years. I think if you don't take time off now, you'll regret it. And you can't make rational decisions when you're stressed. You told me this was your life and couldn't think what you'd do if you sold. If you sell now you might regret it when you feel better."

Ruth sniffed. "I suppose you're right. If I have a day or two off, my head might clear."

"When was the last time you had a day off?"

"When we went to visit Rupert Bird; before that, I don't even remember. Maybe never, except for Sundays."

"*Jah,* but even then you unlock the place to let the workers in. You told me that before. So it's not as though you can switch your mind off and not think about the place of a Sunday. Have two weeks off, and then you'll feel like a new woman."

Ruth stared at Ettie through bleary eyes. "Do you think so, Ettie?"

"I do."

"But it's been busier since all the press about the murder. I thought it might keep people away, but it's done the opposite."

"I'll get a roster going and get some of our ladies to help out. I know quite a few who'd be willing to come in and help."

"Would you do that, Ettie?"

"Of course. I'll organize everything so you don't have to worry about a thing. Stay away from this place for two weeks, and I'll organize three ladies to come in every day except Sunday."

"That sounds *gut*. I don't know why I didn't think about it before, but who will I trust with my key and my recipe?"

"You trusted your manager with the key once. You need to let someone in on some things. How about you trust the manager again?" Ettie suggested.

Ruth nodded. "I suppose I can. He's been with me for many years and he's never let me down."

"Why don't I wait here with you while you tell your staff what's going on, and then I'll walk home with you?" Ettie patted Ruth on her shoulder.

Ruth nodded.

When Ettie got home that evening, she had Elsa-May help her make up a roster with ladies they knew would help at the bakery.

When the roster was done, Elsa-May put Snowy on a leash and all three walked down to make some calls. After workers for the next few days had been confirmed, the two elderly sisters and Snowy made their way home.

"I thought that was a job well done," Ettie said as they strolled along.

"Jah, from what you said she needed a rest. I didn't think Ruth would be the type of woman to break down and cry."

"I was surprised too, but it's not every day you find someone stabbed and dead in your office. It also might have put a strain on her that everyone wants her bread recipe, and her bread secrets, whatever they might be."

"You're right, Ettie. I think that has worn her down."

"It's good that Detective Kelly is finally following up on the knives."

"Ruth said he was heading to talk to Rupert Bird right after his visit with her this morning, seeing that he also had that same knife set."

"Didn't Kelly already know that Melissa resented her father?" Elsa-May asked.

"Stepfather," Ettie corrected. "I don't know if the detective knows that yet."

They walked into their house, and Elsa-May took her pup off the leash. The pup ran around in circles and Elsa-May and Ettie sat down in their living room.

"Let's think about the facts we have so far, Elsa-May. Melissa's stepfather was stabbed in the back while inside the bakery of a person he was trying to buy a bread recipe from. Melissa's mother had disappeared years earlier only to turn up dead. Trying to make his stepdaughter happy, Alan Avery bought a café, and then later, a large building to turn into a bakery."

"*Jah* and I do find it odd that he'd spend so much money without having Ruth's recipe."

"And that would make him desperate to have it, seeing he was spending all that money on the remodeling."

Elsa-May added, "It wouldn't do to have a bakery with no customers. And his bread would've been nowhere near as good as Ruth's."

"So we can assume he *was* there to steal her recipe, he was certain it was in the bureau and then he found her Bible. We're missing the identity of the person with him."

"Who would have gained from his death?"

"Only Melissa. He had life insurance, and we can safely say that the men he borrowed money from aren't coming after her like she'd said because we saw her cozying up to one of them. Ava saw them kissing in the café."

"Are you thinking Melissa killed him, or had one of the thugs kill him?"

"Kelly seemed to think it was a man who killed Alan Avery. It's unlikely Melissa would've done it herself. If she had wanted him dead she would've asked her boyfriend to do it."

"We know that the knives aren't commonly available, and Hugh Dwyer lied to Kelly about the largest knife being a replacement, even when the detective could plainly see that it was."

Ettie sighed. "We haven't heard from Ava about Georgina's death. She said she'd look it up today. I'd like to learn more about Rupert Bird, too. He went funny when I asked if he used to live in the area around Ruth's bakery. He couldn't look me in the eye, and mumbled something about tasting the bread when his family was passing through."

"It's still early in the day. Why don't we head to the library and look it up on the computer ourselves? Ava's got enough on her mind at the moment; it's most likely slipped her mind since she's giddy and in love at the moment."

Ettie nodded. "But we can't take Snowy to the library."

Elsa-May looked down at her pup who was now sleeping on his bed. "I don't see how that's fair. Okay, we'll leave him here. He seems to have exhausted himself."

CHAPTER 18

Later they were settled at the library, and Ettie was looking up information on the Internet while Elsa-May sat beside her.

"I can't find anything here about Georgina Avery's death," Ettie said.

"She could've gone by her maiden name. Or her first married name. She might have still gone by Melissa's father's name."

"That wouldn't be likely if Melissa's name was changed to Avery, and her mother hadn't changed her name."

"Don't worry about that if you can't find it. See what you can find out about Rupert Bird," Elsa-May said.

Ettie did as her sister suggested and concentrated on finding out about Rupert. A few minutes later, she found something and gasped. "Listen to this Elsa-May! You won't believe it. This is a news report from the eighties. A man by the name of Marvin Montgomery was hiking when he fell down an embankment, hit his head and was knocked unconscious. With him were his two foster children, Alan Avery and Rupert Bird!"

"Really?"

"Look; there's a photo of them on the screen. It's definitely the same Alan Avery and Rupert Bird. They're young but you can still tell it's them." Ettie moved away so Elsa-May could get a better look at the screen.

"It's no use, I didn't bring my glasses with me."

"Hang on, then. There's more; I'll keep reading it and then I'll tell you what it says." Ettie read for a few moments. "Marvin couldn't be reached due to the rocky terrain, and one of the boys went for help and one stayed close. The rescuers finally reached Marvin, and he later recovered in a local hospital." Ettie hit Elsa-May in the arm. "They're referring to Marvin as a local man. I thought Rupert grew up around these parts. Didn't I say that?"

"Ow." Elsa-May rubbed her arm where Ettie had hit it. "When did you say that?"

"That's right. You weren't there at the time."

"So Rupert *did* live in the area and he grew up in a foster home with Alan."

Ettie nodded. "Seems as though they both had tasted Ruth's bread as children. And they were most likely competitive with one another seeing that they both wanted to buy Ruth's bread secrets."

"Rupert already has a bakery, is that what made Alan want one?"

"Could be, if they were that competitive."

"Do you think Melissa would know Rupert Bird? Would Rupert and Alan have kept in contact?" Elsa-May asked.

"Well, we can't very well go and ask her," Ettie said. "I've only met her once at her stepfather's funeral."

"*We* can't go ask her, but Ruth could."

"Have you forgotten already that Ruth's having some kind of breakdown? I had to force her to have time off. I don't want to go to her with this kind of news."

Elsa-May scratched her neck. "Then what shall we do?"

"One of us can call Melissa on the phone and ask to speak to Rupert Bird. When she says that he's not there, *you* can say that this is the number *you* were given for him. Then, she might say that Rupert Bird is her uncle, or friend, or some such thing."

Elsa-May frowned at her sister. "What if she asks *you* who *you* are, and what *you* want with him?"

Ettie grinned. "It's worth a try."

"Well, it might be, but you'll have to be the one to make the call."

"Go on, Elsa-May. Your speaking voice is so much better than mine. You're forthright and you sound official."

Elsa-May shook her head, and grunted. "All right, but only on the condition that if we have to do anything else horrible after this, it'll be your turn."

"Okay," Ettie agreed.

"Now find her phone number and I'll give her a call."

Ettie looked up Melissa's number and found her cell phone number attached to her café's listing. She scribbled the number on a piece of paper and handed it to Elsa-May. "There you go. I wrote it nice and big since you don't have your glasses. Call her from the phone over there." Ettie nodded her head to a public phone at the entrance of the library.

Elsa-May snatched the paper from Ettie, and then stared at it. "You'd better write that man's name down in case I get nervous and forget it."

Ettie took the paper back and wrote 'Rupert Bird' in large letters. Ettie heaved a sigh of relief as she watched her sister head to the phone. While she waited, she turned back to the computer to see if she could find any other information about Rupert, or Alan.

"Well, that was a complete waste of time."

Ettie looked up to see Elsa-May back already. "Didn't she answer?"

"She answered all right. When I asked if I could speak to Rupert

Bird, she told me flatly that I had the wrong number with no hesitation in the slightest."

"There was nothing else said?"

Elsa-May shook her head.

"Did you get the feeling she was being cagey, or that she just had never heard the man's name?"

"I couldn't tell. Now what?" Elsa-May asked.

Ettie turned back to the screen. "I'm looking for anything else on Rupert or Alan."

"I wonder what Detective Kelly has found out on his visit to Rupert."

"We should stop in on him on the way home. See if he knows that the boys were raised in the same foster home."

"What about the old man?" Elsa-May asked.

"Marvin Montgomery?"

"*Jah.* I wonder if he's still alive. He might be able to shed some light on things."

Ettie nodded. "I'll see if I can find anything out about Marvin Montgomery. Can't be too many people with that name. While I'm looking, you go and call the station and find out if Detective Kelly's going to be in later today."

"That's a call I don't mind making."

While Elsa-May called the station, Ettie found a phone number and an address for Marvin Montgomery. He lived around fifteen minutes away. Ettie wrote down his contact details while wondering the best way to approach him.

"He's not going to be back until around five," Elsa-May announced before she sat back down next to Ettie.

"I've just found a phone number and an address for Marvin. Shall we call or just go and knock on his door?"

"Going by my call to Melissa, I think it would be better to see him in person. Where does he live?"

"Close by. It'll only take us fifteen minutes by taxi."

CHAPTER 19

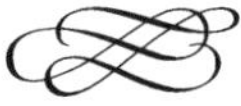

Ettie and Elsa-May stood at the front path and looked at the house of Marvin Montgomery, the man who once had fostered Rupert Bird and the late Alan Avery.

"There it is, Ettie."

"What reason are we going to give him for asking questions? He'll want to know."

Elsa-May said, "We should've brought Ava. She would've thought of something."

"We could say we're interested in foster children and how they cope."

"True, and that wouldn't be a lie. Because we are interested in the boys he fostered." Elsa-May pulled on Ettie's sleeve. "Now, you knock on the door and I'll stand behind you."

Ettie winced. "Me?"

"It's your turn, remember?"

Ettie pouted, and then walked forward and knocked on the door. She looked over her shoulder at Elsa-May, and hissed, "Stand closer."

Elsa-May inched forward.

When the door opened, they saw a man in his late sixties to early seventies.

"Hello, Mr. Montgomery?" Ettie asked.

He said nothing while he looked Ettie up and down. "You after donations?"

"No we're not after anything like that at all. I'm here about foster children. I heard from one of your neighbors that you fostered some children years ago. We were wondering if you might spare a few moments to tell us about your fostering experiences?"

The man took a step forward and peered down the street, first left, and then right. "Which neighbor told you that?"

"I don't quite recall exactly who told me."

"It was probably that old bat next door. I wish she'd mind her own business. She's always watching what I do." He pointed to the house next door. "There she is now!"

Ettie turned to look where he pointed and saw a curtain move. "I can't say for certain, I'm sorry, but can you spare us a few moments of your time?"

He clenched his jaw and looked from Ettie to Elsa-May.

"I'm Ettie, and this is my sister, Elsa-May."

"I suppose you can come in. It'll give that old bat next door something to talk about."

Relief washed over Ettie as they followed the man into his living room.

"I don't get many visitors anymore." He pointed to an armchair, and said to Ettie. "You can sit there." He pointed to the one next to it, and said to Elsa-May, "You can sit there." Then he sat at the end of a three-seater couch. "I always sit here, so I can see the TV better."

"Do the boys you fostered ever visit you?"

He shook his head. "It was my wife's idea. She's dead now. We couldn't have children for one reason or another. They never found out why, but back then it was just accepted. There weren't any of these newfangled tests they have today."

"Sorry to hear about your wife," Ettie said while Elsa-May nodded. "How many children did you and your wife foster?"

"Five all together." He turned his head to look at the clock on the wall. "My show's coming on in eight minutes. Can we make this quick?"

"Yes, we can. You had five foster children, and did you have a mix of boys and girls?"

"All boys."

"And did they get along together?"

"The first two we had for two years before they turned eighteen and they weren't a problem. Then we took in three younger ones the same age. My wife took a liking to one of them, and when his mother died, he became available for adoption; she wanted to adopt him. I told her it wasn't a good idea because I knew the other two would get their noses out of joint. You know how women can get; she nagged and nagged me until I gave in. And you know what I got for it?"

"What?" Ettie asked.

"I don't know which one of them it was, but one of the other two boys pushed me off a cliff and nearly killed me."

Elsa-May gasped. "Pushed you?"

"As sure as you're sitting here right now. I didn't know which one it was. Hugh stayed at home that day because he was sick; he was a sickly boy."

"Hugh?" Ettie asked trying not to choke. *Could that be Hugh Dwyer?* Ettie felt she couldn't ask him what Hugh's last name was.

"Hugh was the one we adopted."

Elsa-May took a turn at asking questions. "So you were looking after three boys all roughly the same age?"

"That's right." He glanced up at the clock again. "Is there anything else you'd like to know? You can come back tomorrow and I can tell you more, but not around this time. If I had my time over I can't say I'd foster again. Not boys, they were too much of a handful, but I've heard girls are worse." He shrugged his shoulders and smiled before he reached for his remote control and flicked the TV on. "Do you ladies mind showing yourselves out?"

Ettie looked at Elsa-May, who said, "Thank you for talking with us."

Ettie and Elsa-May stood up and made their way out of the house.

Once they were on the street, Ettie was the first to speak. "Elsa-May, he said one of the boys pushed him. That means Alan, or Rupert tried to kill him."

Elsa-May nodded. "I know. And do you think the boy he adopted was Hugh Dwyer? Isn't Hugh Dwyer the third man who was after Ruth's bread recipe?"

"*Jah,* he's the one who has the Amish small goods store and attached cafe."

"The three of them all wanted Ruth's bread. I wish we'd had more time to ask him more questions," Elsa-May said.

"I think we did well finding out as much as we did. I was fearful the whole time he'd ask us why we wanted to know all that."

"Me too. My heart was pumping so fast. Now, we have to go tell Kelly what we found out."

CHAPTER 20

"What is it this time, Mrs. Smith?" Detective Kelly asked looking across his desk at Ettie.

"We found a newspaper article that mentioned Rupert Bird and Alan Avery."

"I'm one step ahead of you, Mrs. Smith, we had that information days ago. We know that the two men were, at one point, fostered in the same home."

Ettie and Elsa-May looked at each other.

Ettie said, "Do you also know that the same man who fostered them also fostered Hugh Dwyer?"

The detective opened his mouth and leaned back. "No, I didn't know that. How did you find that out?"

"We visited the man who fostered them today."

"Yes, Ettie and I went and visited the man who fostered all three boys."

When the detective scowled at them, Ettie added, "One of the boys tried to kill him. It was either Alan or Rupert."

"When?"

"Years ago. He was pushed off a cliff. Didn't you find that same article?"

"Yes, we did." The detective nodded.

"Marvin Montgomery told us that he and his wife adopted Hugh Dwyer, and the other two boys were jealous. Well, he said the name 'Hugh' but we're certain it must be Hugh Dwyer."

Elsa-May dug Ettie in the ribs. "Tell him what else you found out."

Ettie said, "We heard that Melissa had a grudge against her stepfather and we also found out that Melissa's mother died a few years ago – was murdered."

"Yes, we've got her possible murder on record. They never found out who did it. In fact, they never proved positively that she was murdered." The detective pulled the same four photos out of his folder and placed them in front of Ettie. "Which one did you see with Melissa Avery?"

Ettie peered at them and tapped her finger on one of the photos. "This one."

"Thank you, Mrs. Smith, that makes my job a whole lot easier."

"What do you mean?" Ettie asked.

"This man is Stuart Tonks and a partial print of his thumb was found in Ruth's office. We've already got him here for questioning. One of my men is talking to him as we speak." The detective stood up. "He's denied everything up until this point, but he might change his tune when we let him know that you've made a positive ID as to him being close to Melissa Avery. If you'll excuse me, I'll go and see if he's said anything yet."

"Wait! You're not going to mention Ettie's name, are you?" Elsa-May asked.

"No." Detective Kelly hurried out of the room.

Ettie and Elsa-May stood up.

"Does that mean that Melissa might be involved?" Ettie asked.

"We don't know that yet. Can we wait and see what he says?" Elsa-May asked.

"We could wait in his office here, but will he get mad when he comes back?"

Elsa-May grinned. "I think we should wait. He never seems happy with us anyway."

Five minutes later, a police officer stuck his head into the room. "Detective Kelly asked me to drive you ladies home."

Elsa-May smiled. "He did?"

"Yes."

They followed the officer to one of the patrol cars.

"This is service," Elsa-May said.

"What if one of our neighbors sees us being driven home in a police car?" Ettie whispered.

"You're sounding like Marvin Montgomery."

Ettie giggled.

"If they say anything, we'll tell them to mind their own business," Elsa-May said.

The officer opened the doors and the ladies got into the car.

"Did you see who Kelly was questioning?" Ettie asked the officer on the way home.

"Yes, I did. He's often brought in for questioning over one thing or another."

"And what was it today?" Elsa-May asked.

The officer glanced at Elsa-May in the rear view mirror. "He said a woman paid him to do it."

"The murder?"

"Yes. They had his prints at the scene, so he's giving up the person who paid him in exchange for a lighter sentence. I'm glad to get out of the station with all that going on. Kelly gets crazy and starts yelling at people when he's on to something like that."

"I'm glad we could be of help to you," Ettie said.

When Ettie and Elsa-May got out of the police car, they hurried into their house. Snowy was there to greet them at the door, dancing on his hind legs to be picked up. Elsa-May leaned down and scooped him up.

"I'll put the pot on for a cup of tea," Ettie said.

"*Gut*. I'll take Snowy out to the backyard so we don't have any accidents inside."

"He knows how to use the dog door." It was too late; Elsa-May was already in their small yard.

When the tea was ready, Elsa-May and Ettie sat at their kitchen table.

"A woman paid him," Ettie said.

"So he says, and I suppose he'd tell the truth if he's after a lighter sentence."

"That's right." Ettie took a sip of tea.

"Who could it have been besides Melissa Avery?"

"I don't know, Elsa-May. Melissa's mother back from the dead?"

"I was thinking of Melissa's mother, but she was found dead after she'd disappeared. It's unlikely they got someone else's body mixed up with Melissa's mother."

"Mmm." Ettie nodded. She waved a hand in the air. "Elsa-May, when I went to Harrisburg with Ruth to talk with Rupert, Ruth mentioned Alan Avery's name and that he was found murdered in her office, and he didn't flinch. It was as though he'd never heard the name. Now we find out that he'd lived with him."

"Okay, but it was a woman who paid that man to do it, so Rupert Bird must be innocent. He might have already heard about Alan's death on the news or something."

"I suppose that could be true."

"Tomorrow, I think we should go and visit Ruth. I'm sure she'd like to know all that we've found out," Elsa-May said.

"I think you're right."

WHILE THEY WERE on the way to Ruth's house the very next day, Ettie leaned over and had the taxi driver take them to the library.

"What is it Ettie?"

"I'm just going to check on something."

When they arrived, Ettie wasted no time in sitting down in front of one of the computers. She sifted through images on the Internet.

Elsa-May had her glasses folded onto the top edge of her dress. She unfolded them, popped them on, and leaned closer to see what Ettie was looking at. "You're looking at books?"

"I'm looking at Bibles. I was just going over everything in my head as I was waking up this morning. I remembered Ruth's Bible didn't look like any Bible I'd ever seen before."

"And?" Elsa-May said.

"And there's one here that looks the same as hers."

Ettie clicked on the picture. "It's a first edition Clovedale Bible assumed to be dated around 1535. It's the first complete English-translation Bible."

"The year 1535?"

"*Jah.* Have a look Elsa-May. Hers is exactly the same as this one." After Elsa-May had a look, Ettie did another search. "It's worth around half a million dollars." Ettie opened her mouth and stared at Elsa-May.

Elsa-May leaned back. "Are you sure?"

"That's what it says here, and I'm certain it's exactly the same."

"I wonder if Alan Avery knew what he had in his hands?"

"The man who killed him can't have known; otherwise he would've surely taken it," Ettie said. "Ruth kept saying the Bible was her most prized possession, and I didn't stop to think that she meant it literally."

"She might not know the value of it," Elsa-May said.

"There's one way to find out."

Elsa-May and Ettie left the library and continued to Ruth's house.

Ruth had let them in just as the detective's car pulled up directly in front of the house. From the doorway of Ruth's home, the three ladies watched as Detective Kelly strode toward them.

"Mind if I come in?" he asked when he reached them.

"You don't look too happy, Detective. Come through to the living room and take a seat," Ruth said.

As soon as he sat, he said, "Ruth, can you tell me what you were doing with a rare first-edition Bible worth hundreds of thousands of dollars?"

"A very dear friend gave it to me. It's my most prized possession."

"Ruth, did you know how much your Bible is worth?" Detective Kelly asked.

Ruth nodded. "It's priceless."

The detective rubbed his chin. "Why didn't you tell me how much it was worth?"

Ruth breathed out heavily. "I didn't want anyone to know."

Ettie raised her eyebrows. Ruth had known all along. Ettie stared at the detective to see what he'd say next. She could see his nostrils flare, and a vein in his temple was throbbing.

"You led us to believe he was after your bread recipe, and you sent me on a wild goose chase?"

Ruth looked down, and her eyes filled with tears. "I just wanted it back. I thought it was valuable, but I didn't know it was worth that much. It's not the money value that's important to me. You see, a dear friend gave it to me and asked me to keep it forever."

"Would that have been William Yoder?" Ettie asked.

Ruth nodded. "It was passed down through his family and came to him. He wanted me to have it so I'd never forget him, and I never did."

"How did you find out, Detective?" Ettie asked.

The detective smiled. "I went over the evidence to see if there was anything I'd missed. When I was looking over Alan Avery's house, I saw he had loads of information on antique and rare books. When I saw the Bible in the evidence room, something clicked." He turned back to Ruth. "We found out what happened in your bakery."

Everyone leaned forward. "Stuart Tonks was paid by Melissa Avery to do away with her stepfather. Stuart Tonks followed Alan right into the bakery, and killed him just as he was stealing your most prized possession, Ruth."

Ruth gasped. "Is that what happened?"

"That's how he tells it." Kelly laughed. "You should've seen the look on Stuart Tonks' face when I told him he walked out of the room leaving half a million dollars behind."

"He wouldn't have been too happy about that," Ettie said.

Ruth sighed. "I had my Bible out one day looking at it when Alan Avery came in to pay his account. He took an interest in it and said he collected antique books. He asked me about it and said it might be extremely valuable. I packed it away and wouldn't let him see it."

“So, is that when you stopped supplying him with bread?” Ettie asked.

Ruth nodded. “It was also around the same time I found out he was opening the bakery, so it wasn’t just that he seemed too interested in my Bible.” Ruth looked at the detective. “Can I have my Bible back now?”

“I don’t see any reason why you can’t, but I don’t think you should go around calling it your most prized possession. I don’t think you should keep it around here anymore either.”

“No, not now that you’ve told Stuart Tonks about it’s existence,” Elsa-May said scowling at the detective.

The detective ignored Elsa-May’s comment and looked at Ettie. “And all the while, Mrs. Smith, you were worried about missing knives.”

Ettie’s lips turned down at the corners. “And I still am. Where did Tonks get the knife to kill Alan Avery? And what of Melissa Avery?"

“She was arrested this morning. We’ve got Stuart Tonks prepared to swear under oath that she paid him to kill her stepfather. He claims he stole the knife from Hugh Dwyer's place, that Dwyer has ties to Big Freddy's gang so Tonks had seen the set before. Naturally Dwyer lied about the knife when I asked about it because he’s been in trouble with the law before.”

“Weren’t Stuart Tonks and Melissa in a relationship?” Elsa-May asked.

The detective shrugged. “Things can change suddenly under

different circumstances. It's not unusual for a man like Stuart Tonks to throw his girlfriend under the bus. There's no loyalty among the criminal element."

Ettie looked at Ruth. "How are you feeling, Ruth?"

"I'm feeling a little better now that it's all sorted and I'll get my Bible back. I can't believe that Melissa would've had Alan killed."

"Money might not mean a lot to you, Ruth, but to some people, that's all they think about," Detective Kelly said.

Ruth sighed. "I don't know how I can keep my Bible now. I might loan it to a museum. At least that way it'll be safe and I can visit it."

"That sounds like a good idea, Ruth," Detective Kelly said.

IT WAS a week later when Ettie opened the oven and pulled out the first loaf of bread she'd made in a long time. She shrieked when she saw it. "Elsa-May, it's okay it's not sinking!"

Elsa-May came into the kitchen to have a look at it. "It does look better. How did you fix the problem?"

"I don't know. I've done nothing different."

"Hmm." Elsa-May looked over Ettie's shoulder at the bread. "Can you cut me a slice and put butter on it?"

"Okay, but I'll let it cool down a little first."

When the sisters left the kitchen, they heard a knock on their front door. Ettie opened it to see Detective Kelly. "Come in, Detective."

"Thank you."

"Hello, Detective Kelly," Elsa-May said. "Come, have a seat."

The detective nearly tripped over Snowy. He looked down at the dog clawing at his shoe. "New addition?"

"Yes, that's Elsa-May's dog, Snowy."

As soon as they were all seated, Ettie asked, "How's everything?"

"I was just driving out your way and I thought I'd drop by. I must say I was quite surprised that you didn't notice that Ruth's Bible wasn't a regular kind of Bible, Mrs. Smith. I had come to think that you had a mind as sharp as an eagle's eye, but the identity of that Bible slipped right on past you."

Ettie nodded. "Just as well you've got the mind like an eagle, Detective. And isn't that what they pay you for? I'm just a regular Amish woman." Ettie and Elsa-May had decided to let the detective think that he was the only one who'd found out the value of the Bible.

Elsa-May stood up. "Ettie's just made some fresh bread. Would you like to try some with butter?"

"Don't mind if I do." The detective threw his head back and laughed.

"What is it?" Ettie asked.

"To think that you thought someone would've been killed over a bread recipe."

Ettie pouted. "Well, it was odd that the three men who'd offered Ruth money for the recipe all had grown up in the same foster house. And one of the boys even pushed Marvin down a cliff."

The detective just smiled and said nothing. Ettie continued, "I've been wondering something."

"What have you been wondering?"

"How did Alan Avery get into the bakery? You said there were no signs of forced entry."

"We found a receipt for key-cutting amongst Alan's paperwork. Alan must have stolen Ruth's key early one morning, had it cut, and then put it back later in the day before Ruth left the bakery. Tonks said he followed Alan to the bakery that night and saw him unlock the door. One of my men found the key in Avery's pocket. Avery's mistake was in leaving the door ajar, inadvertently allowing Tonks to follow him inside. According to Tonks, Avery had no idea he'd been followed right up until the time he had the Bible in his hands. As he drove the knife in, Tonks said, 'this is for Georgina.' Apparently that is what Melissa had instructed him to say."

Ettie asked, "Melissa thought her stepfather killed her mother?"

"She claims her stepfather killed her mother, and that's why she wanted him dead. In her mind it was a payback." The detective rubbed his chin, and stared at Ettie. "I'm the laughing stock now in Harrisburg. I did tell you it was going to be difficult to talk with Rupert Bird since he was out of my jurisdiction."

Elsa-May placed a plate of buttered bread down on the table. "Yes, but who's laughing now, Detective? You've cracked the case, isn't that how they say it?"

Detective Kelly reached for a slice. "Yes." He chuckled and then took a bite of the bread. When he swallowed, he said, "Not bad, Mrs. Smith, not bad, at all."

Ettie smiled, and then pulled a slice of bread off the plate, but Snowy jumped up and knocked it to the floor. "Elsa-May! Look what your dog's done now."

Elsa-May leaned down and lifted Snowy into her lap. "Would you like a dog, Detective?"

~

ETTIE SMITH AMISH MYSTERIES

Book 1 Secrets Come Home

Book 2 Amish Murder

Book 3 Murder in the Amish Bakery

Book 4 Amish Murder Too Close

Book 5 Amish Quilt Shop Mystery

Book 6 Amish Baby Mystery

Book 7 Betrayed

Book 8: Amish False Witness

Book 9: Amish Barn Murders

Book 10 Amish Christmas Mystery

Book 11 Who Killed Uncle Alfie?

Book 12 Lost: Amish Mystery

Book 13 Amish Cover-Up

Book 14 Amish Crossword Murder

Book 15 Old Promises

Book 16 Amish Mystery at Rose Cottage

Book 17 Amish Mystery: Plain Secrets

Book 18 Amish Mystery: Fear Thy Neighbor

Book 19 Amish Winter Murder Mystery

Book 20 Amish Scarecrow Murders

Book 21 Threadly Secret

Book 22 Sugar and Spite

Book 23 A Puzzling Amish Murder

ABOUT SAMANTHA PRICE

USA Today Bestselling author, Samantha Price, wrote stories from a young age, but it wasn't until later in life that she took up writing full time. Formally an artist, she exchanged her paintbrush for the computer and, many best-selling book series later, has never looked back.

Samantha is happiest on her computer lost in the world of her characters. She is best known for the Ettie Smith Amish Mysteries series and the Expectant Amish Widows series.

www.SamanthaPriceAuthor.com

Samantha loves to hear from her readers. Connect with her at:

samantha@samanthapriceauthor.com

Facebook - SamanthaPriceAuthor

Follow Samantha Price on BookBub

Twitter @ AmishRomance

Instagram - SamanthaPriceAuthor